The Deadly Book Club

a murder mystery

Mary Ellen Jackson

E&MJ

For my grandsons

Gerald Mangham, III and Jerron Mangham

Table of Contents

Chapter 1

Marissa Marigny heard the knock at the front door but continued typing the last paragraph. She had overcome the writer's block holding her for several days. As her luck would have it, someone was at her front door. The door knocking was accompanied by a ringing doorbell. Oh, my goodness! This had better be someone she wanted to talk to, and it sure had better be of importance.

Glancing at herself in the mirror by the front door she smiled at the reflection which greeted her. The dark eyes rimmed with long lashes, the button nose and full lips set in a round face. The curly black hair gathered on top of her head complemented the large black rimmed eyeglasses and tan skin tone. She laid down the collar of the white oversized button-front tunic with its rolled-up sleeves over sleek black leggings which gave her the classy no frills look she loved. She looked down at her bare feet with frosty white toenails and smiled. Her one extravagance seeing as she kept her fingernails short. Stretching her back she opened the front door.

Her publicist, Jacky Crenshaw, stormed into the house. She was her usual impatient self. Marissa collected the mail as Jacky fussed behind her.

"Darn! It's about time you opened the door. I thought your nosy neighbors would have called the police by now. I knew you were here because I saw your car in the driveway. Next time park in your garage like normal people do who don't want to answer their door. Where's Maria? Any other time she'd be here cleaning or something!"

Jacky marched past the dining room corner alcove where Marissa chose to write. Marissa closed the front door and followed her, tossing the mail on the side table. She found Jacky in the kitchen. The publicist scanned the refrigerator looking for the salads Marissa loved making.

Today was a pasta salad with spicy olive oil and vinegar dressing. Marissa walked past Jacky's plate preparation and made a fresh pot of coffee. Grabbing a handful of almonds, she sat at the kitchen counter and watched her publicist.

Jacky's saucy haircut was cropped closer to her head than usual but emphasized the natural curl pattern. It was dyed a coppery red with tapered sideburns and a slightly elongated back at her nape. The top was kept long and allowed to fall over on her forehead in lopsided curly fashion.

She glanced at Marissa under the bangs. "I'm surprised I haven't been arrested with all the times you force me to behave like a trespasser. Living in one of Winding Falls most exclusive communities is a plus for you but a minus for me as your publicist."

She returned to the refrigerator where she pulled out items. The blue leather jumpsuit perfectly showcased her spectacular hour-glass figure. The brown-gold almond-shaped eyes glazed in rapture as she arranged food on the plate Marissa offered. The gold hoop earrings flashed against the bronze skin.

"How are you today?" asked Marissa in a conversational tone.

"Don't speak to me. Why haven't you been answering the phone?" said Jacky tossing a few crackers on her plate.

"I've been writing, Jacky. My writer's block has passed. I've come up with a couple of great ideas for a book series."

Jacky looked at her crossly. "That's all well and good you've gotten over your writer's block, but as your friend, would it hurt to at least pick up the phone sometimes and say hello?"

"You're right. I stand accused, and guilty of being neglectful and trifling with our friendship."

"Alright. I did not say all that. What are you writing? Another book of poetry?"

"Not this time. I thought I'd try my hand at a new genre."

"A new genre? Why? Besides your novels, your poetry has been successful and profitable."

5

Marissa smiled. "Not to mention profitable."

"Aren't we witty today?" She took a bite of salad. "What's the new genre?"

"A whodunit in the mode of Sherlock Holmes."

Jacky stopped eating and stared at her. "You're kidding, right? Sherlock Holmes? You've written romance novels for the past fifteen years. Where is this coming from?"

"You're saying I'm sidelined as a one-hit wonder?" asked Marissa with an indignant scowl.

"One-hit wonder? Not with fifteen years of massive success to your credit, let alone bank account!"

"Money isn't everything!"

"Says the one with it. Where is Tony with all this newfound creativity?"

"He'll support me. Anyway, he's still at that conference in Texas."

"I'm sure he'll support you, but something tells me you haven't mentioned this bout of lunacy with him."

Marissa stayed silent. Jacky looked over at her. She had a change of heart to her friend's news.

"I'm sorry Marissa. You're a skilled writer. I guess we all need a break every now and again. Write your whodunit and get it out of your system. You never know. Maybe you'll be the first romance writer to pen whodunits in connection with love stories."

"Thanks, Jacky."

"So, tell me the premise of this whodunit."

Marissa bit her lip. "I don't know yet. I just wrote the first few pages. So far someone is missing, but I don't have... I haven't outlined my characters yet."

Jacky looked up at the ceiling. "Oh boy! Okay, let me get out of here, so you can move forward."

Marissa turned from the dishwasher to follow her friend to the front door. Jacky retrieved her handbag and turned around.

"When is Tony due back home?" she asked.

"Tonight, or tomorrow morning. Why?"

"I won't call you for a few days. I know how you two get whenever you've been separated for a few nights."

"Get out!"

Marissa closed the door on Jacky's snickering. She looked at the wall clock. She called her best friend, Janelle Carr.

"Hey, sweetie. I know it's still chilly out, but I needed to go for a run. Can you get away today?"

On the other end, the woman giggled. "I just got off the phone with Spencer. He's picking up the boys. They have karate practice this evening."

"Oh, great! You want to meet at the park then?"

"Yes! See you in five."

Marissa smiled as she caught a glimpse of a silver framed picture of her and Janelle on a cruise. They looked alike enough to pass as sisters and often did.

Marissa went upstairs and put on a dark pink trimmed in red exercise tank and purple calf-length joggers. She zipped up the purple warm up jacket. She tied on her red and purple running shoes and braided her hair into one plait down her back.

Marissa spotted Janelle's golden four-door truck as soon as she pulled into the Winding Falls Park entrance where the runners met. Janelle, outfitted in a pink exercise set, was doing stretches to warm up. They hugged enthusiastically.

"Oh, I love that color combination," said Janelle of her outfit.

"Thank you, but at least yours is seasonal," Marissa said as she pulled on purple leather gloves.

Janelle giggled. "That's alright. I love my pink. You know, I can't believe it's only January. Any other time we'd be in June by now."

"Valentine's Day is around the corner. Are you and Spencer planning anything romantic? I'm asking because Tony made plans for us to spend the weekend at that new resort in Exeter. It's a surprise."

Janelle stopped stretching to look at her. "How can it be a surprise if you already know about it?"

"He doesn't know I know so to him it's a surprise for me."

"You always were a clever woman. My in-laws are keeping the boys that weekend. Spencer and I decided it would be more romantic to just stay home... like when we were first married without kids."

"That does sound romantic," agreed Marissa.

"Are you seeing a show?"

"I didn't find an itinerary. We're probably just going to mosey around like we did when we were first married, and just wanted to hang out together."

The women laughed and went ahead up the incline. They never talked while running, which Marissa loved. Running freed her mind and allowed her to think more clearly.

Some hours later, Marissa walked into the living room. The wedding portrait on the mantel caught her attention. She first glimpsed the man who would become her husband when she stepped foot on Winding Falls University campus as a first-year student. She remembered looking up into the greenest eyes she had ever seen on a person.

She remembered her final year and being talked into a blind date. After he was introduced as Marcus Anthony Marigny, he leaned close and whispered, "just call me Tony" and winked. They both laughed.

After that date, he came by the campus to pick her up for their dates. On the nights when they did not see each other, they spent time on long-distance phone calls. A year later, they married. The persistent buzz of her phone jolted her out of her reverie.

"Hello baby." The deep mellow voice of her husband brought a smile to her face.

"Hello, Tony. How's everything going?"

"We're done and I'm heading home."

"Oh, that's great. Did you have a good time."

"It was a working weekend. I'll have a good time when I see you."

"Where are you now?"

"On the plane. We just took off. I have a gift for you."

"How soon will you be here? What do you want for dinner? What kind of a gift?"

"Slow down. One question at a time. The plane lands in about an hour."

"Oh! You're on the plane now?"

"Yes, dear wife. I'm on the plane now."

"We'll order in then. What would you like?"

"To see you."

"Yes, but what would you like to eat?"

He chuckled and she changed the subject. "I'll figure it out."

"I thought you would. See you soon. I love you."

"I love you too."

Tony leaned back in his seat and adjusted his headrest. His seatmate gave him the side-eye but minded her business. They had set up he was the non-verbal Neanderthal type. Tony preferred not to be too friendly with women. He was happily married to the love of his life. He had no need for outside friendships with other women. He closed his eyes and thought of Marissa.

Marissa heard wind chimes at the front door. She turned and Tony was standing in the doorway wearing the familiar smile he always wore. He closed the door and shrugged out of his leather jacket. He laid his gun holster on a chair. She smiled. His eyes held hers as he pulled her toward him.

Marissa opened her eyes and looked at the clock. She stretched. It was a little past midnight. She smelled bacon. She dashed into the shower and threw on tank top and gym shorts. Tony saw her coming and slid two plates on the counter.

"Would you put them on the table please?"

"Hmm...this is good, Tony."

"Thank you, baby."

"Where's my gift?"

He looked at her quizzically. "You mean you weren't happy with the gift I gave you earlier?"

She almost choked on her response. Laughing, he patted her back.

"Calm down. I didn't forget you."

He reached under the table and presented her with a little bag. It was a pinky ring with her initials on it. She hugged him around the neck.

"Oh, thank you, baby. I love it."

"And I love you. How's your weekend been? Any writing done?"

"Yes. I finally got over my dry spell."

"Good. What's the travel brochures for?"

"The book I'm writing. I can't decide on a location though."

"Have you ever had a location in your books?"

"No. That was never the emphasis, and no one cared."

"Don't mess with success, baby. Eat your food before it gets cold."

"Honey this is good and all, but I can't eat anymore."

"Give it to me," he said, reaching for her plate. "Where are you going?"

"Upstairs to finish styling my hair."

"Don't go to sleep. You're my dessert."

She smiled but did not look back. She knew he was watching her with that perpetual smile on his face.

Chapter 2

Sitting in his squad car, The Watcher had a perfect view of the front of the police station. He saw his rival talking to a few police officers. Oh, how they loved him! He had to admit though he was a likable guy, and he hoped before all this was over, he would not have to kill him. He was invaluable to the police department in this town. But the wife had to go. Had he known it was her meddling he would have gotten rid of her a long time ago. But this young detective would not have a difficult time getting a new wife, not the way every woman, and a few men, threw themselves at him. He looked in his overhead mirror. He had never been a bad looking guy himself and staying in good physical shape added to his attractiveness. Ah, the day crew were arriving. That last assignment was rough, but this team was formidable. He let his rival enter the building and slipped surreptitiously in along with the rest for the day's assignments.

The Winding Falls Police Administration Building sat on a one-acre lot in Center City. The Major Crimes Task Force was the creation of Captain Fred Murray, a legendary lawman in the criminal justice community. Tony recruited by Murray, hand-picked the eight people, who composed the unit.

This morning the team was reunited after time-off for solving a three-year, multi-town armed robbery spree.

"I thought I would never wake up once I fell in bed," said James O'Neill. His partner, the ever-glamorous Vanessa Benson, walked in and sat at her desk directly across from his.

"You made it to bed," quipped Luis Trevino. "I fell in love with my carpeting for two straight days."

"Bed? No way!" shouted his partner, Priscilla Perez. "After three weeks of tracking those vermin in the woods, I couldn't wait to get in a nice, hot tub of water and scrub the filth away."

The dapper Kevin Gerard laughed. "Oh, you have carpet? I slept on a hardwood floor for three nights!"

"Well boys, not only did I find my bed, but I slept in it, and it was a darn comfortable and glorious sleep!" said Jeanette Johnston.

"Oh, here we go!" said profiler Dante di Giovanni, laughing. "No one told you to follow us into the woods. We could have caught the bad guys without you."

Robin Sloan threw her golden head back in a mock laugh. "Oh, yeah? Buddy, our exceptional tracking skills are why they were caught."

"Ha!" di Giovanni said. The detective sang the opening notes of an aria in his smooth tenor.

Not far away, Tony was in his office listening to his team and grinning. They were always like this after a major case was solved. They had worked together for more than a decade now and behaved more like siblings than partners. He was proud of the work they did and honored they still looked up to him as their leader.

A rap on his open door, and Police Sergeant Stan O'Malley, entered the office with an armful of correspondence. O'Malley took control of the front desk.

"Good morning, Lieutenant."

"Good morning, Stan. How was your weekend?"

"It would have been better had my mother-in-law not showed up," said the cop. Tony grinned. "I believe you say that every year around this time when she visits from Ireland."

"Is that a fact?"

"How long is she here for this time, Stan?"

"A few weeks. She's returning home after Saint Paddy's Day."

"Enjoy." Tony smiled. "Is that for me?"

"Sure is. Have a nice day, Lieutenant. Corned beef special for lunch?"

"Hmm...sounds good. Hook me up, Stan."

"You got it boss."

"Please close the door. Thanks, Stan."

Tony walked across the empty squad room to the well-lit office. He spotted the bodyguard standing outside the door. They nodded to each other as Tony turned to head back to his office.

"Tony, come here a minute." The raspy voice belonged to the silver-haired Murray.

The seated with his back to the door, rose and turned around to greet Tony. Deputy mayor, James Alan Young, a former college football player, was a friend of Tony's from their collegiate years. Young's physique had fared well with marriage and children.

"Hi, Tony. Good to see you," said Young.

"I didn't want to interrupt," said Tony, shaking hands with the deputy mayor. He looked at his boss. "It could wait, Fred. It's not urgent."

"Not at all, Tony," said Young. "I was just about to leave. I know you and your team just returned victorious from that last case. If you need more people, just let us know."

"Thanks, James Alan, but we're managing so far. Everyone works well together, and if nothing else, this last case tested us as a team."

"You've said that for years. Stop it!" Murray grinned. "I'm proud of you and your team. You caught that gang way quicker than any of us imagined."

"It was the team, Fred, not me. A man is as good as his backing."

"Man, Oh, man!" Young grinned. "Humility is great, but let me tell you something, your team is the way they are because you set the bar high. They follow through. But enough shop talk. Are you and Marissa able to make dinner at my home this Sunday?"

"Yes, she told me about it. I'm sure she and Stacie have worked out all the details."

Murray laughed. "Women always do. You enjoy your dinner. My annual hunting trip is this weekend."

"Oh yes, I forgot. Well, you know we'll be having something next week and next month. It never ends with four kids in the house."

Young looked at Tony and the smile left his face. Flushed, he stammered a bit.

"Let me let you go, Tony. Say hello to that beautiful wife of yours for me. Have a great night, Fred, and enjoy your time off. You deserve it, too."

"Thanks, James Alan. Make sure you tell Stacie I'll make her next dinner. I have a bone to pick with her about her last case."

The deputy mayor laughed with full humor. "You two kill me with your legal arguments. I keep forgetting you studied law, Fred. Well, good night, gentlemen."

The deputy mayor walked out into the emptiness of the squad room. Tony turned to his boss who was busy packing files away in his briefcase.

"Good night, Fred. See you tomorrow."

"Not tomorrow, Tony. I have a dental appointment, and I'm off the rest of the week. Must prepare for that symposium next week. That's why the fishing trip. Calm before the storm."

"I hear you, and if you need anything just call me."

"Just keep me abreast of anything happening here. You can always text me any time of the day or night. Although I sleep like a log sometimes, if I happen to be awake, I'll respond. Have a good week and enjoy the dinner."

"You, too. Good luck tomorrow at the dentist."

"Thanks. Say hello to Marissa for me."

"Will do."

Dr. Elsa Santorelli, Winding Falls newly appointed medical examiner, stepped off the elevator to subdue lighting in the squad room. The detectives were gone for the day. The medical examiner smiled when she saw the light on in the office of the detective she came to visit. She lightly knocked on Tony's open door. He smiled in acknowledgement. The heavy blonde hair hung over one light blue eye. The round cheeks set in a round face. The orange sweater dress clung nicely to her hourglass curves. She carried a brown woolen coat.

"Good evening, Elsa. You just missed Fred."

"Oh, shucks! I wanted to ask him a question about something. Oh, well! Next week will be here soon enough."

"That it will."

Tony turned his back when Santorelli stepped into his office. He could smell her perfume. He shrugged on his overcoat and picked up his briefcase and keys. He turned around and she was gone. She was waiting by the elevators.

She pressed the button and smiled. "No sense in hopping on before you."

Tony's instincts perked up as he looked at her. "How's Chris doing?"

"He's fine. How's Marissa?"

"She's fine. Where is Chris?"

"He's away in Belgium at a medical conference."

Tony noticed the irritation in her voice as she smiled across at him. He almost smiled, but he did not want to encourage her. He looked at the elevator doors, and thought they were not moving fast enough.

"I was wondering if you wanted to get a drink at the Policeman's Pub. I usually meet half your team down there on Friday nights."

"I'd rather not know that, Elsa."

Santorelli laughed gaily which made Tony smile. The doors opened. Tony stepped out behind Santorelli, waved to O'Malley at the desk, and went quickly through the side doors to his vehicle in the police lot. He spotted the doctor's orange dress as he turned out of the garage. He timed the changing of the traffic lights. He did not look at her as he sped past to the highway.

Chapter 3

Four times a year, Marissa drove to a Washington Heights estate to attend a woman's book club meeting. The estate belonged to her longtime childhood friend, Tessa Smith. Marissa parked her white sport sedan in the spacious driveway next to the gold-colored truck of her best friend. Marissa thought the beauty of the unexpectedly seasonal warm winter might mean they would be outside.

She walked up the path to the double gates adorned with draping ivy and yellow miniature roses to enter the backyard. She walked across the yard bypassing the French doors to the far side of the pool area where lawn chairs were set up around a lit fire pit. She heard her name and turned around with a smile.

"Good morning, Marissa. You look beautiful in your black and white."

"Thank you, Tessa. You know I love you in that deep blue. I brought my attendance book. I forgot it last time."

"Hmm...you and your record keeping. Have a seat here, sweetie. Let me get the ladies out here."

"What are they doing?"

"Helping Ida Mae with the lunch preparations."

Tessa went into the kitchen through the open patio doors. Marissa sat down and pulled out her attendance book. Jacky brought her a marshmallow-topped mug of cocoa pulling up a seat beside her. Tessa reappeared on the patio followed by women. They greeted Marissa and gathered around with their books.

Marissa walked to where three other women were grouped together. The women all hugged and smooched each other's cheeks. Marissa sat in the fourth available chair next to Janelle.

Two hours later, the book discussion ended.

"Whew!" said Jacky stretching her arms skyward. "That was a good read. Short, sassy but interesting. Excellent book choice."

"Spoken like a true book publicist," said Janelle Carr, smiling and pushing back her long dark hair.

"Have we thought about our next book? I was thinking about us doing a book series. We've never done one of those," said Stacie Young, with her soft voice.

"That sounds interesting Stacie," said Patricia Mendoza, her dark eyes shining with excitement. "What do you guys think?"

Emily Wilkinson pushed a blonde strand of hair out of her gray eyes. "I think a book series seems nice because we can deal with the same characters and see how they evolve with each storyline,"

Marissa piped in. "There's a science fiction series out. I think it's a trilogy. Anyone game for science fiction?"

"I love science fiction. That's a great idea, too," beamed Beth Maynes.

"Let's take a vote on it," suggested Elsa Santorelli. "Although, I think it would be great. Take us through the summer."

"No need to vote," said Tessa. She smiled as the ladies had their hands up in a voting stance. "That's what we're doing then. A trilogy."

"What's next?" asked Marissa, looking at her notes.

"What are we doing for our fifteenth college reunion? Are we going somewhere or what?" asked Angela Rojas.

Lynda Molina, Angela's best friend, looked around the group with a worried frown. "I might not be able to make it guys. The baby's due date is the end of summer."

"Talk about long-range planning! Lynda, our college reunion is after the Labor Day weekend. You'll be able to attend by then. You and baby number four." Jacky with a smirk.

"How far along are you, Lynda?" asked Sierra Smith. Sierra and her husband Thomas did not have children of their own but were godparents to the group's children.

Lynda looked down at her swollen stomach and said, "Five months and counting."

Catori Moon Perry smiled. "I know it feels like forever Lynda, but it will be over soon."

"Yeah, and just think you'll deliver in time to have a beautiful summer," chimed in Emily in her wistful way.

"Well, she won't have that great a summer with a new baby keeping her and Gabriel up all night," said Jacky.

Tessa 's posture tensed. She looked at Jacky with a stern face, and in a cold voice said, "I think having a beautiful new baby in the home is not as odious as you make it seem Jacky regardless of when they have to get up."

Jacky backtracked quickly. "Oh, I didn't mean anything by it Tessa. Just teasing Lynda is all. You know I'm the godmother to everyone's babies."

"Let's talk about something else," said Kristen O'Leary in a loud but firm voice. The Irish beauty deflected arguments wherever she could.

"When Angela mentioned our school reunion, I thought about our club's fifteenth anniversary," said LisaMarie Butler, "which is also on the horizon."

"Maybe we could take a trip somewhere," suggested Vanessa Benson.

"What do you mean by a trip somewhere?" asked Angela.

"I mean, take a weekend trip to Vegas. What do you think?" replied Vanessa.

Carla Santiago frowned. "You're kidding, right? Girl, I have five kids and the oldest is preparing for high school. I don't have the time, money, or energy to waste in Las Vegas. And who is supposed to be watching my kids for the entire weekend while I'm away squandering money?"

"Squandering money? Girl, you got to live a little," replied Jacky.

"Both you and Vanessa are single, and without children. You don't have husbands or families to think about like the rest of us," said Patricia to Jacky. "That's not a good idea."

LisaMarie, nodded her head. "I agree with Patricia. It amazes me how much I spend on things like food, haircuts, and clothes for my two boys. They haven't reached teenage yet, but I shudder to think about the costs of feeding and clothing them."

"You and me both," said Anna Yang. "I keep having renewed honor for the sacrifices my parents made with my brother and I."

"Well, sorry ladies, but I can't imagine spending an entire weekend away from my girls," said Angela. "They're almost teenagers now. I'm trying to spend as much time with them as possible."

"You and me both. Mine *is* a teenager. I hardly see him as it is unless I plan a family dinner or something," said Diana Minnelli.

"Let's not talk about weekends away from our families," said Sallie Anne Lewis. "Instead, how about a day trip somewhere? We could take the ferry to New York, have lunch together, and come back in time to have dinner with our families."

"I like that idea much better," agreed Janelle. "It's like a book club day, but with a different way to meet and socialize."

"It's also less expensive than a weekend away," said Sallie Anne.

"I would like to participate in something like that," said Anna.

Tessa turned to her friend on her right. "Pitch them your idea, Marissa."

"Oh, boy!" grinned Beth, reaching for her lemonade glass. "This should be good. Whenever you two get together, there's always something brewing."

"Oh, hush, Beth," said Tessa. She laughed despite herself.

"I was thinking why don't we attend a book signing for our book club anniversary? Then we could do lunch at the new bistro that's directly across the street from the bookstore," said Marissa.

"Hmm...I wonder whose bookstore it is?" said Kristen, grinning.

Emily laughed. "I saw the book signing promos about a month ago and called Marissa about it. Thank you, Tessa, for prodding our intrepid author."

Stacie said, "I really like the idea of a book signing event."

"Me, too. Count me in!" said Sierra.

"Now, that is an excellent idea!" remarked Diana.

"Let's finalize a date for our work calendars, ladies, so we can all attend together," Elsa suggested.

"Yes, please!" said Lynda. "I'm famished."

"Famished? Come on now, ladies. We can't have the pregnant lady, famished," said Angela with a grin. Lynda pinched her.

As if on cue, Ida Mae Prescott walked onto the patio. She uncovered platters of salads and sandwiches on a long table. Ida Mae was tall with a trim, athletic frame. Almond-shaped eyes and high cheekbones accentuated shiny salt and pepper gray wavy hair set in a golden-brown complexion. She brought Lynda a heaping plate of food while the ladies gathered around the banquet table.

Seated at a patio table for four, Marissa and Janelle shared a private conversation before being joined by Stacie and Patricia. They later pulled chairs over for Tessa, Sallie Anne, and Beth. Across the room, Jacky watched them with a wistful look.

On her way home, Marissa was thinking of what she felt like having for dinner when her phone rang. She stopped at a red light. The car phone picked up the call on the second ring.

"Hello?"

"Hey girl. That was a great idea for the book series. You must have stayed up all night to think of that one."

"Very funny. What do you want, Jacky? I'm busy."

"I didn't get a chance to tell you but, I have a date with a nice gentleman this evening."

"Good for you. What happened to the other guy you told me about a few weeks ago?"

"Oh, he was just for one night. Nice guy, though."

"Okay. Well, enjoy your evening."

"If all goes well, you might meet him one day."

"Who? This guy?"

"Yes. This guy." Jacky giggled.

"Promises, promises. Have a good time."

"No, really," insisted Jacky. "I really like this guy. We just resonate on so many levels."

"Okay. You've said that about all of them at some point."

Jacky laughed. "Well, I may have found my Mr. Right."

"Good for you. Listen, I got to run. Have a good night."

"Thanks. Talk soon."

Marissa walked into the kitchen without a second thought to Jacky's love life. She arranged the yellow bouquet of tea roses given to her by Ida Mae in a vase and set it in the middle of the dinner table. Then she went upstairs to change.

When Tony walked into the kitchen from the garage Marissa had the kitchen table set for dinner. He saw they were having spaghetti and homemade meatballs. He looked in the oven and saw the garlic bread on the warming tray. She was not downstairs, so he went upstairs. She was not in their bedroom. Tony walked down to the next three bedrooms. He walked back down to their bedroom. Tony took his weapon out of its holster and held it to his side. Then he heard a sound coming from their walk-in closet. He looked in. Marissa was sitting on the floor in front of a large box. She screamed before she recognized him. He grinned. He kept his gun from view as he leaned in the door.

"Hey babe. What are you doing?"

"I was looking for my college yearbook. I wanted to do a collage for our fifteenth anniversary."

Tony disappeared into the bedroom to put his weapon away and change clothing. "Have we been married that long? Sometimes it seems longer."

"Very funny. I'm talking about my women's book club. We're celebrating fifteen years soon."

"Congratulations. I hate to interrupt your search, but can I get my beautiful wife to share dinner with me?"

She grinned. "Yes. How was your day?"

"Crazy busy cool."

"Oh my!"

Over dinner they shared a conversation about their day.

"Did you get any writing in?"

"I had a great morning. Then Janelle came over, and we drove to the shopping center. I picked up more undershirts and socks for you. I couldn't remember if you needed anything else."

"No, baby. That was it. Thank you."

"You're welcome."

"I saw James Alan this afternoon. He reminded me we're having dinner with him and Stacie on Sunday."

"Yes, we are. I thought I told you. Anyway, I had Maria pick up your navy striped suit from the cleaners."

"Pass the bread, please. Thanks. What's the purpose of this Sunday's dinner?"

She grinned. "One of the twins won an oratory presentation, so it's a kind of celebratory dinner for him."

"Which twin? Joe or John?"

"I don't remember." She picked up his finished plate. "Are you too tired?"

"What do you have in mind?"

"There's a good romantic thriller coming on in a few minutes. Want to watch it with me."

"Why watch a movie when we can make our own?"

"Is that a, no?"

"Can I take a shower first?"

"Sure. I'll clean the kitchen. We'll eat our dessert while the movie is on."

She caught Tony looking at her smiling. "Stop it, Tony. I really want to see this movie. Janelle said it's a must-watch. Go take your shower. I'll have everything set up in the family room."

On his way downstairs after his shower, Tony lowered the lighting throughout the house. In the family room he walked to the wall-mounted television and turned on the program. Marissa walked over with a tray.

"Strawberry shortcake. I haven't had this since I was a kid."

"Your mama gave me the recipe. I hope you like it. Dim the light on your side, please."

They snuggled together on their oversized sectional. They soon fell asleep and slept soundly through the night.

Chapter 4

It was nine in the morning, and Marissa could not think of how best to start writing. She wondered if trying to switch genres was one of her better or worse ideas. Frustrated, she walked into the kitchen and made a salmon salad. Then she wrote out a grocery list for the following week. The doorbell and her phone rang simultaneously. Jacky sailed in.

"Well, good morning to you, too," Marissa said to Jacky's back.

"So, how's the writing coming along?"

Jacky's voice trailed into the living room from the kitchen. Marissa walked into the kitchen. Jacky was busy inspecting the refrigerator's contents before taking out the bowl of salmon salad.

"There's peach tea in there too," offered Marissa. "The writing is coming. I won't complain."

"Good. Give me what you've written so far."

Jacky busied herself with the salad and pouring the tea. She took her plate and tea to the breakfast table and sat down. Marissa sat on one of the bar stools at the counter. Jacky ate in silence for a few minutes. She wiped her mouth.

"Very good salad, as always. I noticed the macaroni salad. One thing I will say about you is that you stay consistent in your habits."

"Oh? How so?"

"Whenever you have writer's block you resort to making food."

"Preparing a meal is how I think. Remember all the meals I made in the chapter house?"

Jacky let out a little laugh. "Yeah, the cook stayed angry. I'm surprised you weren't kicked out of the sorority house for breaking one of the cardinal rules."

"Please! My grandparents own that building, and my sweet mother is on the Alumni Board."

Jacky remained quiet and busied herself with eating again. "So, what's the problem with the writing?"

"I can't seem to get started."

"Are you still on the kick about writing a crime novel?"

"It's not a kick Jacky."

"Okay, excuse my poor choice of words to describe your sudden infatuation with a genre you are foreign about."

"Why is it so wrong of me to want to expand beyond being a one-hit wonder?"

"Do you hear yourself? You have been a consistent fifteen-year hit wonder. Why mess with the formula?"

"I don't know. I guess I need a challenge."

"Looks like you've found one. What does Tony say about all this?"

"You asked me that before."

"And apparently I'm still not satisfied with the answer."

Marissa smirked. "You get on my nerves. You know that, right?"

"That's what friends, and more importantly, book publicists are for. Now that my tummy's full, and I have a headache from your confession, I think I'll return to work and check on my pension."

"Oh, you are witty today!" exclaimed Marissa, putting the dirty dishes in the dishwasher.

She heard the front door slam, and knew Jacky had left. Her phone on the counter rang.

"Hi Sallie Anne, how are you?"

"Fine, sweetie. I was just calling to see if you wanted to join the girls for lunch this afternoon. Patricia may come, but she said to go on without her if she's too late."

"Sure, the Falls Bistro?"

"Two o'clock sharp."

"See you soon then. I got to get my run in."

"Okay, sweetie. See you soon."

Marissa's friends were seated in the restaurant when she pulled up in the parking lot of Falls Bistro. She looked for Patricia's sleek black sedan with the law enforcement logo on the side windshield. Parked next to it was Stacie's black sport import. Further over, she spied Janelle's truck on the other side of Stacie's car. A blue and yellow sticker was pasted on the right-side windshield of all three vehicles as if it was hers.

Satisfied, her friends were inside, she smoothed down the skirt of the blue, double-breasted wool coat dress she wore. She gathered her handbag and woolen shawl. She looked at her reflection one more time in her compact. Marissa followed the server to the well-dressed women seated in a large circular booth. She sat on the end next to Janelle in a pink woolen suit with a blue collar as they hugged and held hands for a minute.

"We ordered cocoa mugs for the table," said Sallie Anne.

"Oh, that's good," responded Marissa.

"I love that dress, Marissa!" gushed fashion maven Sallie Anne attired in an olive-green wool coat dress.

"Thank you. I love that color green on you."

Beth listened to her friends' compliments of each other with an impatient toss of her platinum blonde head.

"Marissa, listen. I was just about to tell the ladies a news item Sallie Anne brought me this morning. Now I don't have to repeat myself."

Marissa laughed. "Must be juicy if you don't want to repeat it."

Beth's deep blue eyes surveyed Marissa. The women sensed she was about to say something they needed to hear. They all subconsciously leaned forward as Beth lowered her voice.

"Seems Winding Falls has a new crime novelist."

"A new what?" echoed Stacie with a slight smile.

"Who is it?" asked Kristen reaching for a roll.

Patricia sat back with a sardonic look at Beth. "Good one, girl."

Janelle passed the butter dish. "Are you interviewing this novelist, Sallie Anne?"

"Not me," said Sallie Anne, tossing her dark red pixie curls. The golden eyes surveyed Beth with interest. "I had thought we were going to wait a bit Beth to authenticate the rumor."

"Pass the breadbasket, please," said Tessa as she turned to Beth. "Who is this new novelist?"

Beth grinned. "Our resident writer is switching genres from romance to crime stories." She pointed to Marissa.

Janelle looked at Marissa. "Oh, wow! Is it true, Marissa? Will you be putting in some of the details from Tony's cases?"

"She'd better not!" said Patricia in a low voice. "This is not the big city. Marissa will have to continue to use her imagination as she's done in the past."

"That's not fair!" pouted Sallie Anne. "As a writer she comes into great information, and I'm certain it will be in her next whodunit book."

"Whodunit book?" With a frown Kristen's head swerved to look at Marissa. "What is Sallie Anne talking about Marissa?"

Sallie Anne blurted out, "Jacky told me all about Marissa wanting to switch genres from romance to whodunits. Jacky said Marissa wants to be a lady Sherlock Holmes."

To emphasize her comment, Sallie Anne pantomimed a woman blindly in search of clues on the tablecloth. The women shrieked with laughter. A tight smile spread across Marissa's face, and she slapped the table hard. The women were startled.

"Jacky is supposed to be my publicist not a gossip columnist. Second, I am playing around with the idea because I'm tired of writing the same thing year after year. I just shared the suggestion with her this morning. How is it she's gotten it to you this quick, Beth?"

"Calm down, Marissa." Beth swallowed hard. "I didn't know."

Sallie Anne came to the aid of her best friend. "Please calm down Marissa. I apologize for mocking you."

Marissa took a sip of cocoa to calm her nerves. Her hand shook a little. Tessa saw the hand tremor and looked at Marissa with a chagrin look. "That was not for Jacky to do. Besides, there's a difference between a whodunit and a murder!"

"True, Tessa. The police decide where cases fit. Homicides are complex cases, especially in this litigious town," said Patricia, her arms crossed as she looked beyond them to a spot above their heads.

Janelle put an arm through Marissa's. "Are you okay?"

Marissa struggled to control her temper. "I'm fine, Janelle. I need to get Jacky out of my life. I think she's made enough money off me these last fifteen years. Why am I serving a penance?"

Around the table was silence. The women avoided looking at Marissa. Sallie Anne grabbed a menu.

"Here comes our server. Let's order. I'm starving."

Patricia stood up. "Sorry, ladies. I need to go to the office. I need to have a chat with our mayor. If there's something going on, I need to know about it."

"Can we get first scoop when you do?" Sallie Anne stared directly at Patricia impervious to the attorney's mood.

Surprisingly, Patricia smiled. "Sure, Sallie Anne. Thanks for asking."

"Oh, please stay Patricia," Janelle pleaded.

Patricia waved but kept weaving through the tables to the front door. Marissa watched Patricia until she disappeared. She sighed. How she despised Jacky sometimes.

Several days later, Marissa managed to type the first chapter in her new genre, but it was hard going. She decided to type and see where it took her. An hour later she read what she wrote and removed the page. She ambled into the kitchen and thought of baking something. She walked over to the open pantry closet and looked inside. Their housekeeper, Maria Espinoza Sandoval, was restocking the shelves with cleaning items. She looked up from her task.

"Ms. Marissa, I'm trying this new cleanser since Mr. Tony was allergic to the other one. It has a clean scent. Smell."

She offered the bottle to Marissa. "Oh, this one does have a clean smell. Like fresh laundry."

Maria laughed. "That's a good description."

They both heard the doorbell, and then the phone. "I'll be upstairs cleaning the bathrooms if you need me."

Maria used the kitchen stairs to the upstairs floor. Marissa shook her head. Maria never developed a liking for Jacky, and never explained why.

"Well, thank you for not having me hanging on the doorknob for an hour. What are you doing today?"

Jacky strolled in, tossed her tote bag on a nearby chair, and walked through the living room and over to Marissa's writing nook. She hovered over the blank screen.

"What's happening here?"

"Apparently nothing."

"Oh goodness! You could be halfway through a draft. Why are you insisting on killing yourself and torturing me?"

Jacky walked into the kitchen. She washed her hands and opened the refrigerator. Marissa leaned on the counter.

"Shouldn't that be the other way around? Tuna salad in red bowl to your right."

"No, it shouldn't cause you're killing me with this new genre. Thanks!"

"Want some coffee? I was about to make a fresh pot."

"Sure. Any rolls? Never mind, I see them."

"I had lunch with the girls a few days ago. I was told you mentioned me switching genres. Everyone thought it was funny but me."

"So what?"

"Why would you tell Beth and Sallie Anne of all people my story ideas?"

"Oh, don't get all upset. I just think it's funny trying to switch genres in midstream instead of staying..."

"What? Safe? Always playing it safe, uh Jacky?"

"Now look, I'm sorry if I offended you."

"Shut up, Jacky! You don't care about anybody else's feelings but your own. You're my book publicist and that's it! You don't need to be telling my friends my professional business."

"You forget they're my friends too."

"At least I can differentiate between friendship and work!"

"Oh, please! You're just angry because I told them first. Admit it."

"I'll tell you what I admit. I admit it's time we severed our partnership. I'm sick of you!"

Struck by the statement, Jacky looked at her. "Hey, I'm sorry. Really. You're right. That was an invasion of your privacy. I won't do it again. Just stop being angry. I'm sorry."

Marissa left the kitchen. She sat down in front of her tablet. Jacky brought her prepared plate to the dining room.

"You want me to pour you a coffee, too?" she asked Marissa.

"No, I've got it."

Marissa walked into the kitchen and poured herself a cup of coffee. Jacky followed her.

Subconsciously Jacky held her hands clasped together in a praying or pleading gesture.

"Marissa, please forgive me. I'm terribly sorry. I guess I'm taking our friendship for granted. You justified to be angry. I do apologize."

"Forget it."

Marissa walked back to the dining room with her coffee. Jacky followed and tried desperately to think of a topic to ease the tension between them.

"Hey, I'm going shopping for a gown. I have a hot date with the new guy I'm seeing. I tell you he really reminds me of someone."

"What's his name?"

"Al Max."

Marissa side-eyed her. "Al Max? Is that his right name?"

"Oh, look who's got jokes! Yes, it's his right name. He showed me his driver's license."

"Are you guys serious yet?"

"Not yet. I just met him a few months ago."

"A few months ago?"

Jacky did not notice the cruel twist to Marissa's face. Nor did she catch the gleam in her eye. Marissa sipped her coffee. She smiled at Jacky.

"He hasn't been in your bed yet. What are you waiting for? Or is he the one waiting? You know you have no restraint where your bed is involved. Fly the friendly skies on Jacky's bed! Did you tell our friends that! How easy you are. You use your body like a playground. When will you tell *our* friends *that*?"

Marissa's laugh was cruel. She looked at Jacky through dark eyes. She did not notice, nor did she care about the look of embarrassment and hurt on Jacky's face.

Chapter 5

Beautiful to look at but self-absorbed. Why are women oblivious to their personal safety? Lovely home and community but tone-deaf to the dangers out here. Too much isolation from the real world. I can't tell if she's running or jogging because her schedule is erratic. He's such a cautious fellow, and she's careless with her personal safety. What a pair! What a magnificent day it is. Ah! I love spring. I like the fact she wears such bold, bright colors. Easy to keep track of her in these woods where they have mountain cats. Hmm...good speed and distance. Except for that one stretch she mostly runs where there are lots of people. That's a great safety measure. Okay, enough for today. Don't want to overdo it. There's a lovely blonde coming my way. Nice wave and keep it moving. She barely looked at me. Amazing how none of them pay attention to anyone or anything in their natural surroundings. Simply incredible!

It had been a tiring but productive day for Tessa's Salon. Her shop was booked solid for months with many of her long-time clients insisting on scheduled appointments. She smiled. She was grateful for them. They were the reason she stayed as long as she had.

A knock and her salon manager, Marian Brown, walked in. The diminutive beauty stood five feet two inches tall, wore four-inch heels every day, and served sassy attitude with a smile.

"Hey, Tessa. I'm leaving for the day. We have two morning appointments scheduled for tomorrow, and one cancellation mid-afternoon."

"Thanks, Marian. Say, did Jacky Crenshaw call at all today?"

"No, and that's not like her at all. I hope she's okay."

"Me too. Have a good night, Marian."

"You too. See you tomorrow."

Tessa thought a moment. Who would have seen Jacky last? Tessa phoned Marissa.

"Hello? Marissa?"

"Hi, Tessa. Did I leave something behind?"

"No. I'm sorry to bother you at home."

"That's all right, Tessa. What's wrong, sweetie?"

"Have you heard from Jacky at all?"

"Jacky? No. Why?"

"She had a hair appointment early this morning, and never called or showed up yet."

"Wow! He must be a great guy!"

"Tell me about it. He's some kind of man to make her forget about getting her hair done."

They both laughed with gusto for a few minutes. Marissa finally caught her breath.

"Tessa, sweetie, if I hear from her, I'll tell her to call you."

"Thanks, lady. Have a good night."

"You too, sweetie." Marissa laid the phone down.

Reclining on the sectional in the family room, Tony asked, "What was so funny?"

"Jacky missed her hair appointment."

"That was so funny you laughed for five minutes?"

"You're not a woman. Let it go."

Tony looked at Marissa in her tank top and shorts. "Come here."

"No."

"Then I guess I'll have to come get you."

Tony put the remote on the table. Marissa was near to the back stairs. She giggled. By the time Tony jumped over the coffee table, Marissa was halfway up the stairs. She ran into the bedroom where they spent the rest of the evening.

31

Chapter 6

Ah, the exquisite Janelle Nicholas with the face of an angel! You have always been a vision of loveliness. You earned every one of those tiaras they placed on your gorgeous head. Such a beautiful and well-kept home. You're so talented, but again, you always were. What a fabulous kitchen. Pie in the oven? Yes, smells delicious. I'm sure your family will enjoy it.

Now we must get down to business. I don't want to inflict much damage to that breathtaking face. Oh, if you had minded your own business, I would not have to do this. But you and I know there's one person to blame. But don't worry, Janelle, she'll get what's coming to her too. I can truthfully promise you that much.

Now go to sleep, my lovely angel. Rest in peace, the beautiful daughter of Venus.

O'Neill and Benson turned onto the wide street of tree-lined oaks. The homes in this section of upscale Washington Heights were built on the Craftsman-style and tended to sit uphill. They parked in front of an expansive home with a wide walkway leading to a wider enclosed porch. The porch was laid out with floral-patterned and wicker furniture at one end and a dining set at the other.

The interior of the home was a semi-open design with the spacious living and dining rooms seamlessly connected by the placement of traditional furniture. Nothing was out of place.

Benson stooped to look at the sewing basket on the living room coffee table. She walked under an arched doorway leading into the roomy kitchen.

A pie was in the oven. Benson checked the temperature. She spied something out of the corner of her eye. Looking down she saw a woman's leg. Walking around the counter she gazed into the still face of the woman, with eyes and mouth wide open, and bearing the anguished, tortured look that earmarked a violent act of death. Benson staggered back onto the oven door dismay marking her face. O'Neill walked into the kitchen. He looked at his partner, walked around the counter, and saw the body of the slain woman. He stooped down and examined the light bruising around the victim's broken neck. O'Neill turned to his partner.

"I take it you knew her?"

"We were in college together."

"I'm sorry, Vee. Were you close?"

"No. Not really."

"Wait a minute...who found her?" O'Neill looked around for an officer. "Who's our witness, Ben?"

The beefy officer stood on the other side of the counter. "Her son, Spencer Carr."

"Where is he now?"

"In the den with his three brothers and a social worker."

"What's the social worker's name?"

He consulted his notepad. "Angela Rojas."

"How long's she been here?"

"She was here when I got here, and Sam and I were the first officers on the scene. Then you arrived."

"Thanks, Ben." O'Neill turned to Benson with a long sigh. "The grandparents don't live far from here. Let me call them."

"Okay, but the boy needs to be questioned."

"We'll do that when his father arrives, Vee."

"Why wait?"

"You didn't catch the boy's name? His father is Spencer Carr, the personal lawyer and friend of our mayor. Carr will throw the book at us if we violate his minor son's rights."

"You have a point. I'll speak to the social worker." She turned to the officer again. "Officer Frazier, could you tell the social worker I'd like to speak with her, please?"

"Vee, call the lieutenant first. I'll call the grandparents and his father."

Benson wandered into the next room to get away from the kitchen area. The room was decorated in a pink floral pattern with long full windows and airy, gauze drapes. A black and white portrait of Janelle against a pale pink backdrop graced the fireplace. Benson studied the portrait. Then she noticed smaller photos of Janelle with her husband and sons. She smiled at one of Janelle surrounded by her four boys. It was a recent photo. Tears came to Benson's eyes. Gorgeous, sweet Janelle. In the back of her mind as she made phone calls, she wondered how Marissa would take this horrible news.

Benson walked back to the front of the home. She looked in a room and saw the social worker. It was a large room done in checkered patterns of beige and blue. The two smaller boys were playing a board game at a round table in the corner. The middle one watched a television on the wall as he played a video game. A police officer was standing near an open patio door. He nodded his head toward the back of the room.

The social worker and the boy were seated in two overstuffed chairs by a window. They were talking. Benson stood in the open doorway and watched them. Presently the woman looked over and a few seconds later joined Benson on the patio. The boy stayed in the chair with a vacant look on his face.

"Hey, Vanessa. How are you?"

"Hi, Angela. I'm good. I see you got your hands full."

"This is a mess, girl."

"Tell me about it. Poor Janelle. How long have you been here?"

"About an hour now. Got here just before you showed up."

"Has he said anything?"

"The kid's in shock. You can't question him until his father gets here."

"So, I heard. How did you get here?"

"Spencer called me. I'm his godmother."

"Oh, I didn't know that. I would think Marissa would be."

"Marissa was *supposed* to be but when she lost her baby. It would have been too emotional for her."

"Yes, I forgot about that." Benson stared above Rojas head. "Give me something."

Rojas gave a short laugh. "Off the record, what do you need?"

"Off the record? How were things when you arrived?"

"Oh, that's easy. Same as they are now. He had his brothers occupied and even brought them their snacks. He's running on remote, but eventually he'll break."

"Speaking of breaking, I thought of Marissa."

"You and me both, girl. She will lose her mind. She and Janelle were lifelong best friends. I can't believe she's gone myself. Who would ever want to hurt Janelle? Beautiful, sweet, kind Janelle."

"Let me get back to the front room. Is Jesus still grilling Saturday?"

"You know he is! We were thinking of making it a pool party since we're in August now. But with this happening, I don't know."

"Sounds like a good idea. Let me know by Friday. I need to buy a new swimsuit."

"Girl, hush! You could swim in a sack, and no one would care. Once a beauty queen, always a beauty queen."

"Keep it up. Flattery will get you my famous stuffed apple pie as a reward."

Both women smiled amid the tragedy.

Tony arrived in an unmarked car. Dark sunglasses covered his eyes. He stopped and spoke on his phone for several minutes. He was shown to the body still on the kitchen floor. He stooped beside the medical examiner, who was crouched writing on a tablet. Tony inspected the victim's neck wound.

"What happened here, Elsa?" he asked in a low voice.

"The victim was manually strangled. Seems he stood behind her and applied pressure from the back of her neck." She pointed to the side of the victim. "See here. Looks like the pressure was so deep it left an imprint. I have a photo of it if you want to see it."

"Was she physically assaulted?"

"Doesn't seem to be. This was a quiet murder; no struggling involved."

"Excellent work, Elsa."

"Of course, as soon as my full examination is completed, I'll send you my findings."

Tony's attention shifted to the newly arrived husband of the victim. "Thanks, Elsa."

Spencer Carr was a dapper man who emotionally broke down when told his wife was dead. He was restrained from entering the kitchen. He composed himself in a downstairs bathroom. When he came out, he walked straight to Tony and O'Neill, and the men hugged. They engaged in a private conversation. Across the room, Benson studied the three men. Her attention was diverted to a commotion at the front door. A petite woman with a full head of white hair entered after a police escort and was shown to the den. The white-haired man behind her was an older version of his son. The men hugged. Tony beckoned Benson over.

"Detective Benson, this is Judge Carr. I'm taking him to his grandsons. You and James interview Mr. Carr and Spencer."

Tony whisked the judge away before Benson could offer her condolences.

On the patio deck off the kitchen, O'Neill and Benson questioned the husband. The attorney now wore dark wraparound sunglasses that obstructed a clear view of his eyes which annoyed the detective.

"Deepest condolences on your loss, sir," began Benson. "The only question I have concerns any visitors you may have had in your home recently."

"We've had a technician hook up a cable line that fell during the last thunderstorm. That was about three months ago. He never entered the premises."

"What about inside the home?"

"This is a new build. So far, we've no need for appliance upgrades or maintenance."

"Did you or your wife keep a record of any maintenance to your property, such as lawn care?"

"My wife and I consulted on everything in our marriage. She had a good system she used on her private computer. Her room is to your left as you leave the kitchen."

O'Neill spoke next. "Did you speak to your wife this morning?"

Benson noticed the tightening of Carr's jawline. In a voice faint with emotion, Carr said, "No. I was in a board meeting until receiving the call to come here."

"Who called you, sir?" asked Benson. She did not see the look O'Neill gave her.

"I don't remember, Detective."

"Mr. Carr, we're going to speak to your son next if you'd like to be present," said O'Neill.

"Yes. Thank you, Sergeant."

Carr allowed Benson to question his oldest son in his presence in the living room.

"I know this is a difficult time for you, Spencer," began Benson. "I need you to answer a few questions for me. Okay?"

"I understand," he said. He was trying to hold in tears. He resembled his mother.

"How old are you, Spencer?"

"I'm thirteen."

"What time did you return home from school today?"

"About an hour ago. We're let out in time to catch the school bus."

"This is the normal time you arrive home?"

"Yes."

"Are you usually the first one home?"

"Yes, my brothers are in elementary school, and they arrive here after me."

"Walk me through what you saw today, Spencer."

"The front door was open. Mom never leaves the door open unless she's sitting on the porch. It's cold today so she wouldn't be sitting..." He stopped and looked at his father before speaking again. "I saw her sewing basket in the living room. I knew she was here. I walked into the kitchen, and at first, I didn't see her, and..."

At this point he broke down hiding his face in his hands. His body convulsed with tears. His father walked near, and they embraced. He nodded at Benson, and she understood the interview was over. The attorney and his son held tightly to each other as they walked out.

O'Neill turned to Benson. "Let's go check out Janelle's room. We need to look at her computer system."

He walked ahead of Benson. She followed quietly. This was a big home with spacious rooms. They found Janelle's sitting room in a cozy nook on the other side of the front stairs. The area was designed in a color palette of soft pink and off-white. The furniture in this room was in a muted floral pattern made complete with a matching circular ottoman table. On one side of a wall were photos in different size frames of family members and close friends.

"What a beautiful room," said Benson. "I love the frilly curtains. Here's a table full of photos." Benson scrutinized the pictures. They were of varying sizes and flooded the table. "These are all of Janelle and Marissa. I didn't know they knew each other since they were children."

O'Neill looked but did not respond. He picked up the white tablet lying on a side table. He typed several key formations. Benson turned to a tall white built-in bookcase. One of the shelves was stocked with photos. A few were of their sorority members taken over twenty years ago. She barely recognized anyone. She heard O'Neill behind her.

"Give Mr. Carr a receipt. We're taking this tablet as evidence."

They left the room. When O'Neill and Benson entered the living room, they saw the technicians in their white hazmat suits in the kitchen and on the patio outside. Tony walked into the room followed by Bill Holtz, the mayor of Winding Falls.

The mayor directed his questions to O'Neill. "What happened here?"

"Janelle Carr was the victim of a fatal assault this morning."

"I know that part. I'm asking what happened to her."

"The medical examiner states she was manually strangled."

"Is Spencer here?"

"He's in the den with his parents and children."

"Who found Janelle?"

"The couple's oldest son," said O'Neill.

"What a horrible thing for a kid to see..." Holtz shook his head. "Was the boy questioned with his father present?"

"Yes sir," said Benson.

"I'm going to speak to Spencer and the family," said Holtz and left them.

O'Neill turned to Tony. "We need to get Robin to put together something for the news tonight."

"You're right. I'll text her the details," said Tony. "Check the surveillance in this home and along this block, James. Gather as much information as you can about the security along this block and in this community. We've got to hit the ground running on this one. Maybe someone saw something. Be as discreet as possible before this hits the airwaves."

"You might be too late," said O'Neill.

He nodded at the growing crowd of spectators and the arriving news trucks. A uniformed cop walked up to them.

"Lieutenant Marigny, the reporters are asking if anyone from the police department will give a statement about what's happened here. What do you want me to tell them?"

"Someone's already tipped them off this is Carr's wife."

"Have you seen Captain Murray here?"

"Yes."

"Go tell him what you just told me." Tony turned to Benson. "How did the social worker arrive here ahead of the police?"

Benson swallowed. O'Neill looked at her. "Angela Rojas and her husband are his godparents."

"Who are they?"

"Jesus Rojas is a computer programmer. They live in Delsea Park North. They have two daughters."

"Write that up in your report complete with full information on the social worker."

Another man entered the home. He surveyed the room with a solemn expression before he walked over to Tony.

"Afternoon, Lieutenant."

"Chief Hall. The mayor and Judge Carr are also here."

"Good, but I came to see you," said the man. "Walk with me, Lieutenant."

Tony walked with the man away from the house.

Chapter 7

Police Chief Rob Hall was a quiet man and known to be calm-tempered. He and Tony had developed an easy friendship over the years.

Leading the way, Hall stopped on the curb, and glanced over his shoulder to make sure no one was nearby. Tony stood facing him.

"Who was on site first?" asked Hall in his deep bass voice.

"The social worker got here before my detectives."

"Who alerted her?"

"The oldest son. Her name is Angela Rojas and she's the boy's godmother."

"Okay. I can see him calling his godmother. Does she live close by? What do you know of her?"

"She's a social worker and her husband is a computer programmer. They live in Delsea Park North. They have two young daughters."

"Do you think Janelle's murder has anything to do with the gangland case Spencer tried a few months ago?"

"I thought about it until I saw Janelle. This was a quiet murder. The assailant strangled her. There's no other bruises on her body that I could see. I'll wait for the final medical report."

"Okay. What's bothering you then?"

"The wives were best friends. Grew up together."

Hall sighed. "Ah, man! Are you free for lunch? I was meeting Fred. We need to go over a few things about this incident in connection with Spencer."

"Sure."

"I'll get my wife to call Marissa. Those two work on some committees together. I'm sure my wife can keep her distracted until you can get home."

"It was horrible seeing Janelle that way. I've known her for as long as I've known Marissa. They were inseparable, Rob."

"I know. That's how Patty is with her best friend. Come on, let's get back in there."

It was afternoon when Tony stepped off the elevator, waved at the room, and disappeared into his office. He came out moments later with his shirt sleeves rolled up, his gun holster firmly in place, and carrying his tablet. He wore the pleasant expression that was his trademark.

"Okay. What do we have?" said Tony.

O'Neill said, "Our victim is Janelle Carr, a thirty-seven-year-old mother of four. She was found strangled in her kitchen. There were no signs of forced entry."

Benson sighed before saying, "It was such a wholesome home. The sewing kit in the living room with a homemade pie in the oven in the kitchen."

"Pie?" repeated Tony. "Was the oven turned on?"

"No. I checked to see if the oven was off." Benson said. "It was, but it was still warm to the touch."

"The murderer could have turned off the oven or the victim turned it off before she was murdered," said O'Neill. "We found only her prints."

"Was there anything taken from the home?" asked Tony.

"Nothing according to Mr. Carr."

"The house was checked for an illegal way in, and nothing was found. The assumption is that she let her killer in the home."

"Was she molested?" asked Tony.

"The medical examiner stated she was not, so it's not a sex crime."

"Was either one having extramarital affairs?"

"Good question" said Benson, still looking at her notes. "We don't know."

"Did they have any kind of home security system?"

"There was no security system setup for their home."

"Were there any witnesses?"

"None. We went door-to-door asking their neighbors and none saw or heard anything out of the ordinary."

There was silence for a moment as the detectives looked at Tony. Tony smiled. "Vee, I'm told you attended school with the deceased. Is that true?"

"Yes. We were in college together. Before you ask, no, I didn't know her personally. She hung with a different crowd, but she seemed to be a nice person."

"Nice person in what way?"

"She was the kind of beautiful girl you expected to have an attitude thinking the world should grovel at her feet, but she was the exact opposite. She spoke to everyone. A nice person."

O'Neill said, "We've given her laptop to the crime lab to open. Kevin's over there now. As soon as they open it, he'll let me know the contents."

"Excellent work. Okay, I want you to investigate Spencer Carr's finances. Do so as discreetly as possible. Also interview the library where Mrs. Carr worked and see if she has an office. James, interview my wife and her publicist, Jacky Crenshaw. Here's her contact information. If there's nothing else, James I need to see you for a moment."

"Give me a second."

O'Neill picked up the phone. Benson watched Tony walk to his office. She caught a glimpse of her partner eyeing her. She turned her keyboard on.

O'Neill rapped lightly on Tony's door before entering. Tony saw Benson at her desk. He looked at O'Neill who was seated.

"What's bugging you, James? I know that look."

"There's no home security video because Spencer and Janelle didn't think they needed one."

"What about the neighbors?"

"Same thing. No one along that row of homes has home security systems. According to the data I pulled since Washington Heights is an affluent community on the same level as Oxford Circle most of the homes have private surveillance systems."

"Did they?"

"I don't know yet. Waiting on a callback."

"What about the neighbors on their right side? Maybe they saw something. I know Karen is a stay-home mom."

"Karen and Tom are on vacation. Tom's parents were house-sitting but unfortunately were out to brunch with friends."

"So, we have no witnesses of any type." Tony tossed a paper clip across his desk. He watched Benson for a few minutes.

O'Neill, as if reading his mind, said, "Vee can't think of a solid reason why Janelle would have had this happen to her. To tell you the truth, I can't either."

"Well, James, one thing we both know is that people believe in revenge. Remember Spencer used to be a federal prosecutor."

"What's next?"

"Janelle was a part-time librarian. She had a small office in the back that I've had taped off. Talk to whoever's in charge now. Check her office while your there."

"Okay. I'll set up a meeting for tomorrow. Might get more leads." After a pause, O'Neill quietly asked, "What are you doing about Marissa? You know they spoke nearly every day."

"I'm going home now before she sees it on the news. Call me if you need me or anything interesting turns up."

"Take care of Marissa. This is going to hit her hard."

Tony looked at O'Neill and nodded. They walked out of the office together.

Tony did not make it out of the lot right away. Trevino and di Giovanni waited for him by his vehicle. Trevino stood with his hands in the pocket of the red pinstriped suit he wore. The red and black two-toned lace-ups finished off the look. Di Giovanni wore a black leather trench over a black turtleneck and slacks. The detective known for his good looks leaned casually against the driver's door. Tony looked from one man to the other.

"I need an escort home or something?"

"Some interesting things we think you should know about Mr. Carr," said Trevino.

"Write it up in a report, Luis."

"Not that simple, Tony," di Giovanni said.

"If it will help you any, I had a long lunch date with the captain and the chief. We discussed Carr's involvement with prosecuting those gangs. We're going to work on that angle to protect Carr and his sons."

Trevino and di Giovanni exchanged glances. Tony stopped smiling.

An hour later Tony parked in the garage next to Marissa's car. His heart nearly jumped out of his chest when he saw her seated in the family room watching television. He sat beside her and turned off the set.

"Hi, your home early."

"Hello, baby. Long day and I'm tired."

"Patty Hall came over. She left a few minutes before you got here."

"Oh, yeah. How is she?"

"Patty's fine. She brought over some design books. She wants to redo their home. You know, freshen it up some."

"Hmm... What's for dinner?"

"I made a pot roast."

"Smells good. How was your writing?"

"I had a great day. Hey, I saw on the news earlier about a homemaker being murdered. The news reporter didn't seem to know much."

He was more relieved than he needed to be. "It's a brand-new case, that's why. They all run into each other sometimes. Besides this one is different."

"Different? How?"

Knowing she would continue asking, he told her as little about it as possible. In turn, Marissa reminded him of a case he had been involved in when they lived in Chicago. He stared at her for a moment.

"Dear wife, I forgot all about that case. But this is a bit different. This is... is..."

"You must be tired. You're stuttering."

"Cute and funny."

"What's next in your investigation?"

"Finding clues that will lead to the capture of a killer."

"Tony, I was just about to put a cake in the oven. Can we talk some more during dinner? Go take a shower or something."

Tony hesitated for a minute. "Okay." He put the television remote in his pocket.

He took the back stairs to their bedroom. He put his gun holster on the top shelf of the closet, discarded his clothing, and walked into the bathroom. Tony stood under the running water thinking about the scene earlier at the Carr home.

Marissa was pulling a cake out of the oven as Tony entered the kitchen. A quick kiss as she removed the lid from a pot on the stove. She looked at him and smiled. He stood back and looked at her. The soft yellow floral blouse with its low-cut neckline emphasized the smooth neck. The top was tucked into the faded blue denims which hugged the trim figure like a glove. He looked at the bright yellow toenails on bare feet. He watched the curly ponytail as it swung seductively from side to side as she walked. She looked across the counter at him.

"Tony? What's the matter?"

She was giving him a concerned look. He walked into the family room and sat down wearily.

"Come here and sit beside me."

"Okay. What is it? Did something happen at work? Did someone on your team get hurt?"

"Marissa..." He looked at her.

"What's the matter, Tony?" She said it so softly he barely heard her.

"Janelle was found murdered earlier today."

When she finally stopped screaming, she collapsed in his arms. There were no tears. He carried her upstairs and put her to bed. She clung to him, silently clutching his chest until she fell asleep. Tony eased out of bed, dimmed the lighting, and walked downstairs. He had no appetite for food. He put everything away and cleaned the kitchen.

In his den he made a few phone calls. When he hung up, his phone rang steadily with text messages from his team. He called O'Neill and they spoke for an hour. Di Giovanni paid a visit with his friend, Michael Minnelli. The men spoke quietly in Tony's den.

He returned to the bedroom, turned off the soft lighting, and climbed into bed beside Marissa.

Chapter 8

The community was faithfully served by Falls Bank for over two hundred and fifty years. The four-story construction was designed in the Victorian style and modernized by revolving doors. The inside was airy, spacious and cozy. O'Neill and Benson were led down the glass walled hall by a pert redhead in a gray two-piece suit and four-inch heels. She stopped, turned, and pointed to an open doorway. A round man in a light gray tweed suit seated behind a large oak desk, waved them in. He beckoned to two black leather chairs in front of his desk. The office was spacious and made more by a wall of curtain-less windows.

The man looked at them and smiled. Benson saw his eyes were like dark sockets in his head. He was grossly overweight. She studied his hands. Big and meaty with chewed nail beds.

"I'm sorry, Detectives. Long morning. My name is Sam Weathers, accounts manager. What can I do for you again?"

"We'd like to look at the banking account of Janelle Carr. We also need her safe deposit box opened," said Benson.

"I'm sorry, but unless her husband authorizes such a transaction, that's not possible. Perhaps, if you get him to sign a release or something."

O'Neill smiled. He passed across a sheet. The man read it and looked at them again. He picked up his phone, and O'Neill took it from him.

"Mr. Weathers, we don't have time to play games with you. In case you hadn't heard, Janelle Carr, has been murdered. This is a homicide investigation. That piece of paper in your hands is a search warrant. I suggest you get yourself together, or we will shut down this bank."

Benson smiled. "While my partner's looking in the safe deposit box, I will need to investigate Mrs. Carr's bank accounts. Kill two birds with one stone."

Weathers sighed.

In the safe, O'Neill found various certificates, a small pink diary, some jewelry, and a will. He made a copy of the will. He read a few pages of the diary and frowned. Young girls were dramatic. He decided to bag the diary as potential evidence. Besides, his partner loved reading.

In a small room with a microfilm machine, Benson's search produced nothing but tired eyes.

O'Neill was seated in the bank lobby watching customers when Benson joined him. She plopped down in a chair across from him.

"Anything?" asked O'Neill.

"Nothing but sore eyes. Janelle Carr, and by extension, Spencer Carr's professional and personal finances are well organized. They use a tax firm that's highly rated. A woman named Kristen O'Leary manages the family finances at Stonehedge Martine Accountants. The family's legal matters are tended by Stacie Young. She's a partner at Hugo, Larsen, and Young. If there are discrepancies, I couldn't find them. The family's household accounts was managed by his late wife, and she had most of the family's daily expenses auto generated. To be as wealthy as they are, they live well within their financial means."

"Good for them."

"Any prenup agreements in place?"

"No," returned O'Neill. "There's living wills for healthcare, and both had wills leaving everything to their sons, not each other. Which is curious to me."

"What's curious about their wills?"

"Most women expect to claim their husband's pension on his death. So, I'm wondering if she was independently wealthy."

"I can answer that based on what I know about her. Janelle was the only child of two doctors. She was also the only granddaughter of the founder of the women's medical center out in Lakehurst. She didn't need her husband's wealth. She had plenty of her own."

"Well, that answers that." O'Neill tossed the evidence bag with the diary at her. "Some light reading when you have nothing else to do."

"What is it?"

"Her diary at seventeen or eighteen years old. Full of drama, tears, and fears. You'll love it. Classic chick lit."

Benson laughed and stuck the diary in her tote bag.

A few days later, the detectives walked into the airy Winding Falls Public Library and headed to the information desk. They flashed their badges at the receptionist and waited while she paged her superior. Benson pointed out several large urns of beautifully arranged white roses and camellias in the lobby. In a few minutes a small-boned woman with fair, translucent skin, light gray wavy hair, and sky-blue eyes, appeared from the back of the library. She wore a long red print dress with a red bulky cabled cardigan and carried two books she handed to the receptionist.

"Hello, Detectives. I'm Deborah McGhee. How may I help you?"

"I'm Sergeant O'Neill and this is my partner, Detective Benson. We'd like to ask you some questions about a coworker. Is there somewhere we could talk in private?"

"Yes, of course. Please follow me, Detectives. We can sit in here for more privacy. We have coffee, tea?"

"No, thank you, Ms. McGhee, we don't want to take up too much of your time," said Benson. "No doubt you've heard of the news regarding Janelle Carr?"

"Yes, my husband and I saw it on the news last night. Janelle was a wonderful lady. We're going to miss her charming and bright personality."

"How long have you worked here, Ms. McGhee?"

"I've been here for thirty-three years."

"As the head librarian?"

"No, I worked part-time because I had a family to raise. Connie Sheridan was the head librarian."

"How long had the victim worked here?"

"Janelle began working here part-time during her summer breaks in school.

"Janelle began working here part-time during her summer breaks in school. Since she was a young girl, she's been the fabric of this library for as long as I can remember."

The librarian stopped. Tears streamed down her face. She retrieved a cloth handkerchief from her cardigan and dabbed her eyes. She took some time to get herself together. The detectives waited. She regained her composure.

"Excuse me. As I was saying, once Janelle graduated from college, she became permanent. Two years later when Mrs. Sheridan retired Janelle was named head librarian."

"Why wasn't the position offered to you as you'd been here the longest?"

"I didn't want it. I'm the interim now until they can fill the role."

"At the time of her death was Ms. Carr full or part-time?"

"Janelle switched to part-time to be home with her children once they entered school. She often brought them here for the educational programs we have. As they grew older their interests moved elsewhere. But all four boys still take part in the math and science initiatives the library holds yearly. The younger ones are always here on Saturday mornings for our children's programs."

"What were her hours?"

"Janelle worked on Wednesday and Friday mornings. Those days are the busiest times of the week for the library."

"On those days, was the library opened later than usual?"

"Yes. We stayed open until six o'clock in the evenings."

"Who watched Ms. Carr's children while she was in the library?"

"Her best friend would pick them up from school and bring them here. To my knowledge her best friend was also on hand to babysit the boys."

"Who was the best friend?"

"The author, Marissa Marigny."

"How do you know they were best friends?"

"I've been here for a long time, Detective. The two women grew up together. As adults, Ms. Marigny was the only woman who came to the library to see Janelle. Whenever she visited, they would sit in Janelle's office in the back for hours. Sometimes Ms. Marigny would come get her for their lunch dates."

"When was the last time Ms. Marigny was here with the victim?"

"Last week, I believe. Wait a minute, no. A few days ago. They went shopping and Janelle took the rest of the afternoon off. Another lady sometimes visited along with Ms. Marigny. Her name is Jacky Crenshaw. She's the author's publicist."

"How many times did Ms. Crenshaw visit the victim?"

"Maybe twice that I know of."

"These two women were the only private visitors the deceased had?"

"Yes. But Ms. Crenshaw was more than Ms. Marigny's publicist."

"What do you mean?"

"Ms. Crenshaw told me on several occasions that they were all good friends."

"Can you remember, at any other time, anyone else visited Ms. Carr?"

"Oh, yes! Yearly we get a visit from the news anchor, Sallie Anne Lewis. She brings her camera man, and they snap photos of the library and such. They talk about our programs, and whatever best-selling book Marissa Marigny has written. That's so exciting because, really? Who doesn't know the news anchor? That woman is too gorgeous for words."

"How long has the news anchor been interviewing Ms. Carr?"

"Oh, gosh! It's been a few years. It began right after our Janelle ran in a marathon promoting a children's organization. In fact, she and Marissa Marigny ran in the same race. They were very close. I can only imagine the pain Janelle's passing has brought her." She dabbed at her eyes again. "In fact," McGhee continued through sobs, "the beautiful flowers gracing our lobby were sent by Marissa Marigny to honor Janelle."

"Did Ms. Carr ever mention any problems with customers? Someone in her daily life hassling her that she didn't want to mention to her husband?"

"Oh, no! There is no reports of disgruntled customers. Janelle grew up here and everyone knew her. In the years I've been here she is a woman I can honestly say whose personality was always warm and friendly."

"Ms. McGhee, as an observer, did you notice anything out of the way between the victim and her husband?"

"Out of the way?"

"Did she ever talk about him cheating, for instance?"

McGhee looked from one detective to the other with alarm and concern, despite the tears that continually leaked from her eyes.

"Oh, my goodness, no! They were truly a happy couple. He adored her. Often, he would send her a large bouquet of whatever flowers were in bloom, and she would spend the rest of the day blushing because we teased her so. But we loved her dearly."

The grief the librarian felt impacted Benson emotionally. She shifted in her seat and pretended to be note-taking, although she knew O'Neill's recorder was turned on. She was aware of O'Neill side-eyeing her. The librarian continued.

"I'm sorry. I wish I could give you something. I really do. That's why her death is so hard to process. She lived the perfect life. Loving husband, well-behaved children, and great friends."

"Thank you for your time, Ms. McGhee, and your cooperation."

"May we see Ms. Carr's office, please?"

"Yes. It's at the end of this hall. Here we are. I hope you catch whoever took our glorious Janelle away from us."

"If you recall anything else, please don't hesitate to call us."

"Thank you, I will."

The librarian walked away dabbing at the tears falling from her eyes.

O'Neill stood in the doorway of the late librarian's work office as Benson entered and thought of his at-home office. There was one wall with floor to ceiling built-in bookcases. To one side and facing the door was a stained oak table and chair presumably used as a desk. Across from the desk were two golden leather armchairs. Above the chairs on the wall was the Alpha Nu Sorority crest, paddle, and framed membership certificate. Below were various framed commendations from children's organizations.

O'Neill murmured, "She did a lot of work with kids. Being a mother of four children herself, I can see that."

"Hmm... she loved children."

Near a window was a blue cloth armchair with a yellow crochet shawl draped over the arm. O'Neill turned intending to walk out when he noticed the wall of photographs.

"There's Spencer Carr with the mayor on the golf course." Benson squinted at the picture.

There were two men in the background and one looked like Tony. O'Neill's phone buzzed. He walked past Benson out to the main library. Benson moved over to a small table set into the wall's alcove where a collage of pictures rested. Most of them were Janelle and Marissa. The detective studied several small-framed photographs of the two women from childhood to adulthood.

In the larger one, Marissa wore a light orange silk bridesmaid gown. She was seated beside Janelle who wore a white lace wedding gown. They looked alike enough to be sisters.

It was still light outside when Tony pulled into the garage and parked alongside Marissa's car. He checked the odometer on her vehicle. She had not driven in a few days. He walked into the house to dead silence. He looked at the plate in the oven and left it there.

In the dining room alcove, the laptop was closed. He checked the hall foyer. Unopened mail laid on the console. He headed upstairs.

At first, he did not see Marissa under the bed covers. He undressed and took a shower. Wrapping a towel around his waist he returned to the bedroom and walked over to Marissa. He shook her by the shoulders.

"Marissa, get up. We need to talk."

"Leave me alone, Tony. I don't want to talk."

"Get up, and it's the last time I ask."

Tony walked to the bedroom window and stood looking out onto the front lawn. Behind him, he could hear rustling. He heard the shower start. He put on a robe and sat down in the armchair. Marissa came out in a robe. Her hair piled high on her head in a complicated symmetry of black curls, she sat across from him. He studied her. Her face was thinner and her eyes red from crying. Her toenails were painted black. He looked at her. She avoided looking at him.

"Have you eaten today, Marissa?"

"I haven't been hungry."

"Have you written anything?"

"No. I didn't feel like writing."

"Have you been in bed all day?"

"I was tired."

"Do you love me, Marissa?"

She looked at him. "What are you talking about?"

"It's a simple question. Do you love me?"

"Of course, I love you."

"And I love you." He took her hand in his and held it gently. "Baby, I know you've known Janelle longer than you've known me, but don't make me feel like I'm competing for your heart."

"Tony..."

"You've had a terrible shock. I got that. Grieve, scream, yell, go in the exercise room and box a bit..."

Marissa uttered a little laugh. "You're so crazy..."

"I'm crazy about you."

He looked directly at her. The green eyes were intense and focused on her. She remembered the first time she had seen their intensity and locked her fingers in his.

"I'm just sad is all. Seems like we didn't have enough time together. I've known her all my life. I thought we would grow old together as best friends. I think of her boys growing up without a mother." She looked at him and tears began sliding down her face. "She loved her family so much. Junior had a milestone birthday without his mother and, how Spencer loved Janelle.... I wonder how it would be for you if we had...had."

Tony stood up and pulled her close to him. She wrapped her arms around him. They slow-danced to their own music. She looked up at him. He kissed her.

Chapter 9

O'Neill met his partner in the police parking lot as soon as she stepped out of her vehicle. Wordlessly, he drove to a private enclosure in the heart of downtown Center City. They showed their badges to the attendant and found a space on the roof near a fire exit.

Benson looked over at her partner. "Where are we?"

"Spencer Carr Associates. Tony called me last night. Carr wanted to see us."

"Oh, oh! You think the bank manager called him?"

"I know the bank manager called him. Come on, let's get this over with."

Spencer Carr was seated behind a glass desk when they were ushered into his office. It was a large room with two side walls of Plexiglas windows that looked out over the broad avenue below. He sat with his back to the world. Benson looked around the office. It reminded her of a chalk drawing with its glass tables, marble figurines, and black furniture.

Carr stood and shook O'Neill's hand and nodded at Benson. He directed them to the plush black leather chairs in front of his desk. He smiled and Benson noticed how light his eyes were, but she could not tell their specific shade. Carr smiled again, and this time Benson felt a chill run through her body. She noticed Carr's eyes never left O'Neill's face.

"Good morning, Detectives. You've been busy."

"Good morning, Mr. Carr," said O'Neill.

"Would you mind telling me what you were doing yesterday at the bank?"

"We interviewed the bank manager merely as a formality to closing ..." O'Neill cleared his throat. "We wanted to close the finance portion..."

Carr cut in. "Did you find reason enough to close the financial aspects of the case?"

"Yes."

"Is there anything else you believe you might need from me to clear me of my wife's murder?"

O'Neill returned his stare. "No."

"Are you certain, Detective?"

"Yes, Mr. Carr. Very certain."

"Good. If there's anything else you might need from me or my office in the future, James, please give me the courtesy of requesting it through the proper channels."

O'Neill cleared his throat. "While we're here I'd like to ask you about your wife's friends, associates. Anyone we could speak to who knew her well."

Carr and O'Neill stared at each other until Benson felt heated from the silence. Finally, Carr smiled.

"My wife had a core group of women she loved and who loved her. Of course, I don't know them all, except one. She stands out because she is my wife's lifelong friend. Her name is Marissa Marigny. If there are other names you need, I'm certain Ms. Marigny can supply them. Have a good day, Detectives."

Carr pressed a button, and the door opened. He stood still smiling. Two men in black suits with black sunglasses entered the office.

"Kindly escort the detectives to their car."

There was no handshake this time. They were led down the hall in the opposite direction from which they entered. A tight elevator ride with the men standing behind them. They were escorted to their parking spot and watched until they drove off the lot.

In their cruiser with Benson driving, O'Neill made phone calls. He called Gerard first and put him on the speakerphone.

"Hey, Kevin. Have you completed your work on that tablet we turned in?"

"Hey, James, Vee. There's nothing on it but food recipes, holiday menu planning, and grocery lists. She also had a housekeeping schedule. No names of vendors or anything like that. There were files detailing summaries of books she'd read. Sort of like book reviews."

"Appropriate for a librarian," O'Neill murmured.

"There were also a dozen speeches written to a Sallie Anne Lewis."

"What?"

"I know who she is," Benson interrupted. "She's the local news anchor. She does a community segment about once a month."

"Any notes or letters to Ms. Lewis?" asked O'Neill.

"There was an appointment date. I'll send it to you."

"Thanks. Every clue helps."

"Exactly. Anything else you need?"

"Nah, thanks, Kevin. Leave it on my desk. We'll return it."

"Sure."

O'Neill called Tony whose sound as if he were amused. It was difficult to tell as he was always pleasant.

"Are you two, okay?"

"I got the strangest feeling sitting in that ice chamber he calls an office that he was angry and trying to cover it up," said Benson.

O'Neill cleared his throat. "He didn't appreciate us visiting the bank without informing him."

"I'm sure he didn't. How was his demeanor?"

"Sad, hurt, baffled, and of course, angry."

"Of course. Any leads?"

"One, possibly two."

"Okay."

When the line cleared, Benson asked, "I wanted to ask you before. Do you know Spencer Carr personally?"

"What do you mean?"

"Don't play with me, James. You three looked mighty cozy in the Spencer home."

"He's a grieving husband..."

"Hmm... In his grief a while ago, one of the top eagle beagles of Winding Falls, slips up and calls you by your first name."

"And?"

O'Neill's response caught her off-guard. She remained silent. He parked, walked ahead of her into the building, and disappeared.

It was late afternoon. O'Neill stood by Benson's desk in his suit jacket. She hung up the phone and gave him her no-nonsense look.

"You might want to postpone our appointment with Ms. Lewis for another day."

"Why?"

"She gave me an outside address to meet with her."

"Don't speak in riddles. What are you talking about?"

"The news station is doing a documentary series on Janelle Carr. Ms. Lewis and her camera crew are filming the outdoor scenes. She can give us an interview in about two hours."

Benson willed herself not to laugh at the look on O'Neill's face. One thing she could say truthfully about her partner was that he took upholding justice seriously. She waited. She could tell he was controlling his temper by the way he lowered his head at a slant.

"Okay, let's get this over with. Where is she?"

"Out on Old Mall Road."

"Let's go. I'll drive."

They did not speak further. Benson had been working as O'Neill's partner for a long time. She admired him a great deal. He was a data scientist by training and often his reports reflected his knowledge of a crime she missed. She relied on his skills as much as he depended on hers.

They arrived on Old Mall Road and parked a few feet from the various news trucks. Benson looked for and found the tall redhead. Wow! Sallie Anne was truly gifted in beauty. She was seated in a director's chair with a small pillow under her booted feet. Her head rested back on a pillow with her eyes closed. A small-boned blonde dressed entirely in black stood nearby on a phone. She eyed Benson and O'Neill as they walked up.

"Yes. May I help you? This area is off-limits to the public."

"Who are you?" asked O'Neill.

"Anya Petrovski. You need to..."

Sallie Anne opened golden eyes and smiled at O'Neill. "Oh, it's alright, Anya. Hello, James. What are you doing here?" She spied Benson behind O'Neill, and her demeanor changed instantly. "May I help you two?"

"Ms. Lewis, we're here to ask you questions in regard to the late Janelle Carr."

She looked around them and beckoned to someone with two fingers raised. Immediately, the detectives were brought folding chairs to sit in. A small table laden with bottled water and bags of cookies and chips were placed before them. The woman sat on a black folding chair a few steps away. She was now on a headphone.

"Please help yourselves, Detectives." Sallie Anne smiled at Benson. She then transferred her cheerful look to O'Neill. "What do you wish to know about Janelle."

"For starters, how long have you known her?"

"All my life. I don't remember exactly how we met but just that I've always known her."

"We've been told you promoted the library's endeavors at least yearly, is that true?"

"Yes. My husband and I are great philanthropists when it concerns children's needs and wants."

"When was the last time you and your husband promoted such an endeavor with Ms. Carr?"

"We were supposed to get together a few weeks ago to film some behind the scenes activities but with her ......I don't want to cancel it. Her segment brings in rave reviews and high ratings every year." She sighed.

O'Neill asked, "When did you speak or see Ms. Carr last?"

"I spoke to Janelle maybe six or seven weeks ago about the Children's Fund benefit scheduled for this fall."

"And when did you physically see her?"

"Oh, gee, I had lunch with her about three weeks ago. Probably during the same time, she was... she was. "

Sallie Anne put her head down. She abruptly stood up. In her anchor voice she said, "I'm afraid that's all I have for you, Sergeant O'Neill. If you have any other questions or need anything else, please contact my assistant, Anya. Janelle was a sweet lady. Give you anything and I do mean anything if she could. Whoever did this need to be held accountable to the fullest extent of the law. Now, if you'll excuse me, James, I must get back to work."

"Of course. And thank you for your time," said O'Neill.

Sallie Anne walked past Benson with her head held high. They watched as the people who sat at a distance jumped to their feet. There was a flurry of activity around the anchor and suddenly the noise volume rose as people scrambled about in a wild frenzy.

Benson drove away from the site by another exit. She did not want to pass Sallie Anne's entourage of people. Being in these women's presence brought back hurtful memories. At a traffic stop she glanced at her partner in the passenger seat. He was busy typing, but she could not tell what.

Saturdays were always the busiest days for the hair salon. Tessa, in her all-white office, stretched to reach the volume knob on the television. She turned off the set. She could have used the remote but fancied the idea she was getting a little exercise. She glanced at the wall clock. It was past eight fifteen in the evening.

Her eyes fell on the blue silk scarf Janelle had given her one year as a birthday present. She loved it because it matched most of her wardrobe, and she knew Janelle had bought it expressly for her. Tessa looked at the photos she had of Janelle in their sorority house. How she would be missed!

Tessa reached for her car keys and glanced at the group photo sitting on her wall unit. Tessa's thoughts turned to Jacky. She still had not heard from the woman. The only person she knew who Jacky would not stand up was Marissa. She wanted to call Marissa but did not want to upset her more than what she was.

A knock and Marian, her business manager, entered. "I'm out for the night, Tessa."

"Thanks, Marian. Today was a long one."

"Long but good. I'll see you Tuesday morning then."

"Yes, thank you."

"Condolences on your friend."

"Marian, I hate to keep asking you this, but..."

"Did Ms. Crenshaw call by chance and I forgot to tell you?" Marian gave Tessa a sad smile. "I'm worried about Ms. Crenshaw as well."

"Thank you, Marian. Good night."

Chapter 10

Tony was leaning against his private vehicle when Marissa pulled into the police parking lot. He looked at her legs as she walked toward him in a black cashmere coat that came above her knees. The large dark sunglasses obstructed the view of her eyes, but he saw her face was flushed.

"Hi, Tony. I have an appointment with James."

Clutching a small black purse, Marissa tried to walk around him. Tony wrapped an arm around her waist and pulled her toward him.

"This is your first time down here. Everyone knows you're my wife. Remember that and tell the truth. Another officer will be sitting in with James. You're going to be asked about your friendship with Janelle. Routine questions, nothing more. Are you ready?"

"Why aren't you coming in with me? You knew Janelle, too."

"Conflict of interest. Don't worry, I'll be nearby. Okay?"

"Yes."

"Oh, and don't call him James. He's Sgt. O'Neill."

He removed her sunglasses. She smiled and they kissed. They rode the elevator in silence. Tony stood a little away from her conscious of the camera above them disguised as a mirror. He seated Marissa in the interview room and walked next door.

Murray, Johnston, and Gerard watched Marissa look at herself in her compact. The thick, curly hair pulled in an upside-down style showcased diamond stud earring. She stood up, removed the coat, and smoothed down the matching cashmere sweater dress.

The door opened, and the two detectives entered. Marissa gave O'Neill a tight smile. She looked at Benson as if she had never seen her before, nodded, and then focused her attention on O'Neill.

Benson looked at Marissa's hands clasped together on the table, and remembered she always wore lots of rings. The various rings shone brightly on the long, tapered fingers. The white-gold, round-cut aquamarine engagement ring caught and held Benson's attention. She remembered the day Marissa announced her engagement and showed them her hand. Benson recalled the ring was a hefty three carats. She looked at the matching white diamond wedding band.

"Good afternoon, Ms. Marigny. I'm Sergeant O'Neill, and this is my partner, Detective Benson. Would you please say your full name."

"Marissa Marigny."

"Thank you. We won't keep you long. This is just a preliminary question and answer session. If you wish to have an attorney present, that is your right."

"I'm fine, thank you."

"I'd like to ask you some questions about your relationship with the late Janelle Carr."

"Okay."

"Ms. Marigny, how long have you known the deceased, Janelle Carr?"

"All my life."

"Could you elaborate?"

"We lived next door to each other growing up."

"You remained friends for how long?"

"Until she was... until..."

"Okay. Did you attend school together? College?"

"Yes. From first grade all the way up to college graduation."

"You were both at the same university?"

"Yes. She was my very best friend."

"I noticed in her library office you were in her wedding," said Benson.

Marissa smiled, but did not look at Benson. "Janelle was the sister I never had. We stood in each other's weddings. I babysat her sons when they were tiny babies."

"When was the last time you saw the deceased?"

"A few days before..."

"Tell me what you did that day."

"We went shopping at Falls Mall. We bought some exercise clothes, socks, and a few toiletries. She bought a birthday gift for her son, Spencer. He turns fourteen in a couple of weeks."

"How long would you say you two were together that day?"

"Most of the day. It was Janelle's day off at the library, and I was having writer's block."

"Did any of your other friends join you?"

"No, it was just Janelle and me. It was like old times when we would just go off and have fun together. We went to an afternoon cinema at Falls Mall, and then had lunch at that new café next to the bike shop on Old Mall Road."

"What movie did you see at the cinema?"

"It was a romance film with that new British actor. I don't remember his name. He married tennis star, Leda Liz."

"Okay. All the years you've had your friendship, can you recall anyone being angry with the deceased?"

"No. Janelle was a sweet lady. She had kind words for everyone. Whoever did this to her is a monster.... he's evil."

Marissa suddenly bent forward and, keeping her head down, began sobbing in ragged breaths. She clutched the edge of the table. Tony walked into the room, and silently pulled her into his arms. She clung to him sobbing quietly. O'Neill and Benson walked out. Gerard and Johnston returned to the squad room. The captain stayed a few moments watching the couple before leaving.

Tony brought Marissa home. She cried all the way in uncontrollable sobs. His in-laws were exiting their vehicle as he pulled into the driveway. Rose Alexander was an older version of her daughter. Her black wavy hair, streaked lightly with silver strands, was cut to her shoulders, and swung in a heavy curly-wavy rotation about her neck. She smiled with a somber face at Tony, her attention on her child, who was now crying harder. She embraced Marissa and the two women entered the house.

Tony stood rooted to the spot feeling helpless. His father-in-law, Maurice Alexander, walked over to him. He was as tall as Tony, but with a mix of salt and pepper curly hair set off by a matching trimmed beard.

"Hi, Tony. Glad you called us. Janelle's parents called us last week, or rather, her father did. As you can imagine Janelle's mother is taking it hard as well. How are you holding up?"

"One day at a time. I hate seeing Marissa down like this."

"She must work through it on her own timetable, son. This is the first loss she's ever dealt with. She and Janelle were closer than sisters. You know that."

"Yes, yes, I know. I must get back to work."

O'Neill drove past them in Marissa's car. He parked in front of the second garage.

"Hello, Dr. Alexander," said O'Neill, shaking Maurice's hand.

"Hi, James. The staff taking a holiday today?"

The men laughed. O'Neill walked past Tony to the police cruiser. "I'm driving back," he said, getting behind the wheel.

Tony shook his head. "Bye, Dad."

Maurice hugged him. "Don't worry about her, son. We'll be here until you get home. You know your mother-in-law."

"Thanks."

Tony sat in the passenger seat. After a while he looked over at O'Neill.

"Have you contacted the news anchor?"

"Yes. She was dead-end." After a slight pause, "You know something doesn't feel right about all this. The tablet we found at the Carr residence was just for entertainment purposes only. Lots of kid games, a few sites devoted to cooking, needlepoint, and women's online magazines. There was a site devoted to a religious sect whose mission was caring for children. The lecture series concerned the children's mission they both worked together on."

"Okay. Any other leads?"

"I contacted an estate attorney and the family accountant. You know who I mean. We must keep these meetings impersonal. Everyone understands."

Tony smirked. "I'm sure they do. This murder has become too close for comfort. How much have you told Vee?"

"Nothing. I never explain my personal life to anyone."

Tony said nothing. He stared out the side window. He knew O'Neill well enough not to continue the conversation. O'Neill disappeared shortly after parking the squad car. Tony was greeted by Perez and Sloan when the elevator doors opened.

"How's Marissa?" asked Sloan.

"Her parents are with her," said Tony, walking around them.

"She'll be fine, Tony," Perez assured him. "She's just lost her best friend. Something like that takes time."

"Sure does," echoed Sloan.

Tony kept walking to his office where he unintentionally slammed the door. He knew they were trying to be encouraging, but Marissa was his wife, and he was going to take care of her.

Chapter 11

The law firm of Hugo Larsen and Young was in the heart of the Center City business district. O'Neill and Benson parked in the underground garage. The attendant looked at their badges dispassionately and put them on an elevator to the proper floor.

The woman who met them when the elevator doors opened wore a form fitting, black knit suit grazing her knee. The wavy brown hair was pulled into a low ponytail and swung down her back. The black stiletto-heeled pumps were patent leather.

"I'm Lisa Douglas, Ms. Young's paralegal." She extended her hand in a firm handshake. "Please follow me."

She marched down a hallway of glass and turned into a completely different building with walls of closed doors. Halfway near the end of the hall, she stopped before a door knocked once and opened it for them to enter. The woman seated behind the wide desk never looked up. She made a slight wave with her hand and the door closed behind them. O'Neill stared across at the woman.

Benson looked around the office. Light-colored lilac walls with mahogany furniture, a plush sofa in a purple color with a matching chair framed the room. A large plant near the elongated window stood beside a tall statue of Lady Justice on a pedestal. The woman stood up and walked over to them. She extended her hand to them both. Benson remained silent.

"I'm Stacie Young. Please sit down." She beckoned to the plush sofa and sat in the matching armchair. "Sergeant O'Neill, when we spoke on the phone you wanted to discuss Janelle Carr. Is that correct?"

"Yes. We're conducting a homicide investigation into her death. As her personal attorney, we wanted to ask you a few questions."

Stacie smiled. She never took her eyes off O'Neill and barely looked at Benson.

"Let me make my position clear. I'm the attorney-on-record for the legal interests of the four children. There is nothing I can tell you about Mrs. Carr that would help your investigation into her death."

O'Neill smiled. "Thank you for the clarity. However, I did check the records. When was the last time you spoke to or had interactions with Ms. Carr beyond business?"

Stacie smiled and walked to her desk. Benson could not take her eyes off the navy wool suit. She could tell it was expensive by the fit and style. She looked at her feet admiring the navy Italian leather pumps. As Stacie scrolled on the tablet, Benson could not help but admire the beautiful diamond wedding set on immaculate French tipped nails.

There was something about Stacie's mannerisms that irritated her. Then she realized it was the neutral attitude she had displayed toward her. As if they were strangers. Stacie looked up with a smile.

"The last time I saw Janelle was a few weeks ago at lunch. There was nothing different about our time together."

"Was it a business or personal lunch?" asked O'Neill.

"It was a personal lunch. Janelle and I were friends."

"When was the last time you heard from Janelle?"

Stacie sighed. "I would have to say that was the last time I saw or heard from Janelle."

Benson wanted to be heard and seen. She spoke in a louder than usual voice.

"When did you first meet the victim?"

Stacie looked at Benson and smiled. The large brown eyes set in the waterfall of honey blonde hair surveyed Benson coolly. Benson sensed the irritation more than felt it.

"I've known her since our elementary school days. We grew up together."

Benson was not deterred. "Where did this personal lunch occur? The name of the restaurant?"

"We were at the Falls Bistro."

"Would a server recognize you both?"

"I don't know."

"Had you two made any further plans to meet for lunch or dinner?"

"No."

"Were there anyone else invited to this luncheon?"

"We didn't plan lunch dates normally," she said, smiling. "But when any of us were planning social occasions, we would meet up. Sometimes it was no more than a series of phone calls."

"You didn't answer the question. Was anyone else at this luncheon?"

Stacie remained smiling. O'Neill handed Stacie a business card as they rose together.

"Thank you for your time, Ms. Young. If you think of anything that might help in our investigation, please don't hesitate to call me."

"Thank you, Sergeant O'Neill. Enjoy the rest of your day... both of you."

O'Neill walked behind Benson slightly moving her along. Benson looked over her shoulder as they passed through the door. Stacie was seated behind her desk with her hands folded. She smiled with her lips, but her eyes were cold.

Stonehedge Martine Accountants was thirteen floors. The building was glass on three sides. The lobby boasted a mute gray iron staircase offset by scattered plush gray seating areas. The receptionist was speaking in a headset in Japanese; switched wiring and lapsed into Spanish. The detectives exchanged quick glances. They studied him. He was on the thin side with stark white skin, jet black hair that was thick and worn to his shoulders and tied at the nape of his neck. His chiseled facial features were in perfect symmetry. He looked up, connected some wires, and smiled at them.

"May I help you?" he asked in perfect-pitched English.

"We have an appointment with Kristen O'Leary."

"Detectives O'Neill and Benson?" He listened in his headset. He glanced at them sideways. Please sit over there. She'll be right down."

He pointed across the room at a cluster of chairs grouped together. He returned to speaking in the headset. This time it was in German.

Benson had forgotten how tall Kristen was. She was certainly beautiful with her glossy full head of thick black hair and deep sapphire blue eyes.

The honey tan skin offset by the dark green worsted wool pantsuit she wore was a favorite color Benson saw her in at nearly all their book club meetings.

Kristen walked over to them with a huge smile on her face. She extended her hand to both in a firm handshake. Benson had never interacted much with her as she was usually surrounded by the others. As she studied the woman up close, Benson noticed the huge emerald engagement ring surrounded by white diamonds on her finger and the tiny emerald drop earrings swinging between folds of black hair.

"I'm terribly sorry to be seeing you in the lobby, but I was on my way to a meeting. Do sit down."

"We understand, Ms. O'Leary. We won't keep you. We're investigating Janelle Carr's murder. Were you her accountant?"

"Yes. My father managed her family's finances."

"So, you've had a long-term relationship with Ms. Carr?"

"Yes."

"When did you become Ms. Carr's accountant?"

"Right before she married, she kept my services. It's rudimentary stuff. Everything goes to their sons, equally and fully. They have no need of each other's monies."

"When was the last time you saw Ms. Carr?"

"About a month ago."

"In what role? Lunch? Dinner?"

"As a matter of fact, we did attend a fundraiser and dinner together. It was for Winding Falls Hospital. It's the Children's Fund event held every year. It's always great fun."

"How long ago was that event held?"

"It's held every year on the first weekend in November so that would be the end of last year."

"How was Ms. Carr's mood that evening?"

"Same as always. She and Spencer, her husband, danced the night away. Afterward, we shared a lovely dinner on the terrace of the hospital. It was a beautiful evening."

O'Neill stood up. "Thank you for answering our questions. If you think of anything that might be able to help us. Please call."

Benson remained seated. "Excuse me, there was no other more recent time you spent with Ms. Carr?"

Kristen stared at her. "None that I can remember, Detective."

"You both have children. I believe all the children attend the same school. Let me ask you again, was there a more recent time you saw or spent with Ms. Carr?"

"I don't know what you're looking for, Detective Benson, but Janelle and I were on the best of terms. Please leave our children out of whatever it is you're hoping to find."

O'Neill looked at Benson and then Kristen. He smiled and said, "To reiterate, if there's anything you might remember or think of, please don't hesitate to call me."

"Thank you, Sergeant O'Neill. I will."

She walked away from them without looking at Benson. They watched her get into a waiting limousine alongside another woman typing on a laptop. The bodyguard whom they had not seen previously sat in the front passenger seat. They watched the car weave through busy traffic.

O'Neill drove patiently through the maze of congested city traffic. Benson silently wished he had let her drive. She would have hit the highway and stayed on it. She hated city traffic. She glanced sideways at her partner.

"James, do you know Kristen O'Leary personally?"

"No. Should I?"

"You do know Stacie Young though, don't you?"

"What's with the inquisition?"

"I remember what Sallie Anne Lewis said to you."

"What did she say?"

"She didn't see me when she said, 'hi, James,' as if you were old friends. In fact, she slipped at the end and called you by your first name."

"What's your point, Vee?"

"You know these women."

Silence. Then O'Neill sighed and said, "I know a lot of people, Vee. Same as you. You want to pick up a few sandwiches before we go in?"

Benson nodded. The lump in her throat grew tight. She remembered one evening years earlier being taken by her date to the exclusive Riviera Restaurant for dinner. For most of the dinner, she was dimly aware of her date.

Her attention was glued to the table across from the room where Tony and Marissa were dining with di Giovanni and O'Neill and their wives. But also seated at the table with their husbands were Sallie Anne, Beth, Stacie, and Patricia.

She turned on the radio to distract her mind. But she remembered a short time later driving through Olde City, a historic community in Winding Falls Township, when she saw a group of people exit a restaurant. She had to wait at the red light while the group crossed the wide avenue in front of her car. The weather was still warm. She remembered the pretty and colorful silk dresses of the women. Their husbands in light-colored linen outfits. The mighty clique of Winding Falls.

Although her sports car was a bright red import, none of the group looked in her direction. She watched raven-haired Patricia walking in step beside stoic beauty, Stacie. Behind them was the vibrant redhead Sallie Anne walking arm-in-arm with platinum blonde Beth. Last, were gorgeous Janelle and her best friend and twin, Marissa.

It was late when Benson completed details in her report. She emailed it all to Tony with a copy to O'Neill. She had not seen her partner most of the afternoon. His office door was locked. She looked down and realized the lights were off. She did not know he had left for the day. He did so without saying good night as he usually did. She collected her purse and walked past Tony's door. His office was dark.

The elevator doors opened, and she came face to face with Tony and the captain.

"Hey, Vee." Tony had a slight frown on his face.

"Working late?" asked Murray. "We don't pay overtime unless you get shot."

Tony smirked and she giggled. "I had to finish my report for you."

"Tomorrow's another day, Detective. Get on," said Murray. "We're going down. We were upstairs at a meeting with the chief."

"Everything alright?"

"Spencer's wife being the target of some psycho is not alright," said Murray in a low voice.

"How was your hunting trip?" asked Tony to shift the sudden sad mood. "We haven't had a chance to talk since you returned."

Murray smiled. "I could use another one after hearing what happened to Janelle. How's Marissa is the question."

"She's as good as she's going to get, Fred. They were inseparable. Closer than sisters."

"Yeah, I would imagine."

Benson looked at the captain. "Do you have siblings, Captain?"

"No, Vee. I've had the extreme pleasure of being an only child. Spoiled rotten since infancy." The captain laughed heartily which caused Tony and Benson to laugh along with him. When the doors opened, he stepped off first. "Have a good night, you two."

The captain stopped at the front desk and shared a joke with O'Malley. The desk sergeant roared with laughter. Benson walked out to the parking lot with Tony.

"Can I ask you something, Tony?"

"Sure, Vee. What is it?"

"I might have annoyed James earlier today."

Tony smiled. "He's your partner. Work it out."

"I questioned him about his relationship with two people we interviewed today... Kristen O'Leary and Stacie Young. I know them both. We went to college together. We used to..."

Tony stopped her. "Look, Vee. You know James well enough. He likes to keep his personal and professional lives separate. I'm sure we're all going to meet people we've known before. That's the nature of our job. Okay?"

"I know he's super private. I..."

"James left early to attend one of his son's events. He was running late. Don't tell him I told you or I'll fire you."

Benson laughed happily. "Never!"

Tony smiled and shook his head. "Good night, Vee."

"Good night, Tony. Thanks." She waved as she drove past his truck.

Chapter 12

It was late afternoon, and the weather was unexpectedly warmer than it had been. Tony sat in his office and waited on O'Neill and Benson to scroll through their tablets. Murray walked in and leaned against the filing cabinet.

Tony said, "We currently have an open case on Carr. Any updates in your investigation so far."

"No. We have no motive for Mrs. Carr assault. Santorelli has ruled it as a homicide."

"Although he left his fingerprints on the back of her neck, Santorelli said the prints were contaminated."

"We did a walk-through of the home the other day. We found nothing. No broken windows or even unlatched for that matter. Which leads back to the original premise that she let her killer in the home."

"We can safely assume she knew her killer then," said Tony, grimly. "Did you check for surveillance footage?"

"That's what was missing. Mr. Carr informed me the entire unit was taken; even the backup."

Murray looked at O'Neill. "They had a backup unit that was also stolen. This must be someone who knows them intimately."

"Or someone who knows that area because most of those homes have backup units," said O'Neill. "We also doubled back to the bank. Everything's the same."

"Hold on," said Tony, raising his hand. "Did you check with the neighbors for their backup units?"

O'Neill gave him a grudging look. "On the morning of Mrs. Carr's demise there was a minor disruption of service. It was a mere zap that no one paid attention to. That zap reset the program."

Murray frowned. "Why does it feel like you're stating something we should view as important?"

O'Neill almost smiled. "The surveillance system was rigged to reset. Which means effectively destroying the film capturing the exact time of the attack on Mrs. Carr."

"How did you discover the system was rigged?" asked Murray.

"We didn't," responded Benson. "It was our in-house engineer Kevin who told us about the glitch."

"How much are we paying him?" asked Murray. "You all need more money. That's genius of Kevin."

Tony rubbed his hand over his face. "We know Spencer Carr's whereabouts as he was in a board meeting with several dozen people present."

"Easy alibi," mumbled Murray, "especially if meeting was planned."

"He didn't have a reason to murder his wife. No financial gain, no outside friendships, and nothing negative about the couple or their marriage."

Benson said, "I still get chills when I remember our meeting with him. And he had the nerve to say if we wanted anything else, to call and make an appointment."

"I think he wants to be seen as cooperative," cut in Murray. "He has an image to protect. He's the private attorney to the mayor and owns his own successful law firm."

"His late wife was also best friends with a popular novelist whose homegrown, and just happens to be the wife of the local police lieutenant" added O'Neill.

The room went silent. The pleasant look never left Tony's face. O'Neill gave him stare for stare. It was a tense few minutes. Benson kept her head down and tried to think of a way of getting out of the office. Murray looked out the window.

"Okay," said Tony with a smile. "This case stays open until we figure out what's going on. Someone targeted Spencer Carr's wife, and we need to know why and who."

"Maybe one of his white-collar clients didn't like the terms of their agreements," O'Neill said.

"That's a possibility," agreed Tony. "However, until he says something to help us out, we can only guess. Meanwhile, we have other cases to take care of."

Benson looked up with a concerned frown. "Wait a minute! If someone is after Mr. Carr and they attacked his wife, what about his four sons? Shouldn't we be protecting them?"

"Spencer Carr is a former prosecutor, and a smart one. I'm sure his children will be safeguarded. As to our police doing the job, if that's what you're insinuating, that's out the window." Murray stood up straight and walked out the office.

"The funeral for Janelle Carr is on schedule for tomorrow morning," said O'Neill, rising. "Police detail will be tight and security heightened. If you need or want anything else, let me know."

"Okay. Thanks, you two. Have a good night." Tony lowered his eyes to his screen.

Tony hung up the phone with a smile on his face. His order of two dozen yellow roses to be sent to Marissa ahead of the upcoming Valentine's Day weekend were on their way to her. A quick knock, and Elsa entered his office.

She wore a form-fitting red sweater dress with a high turtleneck. The dress was past her knees and seemed molded to the deeply curvaceous body. Tony almost swallowed. He looked down and the picture of Marissa on their wedding day made him smile. His eyes lifted back up. He stared at Santorelli.

"Good evening, Elsa. I'm packing it in for the night. Whatever it is can wait until Monday."

"I agree, Tony." Santorelli smiled. "But I'm here to escort you to the Policeman's Pub."

"Why would I need an escort if I were going to the Pub?"

She giggled. "Sorry. Wrong word. How about go with you?"

"I'm going home."

"Everyone in your department is down there. Shuster's retirement party was canceled last month. It's been planned for tonight."

"Yes, I remember. My team and I took him and his wife, Cora, out to dinner a few months ago."

"Yes, well. Today was his last official day on site."

"I'm going home."

He turned his back and pulled on his parka. He could hear her behind him. She was now buttoned into a black coat. He set the answering service, walked past her, and turned off the lights. She followed him and watched as he locked the door. They rode the elevator in silence. He walked off the elevator behind her and disappeared through a side door to the enclosed parking area. He backed up to a side street and drove a few blocks out of his way to the highway.

It was the end of the day at the beauty salon. Tessa stretched to reach the volume knob on her television. She turned off the set. She looked at the photo she had of Janelle in their sorority house. They were all young! She thought of Spencer and the boys. He had showed up to honor his wife's memory at the luncheon they held for her. They were all crying by the time he left.

A knock at her office door startled her from her daydream. Marian entered. She handed Tessa a black leather ledger and a larger portfolio. She hung a black dress wrapped in dry cleaner's paper on the doorknob.

"The receipts are stapled together in the check book if you want to see them. Our tax guy will be here in a few days. Your dress was delivered while you were out earlier."

"Thank you, Marian. I'll put everything in the safe."

"No problem."

Marian turned to leave. She heard her name and turned back in the doorway.

"Did you call me, Tessa?"

"Yes, I'm sorry, Marian. I wanted to thank you for the large bouquet you sent for Janelle's funeral. That was too thoughtful."

"You all mean a lot to each other. Ms. Carr was a special kind of lady."

"You got that right. Thank you again. I couldn't do this without you."

Marian smiled. "You are sweet for a boss. Have a good night and get home safe. We have a very long day tomorrow."

"Good night, Marian."

Tessa leaned back in her chair. She looked at the security monitor. Marian's husband arrived and they left the shop. She reached for the black dress she would wear to Janelle's funeral and turned out the lights in her office.

The Carr family was prominent in Winding Falls Township. There was constant media coverage in the days before and leading up to the day of the funeral. The couple's four sons were kept away from media scrutiny by their father, and both sets of grandparents.

The church service was attended by every classmate and friend Janelle had ever made throughout her life. The library as well as most of the shops in the area closed for the day to honor Janelle's memory.

At the pulpit, in a voice hoarse with emotion, Spencer Carr spoke to the assembly of people gathered.

"My wife was truly the love of my life. She was everything I ever wanted in a woman and more. I'll always love the essence of the woman she was. When we met, it was mutual love at first sight. We were truly happy together, and though the time was short, the years will live forever in my heart."

He stopped to dab at his eyes with a handkerchief. His oldest son came to stand beside his father. They briefly hugged before the grief-stricken widower resumed.

"There's a lady here who introduced us. She's been a beloved sister to my beautiful wife and I. Marissa, would you please come say a few words?"

Sedated to get through the funeral, Marissa sat between her husband and her mother, in a daze. Tony walked with her to the podium. She held tightly onto his hand. The inscription from her debut novel was read in a low-pitched voice. *"There will never be sisterhood as strong or a friend as dear as what you and I have together. To my forever best friend and confidant, Janelle Nicholas Carr."*

Chapter 13

What is wrong with these women? No one can mind their business. I didn't want to hurt Janelle, but it's not nice to look over someone's shoulder or to spy on them. I hope she's learned her lesson. Here comes this one. Cute enough but won't shut her mouth or mind her business. It would be nice to find a woman who believed in sitting and looking pretty without constantly running her mouth. Look at this one. Can barely get in the house between the packages, the ugly high heels she cannot walk in, and her mouth going at ninety words a minute. My God, she's giving me a headache. I'll give her a few seconds to get settled. Why is her curtains wide open to the world? Any maniac could be looking in on her. What is it about personal safety women don't get? Okay, the show must go on. Oh, still talking. Can't open the door for talking. Yes, yes! Shut up!

On her way home Tessa decided to stop by Jacky's home because she was worried about her, as she had not shown up for Janelle's funeral. When she turned on Jacky's street, she saw the huge white sport utility vehicle with the blue and yellow *ANU* insignia on the right side back window and smiled. But the vehicle parked on the driveway meant Jacky either arrived home a short time ago or was about to go out. Tessa sat in her vehicle and phoned Jacky. No response. Tessa grew alarmed. Suppose Jacky was ill?

She got out of her vehicle and walked up the steps and onto the porch. She rang the doorbell and waited. She glanced over and saw the curtains were open at the picture window. She leaned over and looked through the window.

What she saw made her eyes widen, her mouth drop open, and in what seemed to her to last forever; a long, slow, high-pitched scream emerged from the depths of her being. Tessa could not stop the scream.

Trevino and Perez walked through the mass of police and white-suited technicians to the large house on the hill. It was a traditional four bedroom, three bath home in suburban Washington Heights. The furniture style was Bohemian chic in a floral pattern of pastel colors, mostly in shades of blue and yellow.

Trevino stood in the middle of the spacious front room. "Did she own a bookstore? There's stacks of hardback and paperback books everywhere you look."

"There's a shopping bag shoved behind this chair."

"A bag of books?"

"No..." murmured Perez. She pulled out the items. "We have two evening gowns, and a lacy bra and thong set."

"Whoopee! Someone had a hot time planned."

As Trevino walked toward the kitchen, he spied a suitcase leaning against a hall closet.

"What's in there?" he pointed.

Perez opened it. "Nothing."

They walked into the kitchen. They walked over to the counter and examined the takeout tray of untouched food laid open.

"She didn't get a chance to eat her meal," murmured Perez. Then she frowned. "Something's moving among the contents..."

"This food has sat open on this counter for a long time, Priscilla. Looks like maggots to me." Trevino looked behind the counter while Perez shrunk back with a disgusted look on her face.

"Have you seen a purse yet? Looks like she went shopping, but I haven't seen a purse yet."

Perez found the purse on the window seat. "Here it is. Her driver's license says she's Jacky Crenshaw." She showed the license to Trevino.

"Very pretty woman," he murmured. "James and Vee have been trying to contact her for weeks."

Perez looked through the purse Trevino gave her and laid out the times on the counter.

"Hey Luis, this is a love letter written to some anonymous guy."

"Looks pretty old to me," said Trevino, eyeing the faded paper. "Is there a name in the letter?"

"No."

"Have it analyzed by the Crime Lab."

They retraced their steps back to the living room and found the study. It was a bright room with pale yellow wallpaper. The furniture was clothed in small blue floral print.

"This is definitely a woman's home." Perez said as she walked about the room. "What? No books in here?"

"Television on wall."

On a table Trevino looked at a collage of photographs of young women at events on a college campus. It was obvious the pictures were from years past. He noticed the deceased at once. She had a spectacular figure and was not shy about showing it off.

In a small desk drawer, he found a blue and yellow floral book. It was mostly blank with several pages of doodles. He bagged it and looked at a calendar page. He snapped a picture of the page, and they returned to the living room.

The body of the deceased woman had been taken down from the noose and was laid out on the floor. She wore a black opaque catsuit with black knee-high boots completing the look. Tall and statuesque, she reminded Trevino of a bronze Amazonian goddess. He examined her neck. It was smooth and unlined. The marks from the frayed synthetic cord that had been around her neck a faint line. He looked at the coffee table. He examined the built-in wall bookcase where the hook was planted.

Perez upstairs examined the one decorated bedroom. The walls and floor carpet were a pale blue. The bed linens and window curtains were a pastel yellow. The custom bed frame and furniture were Robin's egg blue. Perez walked around the room. Everything was frilly and light. The walk-in closet held pantsuits and evening gowns. One wall held shoes and handbags.

Downstairs Trevino felt a gust of wind and looked around. Santorelli walked through the door, and over to the body on the floor. She took a few moments to examine the victim's neck area.

"What happened here?" she asked.

"Friend checking up on her found her. What do we have, Doc?"

"I see the rope burns around her neck. I'll know for certain once I do lab work on her."

"How long has she been dead?"

"Looks like about three to four weeks."

"We'll need to check if there were any missing person reports filed on this woman," said Trevino as Perez joined them.

Outside Trevino followed by Perez, walked over to the tall police officer who stood on the curb across from a group of women who stared at him with unabashed shame. He ignored them as he wrote in his notepad.

Officer Emile Cousins was tall, with light brown skin, black curly hair, black slanted eyes, a short nose and full lips. He was very handsome with a no-nonsense attitude.

"Officer Cousins, where's the person who called this in?"

"The witness is over there," said the officer, pointing across the street. "She's sitting in the squad car."

"Thanks, Emile."

"No problem, Luis."

The officer ignored Perez who felt slightly insulted. She studied the woman as they walked toward her. She had long red curly hair, large dark greenish-brown eyes, and a straight nose that was turning red on the tip. Perez assumed she was a natural redhead due to her light skin coloring and the faint brushing of light freckles across the bridge of her nose.

Trevino touched her arm. "I have a call from Tony. You talk to the lady, I'll be back."

He put the phone to his ear as he walked away. Perez looked in the car at the woman.

"Ma'am, I'd like to ask you some questions."

"Sure, Detective."

"What is your name and relationship to the victim?"

"My name is Tessa Smith. I'm her friend and hairstylist."

"What made you drive over to her house tonight?"

"She had an appointment a few weeks ago that she did not keep and didn't call to cancel."

"Do you drive to all your clients' homes when they don't show up for appointments?"

"I've known Jacky for twenty years, and she's been my client almost that long. No, I would not do it for anyone else, but Jacky was a close friend and client."

"So, you drove out of your way to this client's home?"

"I live not far from here, ma'am. And I've already told you I have known her for twenty years."

"So, you've said. Was this the first time in the twenty years you've known her for the victim not to show up for a hair appointment?"

"No, this was not the first time..."

"Did you call her?"

"Yes, I called her several times. I even called her friends."

"Who?"

"Well, I called Marissa because..."

"Marissa, who? Be specific."

"Marissa Marigny.....she's a writer. Jacky was her friend and publicist."

Perez pretended she was writing to gather her thoughts. Friend and publicist? She said, "When you called Ms. Marigny, had she seen or spoken to the victim?"

"No."

"Did you call any other personal friend?"

"No."

"The last time the victim didn't show up for an appointment, did you visit her home?"

"No. No, I didn't."

"But this time you felt the need. Why?"

"I don't know, Officer. Something seemed off this time. I can't explain it."

"What happened when you got here?"

"I saw her truck parked in the driveway and knew she was home which was strange."

"Go on... what was strange about the victim's vehicle parked in the driveway?"

"She never parks in the driveway. Always in her garage."

"How do you know her parking habits?"

"I sometimes take this route to my home. I told you; I don't live far from here."

81

"You stated her appointment at your salon was weeks ago. Why stop here today?"

"I told you. I couldn't get in contact with her..." Tessa could not take any more questions. She tried to control the flow of tears suddenly engulfing her and could not. "Poor Jacky. Who would do something like *this* to her? She was the sweetest thing...sweetest..."

The tears fell uncontrollably from Tessa's eyes. She put her face in her hands and gently rocked back and forth. Trevino walked over, his deep blue eyes like slits. He spoke quietly to Tessa. Then he beckoned over two police officers.

"Ms. Smith, Officer Frazier will escort you home. Officer Allen will follow your car and make sure you get in safely. Okay? If we have any further questions, we'll call you. Please accept our deepest condolences on the loss of your friend."

Tessa looked up at Trevino. Her voice husky with emotion, "I don't believe Jacky did this to herself."

"Why not?" urged Trevino. His adrenaline flowed. His senses quickened. He needed to hear what this woman would say.

"Jacky was a lover of life. She had met this new guy and was excited about him. I had seen her a few weeks earlier at our book club, and she spoke of him then to me."

"What's his name?"

"That's just it. She can be so silly sometimes. She wouldn't tell me his name. But she had made a hair and nail appointment because they had planned a trip together somewhere."

Tessa cried softly again. Trevino helped her out of the police car and walked her to the police officer's car. He stood on the sidewalk and watched as the cars moved down the street.

Perez was seated behind the wheel of their squad car. Trevino beckoned for her to move over. Behind the wheel, he looked over at Perez who stared out the side window.

"What the hell was that?" he asked in a gruff voice. "You don't provoke a witness. What's the matter with you?"

"How do you know she's a witness? She could have killed her for all I know."

"Well, I know she didn't kill her because she doesn't have the strength needed for the lifting and carrying that was necessary. Second, she's known the woman a long time. Those were real tears."

Perez kept her head turned. Trevino started the car and drove in silence. Perez cleared her vision. She turned to her partner.

"Where the hell are you driving to?" She finally asked.

"I was wondering when you'd notice. What's bugging you?"

"That woman did not kill herself, Luis."

"I know. She had a weekend planned with someone. She bought two evening gowns, and an underwear set."

"I saw the outfits, too" said Perez, slumped in her seat. "How did you come to the conclusion she was going out on a weekend?"

"The dated receipt for the clothing, and she had made a hair and nail appointment. The friend, who's also her hair stylist mentioned it, and the empty suitcase by the front staircase. A weekend was planned with someone," said Trevino. "And then, there's the old love letter. Maybe a rekindled romance?"

"I wonder why she didn't fight back."

"Only one explanation, Priscilla. She knew her killer."

They were silent for the rest of the trip to the precinct.

Chapter 14

The ABC Publishers House was a multi-story structure in the heart of Center City. Trevino and Perez rode the elevator to the fifteenth floor where doors opened to a long desk behind which sat a dark-haired woman with a headset on. Directly behind her was a solid wall of sliding doors.

The woman stopped talking into the headphones and smiled at them. "Good morning. May I help you?"

"Good morning. Detectives Trevino and Perez from Winding Falls Police. We're here to see Paul Boleyn."

"Thank you. Just a moment, please."

It took one minute for Paul Boleyn to walk through one of the multitude of doors. He was taller than Trevino but thin and pale. His skin looked translucent with a light coating of dusky pink coloring underneath. His hair was grayish black and combed straight back. He had a thin mustache atop thinner lips. His eyes were dark and piercing. He reminded Trevino of a hawk.

They followed him down a long hall. Boleyn walked with the grace of a dancer. He wore a dark gray striped worsted-wool suit that was slightly British in design with its double-breasted close to the body fitted jacket, and thin legged trousers, They were led into a large office and seated in plush leather chairs. Boleyn planted himself behind his expansive desk.

"What a tragedy for ABC Publishers House," said Boleyn, his face contorted into an image of pain. "What can we do for you at this sorrowful time, Detectives?"

Trevino did not like him. "Mr. Boleyn, what is your position here?"

"I'm vice president of the legal department."

"Why are we speaking with you?" asked Perez.

"Due to the nature of Ms. Crenshaw's death, and her high public persona within the company, we don't want to have any negative press on ABC Publishers House, or her."

"How long did the deceased work here?" asked Perez.

"She was hired immediately after college."

"On the ABC Publishers House website, the deceased is listed as vice president of marketing. How did she become vice president before age thirty?" asked Trevino.

"I believe it was the third month she was employed here she brought in two manuscripts. One was by Jerry Reeves, and the other by Marissa Marigny, and the rest is beautiful history."

"What was her age when all this beautiful history occurred?"

"She was twenty-two I believe."

"Let me repeat the original question with a rephrasing. How did the deceased become a vice president at age twenty-two?"

Boleyn's jawline tightened. "She began as an assistant editor. She brought in the two writers who became best-selling authors. That's all I know."

"How did she come upon these new writers?"

"I believe as college friends. Both writers have been highly profitable. In the course of her time here, Ms. Crenshaw oversaw ten successful authors. Their works are in continued rotation for reprints."

"Mr. Boleyn, keep in mind that discretion does not apply to the dead. Also, keep in mind if you intentionally withhold information that could help us solve Ms. Crenshaw's murder, we will prosecute you to the fullest extent of the law. Do you understand?"

Boleyn frowned slightly. "I understand that, Detective. What is your question about Ms. Crenshaw?"

"Do you know anything about the deceased personal life?"

"I believe she was seeing someone. She seemed happy and would return sometimes from long lunches with a smile on her face. My observations only. She did not talk to me about her personal life. If there are no more questions, I will take you to Ms. Crenshaw's office. Her things will be cleared and sent to her family by this weekend. Her private assistant is Liz Townes."

Boleyn stood up as a sign the meeting was over. Trevino and Perez stayed seated. He looked from one to the other and put one hand in his pocket while the other he balanced on his desk. Trevino took out his notepad. He flipped slowly through empty pages. The lawyer looked at Perez who stared at him. He sat down. Trevino closed his notepad and stared across the desk at Boleyn. The minutes ticked by.

"Were you and Ms. Crenshaw ever intimate?"

"We did not date," said Boleyn, stiffly.

Trevino smiled. "That's not what I asked. Let me put it another direct way since you are an attorney. Did you and Ms. Crenshaw ever have sex?"

Boleyn's face turned so red it appeared purple. Perez thought he was going to be ill. He looked beyond them as he spoke and some of the subtle arrogance left his demeanor.

"It was a long time ago. We were students. I was in graduate school."

"How long did the sexual relationship last?"

"A few weeks. We both were very busy and could not sustain a relationship."

"And when she began working here?"

"Never."

"At the time of her death, was Ms. Crenshaw involved with anyone at ABC Publishers House?"

"Not that I'm aware."

"One final question for you," said Trevino as he rose from the chair. "Was the deceased a publicist or a marketing executive?"

Boleyn frowned. "Ms. Crenshaw was never a publicist. She started here as an assistant editor. With the two successful manuscripts and her degree in marketing is how she managed to parlay her ..."

Boleyn stopped speaking when he met the hard blue squint of Trevino's eyes. He said nothing else. Boleyn waited a second and then walked them to the elevators. He left them without a word.

The elevator doors opened on the fourth floor where an Asian woman greeted the detectives. She was slightly taller than Perez but not Trevino. The olive complexion matched the auburn-tinted, chestnut brown hair and downcast eyes. She smiled with her lips, but the eyes were focused.

Wearing a light beige silk dress that was loose but flattering she walked toward them with extended hand.

"Hello, my name is Liz Townes. I'm Ms. Crenshaw's personal assistant. After you've finished, I..."

"Excuse me. My name is Detective Trevino, and this is my partner, Detective Perez. We're from homicide. We'd like to ask you a few questions about Jacky Crenshaw."

The smile left the woman's face. She looked from one to the other. "I'm sorry. I was told she committed suicide."

Trevino said, "Can we move out of the hall?"

"Oh, of course," said Townes.

She opened the door behind her. They followed her into an office. The assistant noticed them looking around.

"This is my office. Ms. Crenshaw's office is through that door."

"Who told you Ms. Crenshaw committed suicide?" asked Perez.

"Mr. Boleyn."

"Do you keep her appointment calendar?"

"Yes. I keep both."

"Both?"

"I keep track of her business life and her personal life."

"Would you know where she was three weeks ago on this day?"

"She didn't come into the office that day."

"Was it her day off?"

"She rarely took days off. When she did, she told me prior to doing it."

"Did she do that this time?"

"No."

"Were you concerned? Did you call her?"

"Yes, I was very concerned. We had a budget meeting scheduled. She loved attending those. She was also quite the workaholic."

"Did you locate her?"

"No, and that's what is strange about all this. Ms. Crenshaw would never ever just disappear and no one hear from her. She just didn't do that."

"How long have you worked for the deceased?"

"Going on thirteen years now. She was a great boss. Helped me plan my wedding and gave me this beautiful necklace as a wedding gift a few years ago."

"Would you know if she was seeing anyone?"

"She might have been. She rotated her boyfriends. But understand she didn't talk to me about her personal life. Her best friend was the author, Marissa Marigny."

"How would you know who her best friend was?"

"Oh, she was always saying it."

"How long was it before you reported her absence?"

Townes sighed. "Sixteen working days... after the police called here for her twice."

"Who did you report her disappearance to?"

"Mr. Boleyn. It's protocol due to Ms. Crenshaw's status in the company. Her office is through that door. Everything will be cleaned out on Friday because that's when your department said we could move things. Right now, it's just as she left it. I hope you catch her killer."

"You don't believe it was suicide?"

"Not at all! The woman loved life and living too much."

"If you didn't discuss her personal life with her," said Trevino, "how would you know she loved life and living?"

The assistant stared at Trevino for the space of a minute. With thinly veiled contempt, she spoke through clenched teeth.

"Look, Ms. Crenshaw was good to me, okay? She dated a lot of men. She didn't talk about any of them in detail. At least, not with me. But everybody knew she got around. Her personal appointment book is in the bottom right-hand drawer."

"One last question," said Trevino. "Did you call Ms. Marigny when Ms. Crenshaw didn't return your calls?"

"No."

"Why not?"

A momentary silence, then, "I assumed she was with a man."

Trevino reached around the assistant, and pushed the door closed. He stood in front of it.

"Hold on a minute. This is a police investigation not a conversation with your husband. Why would you assume Crenshaw was with a man? Had she disappeared previously with a man?"

The assistant looked upward. She closed her eyes and sighed. "A few years back, she met some guy, and lost track of time. I covered for her."

"How long was she gone?"

"As I recall, about a week or so."

"Thank you for your honesty," said Trevino with full sarcasm. He stepped away from the door. Townes exited the office quickly. Trevino and Perez exchanged looks.

The detectives turned to survey the office. It was mid-size and a replica of Jacky's home study. There was a wall decorated with book covers of the best-selling authors represented by her. On another were many photographs of her at social events. They leaned in to study them.

Perez murmured, "Crenshaw is solo in many of these or with the authors. None with a man that I see."

"Hmm... these are of Marissa Marigny, and she's with Tony," said Trevino as he studied the photographs.

Marissa held hands with her husband and looked directly at the photographer. Crenshaw leaned in on Marissa's side to close the space. Trevino studied each picture minutely before he moved to the next. Perez walked around the room and over to the desk. She found a memo pad with underlined names. She took a pic of the item.

Trevino was now seated and still stared at the photographs.

"You ready?" asked Perez.

"Come over here. Look at the spacing between these two women. Supposedly they were best friends yet the substantial spacing is problematic."

"Problematic? Why? I don't see that, Luis. They're adult women not schoolchildren. Besides, in both photos, Marissa Marigny is there with her husband. No woman is going to chum it up with her pals, and her lover is nearby."

"I think you're wrong in this instance. I was at the funeral for the Carr woman. Ms. Marigny was surrounded by a group of women, and they were hugged up under each other the entire funeral. As I recall, there were men around them that I'm assuming were their husbands."

"Well, grief over losing a mutual friend is different. Of course they would be together."

"You're working hard to make me believe these two women had a relationship. Look at these two photographs and tell me what you see."

"I see three people posing for a picture."

"Right. Now look over here in the corner. Who is that with Ms. Marigny?"

"Oh, that's Sallie Anne Lewis, the news anchor," said Perez, staring with intent at the photograph.

Both women were photogenic. They stood side by side in sparkly evening gowns with their arms wrapped around each other's waists, and their husbands behind them.

Trevino's voice cut into her reverie. "Now look at this bottom picture. It's the same event. Notice how far apart the deceased and Marigny are standing?"

Perez looked shamefacedly at Trevino who was giving her his I-told-you-look.

"Okay, she and Crenshaw weren't warm and fuzzy, but that doesn't mean they weren't friends."

"What is friendship to these women? Look at these pictures. There is only one of the deceased here with a gathering of women. I'm thinking it's a college photo taken many years ago by the looks of it. I saw an identical one in her home. But what about the following years? The hairstylist said she had known her for twenty years. No personal photos are here with her either."

"She was a white-collar professional, Luis. Why would she have pics of babies and puppies when she was single? Would you expect the same of single men?"

"No. I would expect pics of him hunting, fishing, adventure traveling with scores of beautiful women on his arm." Trevino sighed. "It's about perspectives, Priscilla. All these pictures of the deceased, and not one of them in a non-professional setting. Where's a pic of her and her women friends?"

Perez did not argue against Trevino's comments this time. He looked across the desk at her.

"What did you find?"

"In the last drawer I found a stash of letters. They were written eighteen years ago and tied with this pretty red ribbon."

"What's that tiny object in the other bag?"

"I found this diamond engagement ring."

Trevino whistled. "Wow! Where was it?"

"In the bottom drawer with these letters. I wonder what happened? No woman keeps an engagement ring this long without some deeper meaning attached."

Trevino sighed. "You're such a romantic, Perez. What were you snapping pics of?"

"The memo pads have names underlined."

"What names?"

"Beth Maynes, Tessa Smith, and Patricia Mendoza. I don't know who the Maynes woman is, but we know the last two."

"Let's get them all in for questioning. What was interesting about the calendar?"

"On her personal calendar there's stuff written in code." She flipped the book across the desk.

"Hmm...letters and numbers and not in order. Very few are the same."

"Should we turn it over to the Crime Lab? Maybe they can crack the codes."

Trevino tossed it back to her. "Not worth the time and effort. The last two months are empty pages. She had no codes for her killer."

They rode on in silence.

A woman's laughter was heard from the other side of the captain's door. Tony knocked once and entered followed by Trevino.

"Well, it's about time you two got here. Priscilla and I were just about to order in dinner and a movie."

Trevino sat on the bench by the door. Tony smiled and sat in the chair opposite Perez. She opened her tablet.

"The deceased name was Jacky Crenshaw. She was single, lived alone, and worked for ABC Publishers House as vice president of marketing. She was found strangled in her Washington Heights home."

"Who found her?" asked Murray wearily.

"Tessa Smith, her friend and hair stylist." Perez did not look at Trevino. "Ms. Smith filed a missing person report five days before discovering her friend."

"How did the victim die?"

"Death by supposed hanging," interjected Trevino's gruff voice.

"Supposed? You sound skeptical," said Murray as he scrolled through text on his computer screen. "Hasn't her death been confirmed as a suicide?"

"It's' been upgraded to undetermined. Someone helped her have a short life."

"The autopsy discovered no foul play. There was no DNA on her that hasn't been checked." Perez looked at her partner. "There were no defense wounds anywhere on her body. She committed suicide."

Trevino's dark blue eyes sat on his high cheekbones like slivers of lightning. The thick black hair flopped over his forehead as he gazed at her with squinted eyes.

"Kindly use some mathematical theory to explain to us how a woman that tall managed to hang herself, Priscilla. While you're at it, also explain why we found no step stool or anything else that she could have used to propel herself three feet off the floor. We'll wait."

"I share Luis' skepticism." Tony said. "An autopsy showed the victim was five feet eleven inches tall. Look at the crime scene photos. The low table was within distance for her to push off from. But it was not strong enough for her to stand on, and it was perfectly aligned to the floor."

"Meaning there were no scuff marks on the table or the floor. And there wasn't a chair or ladder nearby for her to use. Keep in mind she was five feet eleven inches tall. Someone did the job for her," said Trevino. "But for now, all we have is speculation and supposition."

"She was single. Did she have a boyfriend? Someone she was seeing?" asked Murray. He frowned as he examined the photos.

"We spoke to coworkers at the publishing house who stated they suspected she was seeing someone."

"That was also the same thing her hairdresser stated," said Trevino. He gave Murray a picture of the letter encased in plastic and a picture of the engagement ring.

"Wow!" said Murray. "That's some ring."

"There were no other prints on either item but Crenshaw's," said Perez.

"Were you able to get these items analyzed?" asked Murray.

"Stefanie's team determined the letter to be aged by fifteen years or more. The style of writing is slanted and suggests a left-hand writer. The ring was very expensive and is currently being traced. We also found several more letters in her office." Trevino tossed the pack on the desk.

"Forensic determined those letters are at least fifteen years old, which means they were written when she was in college," said Perez.

"Could we suggest a college boyfriend who might have resurfaced?"

"If that were true, wouldn't she have mentioned that fact to her friends and coworkers?" Tony asked.

Trevino looked at Tony who now stood behind Murray's chair looking at the items on the captain's desk.

Trevino smiled. "Not all women behave the same with their romantic lives, Tony. No one could say with conviction whether she was currently dating or not, or with whom."

"Luis is right. We even checked with her assistant, Liz Townes, and even she said the deceased wasn't a kiss and tell kind of girl."

"That secrecy might have been her undoing," murmured Murray as he continued to look at the photos on his screen. "Okay. Talk to the hairdresser again since she claimed friendship with the victim."

"Hairstylist." Perez said.

"What?"

"Tessa Smith is the hairstylist who claimed she was the victim's friend," said Perez. "No one says hairdresser anymore. It's hairstylist."

Murray stared at Perez until she blushed a deep red. The silence went on. Trevino put a stick of chewing gum in his mouth and smirked.

Tony cleared his throat. "Could we address the elephant in the room? Priscilla, the victim's official title on the website was vice president of marketing. Did you ask if that was her only job role?"

"We were told she started as an associate editor. When did she become your wife's publicist?" Perez looked at Tony.

"As far as I know she's always been Marissa's publicist."

Murray asked, "So, which role is the right one?"

"The company attorney stated the victim was the vice president of marketing," said Trevino. "I doubt if he would lie about it."

"So, why was she posing as a book publicist, and not as a marketing director or whatever?" Murray asked. He turned to Tony, "Does your wife know?"

"That's what we need to find out." Tony looked at Trevino. "Luis, have

Marissa come in for questioning. See if she knows why a marketing executive would shadow as her book publicist. Also, question Jerry Reeves."

"Wouldn't it be better to talk to your wife yourself?" asked Perez.

"If I weren't a cop that would be okay, Priscilla. But we must play by the book. We can't risk contaminating the evidence and having it thrown out in court if something materializes in the future."

"Okay," said Perez.

"Who's Jerry Reeves?" asked Murray.

"The author who came on the same time as Marissa," said Tony.

"We also have an interview scheduled with Beth Maynes and Tessa Smith," said Perez. "We've also called in Sallie Anne Lewis."

"Why? Who is this, Beth Maynes?" asked Murray.

"She produces the evening news. She was penciled on the deceased business calendar for a two-hour meeting. Smith is the friend." Perez let that sink in before saying, "Sallie Anne Lewis is..."

"I know who she is," Murray interrupted. "She's that gorgeous redhead anchor on the evening news. I always tape that segment just to look at that beautiful face. Simply stunning woman."

Perez looked at Trevino and Tony. They were both nodding their heads in silent agreement with Murray. She held back her irritation.

Trevino stood up. "I've also sent for Patricia Mendoza."

Tony and Murray looked at the detective. Tony said, "You did what?"

"Her name is also on that memo sheet. If we're bringing in a television producer, a news anchor, and God only knows who else, then why not the district attorney?"

"I'm getting a headache," said Murray. He put his head in his hands. "I think I'll drink my lunch."

Tony smirked and Perez laughed. Trevino smiled and walked out. Tony walked back to his office with an empty coffee cup. He closed the door carefully and sat behind his desk. He pretended to be reading when Trevino and Perez left for the day. The squad room was now empty. Tony closed his blinds and sat still in his office.

Several weeks had passed since Janelle's funeral and signs of spring was everywhere. Marissa was eating dinner with him again. She was back at her writing. How could he tell her another one of her close friends had died?

It was late when Tony pulled up in the driveway to his home. He sat looking at the house and trying to gather his thoughts. He walked into the kitchen and noticed the stillness and the darkness. As he neared the staircase, he felt a presence and was on one knee with his gun drawn when he heard the sharp intake of a female voice. He turned on the lights and put his gun in his holster. Marissa came out of the corner where she had backed up when she saw him withdraw his gun. She came to him, and he hugged her.

"I've told you before to never walk around quietly like that in the dark," he said into her hair as he hugged her tightly to him.

"I'm sorry. I forgot. The bulb in the lamp blew out upstairs."

"Well, now that you've got my adrenaline flowing..."

"I was coming into the kitchen to get a replacement bulb."

"It's okay, baby. I'll change it. What are we having for dinner?"

"Baked chicken with eggplant lasagna."

"Hmm... smells good. Let me shower and change. I'll take care of the bulb, too. I'll be right back."

By the time Tony returned Marissa had warmed up his food. He smiled as she handed him his plate. She sat a green salad before him.

"Nothing like a home cooked meal. Where's your plate, baby?"

She grabbed a handful of pecans. "Oh, I'm not hungry. That's for you."

"Thank you." He eyed the black and white striped pullover and matching sweatpants. "Did you run today?"

"No. I was going to, but I just didn't feel like it."

She poured them both cups of coffee and sat beside him. She picked up the television remote and turned it on. He waited a few seconds and turned it off.

"Tony, I was going to turn it to the news."

"I'd much rather spend some quiet time with you."

He finished eating and took his dishes to the dishwasher. He took her by the hand and went into their family room. He pulled her down on his lap and kissed her. Then he sat her on the sofa.

"Don't you want to know what I made for dessert?"

"I have to tell you something."

"Okay, what is it?"

"It is believed Jacky Crenshaw committed suicide. We haven't released the information to the press yet, but it will be on the news."

"Suicide? She committed suicide?"

"That's how it appears, but we're still investigating."

"Wow. Thank you for telling me. I'll have to call my publisher later after the news breaks."

Marissa walked into the kitchen and turned on the dishwasher. Tony watched her wipe down the counter and set the coffee timer.

"I thought you'd be a bit broken up over your friend's death."

"Of course, I'll send condolences to her family. I'm sorry she ended her life."

Marissa swept the floor. Tony watched her take the filled recycle bag to the bin on the patio. She looked at him.

"What more do you want me to say?"

"Nothing, I guess. She was your publicist for such a long time."

"Yes, now I have to break someone else in."

She turned away from him and began drawing the curtains across the patio doors. Tony headed to his den.

"So, you don't want dessert?"

He turned to look at his wife. Only then did he see the tears sliding down her face. Wordlessly, they embraced, and he could hear her sobbing.

"Oh, Tony, I'm going to miss her so much."

"I know. I know you will."

Later in their bedroom they watched a game show on television. During a commercial break Tony glanced at his wife.

"Baby, you'll have to come into the station for questioning."

"Questioning about what?"

"Your relationship with Jacky."

"They think I know what happened to her?"

"We're trying to catch her killer. We had to ask you when Janelle was... remember? Anything you can tell us about Jacky will help in the investigation."

She nodded. "Okay. Is the police questioning all my friends?"

"Do we need to? Jacky had a close relationship with you, or that's how it appears so far."

"Jacky was my publicist, but Janelle was my best friend."

"I know you and she had a close business relationship all these years. Just be honest and upfront as much as you can. Okay?"

"Okay. What are they going to ask me?"

"I don't know, baby. Where are you going?"

"To find something cute to wear for my appearance at the precinct. I want to look nice."

Tony watched her disappear into the walk-in closet. He shook his head and turned the television channel to sports. He would never understand women.

Marissa waited until Tony stepped into the shower. She dialed the private number.

"Hi, sweetie! Is this a bad time for you?"

"No. Perfect timing in fact. Eric's taken the girls to a father-daughter movie," said Patricia. "What's going on?"

"I've been called in for an interview about Jacky," said Marissa as she gazed at the polish on her toes. "Tony just told me I have to get interviewed about Jacky since I've known her for a long time."

"So, what's the matter?"

"What should I admit knowing about her?"

"Nothing. Let them ask the questions. Take your time and listen. Sip water, count on your fingers, but don't give definitive responses."

"Okay."

"Listen, sweetie. I have a feeling they're going on a fishing expedition. They've called Sallie Anne and Beth, too."

"Probably because of her connections with the media."

"They've called me in too. I'll tell you about it later. Don't worry."

"Oh, I never worry, sweetie. I just want to keep us all safe."

"I know. We'll be fine."

Marissa hung up and decided to paint her toenails.

Chapter 15

Patricia Mendoza arrived on time in a chauffeured limo accompanied by her personal bodyguard. Doors were opened and voices subdued as she marched down the hall with her head held high. She nodded at passing police officers. She was led to an interview room by a starstruck police officer who blushed and gushed when Patricia nodded her thanks.

Sloan, in the observation room, eyed the district attorney's outfit with envy. Patricia wore a black chalk striped wool pantsuit over a white cashmere pullover. Her long dark hair was loosely pulled into a wavy ponytail. Sloan gazed at the white gold hoop earrings, and the matching bracelet on Patricia's left wrist.

Di Giovanni stood when she entered the interview room.

"Good morning, Ms. Mendoza. I'm Detective di Giovanni. Please have a seat. Thank you for responding quickly. As I relayed to you during our phone call, we found your name on the work desk of the late Jacky Crenshaw. Our focus is on finding her killer."

She nodded and sat with her hands folded watching the detective. The white gold wedding band caught the fluorescent light and Sloan's eyes. Turning on the tape recorder, di Giovanni named time, place, and persons. He opened his folder.

"Would you please state your full name."

"Patricia Ramos Mendoza, District Attorney of Winding Falls."

"Thank you. Ms. Mendoza. My understanding is that you're the first Hispanic of Mexican descent, and the first woman to head the district attorney's office here in Winding Falls, correct?"

"Yes."

"How long have you held that position?"

"Eight years now."

"What was your previous position?"

"Assistant district attorney."

"Where did you earn your law degree?"

"Winding Falls University School of Law."

"What was your undergrad major?"

"Political Science."

"Thank you. The following questions will deal primarily with your time spent at Winding Falls University."

"Okay."

"Ms. Mendoza, who were you close to during your entire four years on campus?"

"On campus? I guess that would have been my roommate."

"Who did you room with during your time on campus?"

"Stacie Young."

"The entire four years?"

"Yes."

"Were you dating anyone?"

"Not the first two years, no."

"When did you begin dating?"

"I met my husband during my third year. We began dating seriously the following year and married a year or so later."

"Who is your husband?"

"Eric Mendoza."

"The Superior Court Judge?"

"Yes."

"Judge Mendoza was your only boyfriend?"

"Yes."

"Do you remember Jacky Crenshaw?"

"Yes."

"Was she dating anyone?"

"I don't know."

"You shared living quarters for four years. You didn't talk about your boyfriends or anyone asking to date you?"

"My roommate and best friend was Stacie Young. I don't remember much about Crenshaw."

"But you knew she was dating someone?"

"She was man crazy. Every day there was a different one. I have no idea who she was dating seriously, if at all."

"Who was Jacky's best friend among you all?"

Patricia thought carefully before responding. "I don't know who her best friend could've been. I don't know who her friends were. She tried to adopt Marissa. Oh, she was suffocating poor Marissa that first year. We would be in our room, in class or anywhere on campus, and here would come Jacky wanting to speak to Marissa or trying to join us at some public event."

"Marissa who?"

"Marissa Marigny."

"So they were close?"

"Marissa's best friend was Janelle Carr."

"How do you know that?"

"Because we were friends in high school before entering college."

"Was the late Ms. Carr friends with the deceased?"

"No. Janelle was a sweet, wholesome girl. She was adventurous and outgoing but not man-crazy like the deceased. Janelle could paint, dance, and play the saxophone. She and Marissa studied in France one summer while Stacie and I were in Mexico."

Di Giovanni looked at her face. It was one of the rare occasions the district attorney's face was free of scowl lines. She was more beautiful than he had ever seen her.

"So, your certain there was no boyfriend in Jacky's life?"

"I didn't say that. She had plenty of love interests."

"I thought you didn't know any of her boyfriends."

Patricia laughed. "The deceased was man crazy. She was always in the company of men."

"Can you think of any reason why anyone would want to hurt the deceased."

"No."

"Ms. Mendoza, there was a message on her desk to call you. What can you tell us about that?"

Mendoza shrugged. "I have no idea why she wanted to talk to me."

"Had she ever called you before?"

"Once or twice to chat."

"Chat about what, Ms. Mendoza?"

"Girl talk, Detective."

"Give me some examples. I'm not a woman."

Patricia was both angry and irritated. The detective saw it in the flash of her dark eyes and the way she tried to control her breathing.

"She talked about whatever book she was promoting. I'm a great fan of Marissa's novels. That's it."

"Marissa Marigny, the book author?"

"Yes."

"Did you and the deceased ever hang out together?"

"No."

"Why not?"

"Different lifestyles. She was single. I'm married with children."

"No lunch dates? Saturday morning shopping trips?"

"No, Detective. We weren't close friends."

Di Giovanni laid a clear plastic packet containing a letter with faded writing on the table. Mendoza never looked at it.

"Have you ever seen this letter?"

"No."

"She wrote it to someone while she was in college."

"I don't know who she was dating. I never met any of them. She didn't share any details about her men. Not that any of us really cared. Maybe they were grad students because they had off-campus housing."

"How do you know about off-campus housing, but don't know who the men were?"

She sighed. "It's just speculation on my part, Detective. Jacky had a car, as we all did, and she was always leaving the campus. I'm assuming she was meeting men, and they lived off-campus."

Di Giovanni pushed the engagement ring, encased in plastic, toward the district attorney. "Have you ever seen her wear this?"

"Wow! That's a gorgeous ring..."

"Did you ever see Crenshaw wear this ring?"

"No. Does it belong to her?"

"Do you remember any complaints about a persistent suitor? Someone who wouldn't take no for an answer?"

"No."

"That's all the questions I have. Thank you for coming in Ms. Mendoza."

Di Giovanni walked the district attorney and her bodyguard to the lobby. He watched them climb into the waiting limo.

Di Giovanni was seated in Tony's office when he walked in. Tony walked around to his desk and sat down the pile of folders he carried down. He tossed a few manila envelopes to di Giovanni. The men studied folder contents quietly.

"What happened with the district attorney?"

"Nothing. She knew nothing about the suicide victim but quite a lot about the Carr woman."

"I listened to the taping. I got the feeling she didn't care for the deceased."

"Nice polite way of putting it."

"Hopefully we have some luck with Marissa."

"Yeah. Hopefully."

A gorgeous day but a bit on the chilly side. Spring is such a temperamental season. Ah! Is that the princess I see up ahead? Yes, it is! How wonderful for me. Love the black and white jogging set. She has some beautiful black hair...long and curly. She doesn't usually run with it hanging loose like that. Where the heck is she going? Oh, some of the girlfriends are out today. They must be meeting in the park. Wait a minute! They're not running. Why is everyone seated? What is that? Boy, sometimes I despise women! But I must keep going. I don't want to draw attention to myself by stopping. I can turn around up there by that large boulder with everyone else. Let's see what's going on now. They're in some kind of huddle. Yes, this group is good at keeping secrets.

Chapter 16

In the lobby a few hours later, Trevino stood by the front desk in the Winding Falls Police Administration Building. He spotted Marissa as she walked up the side entrance to enter the building. She wore large dark sunglasses, but he recognized her from the times he covered surveillance in Chicago when Tony was undercover. He waved at Stan, the desk sergeant, and approached Marissa. He extended his hand which she shook. She had not changed much.

"Ms. Marigny? I'm Detective Trevino. You're here to see me."

"Hello, Detective. No, I'm here to see my husband."

"I need to ask you some questions. You can see your husband afterward. Come with me, please."

They took the elevator upstairs. She was wearing a deep blue cashmere coat and low-heeled beige pumps. He realized she was tall as Perez, who was a whopping five-foot ten in stocking feet. He pegged Marissa at the same height. The perfume she was wearing was soft and feminine. He caught a whiff of it every time she moved. He led her to an interrogation room and watched her as she looked about before taking off the coat and sitting down.

She wore a deep blue checked cashmere dress that slid over a curvy figure. The long black curly hair was combed back off her face and secured on the side with a yellow barrette. She clutched a beige handbag in her lap, removed the large sunglasses, and surveyed him with deep brown, droopy eyes.

She was striking in her beauty, and aware of it, but she did not act on it. That aspect alone intrigued him, and the fact she was guarded. He could see it in her eyes whenever she allowed herself to look at him.

Perez walked in and sat in the chair next to Trevino. Marissa ignored her, which silently amused Trevino. Marissa opened her purse, moved stuff around and pulled out a small tube of hand cream. Then she put it back and looked at Trevino. Perez eyes locked on the large aquamarine and white diamond wedding set on Marissa's hand. In her ears were matching drop earrings.

"Would you like some coffee, tea, or water?" Trevino asked.

"No, thank you."

"These questions concern your relationship with Jacky Crenshaw."

"Okay."

"Would you please state your full name."

"Marissa Marigny."

"When and where did you first meet the deceased, Jacky Crenshaw?"

"We met our first year as students at Winding Falls University."

"Did you room together?"

"No."

"Did you become friends at some point?"

"We became friendly."

"Friendly but not friends?"

"Friendly as in cordial, Detective. My best friend was Janelle Carr."

"Did you have any other friendships?"

"Yes, and I'm still friends with them."

"But not with the deceased?"

"We had a working relationship."

"If you weren't friends in college the four years you were both there; how did a working relationship develop after graduation? How did Ms. Crenshaw become your publicist? Tell me the story."

Marissa stared at Trevino for a few minutes. It was a solid look devoid of emotion. The faint image of a smile played around her mouth.

"She brought an unfinished manuscript of mine to her new boss. He liked it and signed me to a contract."

"How did she get the unfinished manuscript?"

"By guile."

"Where was the unfinished manuscript that the deceased could steal it?"

"It was in my bedroom on my dresser."

"What bedroom? In your college dorm, an apartment, or your parents' home?"

"My parents' home. I moved back home after college."

"If you weren't friends, why was the deceased at your home and in your bedroom?"

"I was newly engaged. I was planning my wedding. She was a member of the wedding party."

"Was she in your wedding?"

"No."

"Why not?"

"After she stole the manuscript, I no longer wanted her around."

"How do you know she stole it?"

"It was revealed later."

"How did you know it was stolen beforehand?"

Marissa was silent and did not look at Trevino. Finally, she said, "I assumed it was her, and later found my assumptions accurate."

"When was your first book published?"

"I don't know. Sometime around my wedding. When we returned from our honeymoon, I had a thousand calls from ABC Publishers House. That's when I found out she had brought it to her boss."

"So, you became friends?"

"No, we became business partners."

"What was the controversy with your third book?"

She seemed confused and sighed. "What are you talking about?"

"I noticed a news clip in Ms. Crenshaw's office. The headlines were screaming about a controversy about the third book."

"Oh, that," Marissa's tone was slightly dismissive. "All of my novels are written with the women characters as heroes. What you'd call chick literature. I thought I'd try something different and made the hero a man, but my readers didn't like it, so I returned to my earlier style."

"Did you and the deceased have a falling out prior to her disappearance and subsequent death?" asked Perez.

Marissa looked across the table at Perez. Her eyes were dark but to Perez surprise Marissa had an almost smug appearance.

"Ms. Crenshaw and I had a professional working relationship. I don't know why that's difficult to grasp. We did not always agree when it came to an idea I suggested for a book or theme. Prior to her disappearance and death, however, we were not at odds with each other."

"When was the last time you saw or spoke to the deceased?" asked Trevino.

Marissa frowned and looked down at her hands. She sighed again. "If I remember correctly the last time, I saw Jacky was when she dropped by my house one afternoon."

"Do you remember when that was? The date?"

"No, I don't."

"Was it the week of her disappearance? The week before that?"

"I don't know when she disappeared."

"Did you receive a phone call from anyone asking about her?"

"No."

"No one called asking if you had seen or spoken to the deceased?"

"If they did, I don't remember."

"When the deceased came to your home, what was the purpose for her visit?"

"I'm beginning a new book. We went over the manuscript."

"How was her mood, temperament? We're trying to figure out her state of mind prior to her disappearance, Ms. Marigny."

"She was in good spirits."

"Why? Did she tell you?"

"She had a date with a new man."

"Did she tell you anything about the man?"

"No."

"Did she ever discuss her dating life with you?"

"No."

Perez cut in. "Ms. Marigny, you and the deceased were college friends. Later, you worked together for over fifteen years. Do you expect us to believe she didn't share some aspects of her personal life with you?"

"I don't care what you believe or don't believe, Detective," said Marissa in a dismissive voice.

"Ms. Marigny, one final question," said Trevino, giving Perez a death stare. "Were you aware Ms. Crenshaw was vice president of marketing?"

"What?" Marissa stared at Trevino. "No. She was my publicist. That's all I've ever known her as."

"Don't you find it strange that she would continue to work as your publicist when she was vice president of marketing?"

"I don't know what to say to that, Detective."

"Did you have a boyfriend that year or anyone you were interested in?"

"No." She frowned slightly.

"What about Jacky Crenshaw?"

"What about her?"

"Was she dating anyone?"

"I don't know."

Trevino laid a letter encased in clear plastic on the table pushing it toward Marissa. She looked at the letter but made no move to touch it. She looked at Trevino.

"Ms. Marigny, that's a letter Ms. Crenshaw may have written to a young man she was dating while attending college."

"I can't tell you what I don't know, Detective."

"You've never seen that letter before now?"

"No."

"Do you know what hand Ms. Crenshaw wrote with?"

"I think she was left-handed."

Perez placed the engagement ring encased in plastic on the table. She moved it gently across the table toward Marissa.

"Have you ever seen this ring before?"

"No."

"We found it with the packet of love letters to the unknown lover." Silence. Trevino asked, "Do you know who gave her the ring?"

"No."

"But you know she had a boyfriend."

"She liked every guy on campus."

"She never shared details with you about a specific guy?"

"What kind of details?"

"Details like his name, age, school major, hometown. All the information people want to know about each other when they're dating."

"I don't think she ever told me about a specific guy."

"Were you and she best friends that first year?"

"She just wanted someone to talk to."

"What did she talk to you about?"

"The guys on campus."

"What did she say about them?"

"I really don't remember, Detective. I was hardly ever listening to her."

"Ms. Marigny, this is a criminal investigation. Someone has killed a close friend of yours. We need to find the missing piece for this puzzle. Only Jacky Crenshaw was dating during your first year as undergrads. Who was he?"

Marissa took a mint out of her purse, and carefully put it in her mouth. She sat looking at her fingernails for a minute. Perez felt heat rising in her neck. She glanced sideways at Trevino who sat calmly watching Marissa. Finally, Marissa sighed. She began to speak slowly.

"Detective, my very best friend in the whole world was Janelle Carr. I can talk to you about Janelle all day and all night. I don't believe there's anything about Janelle I don't know. However, Jacky was just some girl who needed someone to talk to occasionally. I'm not a rude person so I indulged her. But she and I were not personal friends."

"If you weren't friends, why was she always around you? You must have encouraged her attention in some way," Perez said.

"And that is what we're trying to find out. What did she talk to you about? Was that the secret you had between you?"

"Secret?" Marissa frowned.

"Was her having a boyfriend a secret?"

"If that was her secret, I don't know anything about it. We didn't hang out together."

There was silence. Trevino watched Marissa subconsciously play with the rings on her fingers. She said nothing else.

"Well, thank you for coming in, Ms. Marigny. I can take you to your husband's office now."

"No, thank you. I'm rather tired. I'm going home."

She stood up and put on her coat. He caught the scent of her perfume again. It intoxicated his senses. She took the dark eye shades out of their carrying case but held them in her hands.

"Let me walk you out, Ms. Marigny." He opened the door for her.

"Thank you, Detective."

Perez stayed seated. Trevino walked Marissa to the elevators. They did not speak. He put on his dark shades and watched as she caught the attention of people alike. He went with her across the lot to her car which faced the street. He opened the car door for her. She did not give him a second glance as she drove by. He looked after her car deep in thought.

When Trevino returned to the squad room, Tony beckoned him into his office.

"Did you watch the interview?" Trevino asked sitting down.

"Yes, I did."

"I thought your wife was forthright in her responses."

"Maybe Mendoza was but Marissa wasn't forthright about anything you asked her."

Trevino gave Tony a measured look. The Puerto Rican detective spent much of his storied career operating undercover in drug cartels. He learned long ago how to read people, and he knew Tony was crazy about Marissa. Which meant, cop or not, he had to temper what he said to him about his wife.

"You do know your wife is grieving the loss of her friends, right?"

"Her grief has nothing to do with responding truthfully to questions."

There was silence for a minute. Trevino did not look at Tony. "I thought she was quite open with most of her responses."

"She was also lying through her pretty teeth."

"At what point?"

Tony's green eyes were half shut in anger. "All of it. I know my wife, Luis. She's covering up something she knows about Crenshaw."

"Well, we're on the same page there, but to be fair to your wife, I don't think she and this Crenshaw woman were close. I also believe Crenshaw was something of a party girl. It's obvious even now that they were worlds apart in that area."

"Yeah, Marissa was very shy back then."

"She still is, Tony. She's also reserved and conservative. Some aspects of our character traits stay even as we age."

Tony glanced at Trevino and changed the subject. "When is Jerry Reeves due in?"

"Next week." Trevino looked at a small pad in his hand. "We're also meeting with Beth Maynes, and I've called in Tessa Smith."

"What does Beth do again?"

"She's a producer for a news station and Smith is the woman who found the victim."

Tony's desk phone buzzed. He looked at Trevino. "Crime doesn't sleep, Luis, even when we do. Walk with me. I need to update the captain."

"Have you read O'Neill's report on the armed robbery in Olde City last night?" asked Trevino.

"Yes, and I repeat, crime doesn't sleep. What's your take on it?"

"Let me walk you to the captain's office. I don't want to repeat it twice."

"You're sounding like me now."

"You wish!"

They both laughed as Tony closed his office door.

Chapter 17

O'Neill walked into the interview room unprepared for the news anchor's overt flamboyance. From her shaggy layered red hair and light hazel eyes to the luminous glow of her skin she was a vision of loveliness. She wore a purple silk dress with a purple print neck shawl. The diamond studs in her ears glowed between the folds of hair caressing her cheeks and collar bone. She was accompanied by a small, trim man attired in a gray worsted wool suit.

"Good afternoon, Ms. Lewis. I'm Sergeant O'Neill. Please have a seat. Could you state your full names and titles for the record."

"Sallie Anne Braithwaite Lewis, journalist."

"Charleston Claiborne, Esq., attorney for Ms. Lewis."

"Thank you, Ms. Lewis, Mr. Claiborne. Ms. Lewis, what is your occupation?"

"I anchor the Winding Falls Evening News."

"How long have you held the position of anchor?"

"Thirteen years."

"What was your position before becoming anchor?"

"I was a news journalist in the field."

"What is your degree in?"

"Broadcast Journalism."

"Where did you earn your degree?"

"Winding Falls University School of Communication."

"The questions I'm about to ask you deal with your relationship with Jacky Crenshaw."

Sallie Anne sat straight, and whenever O'Neill looked at her, she flashed a brilliant smile.

"Ms. Lewis, who did you room with during your time on campus?"

"Beth Maynes."

"Who else did you room with?"

"Beth is my best friend."

"Who else in your group stayed together the entire four years?"

"I'm not sure."

"Do you remember having to speak to security about a persistent suitor? Someone who wouldn't take no for an answer?"

"No."

"Were you or any of your friends dating as first-year students?"

"I wasn't, and I don't think the other girls were either. Everything was so new and exciting."

"What about Jacky Crenshaw?"

"Who?"

"She committed suicide."

"Oh, yes. That was sad."

"When you were in college together do you know who Jacky dated?"

Sallie Anne frowned. "Who she dated? No. Why would I?"

"Do you remember who Ms. Crenshaw's best friend was?"

"Our first year I think she wanted to be Marissa's best friend. She pretty much stalked the girl around campus." She smirked at the memory. "But they weren't friends. I think Marissa helped her out of a jam."

"What kind of a jam?"

Sallie Anne's attorney leaned in and whispered in her ear. She looked wide-eyed at O'Neill and smiled.

"That's all I know on that."

"You don't remember what the jam was?"

"Poor choice of words, Detective."

"But they were close?"

"Close? Who?"

"Crenshaw and Marigny."

"No indeed not! Marissa's best friend was Janelle."

"Janelle who?"

"Janelle Carr. Our beautiful, sweet Janelle."

"Well, their friendship must have been deeper than you realize as Jacky Crenshaw became her book publicist."

Sallie Anne indulged in a small giggle behind her well-manicured hand. She looked directly at the detective.

"James, we're all considered friends because we're sorority sisters. But trust me when I tell you that woman was not Marissa's best friend. I don't want to speak ill of the dead, but she wasn't, and that's the truth."

"How can you be so sure they didn't become best friends?"

"Marissa and Janelle have been best friends since kindergarten days, that's why. Now Marissa's really close to Patricia, but that's to be expected as they're the only ones left from the foursome."

"What foursome?"

O'Neill could see in the anchor's eyes she realized her mistake. She smiled with her entire face.

"I don't remember the exact number. But we would pair off in groups of fours."

"Ms. Crenshaw didn't fit in?"

"She was not only an out-of-towner, but kind of pushy."

"What about the love interest?"

"For whom? That woman? I don't know anything about her personal life."

"Based on what we've discovered she seems to have always had an active dating life. Surely as sorority sisters you were aware of who she might've dated among the fraternities?"

Sallie Anne's face turned red. Whether from anger or embarrassment, O'Neill could not tell. He hoped his partner was in the next room.

"I wouldn't know. She seem to date the entire campus of men!"

The attorney whispered in her ear again. She looked across at O'Neill and the hazel eyes were now a muted green. She grinned with closed lips and softened her tone.

"I mean she was a pretty girl. Guys were lining up to talk to her, and she loved dating and going out. She didn't seem like the type to settle down."

"Have you seen this letter?"

Sallie Anne and the attorney leaned forward and looked at the letter. They looked at each other and then O'Neill. Sallie Anne shook her head.

"I've never seen this letter. It looks kind of old."

"Can you think of any reason why anyone would want to hurt her?"

"No, I think on the face of it, she was pretty harmless."

"Did you and Ms. Crenshaw ever hang out after graduation?"

"No."

She looked at him with a frown as if he had insulted her. O'Neill decided to push the envelope.

"Why not?"

Sallie Anne flashed a huge smile. "Because I usually went home to my family. I don't know where *she* went."

"Usually? Where did you go when you didn't go home to your family?"

"Sometimes shopping."

"Alone?"

"I told you. My best friend is Beth, and when I'm not with her, I'm with my husband and daughters."

"Did you ever go shopping with Ms. Crenshaw?"

"No."

"Why not?"

"I didn't want to."

"Well, that's all my questions, Ms. Lewis. Thank you for coming in."

Sallie Anne gave him one of her bright smiles and stood up. Her lawyer made a sedate nod and followed her out the door. O'Neill thought he looked relieved it was over.

O'Neill walked into the squad room. He sat down at the desk across from Benson. She handed him a coffee and sandwich. He smiled his thanks as he bit into it.

"Did you watch the interview?"

"Of course."

Tony appeared and pulled over a chair. "Let's talk about your interview."

"Ms. Lewis was aware of Crenshaw but did not seem to know her. It was like she knew of her," said O'Neill as he sipped coffee. "To be honest, I found that part disconcerting. How do you spend twenty years with people and not know them?"

"When you're sheltered in your own little group," said di Giovanni. He turned off his computer monitor. "When you insulate yourself away from the larger community."

"Exclusivity rather than inclusivity," said O'Neill.

Gerard countered with, "most women do this within their groups."

"All people tend to exhibit this type of behavior within their selective groups," corrected di Giovanni.

"What was your assessment of the Lewis interview, Vee?"

Benson sighed. "She seemed mildly arrogant. There were snatches of mean girl like when she described Crenshaw dating everyone on campus or something like that."

"Yeah, I caught that when I asked who the deceased may have dated among the fraternities." O'Neill smiled.

Sloan laughed. "I'm sure she didn't want to think of her husband once having the hots for Crenshaw."

Gerard and Perez tried to cover their laughter by coughing while their colleagues laughed heartily. Tony grinned. He turned to di Giovanni who was scribbling on his tablet. He looked up and smiled.

"Colleagues, the only thing I will say about my interview with our intrepid district attorney is that she was as open as she was going to get. I pulled out a few caveats. The most important one being that the source of our inquiries lies with a local writer. We can't afford negative publicity when it concerns one of Winding Falls most famous celebrities. The goal is to tread lightly but firmly."

Benson spoke with irritation in her voice. "So what you're saying, Dante, is Ms. Marigny's celebrity status is more important than solving the murders of two innocent women."

"I interviewed Ms. Marigny, and her celebrity status didn't influence the type or depth of my questions," shot back Trevino.

"But we will not treat her like a common criminal," said di Giovanni with a smirk. "This maniac killed these women with impunity. Unless they were part of a higher order crime syndicate, which we know they weren't, our goal is to find him and stop him."

Tony smiled. "Luis conducted the interview with Marissa. What I will say is there's an underlying current to the responses of these women I don't like."

"I agree with you, Tony." O'Neill threw his wrapper away. "None of them liked Crenshaw but loved Carr and its evident in the way they've responded to questions about them. But their dislikes aside, we need to know what it is they dislike so much about Crenshaw, because that will be the key to finding this killer."

"Exactly."

"Wait a minute!" Benson's tone was mocking. "I know you are all married except for Luis and Kevin but come on now. Not to speak ill of the dead, but the deceased was a party girl and the others weren't. They're all married women now in settle relationships. Do you really think they care about a free-swinging bachelorette?"

Di Giovanni smirked. "Vee has a point. I don't hang around with the still single guys from my college days either."

"That's not altogether true either, Dante," said Trevino. "My bowling team is married couples and single folks. The golf games is full of married, divorced, and single guys. Not to mention the family events I get snagged into. Every one of my sisters is married."

Gerard laughed. "Yeah, many of my cop friends are married and we hang out sometimes. I even get invited to their homes for dinner and such."

"That's because their wives are trying to fix you up," said Sloan with a grin.

"Yes," agreed Gerard with a grin matching hers. "I know."

Tony cut into their banter. "Next week I want Priscilla to interview the producer, and Luis manage the witness who discovered the body. Thank you everyone for your work today. Enjoy your weekend."

The detectives looked at each other. Tony walked back to his office. For the first time in a long time, he wore a pensive expression.

Chapter 18

Perez watched as two men entered the interview room where she sat. The first man was tall, tanned, and athletically built with black hair and eyes. He had a rugged handsomeness about him. The second man was similar in looks. His dark blonde hair was conservatively cut and tapered into short sideburns. The silver horn-rimmed glasses shielded piercing blue eyes.

The woman walked in the room behind them. An ice blonde, her thick mane fell attractively over her shoulders with side swept bangs that emphasized wide set deep blue eyes, arched eyebrows, a snub nose, and slightly full lips. The white wool suit made her light olive skin glow. She extended a hand to Perez. The grip was firm.

"I'm Elizabeth Maynes. This is my husband, Sam Maynes, and my attorney, Bill Jones."

Maynes looked at her and nodded. The second man merely blinked.

"I'm Det. Perez. Please sit down, folks."

Tony watched the proceedings in his office on his monitor. He sent Trevino in the room as moral support for Perez. The two men glanced at the detective as he entered the room. Then they focused on Perez.

"Ms. Maynes, we'll start off with routine questions about your relationship with Jacky Crenshaw."

"Okay," she replied in a small, breathy voice. She held hands with her husband.

"Ms. Maynes, what is your occupation?"

"I produce the evening news."

"How long have you been a producer?"

"About thirteen years."

"What did you do previously?"

"I wrote news assignments."

"Where did you earn your degree?"

"Winding Falls University School of Communication."

"What was your degree in?"

"Broadcast journalism."

"Any other education?"

"I have a graduate degree as well."

"Thank you. I want to ask you about your time at Winding Falls University when you were an undergrad."

"Okay."

"Do you remember spending time with Jacky Crenshaw in college?"

"Who?"

"Jacky Crenshaw?"

"No. We never hung out together."

"Weren't you in the same dorm?"

She smiled. "I don't remember. I moved into sorority housing before school began."

Perez stared at her. She pushed a composite photo across the table. Beth, her husband, and the other attorney leaned forward to stare at it. Perez stared at the large sapphire blue wedding set on Beth's hand.

"Are you in that photo, Ms. Maynes?"

"Yes, I am. Where did you get this?"

"I'll ask the questions. Isn't Ms. Crenshaw in that photo?"

There was a slight pause. Beth took a minute staring at the photo. After conferring with her husband in a low voice, she looked up with a smile.

"I'm not sure."

"Where was this picture taken, Ms. Maynes?"

Beth's deep blue eyes surveyed Perez and then Trevino. She looked back at Perez and let her eyes wander the detective's face and hair before examining her black button-front shirt and suit jacket. With a subtle smile she looked at the photo again.

"This picture was taken the day I pledged my sorority."

"What's the name of your sorority?"

"Alpha Nu Sorority."

"Did you live in the chapter house?"

"Yes."

"Did Jacky Crenshaw also live in the chapter house?"

"I don't know."

"You don't know if she was in the chapter house with you?"

"I guess she was, but I don't remember much of her. She wasn't......part of our circle."

"Who made up your circle, Ms. Maynes?"

"Oh, gee," she giggled a little. "Let's see, I only remember us by our married names now. Is that alright?" She asked with wide-eyed innocence. When Perez nodded, she continued with a smug smile. "Okay, there was me, Sallie Anne Lewis, LisaMarie Butler, Marissa Marigny, Janelle Carr, Stacie Young, Patricia Mendoza, and Tessa Smith. They're all in the photo you have here."

"Yet you can't pick out Jacky Crenshaw?"

Beth blushed a deep wine color and looked at her nails.

"What about boyfriends?"

"Boyfriends?"

"Weren't any of you dating? You didn't have boyfriends?"

"None of us in my circle had boyfriends until midway our time there. For me, my first two years were spent primarily studying, and hanging out with my friends. I met my boyfriend who is now my husband at a fraternity party, but we didn't date seriously until our third year. I've never had any other suitors."

"Did Jacky Crenshaw have a boyfriend?"

"Who?"

"The deceased woman, Jacky Crenshaw?"

"I don't know."

"Ms. Maynes, do you remember having to speak to security about a persistent suitor? Someone who wouldn't take no for an answer?"

"No."

"You never encountered an aggressive male?"

Her husband interrupted. "My wife responded to the question, Detective. Move on."

Perez glanced at Maynes sideways. She looked at her notes.

"Ms. Maynes, who was Jacky Crenshaw's best friend among you all?"

"I don't know. What I vaguely remember is her always trying to hang under Marissa. She followed her around like a starstruck fan. Marissa would sometimes hide out in our rooms to avoid her."

"Did Marissa ever tell Jacky Crenshaw to leave her alone?" The edge in Perez's voice seemed to sober the smugness that had fallen on the three.

Beth sat up straighter. "I don't know. What I do know is she stalked Marissa around the campus. Marissa and Janelle were lifelong best friends, and there was *no* room for Crenshaw."

The boom in Trevino's voice filled the room. "You were all sorority sisters and living in the chapter house, yet you never socialized with Ms. Crenshaw?"

Beth's face did a slow blush. Jones said quietly, "Ms. Maynes has responded as best she can remember. Move on, Detective."

Trevino turned to Jones. "Make that the last time either one of you says that to us. We're conducting a murder investigation."

Jones said, "The cause of death was ruled as a suicide."

"You should have checked with the current coroner's report. Ms. Crenshaw's death has been ruled as undetermined." Trevino looked at Beth. "Let's stop playing games, Ms. Maynes. How many of you were dating or had boyfriends? Whether it was year one, two, three or the day before you graduated?"

Beth stiffened. Neither of the lawyers nor her responded. She swallowed hard and sat up straighter.

"As I've already told you, I met my husband during our first year, but we didn't start dating until our junior year, and we married directly after college."

"What about Ms. Crenshaw?"

"Who?"

"Jacky Crenshaw. The woman who's the topic of this interview. Did she have a boyfriend?"

"I don't know. I believe she had written some kind of note about a broken heart. I think it was her. I'm not sure." She shrugged. "I just don't remember her all that well."

Perez shoved the faded letter encased in plastic across the table to the woman.

"Is this the letter you're referring to? Have you ever seen this letter before?"

All three leaned forward to look at the item. Beth, with a frown, shook her head. "Hmm no, I've never seen it. Was it her that wrote this?"

Perez pushed the plastic evidence bag with the ring toward her. "Have you ever seen this ring?"

"Wow! Who does that belong to?"

"Jacky Crenshaw. Had you ever seen her wear it?"

"Wear what? The ring?"

"Yes. Had you ever seen her wear it?"

"No." She emitted a small chuckle. "Now something like *this* I would definitely remember."

"Let's move up to the present time. Had you and Ms. Crenshaw ever hung out after college?"

"No. Why would we?"

She asked the question with such sincerity; Perez was momentarily stunned for a response. She cleared her throat. "There was a message on Ms. Crenshaw's desk from you. Why did she need to contact you?"

Jones responded in a clear voice. "What was the date, Detective?"

Perez shoved a picture of the calendar page across the table.

"Oh, this... She usually informed me of any new book releases or author book signings to hit our local area. We always played up local events on our community spotlight segments."

"Did she call you?"

"No."

"You didn't think it odd she never returned your call?"

"No, not really." Again, she chuckled. "I usually spoke to Liz Townes, her assistant. Come to think of it, I might have spoken to Liz."

"Can you think of any reason why anyone would want to hurt Ms. Crenshaw?"

"No. I can't."

"Thank you," said Perez and stood up. "Thank you both for coming in."

When Maynes opened the door for his wife he gave Perez a perfunctory nod. Jones followed the couple without looking at either detective. All three walked down the hall without looking at anyone they passed.

Chapter 19

Trevino answered his phone, stood and put on his jacket. He popped a breath mint in his mouth. Perez looked up from her reading.

"Where are we going?"

"We're not going anywhere. I'm going to interview Tessa Smith." He looked at Perez. "You sit this one out. After your last encounter, I need her open to my questions, not reliving the last time she saw you."

Before Perez could respond Trevino was at the elevator doors when Tessa stepped onto the floor. Tessa smiled when she saw the detective. They exchanged pleasantries, as he guided her to the interview room. Perez walked into the surveillance room next door. She studied the woman.

She was undeniably tall and in excellent physical shape. Perez was impressed by her wide shoulders. The red loopy curls were loose and spilled past her shoulders. The medium charcoal gray wool pantsuit fitted her heavy hourglass curves. The white silk turtleneck emphasized the large eyes and crimson-lined full lips.

Perez looked at her partner. He never took his eyes off the woman. She looked at the woman. It was a mutual attraction moment. Perez wanted to enter the room but thought better of it.

In the room, Trevino and Tessa smiled pleasantly at each other.

"Ms. Smith, thank you for coming in this afternoon. I'm Det. Trevino who you spoke with on the phone." He opened the folder so he could stop looking at her.

"I remember you, Detective. Where's your partner?"

Trevino sensed Perez was next door looking through the double mirror. With tongue in cheek he said, "My partner is currently busy on another project. Let's get into this. Would you please say your full name."

"Elizabeth Smith, but my friends call me Tessa."

"What university did you attend?"

"Winding Falls University."

"What did you study?"

"Nursing."

"When and where did you first meet the deceased, Jacky Crenshaw?"

"We met as students at the university."

"Did you room together?"

"No."

"Ms. Smith, several weeks ago, you reported finding your friend Jacky Crenshaw in her home. For purposes of clarification, would you please go over that evening again."

"Sure, Detective. Jacky had missed a hair appointment two or three weeks earlier. In the twenty years I had known her, she never skipped out on an appointment. She always made them because she loved getting her hair done. I also run a full-service salon."

"What does that mean?"

"Oh, we also do facial massages, manicures and pedicures."

"Did the victim get the full service?"

"Oh, yes. All the time. She led a very active professional and social life."

"Okay, so she didn't make her appointment this time."

"Wait a minute," said Tessa. Her soft voice elevated slightly. "You don't understand, Detective. Jacky was not wishy-washy about her personal image. She loved looking good. If she thought, she would be late she would call me right away."

"Did she always call you or the stylist?"

"She would call me. I was her personal stylist."

"So, she made an appointment she didn't keep?"

"She didn't have to make an appointment, Detective. She was one of my permanent clients. I have a select few clients who only see me."

"And Ms. Crenshaw was one of those clients?"

"Yes, she was."

"What was it that bound you two together?"

"We were in the same sorority, and we hung out all the time together."

"Did you also hang out together after college?"

"Yes. Every year we took a vacation somewhere. We're the only two of our close friends who aren't married with children, and that's what I believe made our bond so tight."

"Okay. I can see that. Did she ever not make an appointment date to get her hair and nails done?"

"No. She was never late, nor did she forget her appointments."

"So, we've found she was punctual about her visits with you. Who did you contact when you couldn't get hold of her?"

"I called Marissa."

"Marissa who?"

"Marissa Marigny."

"Why? Are they best friends?"

"Oh, no!" Tessa said with a frown. "She's Marissa's publicist. They're always in contact over her books."

"I see. How did that conversation go between you and Ms. Marigny?"

"It was short and sweet. I asked Marissa if she had heard from her."

"Had she?"

"No."

"Did you call anyone else?"

"No. I just assumed she would show up."

"Why did you eventually put out a missing person bulletin? It says here you put out a bulletin a few days before you found her. Why didn't you just stop at her home if you had her address?"

Tessa sighed. "Detective, we're adult women. Neither Jacky nor I are married... and Jacky... Jacky traveled a lot. When she was home, she was always on the go. Hopping from one event to another. I don't intrude on any of my friends, married or single, so I wouldn't just drop by her home."

"Yet, you did, Ms. Smith. Why?"

"When Jacky didn't show up for Janelle's funeral... I just knew something must have happened because Jacky wouldn't miss such a sad occasion among us."

"So, you were assuming wherever she was she would have heard about the funeral?"

"Yes."

"Was the victim close to Ms. Carr?"

"I can't speak on that. But we were all friends, so Jacky would have attended the funeral because she knew how important Janelle was in Marissa's life."

"Have you ever seen this letter?"

Tessa leaned forward and appeared to read the letter. She straightened up.

"It looks like a love letter."

"Have you seen this letter before now?"

She shook her head. "No."

He put the bag with the engagement ring on the table and slid it across to her.

"What about this ring?"

"Wow! That's a beautiful ring. I've never seen her wear anything like this."

Trevino listened. "My final question, Ms. Smith. Do you know of anyone who might have been angry with the victim?"

"No. Jacky was a friendly person. Very easy to get along with. She had a fun-loving personality."

"She was single. Do you know of any of her romantic partners? Any names?"

"Jacky was a romantic, but she was private about it. She never told us any of their names or even showed us their pictures. Half the time I didn't know whether to believe her or not."

"Was she like that in college? Secretive about her dates?"

"Yes. Very much so."

"You mentioned you were in a sorority together. What was the name of that sorority?"

"Alpha Nu. We pledged together."

"So, you two saw a great deal of each other through all of the gatherings and events on campus."

Tessa smiled warmly. "Are you also a member of a Greek organization, Detective?"

"Omega Pi Fraternity."

They smiled at each other again. After a few seconds, Trevino looked down at his blank note pad and cleared his throat.

"Who was your friend attracted to at the Greek dances? Do you remember?"

"I have no idea who Jacky was attracted to. She seemed to like and appreciate all men and the feeling was mutual."

"Did she date a lot?"

"I... I can't answer that, Detective. Jacky was a workaholic. She played as hard as she worked."

"I meant, in college. Did she date a lot?"

"I don't know what you mean by a lot, Detective."

"More than you, Ms. Smith?" Trevino smiled a little.

Tessa blushed. "She dated more than any of us, Detective. How she managed to graduate on time is beyond me. She was a very popular girl."

"One final question: she was single and childless. Who gets the bulk of her estate?"

"Gee, I would think it would be her parents. They're still alive in South Carolina."

"Thank you." Trevino stood up. "Thank you for your time, Ms. Smith. Let me walk you out."

They smiled at each other again. They rode the elevator in silence. He walked her out through the front of the building. She pointed to a creamy golden-hued four-door luxury sedan. He walked her to it and held the door. She smiled at him. Black shades covered the dark greenish-brown eyes.

"How tall are you?" He asked as he leaned in her car window.

She smiled, revealing dimples on each side of her lips. He stopped looking at her and straightened up.

"I'm exactly five feet eleven inches, Detective."

"Thank you."

He watched her angle the vehicle into traffic. He saw the logo on the license plate and smiled. She was undeniably his type.

Trevino was deep in thought when the elevator doors opened, and his partner greeted him. He walked past her to his desk, took off his jacket, and sat down.

"What do you think?" he asked Perez.

"I don't know, Luis. For most of it I believe she was being truthful."

"What part don't you believe?"

126

"I think she knew of the ring but not the letter."

"Explain."

"She said she'd never seen her wear it."

"Yeah, I heard that, too." He peered across at Perez. "What's bugging me about that statement?"

Perez smirked. "She's never seen her wear it which means she, Ms. Smith, knew of the ring. She may know of its origins as well."

"Ms. Marigny denied knowledge of the ring too."

"But I believe both women knew of that ring's existence. Maybe they forgot about it? The ring is old."

"Or maybe they assumed she'd pawned it or sold it. Who keeps an engagement ring when you never married the person who gave it to you? I wonder why she never returned the ring?"

"Maybe he didn't want it back. That happens."

"What's your thoughts on the letter?"

"Hard to say. She seemed to read each line. I don't think she'd seen it before."

"I don't either. She did read it. All the way through. Did we find a phone in Crenshaw's belongings?"

"Yes. I believe she had two phones." Perez pulled up an inventory sheet. "Yes. Both were used as business phones. Lots of numbers associated with editors, publishers, printing houses."

"On both phones?"

"Yes. Many of the numbers were repeated. The ones that weren't repeats belonged to restaurants, hotels, and family members."

Perez pulled a yellow manila folder from her correspondence bin and lightly tossed it across to him. He skimmed through it briefly and tossed it back.

"Want to grab a bite, or do you have plans?"

"Mike is working late tonight. Come on, I'll treat you to a burrito dinner."

"Drinks on me."

They shut down their systems. The entire time Trevino held images of Tessa Smith in his mind's eye.

Chapter 20

It was late but Trevino waited. He hung up the phone as the tall, dark skin man stepped off the elevator. He was well-built man with broad shoulders, a clean-shaven pleasant face and wearing close-cropped hair. Trevino admired the light-yellow wool suit with a flaming red silk pocket square sticking jauntily from the buttonhole, and matching loafers. The white silk shirt with French cuffs completed the look.

"Hello, I'm Jerry Reeves," he said in a deep bass voice. "I have an appointment with a Det. Trevino for six o'clock today."

"Good afternoon, Mr. Reeves," said Trevino, clasping the man's hand in a firm handshake. "I'm Det. Trevino. Please follow me."

Trevino led the way to the interview room. The men sat down on opposite sides of the table from each other.

"I apologize for my tardiness. Traffic was a nightmare."

"No worries. Mr. Reeves, as said in our first phone call, this is a simple inquiry about the deceased, Jacky Crenshaw."

"When my publicist informed me, you wanted to speak to me, I was intrigued and only a little confused. The papers said Jacky's death was a suicide."

"Mr. Reeves, I'm not going to insult your intelligence. We have reason to believe Ms. Crenshaw's death was not a suicide. We're gathering information from people who've known Ms. Crenshaw intimately. Would you say you're one of those people?"

"Yes. I knew her all my life."

"When did you first meet Ms. Crenshaw?"

"I met her at a birthday party," Reeves smiled at the look on Trevino's face. "We were both about four and five years old. We grew up together."

"It's my understanding she was your publicist."

"She was never my publicist. She stole my unfinished manuscript and gave it to the man she was seeing on the side."

Trevino frowned. He sat back and folded his arms. He looked beyond Reeves.

"How did she steal your manuscript?"

"She waited until I fell asleep."

"Tell me the story, Mr. Reeves."

"We dated a little bit in high school and attended junior and senior proms together. We both attended Winding Falls University."

"Did you continue your relationship in college?"

"No. She made it very clear it was over between us the summer before school began."

"Tell me the story about the manuscript."

"Fast forward a little past graduation, and we run into each other again. We stopped at one of those diners and got to talking about post college job searches and so on. I had been hired to be one of the writers for a new television series. I was super excited about it. Anyway, she came home with me that night. I must have been drunk or drugged because I don't remember telling her about the book I was writing."

"So when you woke up the next morning she was gone with the book?"

"Right. She had also wiped my hard drive of the original draft. I had no way to prove it was mine. Anyway, I didn't hear from her again for several months. Then one day I received a call from Paul Boleyn. I was asked to come in and the rest is history, as they say."

"She became your publicist when?"

"Let me repeat. Jacky was never my publicist, Detective. My publicist is a man. Jacky was given credit for discovering me when I blew up. Paul did the right thing as he recognized real talent. We've been friends ever since. As for Jacky, I never saw her again except for the occasional publicity book tours or a glimpse in a café or something like that."

"An odd question...," said Trevino.

Reeves smiled. "I'm listening."

"If you had to describe Ms. Crenshaw, how would you?"

"Beautiful, brash, arrogant, smart, sneaky, manipulative, needy, vain, and generous." Reeves smiled again. "I used to think that someday she would come to her senses, and see I was the man for her, but that never happened."

"Have you ever met any of her men friends?"

"Why would I have wanted to? Why torture myself over a woman who was a user and abuser?"

"Abuser, Mr. Reeves? In what way?"

"She knew how I felt about her since middle school. When she stole that manuscript, it wasn't for my benefit. It was to give to some woman friend who was having writer's block. She wanted the woman's work seen by the publishing house she had just gotten hired by."

Trevino's heart pounded in his ears. He felt as if he could not breathe. He looked at Reeves and envisioned Tony in the room beyond.

"Do you know who the woman friend was?"

"No."

"Were you curious? Did you ask?"

Reeves looked at Trevino with an amused grin. "Not really. What would that have done anyway?"

"How did you find out she was going to give your manuscript to this woman?"

"Paul told me."

"Did he tell you whether the woman knew or accepted this transaction?"

"I don't know if she knew or not as it didn't take place."

"So what happened?"

"Paul convinced Jacky to send the woman's own writings. Meanwhile, Paul gave my manuscript to an editor. The editor contacted me for an interview. When I did the interview, I brought along a draft of a sequel to the stolen manuscript. That's what sold them in the original manuscript of mine that Paul later had an opportunity to give them. What's odd is that I write deeply researched historical dramas. I have no clue the writing style of the other person."

"Did you ever confront Ms. Crenshaw on her duplicity?"

Reeves gazed thoughtfully at Trevino. The man was massively built and looked more like a Taino Indian god than a Puerto Rican detective. Reeves liked him. His gaze moved from the detective to the large glass behind

130

him. He wondered who was in the next room. He returned his attention to Trevino and sighed.

"No, Detective. The ball was in her court anyway."

"Mr. Reeves, a final question to clear up something. Did you at any point in your relationship with Ms. Crenshaw, give her an engagement ring?"

Reeves smiled. "No. The one-nightstand aside, she kept me firmly in the friend zone thereafter."

He looked past Trevino; his eyes conveyed a faraway sorrow. He blinked a few times, becoming aware of the present. With a slight smile, he focused on Trevino.

"By the way, you didn't ask, but I'm happily married to my soul mate for the last thirteen years. I met her on a book tour. She's a poet, teaches poetry to middle schoolers, and is the mother of my three beautiful children. I'm a happy and blessed man. I got a second chance at real love. I wish Jacky well. Wherever she went in the afterlife."

Trevino stood in the lobby watching Jerry Reeves ease the dolphin gray two-tone Cabriolet convertible parked in front of the building into traffic. Trevino smiled. It was a tight squeeze, but somehow the man made it.

Tony was looking absently into the darkened squad room when Santorelli walked into his office. She smiled and sat in the chair close to his desk. Tony smiled abstractly. Santorelli smiled back. They continued to stare at each other. Santorelli felt awkward. She wet her lips.

"It's been a long day," she began conversationally.

Tony said nothing. He smiled. His phone rang, and he answered it on the third ring still watching her.

"Homicide. Lieutenant Marigny." He smiled at her. She returned his smile. "Hmm...yes. Thanks."

She watched as he lowered his head and locked his desk drawer. Something happened somewhere. She waited. Her beeper had not buzzed.

Tony hung up, pulled on his jacket, and waited for her to walk out ahead of him. He locked his office door and rode the elevator with her to the first floor. She followed him off the elevator. She stopped as Tony hopped in an unmarked car. She watched the car until it disappeared out of sight.

Chapter 21

The ABC Publishers House left a second message that Marissa listened to while drinking her morning coffee. They were adamant about her interviewing potential publicists to replace Jacky. She wrote down the details of the message. The caller was attorney Paul Boleyn. She liked him but she needed some advice. She called Patricia's private office number.

"Hey sweetie, are you okay?" The prosecutor's voice was quiet but direct.

"I don't mean to bother you at work. Do you have time for a lunch date today? I need your sound advice about Jacky's replacement."

"How'd your interview go?"

"I'll tell you at lunch."

"Okay, I'm free at noon for a couple of hours. Good for you?"

"Great. The Falls Bistro at noon. I'll make reservations."

"Okay. See you then."

Promptly at noon, Marissa eased her car into a parking space in front of the Falls Bistro restaurant and looked around for Patricia's black sedan. Seeing it parked further over she smiled. Smoothing the skirt of the beige belted pantsuit she wore; she grabbed her black clutch and took a final glance at her reflection in her overhead mirror. Walking behind the server she spotted Tessa, Kristen and Stacie seated beside Patricia. They grinned and hugged each other.

"I wanted this to be a private meeting, Patricia," Marissa said, curtly.

"There's a method to my madness, darling," said Patricia. "We ordered appetizers and drinks for the table."

"Hey ladies," said Stacie to someone behind Marissa who turned to see Sallie Anne and Beth approaching. The ladies took their seats. Sallie Anne leaned over and took her hand.

"How are you, Marissa?"

Marissa removed her hand. "I'm fine. How are you doing?"

"I just can't stop thinking about poor Jacky," breathed Sallie Anne.

"Knock it off, Sallie Anne!" snapped Patricia. "You didn't care for her all that much. No one wants anyone to die but stop with the fakeness."

"Ladies, please, let's not fight," said Kristen looking down at her manicured hands.

"Beth, I like your new short, layered hairdo."

"Thank you, Tessa," Beth said tossing her head about. "I'm not used to it being this short. I think I'll let it get a little longer but keep the layering."

Stacie nodded her head in agreement. "Yeah, that cut will look great longer."

Tessa beamed. "Thank you, ladies. I do my best work on all of you."

"I need to do something with this mess," said Kristen, shaking her dark wavy tresses.

"My dear, if ever there was a gal who could get by with all those luscious waves, it's you!" said Stacie as she sipped her drink.

"Oh, please," breathed Kristen. "The natural curls of Marissa and Tessa are outstanding. I wish my hair curled instead of just lying about lumpy."

"Not to mention our golden beauty," said Marissa to Beth, who merely smiled. "I love the highlights, sweetie."

"Thanks, Marissa. You're always so sweet," said Beth.

Patricia said, "I almost forgot. I need to push back my hair appointment, Tessa. Eric and I are taking the girls on a family cruise that weekend."

"No problem, sweetie. Just call me when you want to come in."

Sallie Anne inched closer to Marissa. "Patricia told me you have to look for a new publicist?"

"Yes, the legal department left a message again last evening. I've never had to do that. I knew Jacky, and she just naturally filled the shoes there. I will have to interview people I don't know, pick one, and hope they fit the bill."

Beth looked at her. "I know you're better at research than talking to people. Why not do social media type interviews?"

Sallie Anne moved forward in her chair. "Hush, Beth. I know someone she already knows who fits the bill."

Patricia leaned on her arm smiling at Beth. "I have a feeling it's why your best friend wrangled an invitation to this lunch."

Beth's surprised face made Marissa laugh out loud.

"I thought...you mean we weren't invited?" asked Beth, wide-eyed. The women seated at the table laughed.

"Hush, Beth," said Sallie Anne with a mischievous gleam in her hazel eyes. She turned to Marissa. "Marissa, do you remember when you used to babysit for my brother's daughter, Nicole?"

"Oh my! That was eons ago, Sallie Anne."

"Eons is right. She's now recently turned twenty-two with a degree in English Literature, and three years interning in the news station's research department. She would make a perfect publicist for you."

"Good suggestion, Sallie Anne," said Tessa. "Nicole is an extrovert and would be comfortable around high-profile people. She's also familiar with your books, Marissa."

"How do you know she's familiar with my books?" Marissa asked Tessa.

"Because we always discuss one of your books when she comes in for her hair appointments. Doesn't matter if it's a book she's read or one of your latest ones."

"Nicole is a sweetheart. Does she have a resume?" asked Marissa.

Sallie Anne smiled. "Yes, she does. I will text you her information right now. Her full name is Nicole Braithwaite."

"Thank you, Sallie Anne."

"Of course, sweetie."

Patricia raised her cup. "Cheers to Nicole!"

The ladies raised their cups in unison. Business settled; Marissa glanced around the table at her friends absorbed in choosing their lunches. Once the server had taken their order and left, she spoke in a semi-subdued voice.

"I was interviewed by the police a few weeks ago."

"Okay." Beth focused her deep blue eyes on Marissa. "So, what happened?"

"They wanted to know who Jacky was dating in college."

"College? They think her murderer was some guy from college?"

"Wow, just wow."

Beth's eyes squinted. "Who was Jacky dating? She always kept her private life to herself." She peered at Marissa. "Well, she did tell you some things."

"She certainly did." Stacie remarked. She stared at Marissa. "Did you tell the police anything?"

Marissa stared back. "Like what, Stacie?"

"I don't know. That's why I'm asking. College was a long time ago. Why would they be questioning you about Jacky's dating life that long ago unless they knew something?"

"Well, Stacie, I don't know what they could possibly know, and I refuse to go on fishing expeditions. The short answer is that I don't know...then or now."

Patricia intervened. "Don't worry, ladies. Our fearless writer was not caught off-guard. However, based on the questions asked, seemed like the police were trying to piece together Crenshaw's love life and whatever men she may have dated."

"The more things change, the more they stay the same. Even in death she's still shadowing you."

"Well," said Beth, setting her cup on the table. "Marissa isn't the only one of us the police has called in. I had to meet with them over a week or so ago, too. Remember?"

"Don't forget about me," echoed Tessa.

"Or me," said Sallie Anne with a smirk.

"No!" uttered Kristen. "What did you all do? What did they want? Why did they call you all in?"

"Hush, Kristen, and let them answer."

"They wanted to know about Jacky, of course!" responded Beth. "But they were asking about her love life. Who she dated in college. Much like they asked Marissa."

"Yes, same here," said Tessa, and sighed.

"Maybe one of her lovers did her in."

"Wild as she was, I wouldn't doubt it."

"Come on, ladies. Let's not stoop too low to the ground," said Kristen. "None of us liked her but let's not speak ill of her passing... especially with how she passed."

"What a strange woman she was. I never understood her."

"They showed me a beautiful engagement ring," Beth continued, absently stirring her spoon in a near empty cup. "I've never seen a design like that before." She abruptly turned to Tessa. "Did they show you the ring?"

"Yes," Tessa said quietly. "I remembered it. She wore it that weekend."

Sallie Anne frowned. "They never showed me that ring. Thank goodness!" She looked across at Marissa. "Did they show you the ring?"

Priscilla's dark eyes flashed. "Why the hell was she still holding on to that ring?"

"Maybe to blackmail him later?"

"More like to hold us hostage with her..."

"Stop this! Jacky was a woman same as all of us. I think she might've loved the guy back then, but it didn't work out."

"Kristen, you're one of the most romantic women I know, but I agree with you this time."

"Well, I don't. For all her slick ways, that bit of nostalgia was foolish. She's been engaged several times. She got rid of those rings but keeps this one?"

"An ode to the past. Who can understand crazy?"

"Hmm... I wish I didn't have to return to work. This is a day for a stiff drink."

"Except of course, you don't drink."

"Why can't I start now?"

Giggles ensued for a few minutes. The server arrived to take their dessert orders. Once he walked away the ladies resumed their chatter.

"A handsome detective interviewed me. His name was L u i s Trevino. He's either Italian or Spanish. He had the most gorgeous blue eyes."

Tessa blushed when she noticed the ladies smiling.

"Hmm... someone's got a crush."

"I know who you're talking about," said Marissa with a wide smile. "He *is* very good-looking. He's not married either."

"I knew you would know," said Tessa with a little pout of her lips.

"I think it's time for a little dinner party," mused Marissa.

Tessa blushed. "If invited I would surely attend."

"I'm sure you would," said Patricia.

Sallie Anne raised her voice. "Well, I was lucky. James interviewed me."

"Was Vanessa with him? They're partners, you know," said Marissa.

"No. It was just James."

"Did he want to know about Jacky's love life as well?"

"Actually yes, but of course, I knew nothing. He did show me that ancient love letter of hers."

"Why was she holding on to that crusty love letter anyway?"

"Another ode to foolery."

There was silence at the last comment. Marissa looked under eye at the women around the table.

"I found out from the detective something none of us knew, and I confirmed it with Mr. Boleyn."

The ladies were quiet as they looked at Marissa whose face was a mix of anger and frustration.

Patricia sat up straighter in her chair. "What happened, Marissa?"

"Jacky was a vice president in the marketing department."

"Was she newly promoted?" asked Tessa.

"No. That was her primary position. She'd never been a publicist."

"What?" said Kristen. "But she was your publicist... I don't get it."

"She was never a publicist... mine or anyone else. She was in the marketing department."

"Jeez! We should've checked out the website a long time ago," said Stacie, looking away.

"Why would we have done that?" asked Priscilla. "We were all beginning our careers. We weren't even socializing as much as we are now."

"The success of Marissa's books came hard and fast, and Jacky was instrumental in that," said Kristen, before adding, "I just thought she was paying penance for all the problems she caused."

"I get it," Patricia said. "As always, she lied, so she could still be in your life, Marissa. She must've wanted to be your friend something awful."

"Obsessed is what you call it," said Tessa. She wore a look of sadness on her face.

"Crazy is more like it," the murmured reply.

"Once again, we've all fallen victim to her antics."

"Here comes our desserts," said Kristen, quietly. She watched as the server approached.

"Good. Maybe I'll order some wine to go with it."

"Let's talk about something more pleasant, shall we?"

"I'm glad the weather's warming up. I need to spend a weekend in the backyard sprucing it up."

"You and me both. We're supposed to be coming into a warm spell."

Kristen put her napkin on her lap. She looked over at her friend. "By the way, Sallie Anne, where does Nicole live now?"

"Around the corner from all of us," said Sallie Anne, "with her parents."

"Life can be great sometimes," murmured Patricia.

"She's returned home," said Tessa matter-of-factly. "Ida Mae mentioned the other day about hosting a tea party."

"Oh, yes, Tessa! We love your tea parties."

"Will you come, Marissa?"

"Yes, I will come. Janelle would want us to go on with our lives."

"Yes, our bright and beautiful Janelle."

"Let's have it in her honor. Bring out all her old photos... and her tiaras."

"That's a marvelous idea."

"Don't forget about your dinner party for Tessa and her crush. I'll help with anything you need, sweetie."

"I'll help, too. We are invited, aren't we?"

"No, not this time. I want it to be a foursome."

"Uh, no. He mustn't know he's the target of your matchmaking dear. Invite us all with our husbands in tow."

"I agree. I know a wonderful caterer Marissa you can use so your gal Maria is not swamped with extra work."

"What a considerate darling you are!"

"More time to plan and shop."

"Now, what are we all wearing for that glorious dinner!"

Marissa was happy and smiled throughout the rest of lunch.

Chapter 22

The Captain was not in a good mood. "I have exactly twenty minutes to listen to your findings. Then I'm out to a meeting. My life used to be so exciting and... and..." He slammed his coffee mug on his desk and looked at them. "Well? What are you all waiting for?"

Perez said, "The interview I did with Beth Maynes concerning Jacky Crenshaw went nowhere. I got the impression she was there for the story somewhere down the line. She did not know anything about the deceased and was not interested in talking about her. She appeared to want to know what I was going to ask."

Trevino grunted his agreement. "You hit it on the money, Priscilla. I got the same impression. She talked about her own courtship, and didn't field any questions about Crenshaw or any of the others."

"But I think she knows more than she's willing to tell. She gave off a 'dead men tell no tales' type of coyness," replied Tony.

"I think the husband briefed her on what to say," said Trevino. "She's not a lawyer. She was too guarded."

"Who's the other guy?" asked Murray watching the interview replay on the computer monitor. He had turned off the sound.

"Another lawyer from the same firm as the husband," said Perez.

"What does the Maynes woman do again?" asked Murray as he zoomed in on Beth Maynes face.

"Beth Maynes produces the evening news," said Perez. "She attended college with the deceased."

"So what?" asked Murray as he turned his gaze on Perez. "Did you question everyone the deceased attended college with?"

Trevino said, "Ms. Maynes was one of the people whose names were on a telephone message pad in Crenshaw's office."

"Hmm..." Murray said. He returned to look at the monitor. "I've met that guy seated beside her husband before somewhere..."

"Bill Jones is William Jones, Jr., the son of Judge William Jones who sits on the Criminal Court in Westchester," said Trevino.

"Thanks, Luis. That would have kept me up all night."

Perez was looking through her notes. "The Maynes woman gave us an impressive list of names as part of her circle of close friends."

Trevino took a photo out of his pocket and passed it around. The detectives stared.

"That's Tessa Smith. She was friends with the deceased woman."

"How tall is this woman?" asked Murray.

"She's five feet eleven."

"Impressive," murmured Murray as he stared at the photo. "She's a looker, too. Beautiful hair color."

"What's important about her height?" asked Perez.

"I don't know yet," replied Trevino. "It's just interesting to me they're all over five feet six." He sighed. "Hell, it may mean absolutely nothing in the long run."

Tony said, "Marissa is an even five feet ten inches in stocking feet. Janelle Carr was the same height, but Jacky Crenshaw was taller."

Perez looked at her notes. "Thanks for Marissa. I didn't know that. The Crenshaw woman was five feet eleven."

Trevino sighed before saying, "I did question the hair...stylist, Tessa Smith, about her relationship with the deceased. She didn't know any intimate details because the deceased kept her dating life private. But the Smith woman described her as a fun-loving, punctual woman who didn't leave her appointments hanging. Other than that, we got nothing."

"Wait a minute, your wife is in this pic," began Murray in a faint voice.

He looked at Tony and then back at the photo. "There's the news anchor, and the deceased publicist."

"Aw, jeez," murmured Perez. "We've might've stumbled on a revenge type killing."

Trevino looked at her. "Revenge type killing? You mean the publicist?"

"No theories," interjected Tony in a loud voice. "The publicist was a single, white-collar professional who hawked books for a living."

"So, tell me why the producer felt the need to bring two attorneys to answer routine questions about these women in her circle?" asked Perez.

Murray laughed. "Jones acted as the producer's attorney on record. Most wealthy people have attorneys on retainer."

"And that is what is known as covering your backside, especially with a line-up like that." Tony turned to Trevino. "How'd your interview go with the writer, Reeves?"

"Very well. The guy is a straight-from-the-hip shooter. I'm going to check out his life story though and get back to you."

Murray stared at Trevino. "What was the deceased relationship with him?"

"She used him to get her foot in the door of the book publishing company. To put it bluntly, and not speaking ill of the dead, the Crenshaw woman was a cold, calculating femme fatale who used men to get where she wanted to go and discarded them later."

"Maybe one of those discarded men caught up with her," replied Murray. He looked at the image of the deceased woman on the screen. "We seem to be running into dead ends. As Tony would say, the Crenshaw woman committed suicide. You can work on her case during your downtimes. Is there anything else?"

Murray's phone rang. Everyone filed out. Tony looked back as he pulled the door close. Murray's fingers was flying across the keyboard as he spoke police jargon into the mouthpiece.

Tony was in his office completing a file when Murray knocked on his door and waved as he left the station for the day. Tony saw the bulging briefcase in one hand, and the brown shopping bag in the other. He smiled and shook his head. Murray was a class act.

Across town, Marissa parked her white sport sedan in the parking lot of the Falls Bistro. She smiled at her reflection in the overhead mirror before she added a light pat of foundation powder to her forehead. She was having lunch today with her friends and Sallie Anne's niece. She smoothed the skirt of the blue belted wool suit as she followed the server.

Beth was all smiles as Marissa approached. Stacie, Tessa, Kristen, and Patricia waved from across the table.

"Hi, sweetie. You look beautiful, as usual," said Beth.

Marissa sat down. "Thanks, Beth. I don't have to tell you white is your color. Hi, ladies. What's to drink?"

"The server is bringing a carafe of coffee for you and Patricia, and a teapot for the rest of us," said Tessa with a grin.

"Okay, table rules," said Marissa. "No talking about anything but television programs. Make that comedy shows, fashion, and art."

"The Art Museum is having a showing of Rodin I believe. That begins the first of next month."

"The Library is scheduled to have a massive book sale, too."

"Oh, hi ladies," said Tessa.

Marissa turned to look behind her at the approaching women. Sallie Anne, in a dark blue bouclé dress suit that was eye-catching as well as appealing on her lithe frame, was all smiles as she approached the table. Following her was a young woman with long brown hair, a honey-beige complexion, and large brown eyes, snub nose, and full lips.

In a breathy voice, Sallie Anne said, "Marissa, you remember my niece, Nicole Braithwaite?"

"Hello, Nicole. It's so good to see you again."

"Hi, Ms. Marigny. Thank you for the invitation to lunch. This bouquet is for you." Nicole handed Marissa a bouquet of yellow roses wrapped in blue tulle.

"Call me, Marissa. Thank you for the flowers. I love them."

"I love your dress," said Patricia to Nicole who wore a blue tweed dress under a yellow tweed coat.

"Thank you."

"So how long have you been job hunting?" asked Marissa.

"I'm currently working as a teacher's aide. I don't want to teach," she said as she reached for her plate from the server.

Marissa watched her with a little smile on her face. "I recently lost my book publicist, and your sweet aunt suggested you might be persuaded to consider the post."

Nicole's face broke out in a broad smile. "Really? I would love to be your publicist. I have every book you've ever written. I took a few courses taught by Jacky Crenshaw at the university and learned her style and some of her strategies for book promotions."

"Well! I like the fact that you've prepared for your future. Tell me, because I forgot to ask, are you a member of Alpha Nu Sorority?"

Nicole's eyes lit up. "Oh, of course! I lived in the house for three years. I loved every minute of it!"

Every female at the table smiled engagingly at the young woman. Glasses were raised and clinked together in a celebratory toast.

"When can you start or wish to start?"

"I need to give my present employee notice. How about in two weeks?"

Marissa smiled. "This is what you're going to do, Nicole. You take your two weeks from your former employer and do a grand slam job. Then take a week with pay to rest up, gather your wardrobe together, and look through this portfolio. Then you can begin bright and fresh the first day of the month."

Nicole smiled through happy tears. She hugged Marissa tightly.

"And" continued Marissa, "don't worry about anything. I'll take care of all the details myself. You just need to show up on your start date."

The women finished their lunch. While their friends returned to work, Marissa and Tessa took Nicole shopping. When Marissa arrived home, she called Paul Boleyn.

Once she finished, she changed into a sweatshirt and jeans and sat down at her computer terminal. The words flowed effortlessly.

The Policeman's Pub was crowded as it was nearly the weekend. Trevino raised his hand for Tony to see him among the throng of people. He sat across from Trevino in the booth. Trevino could see who entered the front of the bar and Tony could see who entered from the back. They waited for the server to approach their table. She tossed her long hair over her shoulders as she placed drink coasters in front of them.

"Hi, guys. How's Winding Falls finest this evening?"

"Trying to stay alive, Angie," said Trevino.

"I hear you, Luis. You want your regulars?"

"Yes."

"How's school going, Angie?" asked Trevino.

"It'll be great once I graduate."

Tony and Trevino watched Angie Mancini walk to the bar. The dark hair swung from side to side across her waist. Her favorite attire was a snug tank top and equally snug shorts of any color. In colder months she wore a long sleeve snug pullover and snug fitting slacks.

She returned carrying their drinks. She placed sparkling water in front of Tony and gave Trevino a bottle of non-alcoholic beer. They gave her a tip and watched her walk away.

"Cheers," said Trevino. He sipped his drink and waited.

"Luis, something is crazy with all this. I never heard the story of someone passing off their manuscript as Marissa's. She's been writing since I've known her."

"You think he was lying or at the most exaggerating?"

"No. I've read three of his books. His style is so far from what Marissa would ever write... Just no, and as proud as Marissa is, I doubt she was in on the duplicity."

"Yeah. I don't think the writer in question was your wife either. Ms. Crenshaw seemed slick."

"She was an opportunist, Luis. He was a fool in love. When haven't we been in similar situations?"

"She saw two women before she was killed. I mean, before her suicide. One of them is dead and the other doesn't appear to know much about her. But you and I have an instinct that something isn't right."

"What about that engagement ring? Has it been appraised yet?"

"It's a custom-made vintage design. It's been appraised at a cool six million. But who it was originally sold to is still being investigated."

"Is that today's market value?"

"Yes. Our jewelry expert thinks it was a family heirloom because of the intricate design of the setting."

"Who would've given her a ring like that?"

"You mean, and let her keep it?"

Neither man spoke further. They enjoyed their drinks in agreeable silence.

On a cloudless weekend, Tessa held a private memorial service for Jacky in her home. Once they were all assembled in the garden, Emily brought in a bird cage covered with a white cloth. On the patio Catori released a white

144

dove into the sky. She explained the dove symbolized Jacky's transition into the universe. The women hugged each other. After a moment of silence, the women returned indoors. They enjoyed shrimp tacos, seafood salad and peach mimosas, while playing a rousing game of Bingo.

"Hmm... I love these mimosas," murmured Patricia. "You must give me the recipe, Tessa."

Tessa smiled. "Actually, I used Stacie's recipe this time."

"What's the secret ingredient, girl?" asked Angela.

The question made the flaxen-haired beauty grinned. "Adding a little bit of peach-flavored liquor to the container."

"Oh, my!" said Lynda, smiling broadly. "You would think I would have picked that up the way I love peaches."

The women laughed. Angela and Kristen brought more pillows to prop behind Lynda's back. Her pregnancy was obvious now. Anna gave her a manicure. Beth and Elsa were polishing her toenails much to her delight. Marissa sat in a slight daze. Janelle would have sat beside her in the past. She listened to her friends as if in a wind tunnel.

Across the room Trevino sat with Tony. They devoured plates heaped with food given to them by Tessa. They observed and listened as they ate. Trevino looked at Tony.

"How did Marissa take the news about Crenshaw?"

Tony watched Marissa. "She was sad. She told me this morning she hired someone new as her book publicist."

"That's good. Do you hear what they're all talking and laughing about?"

"Yeah, clothes, hair, and makeup. What else do women talk about?"

"Apparently not their dearly departed friend who recently committed suicide. The grief disappeared with the dove it seems."

Both men remained quiet for a long time. Tony remembered how carefully Marissa picked out the bright orange dress she wore. He studied the gathering of women. They were all in a multitude of summery colors, although it was still early spring.

Chapter 23

As she maneuvered her car in the designated parking slot, Anna Yang, reflected on the unseemly deaths of Janelle and Jacky. She was pleased the school semester was almost over. She needed time away from Winding Falls with her family. She and her husband planned a month-long trip to China with their two children. She was happier than she had been in months.

Today was her first day back at Primrose Elementary School after a short spring break. Anna unlocked her classroom door and put her cardigan on the coat rack with her tote bag. She put her purse in her desk drawer. She needed to water the plants. The instructions for their care had been written in detail and left for Mr. Bixby who promised to look in on them periodically until she returned after the break.

Anna's back was to the person who lifted her up by her neck and held her midair tightening his grip on her neck as she flailed about. Then she felt the heavy cord; suddenly she was yanked off the floor. Her last thought was she hoped her class did not find her like this.

Rose Henderson heard the voices of children outside her office window. She glanced at the clock on the wall. It was five minutes past the last bell. Whose class was still outside? As she exited her office a teacher informed her it was Ms. Yang's class. She stopped in her tracks. This was unusual behavior for the long-term teacher. She guided the youngsters into the auditorium and had the resource counselor watch them while she found out what was going on with Ms. Yang. The thought struck her that the teacher might have taken ill as her car was still on the lot.

The classroom door was locked, but the lights were on. She unlocked the door and walked in. Everything seemed in order. She saw Yang's sweater and tote bag on the coat rack. As she turned to leave the room, Henderson spied legs on the floor beneath the teacher's desk. She walked cautiously closer arching her upper body sideways to get a better view. What she saw on the floor caused her to open her mouth and emit a loud, long piercing scream.

A speeding emergency vehicle sped by as Johnston and Gerard entered the parking lot of Primrose Elementary School. They put on white hazmat uniforms and silently weaved through a crowd of loud and indignant people. Johnston managed to show a small man on the other side of the double doors their police badges, and he pushed the door open. Gerard helped him close it against two parents trying to force their way into the building.

"Thanks for your help." The man stared at the faces of the enraged people banging on the doors.

"Who was in the ambulance?" asked Gerard.

The question temporarily distracted the man. He turned to them. "The ambulance was taking Mrs. Henderson to the hospital. Poor woman collapsed. I called her husband."

"Who is Mrs. Henderson?"

"Our assistant principal. She found the body of Ms. Yang."

"Where is the body?"

"In the classroom."

"Thank you," said Johnston. "What's your name?"

"Alvin Bixby."

"Is Ms. Yang's car on the premises?" asked Gerard.

"Yes. It's parked out back. It's a black, two-door import."

Gerard moved away to send text messages.

"Where do you live, Mr. Bixby?" asked Johnston.

"Eastview on the west side."

"Are you married?"

"I'm a widower."

"How old are you?"

"I just turned eighty years old."

"What's your job here?"

"I'm the school custodian. These days they call us building managers."

"Are you the only one?"

"Yes."

"What are your hours?"

"I work Mondays through Fridays from eight in the morning until four o'clock in the afternoons."

"How long have you been at this school?"

"The last twenty years."

"What was your occupation before this?"

"I was a mechanical engineer at Freeman Airfield."

"Were you here when the assistant principal found the body?"

"Yes, but I hadn't entered any classrooms. I was in the teachers' lounge having a cup of coffee with Doctor Abernathy."

"I noticed the cafeteria when we drove in," Gerard said as he walked up. "Who serves the children lunch?"

Bixby smiled. "The mothers who belong in the local parent-teacher group, the PTA. It's my understanding that they take turns volunteering as cafeteria workers. Doctor Abernathy could tell you more about them."

"Thank you for answering our questions. Can we see the classroom now?"

Bixby directed them to the classroom. There were small potted plants on the windowsill with the names of the plants neatly engraved on an index card and placed under clear plastic. Brightly colored balloons with the children's first names on them framed windows. Textbooks were stacked neatly on the three-foot tall bookshelves that lined underneath the windows. The room was light, airy and colorful.

Johnston and Gerard examined the body of the woman laying prone on her back. In death she appeared to be sleeping. She was beautiful with honey-colored skin and dark brown wavy hair. There were no visible markings. Johnston reached across the body.

"This is a piece of odd-colored cloth that was underneath her." She bagged it to examine later.

"Her jewelry and clothing are intact," Gerard said. "I wonder if the killer posed her."

"She's missing a shoe."

"There it is. It's under that desk."

"Leave it for forensics."

Johnson looked at the purse and cardigan hung on the coat rack. She found the victim's wallet and driver's license.

"Her name is Anna Yang. She just turned thirty-six. Two kids by the pictures here. She lives in Washington Heights," said Johnston. She replaced the billfold.

"What's in the tote bag?"

"Let's see, there's a ball of yarn wrapped up in this blanket she was knitting, a paperback book, and a lunch kit."

"Okay."

"See if the teacher next door is in any condition to be interviewed. I'm going to speak with the principal."

"Here comes the medical examiner. Let's get a time of death."

Santorelli nodded to them and bent over the body. Johnston knelt on the floor beside her. Gerard leaned against a wall and watched the growing crowd outside the classroom window. Police had arrived and set up barricades. He watched several news trucks park on the grass alongside the school. He sent Tony a text message. Santorelli and Johnston stood up. Santorelli removed her eyewear. She reached for the tablet the technician held.

"How long has she been dead, Doctor?"

"A little under three hours," Santorelli said. She sighed. "She was manually strangled from behind. I don't think she even knew what was going on."

"Strangled from behind?"

"See the indentations on the back of her neck? He manually crushed her windpipe which is why all the markings are on the back of her neck. See this lump here? He might have severed her spine as well."

"Man! She's a tiny little thing," Gerard blurted out. "She can't be more than five feet."

Santorelli sighed again. "Yes, she was the smallest. I'll send the medical reports when I've completed the autopsy."

"Was there any kind of struggle on her part?"

"No. Either she knew the person, or she was caught off-guard. I'm in no position to say which."

"Thanks, Doctor." Johnston turned to Gerard. "I'm going to visit the principal. See if the car is still on the premises."

Gerard found the car. It was sandwiched beside a bright yellow French import and a white four-door German-model.

The car was black, two-door, and a hatchback. The passenger side was unlocked. The interior was gray leather. He looked in the trunk. It was clean as a whistle. Gerard scratched his head. He sent a text to Johnston and read the one she sent him.

He walked to the front of the building and discarded his uniform. On his way inside the school through a side door, he thought about his life in Haiti when he was orphaned during one of the island's uprisings. He was barely three months old. He never knew his parents.

Police sirens returned his attention to the petite teacher's body in the classroom. What kind of monster could do this, and why?

The principal of Primrose Elementary School was a small, intense man with dark red curly hair and light green eyes. Johnston watched him walk toward her in his purple suit and thought he fit in with the school primary colors. He extended his hand.

"Good morning, Detective Johnston, I'm Doctor Jude Abernathy. Come into my office, please."

"Thank you. Doctor Abernathy, I just have a few questions this morning."

"Of course. Please sit down."

"How long has Ms. Yang taught here?"

"She was hired fourteen years ago."

"What grade and what subjects did she teach?"

"She taught fourth grade math and science courses during the normal school year. Last year when her youngest entered junior high she signed on to a mentoring program to act as a math and science mentor for the summer."

"Did she always report to work early?"

"Yes, most of them do. We're in the second quarter of the school year after spring break. Many want to set up their classrooms, go over curriculum and that sort of thing. Sometimes we have early morning meetings which many teachers favor as three-fourths have families of their own to get home to in the afternoons and evenings."

"Did Anna Yang have any problems or issues with a student or their parents?"

"Mrs. Yang was a much-loved teacher."

"Did she have another teacher here who knew her personally?"

"Her closest friend here was Mrs. Amber Greene. She teaches social studies and art. Otherwise, Mrs. Yang kept to herself. I was told by someone she had a vibrant group of women friends outside the classroom, but I wouldn't know them."

While he was speaking, Johnston sent Gerard a text message. She asked the principal, "Who has keys to the classrooms?"

"Mrs. Henderson, the building manager, and me."

"Who is the building manager?"

"Alvin Bixby. You might have seen him in the hall?"

"Yes. How long has he worked here?"

"Twenty years, I believe. Mr. Bixby has two wooden legs from a childhood illness. He's also a former engineer. Do you need to speak with him?"

"No. We already have. Is there a monitoring system here? Cameras?"

"Only for outside the building and only operable on the weekends."

"This school teaches first to eighth grade?"

"Kindergarten to eighth grade."

"Any children bused in from the city?"

"No. This is a private school in that we don't solicit federal funding."

"Where does the money come from to sustain and maintain the school?"

"The parents in this community and other... private donors."

"Who helps in the school cafeteria?"

Abernathy frowned slightly. "The mothers who belong to the school's PTA group. It's a volunteer service they enjoy being committed to for the well-being of their children."

"Who heads the PTA group, Doctor?"

"Elsie Lancaster Smythe. Do you need to question her?"

"Yes." Johnston looked at her notepad. "Anna Yang is married?"

"Yes, her husband, Bruce Yang, teaches advanced honors in science and math at the high school."

"High school?"

"Yes, Primrose High School which is about four blocks from here."

151

"Thank you for your time, Doctor Abernathy. If you think of anything else, please don't hesitate to call us."

She left him with her card which she saw he filed in an index card box.

Gerard read Johnston's text. He saw Bixby at the end of the hall with his mop and bucket. He was about to enter a darkened classroom.

"Mr. Bixby, I don't mean to bother you, but I have a question."

The older man turned to look at Gerard. He was small in frame and barely reached eye level to Gerard. He nodded his head, amicably.

"What can I help you with, Detective?"

"You mentioned previously the deceased teacher had a friend in the school?"

"Mrs. Amber Greene right next door to her. She's in there now. Her children are outside for recess."

"Thank you, Mr. Bixby."

The custodian waved and turned away. Gerard retraced his steps. He tapped on the door and entered the room. The teacher was seated at her desk writing in a journal. She was a dark brown skin African American woman with thick, shoulder-length black hair. The almond-shaped dark eyes, full cheeks, and lips were attractively situated in the round face. She reminded him of a long-ago girlfriend.

The woman's smile displayed hesitation mixed with caution. Gerard took out his badge. The smile relaxed as she indicated the chair next to her desk. He sat down and took out his notepad.

"Mrs. Greene, my name is Detective Gerard from the Winding Falls Police Homicide Division. I'm investigating the death this morning of a teacher found on school grounds."

"You mean poor Anna?"

"Anna Yang? Yes. Were you here this morning?"

"Yes, I was. Anna and I were usually two of the first teachers to arrive after holidays to reopen our classrooms."

"How long have you worked at this school?"

"I've been here the last twelve years."

"Where were you previously?"

"I taught at Lakehurst Elementary for four years. When my husband was promoted, we settled in Winding Falls."

"What does your husband do for a living?"

"He's an airline pilot."

"Do you have children?"

"We have two sons. They're in third and fourth grade here."

"What was your relationship like with the deceased?"

"Anna? We were colleagues and work friends."

"Explain what you mean by work friends, please."

"We were friendly together and often ate our lunches or went shopping on our lunch breaks. That was the extent of it. When school was over, we went to our respective homes and lives."

"In the times when you ate lunch together or went shopping, did she ever discuss her marriage or friends?"

Greene smiled. "We talked about our children, mostly. Never about our marriages or husbands. I got the impression they were a good couple. Every year I've been here, he always sends white flowers for her birthday. I didn't know her friends. She was a private lady."

"One last question, Ms. Greene. What subject do you teach?"

"I teach third and fourth grade social studies and art."

"Do you know of any disgruntled parent or anyone who would want to harm the victim?"

"No, Detective. Anna was the sweetest woman you could ever meet. She had a wonderful sense of humor and loved telling me jokes. I will miss her so much. I pray you catch whoever committed this atrocity."

"We will, Ms. Greene," Gerard promised.

Chapter 24

Murray studied each photo of the crime scene in minute detail. He made remarks on a pad as he circled his copies. Gerard and Johnston sat transfixed and stared at the top of the captain's white curly head. Tony knocked and entered. He looked at his two detectives and then at Murray's bent head. He coughed slightly. The captain looked up. The blue eyes were deeply troubled, and the dark rings emphasized his lack of sleep and rest.

"Have you seen these?" Murray pointed to the photos on his desk.

"Yes. You and I have a meeting to attend with the..."

"I'm tired of these damn meetings!" Murray exploded. "This is a damn kindergarten teacher for Christ's Sake!"

Tony calmly said, "We don't know if it's the same guy yet. The autopsy hasn't come back. I think..."

Murray cut him off. "We have two women who've been strangled and hung. This poor little thing received both treatments. I'm in no mood to hear some philosophical..."

"Fred, you're going to have to calm down," said Tony, raising his voice a tad above. "It's too early in the game to call the shots. You know that."

The captain looked back at the photo spread on his desk. He blew out through his mouth and glanced over at Johnston.

"What's your take as a trained nurse, Jeanette?"

"The victim's death was overkill. He strangled her and then he hung her up... as small as she was, a good slap might have proven fatal. There was no signs of struggle on her body, or in the room."

Murray nodded and looked at the Haitian detective. "Kevin, you're an engineer. What's your theory on this killer?"

"I think he was in the room when she arrived."

"Confirm your hypothesis."

"The medical examiner gave us a two-hour window as time of death. She was discovered at eight-thirty-two."

"When does the school day begin?"

"Eight o'clock in the morning."

Murray shook his head. "I see what you mean. Something's wrong. I'm sure the teacher wasn't there at six-thirty."

"I checked the security systems the school uses to open and close doors; emergency exits and so forth. Nothing was out of place."

"Did you find evidence he was lying in wait, so to speak, for this victim?"

"No, sir. But the medical examiner said he choked her from behind, so I believe he was already in the room."

"We'll double check with the examiner again regarding the time," said Johnston.

"Does the school have a surveillance system?"

"No."

"When are you speaking to the husband? Get an understanding of when she left her home and may have arrived at the school. Was she having an affair? Did she meet a lover on her way to school or even at school? Questions you may not consider but should ask. Also, see if you can get the maintenance report on her vehicle. Might help with figuring out how much or how little she drove." He looked at Tony. "Anything you think I've missed?"

Tony shook his head. The captain's desk phone rang. He closed his eyes as he listened to the voice on the other end. He waved goodbye to his detectives. When Murray got off the phone, he grabbed his briefcase, nodded at the detectives in the squad room, and ran to the elevators where Tony was waiting.

Johnston and Gerard drove to Primrose High School. It was a sprawling, three-story building that sat on one acre of land. Gerard took one look at the oversized parking lot full of vehicles and parked on the grass near a fire lane. Johnston put the police placard on the dashboard.

"I see there's no dress code for the high school," said Johnston.

Most of the students were in shorts, male and female, with book bags firmly strapped on their backs. They stopped a student who directed them to the teacher's lounge on the second floor.

Bruce Yang was a handsome man who hid his grief well. He bowed and led the way to his classroom. It was bright, full of desks and chairs, and sterile. In one corner, behind his desk, a red ceramic tea set sat on a black lacquer table.

"May I offer you some liquid refreshments?" he asked.

"No, thank you, Mr. Yang. We won't keep you long," began Johnston. "How long have you worked at Primrose High School?"

"This will be my seventeenth year."

"How long had you and Mrs. Yang been married?"

"We married right out of college. In another week it would have been fifteen years."

"When was the last time you saw your wife?"

"In the morning before we both departed for work."

"Was there anything in her demeanor that would seem out of the ordinary to you?"

"No. My wife's demeanor and mannerisms were the same as always."

"Did she ever speak of difficulties with a work colleague?"

"No. She loved teaching and knew all the faculty. She was liked and respected."

"Would you know any of her friends outside of the teaching community?"

"No. My wife and I did not intrude on each other's personal hobbies. I do know she had many women friends, but I do not know any of them personally."

Gerard asked, "Does your wife have an office or den in your home we might look at?"

"Yes. She has a private space. Often, she entertains her friends there."

"We'd like to take a look at it."

"Whenever you wish, Detectives."

"Thank you, Mr. Yang, for seeing us on such short notice."

"It was unfortunately for me an honor to meet with you."

"Here's our card. If you think of anything else, please call us."

"Thank you, sir. I will."

With Johnston behind the wheel, Gerard called Tony.

"Good morning. How's it going?"

"Good morning, Tony. We need you to do something," said Johnston.

"Legal or off the record?" asked Tony. Humor was in his tone.

Gerard smiled. "Neither. We want a search warrant for the Yang home. Even though he's given us verbal permission."

"Okay. No problem. I'm going to speak to Judge Byrne directly. Where are you headed now?"

"We have a lunch interview scheduled with the president of the PTA."

"Okay. Stefanie texted me last night."

"Last night? What did she find?"

Tony hung up without responding. Johnston eased off the highway.

"Lunch interview?"

"Her words, not mine."

"Wow!"

Gerard grinned.

The detectives sat in the driveway of the spacious home nestled among large trees. The neighbor's property was slightly obstructed by a wall of lined hedges offering privacy and beauty. The front lawn was meticulously cared for, and the driveway newly paved. A mix of blue and pink hydrangeas graced either side of the home.

They walked up to the front door painted a bright pink. A squat middle-aged woman opened the door. She gazed up at them.

In a raspy voice she said, "Detectives Johnston and Gerard? Please come in."

They entered the furniture laden foyer. The woman directed them through a side door into the light gray multi-hued decorated living room through into another fully furnished area. Johnston noted the hydrangeas out front through the long windows. The woman guided them to a floral sofa.

The coffee table was laid with a triple-tiered silver tray stacked with an array of various sandwiches, cookies, and small cakes. There was a silver tea pot and a glass pitcher of lemonade.

"Mrs. Smythe will be down shortly. The food is for you. Enjoy. If you need anything else, my name is Anna."

While Gerard helped himself to the food, Johnston surveyed the home. The color scheme here was light gray with touches of deep pink and gray. The room was divided in half. They were in the seating area composed of two sofas and several chairs. At the other end of the room was a round table with a chess set on it.

A slight rustle at the door drew Johnston's attention. The woman who entered the room was tall and slim with a heart-shaped face offset by a head of thick, golden hair. She wore a long flowing gown in a bright red color and streaming with ruffles from neck to the floor-length hem. She smiled as she sat on the matching sofa opposite them. The multitude of rings on each hand flashed as she waved them about whenever she spoke.

"Detectives, I'm Elsie Lancaster Smythe."

"Ms. Smythe, we're from homicide, and..."

"Oh, I know why you're here, Detective," she said dismissively. "Jude called me yesterday. Poor Anna. We're all just devastated by what happened to her."

"Yes. Ms. Smythe, we were told the president of..."

"Yes, I am. I've been the elected president of our school's PTA Board for the past nine years. It's an honor to be able to serve our school children and community."

"How many of your children attend Primrose Elementary School?"

"My two little girls who are in the eighth grade."

"How long have you known Anna Yang?"

"It would be about nine years now."

Johnston squinted. "Why were you interested in becoming a PTA parent when you didn't have a child..."

"Oh, no! My older son attended the school as well. He's now in the ninth grade at Primrose High School."

"How many children do you have in total, Ms. Smythe?"

"Four. My youngest is a toddler."

"What was your relationship like with Anna Yang?"

"We got along well. We knew some of the same people. She was a lovely woman."

"Do you also teach school?"

"Heavens, no!" Smythe giggled and shook her head slightly. "We both knew the author, Marissa Marigny."

158

Gerard stopped chewing and stared at Smythe. He glanced at Johnston who appeared to be writing on her notepad.

"How did you know Ms. Marigny?" Gerard asked. He had sat his plate down.

"Ms. Yang and I worked with Marissa on the Children's Fund charity event one year. Another time I reached out to Marissa to find someone to tutor inner-city children in science. Marissa referred me to Anna. That's how we're all interconnected."

"When was the last time you saw or spoke with Ms. Yang?"

"I didn't speak to her per se. I saw her, or rather, we passed each other as I was picking up my daughters."

"When was that?"

"Maybe sometime before spring recess?"

"How did Ms. Yang seem to you?"

"She seemed fine. Her quiet presence was always appreciated in a busy environment like the school."

"Have you ever interacted with Ms. Yang beyond school or..."

"No, Detective. My only contact with Ms. Yang was through Marissa. Other than that, Ms. Yang and I lived worlds apart."

"What does your husband do for a living, Ms. Smythe?"

"He's an attorney at Smythe and Smythe Law Firm." She smiled. "In case you're wondering, my husband is the grandson of the founder of the firm."

"Do you work?"

She frowned condescendingly at Johnston. "Not in the way you mean, Detective. I work taking care of my family. I also manage my family's philanthropy pursuits."

"Have you ever met the deceased husband?"

"We might have met at the charity fund. I do recall Anna attended with an Asian man."

Johnston turned to Gerard. "Any other questions, Detective?"

Gerard shook his head, and they stood up. Smythe walked them to the front door and closed it promptly as they descended the steps.

With Gerard driving, Johnston sat and looked out the side window. She finally turned to her partner.

"What's your impression of Smythe?"

"One word. Pretentious."

"Snob would be another one."

"There's more but let's leave it there," said Gerard as he angled their vehicle onto the ramp taking them into the city.

"I have a feeling Ms. Smythe will be the next president on the high school PTA board."

"Do high schools have PTA boards?" asked Gerard.

"Of course they do!" Johnston reached for her phone that buzzed. She read the text message. "Tony wants us to see Stefanie before we return to the office. The search warrant will be on my desk."

"Did you hear she knows Tony's wife?"

"Yeah, I heard. More name-dropping than anything."

"Not so much, Jeanette. Ms. Marigny is the daughter of a socialite. Ms. Smythe has that old money look about her, too. They might know each other. Did you get a good look at that house? Lots of antiques..."

"Was the food good? The way you wolfed it down, she probably thought we don't get paid enough."

"Well, her thoughts on that subject would have been on the money."

Johnston tried not to smile and lost.

The Crime Lab was found behind the Medical Examiner's Building and reached through a glass-lined walkway. The detectives were met at the elevators by Stefanie Symonds, the director of the laboratory. With her light brown skin, black tapered bob haircut complete with bangs, she looked younger than many of the technicians she supervised. At five feet six inches in height, she was petite of frame and the sneakers she wore added to her gamin look.

Her arms were crossed when the doors opened.

"Well, it's about time you two showed up. I've been waiting for hours," she said, laughing.

"Knowing you, that's not an exaggeration," Johnston remarked.

"Jeanette ordered a second helping of key lime pie," said Gerard.

"Very funny," said Johnston. "What do you have for us, Stefanie?"

Symonds smiled. She pressed the elevator button again. "We're going across the way."

160

Across the way meant they walked to a second elevator that Symonds unlocked with her palm and rode it to the roof. They took the skywalk across to the next building, and down to the basement. They were given hazmat suits and goggles by a technician. The detectives followed Symonds past various cubicles with busy medical specialists. She stopped walking and pointed to an open cubicle.

"There's your vehicle. It's clean as a whistle."

Gerard sighed. "You found no trace evidence of anything?"

"Why bring us down here, Stefanie?" asked Johnston. Her irritation was clear on her face and in her voice.

"We didn't find trace evidence because this vehicle was thoroughly cleansed. What was forgotten though was the tracking device installed underneath the trunk hood."

The detectives perked up. "Where is this device?"

Symonds smiled and reached inside her lab pocket. "Here you are."

She placed the device in the middle of Gerard's outstretched hand. The device was in the shape of a gold coin. It had been placed in a plastic bag.

Gerard smiled. "Have you traced it?"

"We're still looking into who the buyer is. Seems it was bought a long time ago. There's a serial number that's been rubbed off. Whether intentionally or through wear and tear I can't say until we've run the tests. We'll keep you updated though. We'll need to keep the device. Here's a copy of it for your records." She handed him a glossy colored print.

"Thanks, Stefanie."

Johnston stepped forward. "I have another question for you, Stefanie. What is the mileage on this vehicle?"

Symonds read the chart a technician handed her. She scanned the page.

"It says here this was a new vehicle in excellent condition. It's two years old. The log we found in the console shows steady maintenance upkeep." She flipped the paper. "The mileage is very low. I imagine they have a second car since she has children. This car was used for transporting her back and forth to work."

"Because of the low mileage?"

161

"Yes, and because having children there's nothing in the car that says that. My sister has a toddler. I don't know which is messier; the house or their cars."

The detectives walked around the car before waving at Symonds and leaving the site. In their car, as Johnston drove, Gerard examined the photo of the coin. He studied the image on the back of the coin. It was familiar. Why?

Chapter 25

Early the next morning, Johnston and Gerard visited the Yang home. It was a modern two-story dwelling in Washington Heights. Johnston pulled up behind a large black sports utility vehicle parked in the driveway. Gerard glanced in the driver's window at the car's black leather interior.

The front door, painted a carnelian red, was opened by a smiling young boy followed by a girl of similar age. They stared at the detectives. A man walked to the door. He spoke quietly and the children moved back.

"Good morning, Mr. Yang," said Gerard. He handed him the search warrant. "We're following up on inspecting your late wife's personal space."

Without looking at the document, Yang stepped back and bowed. They entered. Johnston looked at the children.

"What are your children's names, Mr. Yang?"

"Michael and Susie. Michael has just turned eight and Susie is six. They are good children. They asked about their mother. I'm waiting for my sister. She is a child psychologist."

Johnston nodded. "I understand. Would you and your children please wait in another room."

"Yes. That is a wise suggestion. I shall take them to the garden. My wife's room is to your right, Detectives."

They watched him move silently away. The home was an open space concept and minimally furnished. They found the room through a sliding door.

"This is nice," remarked Johnston as they entered the bright room. The walls were an off-taupe coloring with light wooden flooring. Bits and spots of red were seen in the red print pillows on the long settee, an end table and a small chair placed under a brown wooden desk. The wall unit was brown wood as was the coffee table. An abstract in shades of gray and taupe hung on the wall.

"There's her laptop."

It was open with a picture of a Chinese New Year parade as the screensaver. Gerard wrote out a receipt for the laptop. He joined his partner in front of the wall unit. She was staring at a photo of a much younger Anna Yang in white linen seated among white orchids.

Tony walked into his office with mail in one hand, and a Styrofoam cup of steaming coffee in the other. He had barely sat behind his desk when Gerard and Johnston knocked and entered his office.

A few minutes later, Tony smiled pleasantly. He folded his hands atop his desk. He wore such a pleasant expression that both squirmed under his gaze. Johnston shrugged her shoulders catching glimmers of silvery thread highlighted in the snow-white crown of hair. Gerard turned redder than his normal cinnamon-tinged complexion.

"Let me get this straight. You two are telling me there is no clear motive for this lethal attack on an elementary school teacher."

Johnston said, "We have not found anyone willing to state the woman had committed any wrongdoing against anyone."

"She and her husband tutored kids in math and science on a volunteer basis. Mrs. Yang worked for the rights of the unborn and children. She and her husband funded an orphanage for abandoned children in their native Singapore."

Tony could hear the emotion in Gerard's voice. He looked at Johnston.

"Both are highly respected in the education community." She looked at her tablet. "What we received from the medical report is that she was lifted bodily to a hanging rope placed around a ceiling pipe."

"She was light enough and the pipe heavy enough to sustain her weight."

"What medical report are you looking at?" asked Tony with a frown. "The report I received states she was strangled."

"Initially that was the thought until tests were done that showed clearly the pattern of violent abuse this victim endured," said Johnston.

"She was strangled and then hung?"

"Thankfully it was over in a matter of minutes," said Johnston. She glanced sideways at her partner who was now silent. "There was no prolonged suffering or pain."

"No one saw or heard anything?" Tony asked.

"No. It was just another school day."

"How tall was Anna Yang?"

Gerard cleared his throat. "She was four feet eleven inches. The words tiny and petite would describe her."

"We did search the Yang residence this morning before we arrived here," added Johnston. "Her small den held lots of family pictures. We also found school pictures. Nothing stood out. We gave her personal laptop to Stefanie's group."

"What did they find on the laptop?"

"Stefanie sent me the contents on the hard drive as well. There's nothing but schoolwork. Curriculum, tests, pop quizzes, grades and so forth."

"What about DNA evidence?"

"The Crime Lab could find not one trace of DNA that was foreign to the class, teacher and students. Which is interesting given she was murdered in her classroom," said Gerard. "That's what I don't get."

"Why are you assuming her killer was a man?" asked Johnston.

"In other words, he could have been she," finished Tony. "I agree and disagree, Jeanette."

"Are you playing devil's advocate, Tony?"

"No. First, a woman would not have the strength to lift the victim without some DNA depositing itself somewhere on the victim. Second, a tall man could easily lift her with one arm."

"We found no one in her life who would've harmed her. For all intents and purposes this might have been a case of mistaken identity," stated Gerard. He shoved a photo image across the desk to Tony.

"Stefanie's team found that tracking device under the trunk hood of Yang's car which, by the way, had been meticulously cleaned."

"It wasn't a random event as someone wants us to believe," Tony murmured as he studied the photo. "Otherwise, what would be the purpose for murdering an elementary teacher on school grounds?"

"Someone was following her for a reason," said Gerard.

"Does the husband have a car?"

"Yes, but it's of a different make and model."

"In other words, you wouldn't mistake the vehicles?"

"No." Gerard sighed. "Should we keep it open?"

"Yes. In your downtimes, you might want to go over something again."

Gerard grinned. "Never heard of downtime used in that way before. You keep coming up with ways to make us work these cases in our sleep."

Johnston laughed. Tony smirked.

Tony yawned and reached for another report. He looked at the clock. He debated reading one more report. A rustle at the door. Santorelli was standing there in a bright red form fitting dress and carrying a beige trench.

"Hi, Elsa. Working late?"

"I was until a few minutes ago. Time to unwind."

"Okay."

She walked in his office and sat down. The dress was cut low in the front and looked like any minute her entire chest would be exposed. Tony decided it was time to go home.

"I was just about to close shop," he said.

She smiled. "Good."

She rose. The tight dress was dipped lower in the back. Tony jumped up and threw on his jacket. He slammed drawers shut. He was aware she slipped out. He lowered the lights and locked his office. He stood in the darkened squad room and peered down the hall to where the elevators were. He waited until she looked down at the other end of the hall and disappeared into the shadows at the opposite end of the room. He took the back stairs down to the lobby. Desk sergeant O'Malley showed no surprise to see him exit the lobby from the back stairs. They nodded good night to each other.

The funeral service for the former Anna Wong Yang was private and held in Chinatown. A week later the ladies in the book club gathered for a private vigil at Tessa's home. Seated in white silk covered chairs, each woman wore a black dress. A large mural of bride Anna in a traditional Chinese wedding gown of red and gold surrounded by her friends on her wedding day was behind Marissa. She read from her third book of poetry a passage in which she described *Anna Wong Yang* as *"the smallest angel among us."*

Chapter 26

What a beautiful house. I've often wondered how people could be so frigging stupid. They spend thousands of dollars on a high-tech security system and then leave the doors and windows wide open. Taunt me if you will? I hope the kids are not here. I don't want to hurt them. They're innocent in all this. Let me check their bedrooms though in case. The twin girls are sloppier than their brothers. That figures. Some gorgeous looking children. Well, they're almost young adults now. James should have no problem remarrying. What woman in her right mind wouldn't want to be the deputy mayor's wife? Especially a young and good-looking one? He should be out-of-town this weekend. He said it was some kind of legal convention. It couldn't have come at a better time. She's the one I'm after. Miss big shot corporate attorney. Yes, pretty and quiet but deadly to the core. Always minding someone else's business and being helpful.

Okay, this is the suite. Wait a minute, James is home? Oh well, this could work in my favor. I'd better manage him first though. He's a lot bigger and stronger than she is. One good blow should do it with a little extra. Now for her. Uh oh, she woke up...

Tony received the emergency signal from Trevino as he exited the bathroom. He looked at the text. He grabbed a pullover and sweatpants and dressed hurriedly in the hall. Tony walked through wooded paths on the outskirts of Oxford Circle until he came to the winding path that took him behind the back entrance to Mockingbird Road and the narrower path to the rear of the home. He had hollowed out this route many years ago, and one other person knew of its existence.

He came to a boulder, stopped and surveyed the entire area from an inconspicuous spot. What he saw filled him with dread and sorrow. It was a mob scene below. There were cars and trucks of every description parked wherever they could find a spot. He saw the media barricaded off to a square lot, and heavily guarded by the police. Another news van arrived, and he saw the leggy anchor, Sallie Anne Lewis, appear. He watched her scout the perimeter of the barricades seeing the grounds. Then he saw her smile up at a police officer before another one walked over. Tony smiled. Nothing like a pretty woman to get men motivated.

He heard voices close by. Mayor Holtz was standing with Chief Hall, Captain Murray, and several people in dark suits on the side lawn.

He turned his attention to the house and entered the home through an open side door. The room was flooded with people in white hazmat suits. He was given a hazmat suit and goggles. The photographer was busy snapping shots of the room from all angles. Tony looked around. There was nothing out of place, and no broken windowpanes or door frames. Tony walked through the dining room into the living room, seeing how neat and orderly everything was.

Trevino came to the second-floor railing, saw Tony below, and whistled softly to get his attention. Tony took the stairs two at a time. The master suite was directly at the head of the stairs. Standing in the doorway to the bedroom Tony let out a breath at the bloody horror before him.

The room was covered in blood from ceiling to floor. Huge globs of blood splatter decorated the once cream-colored walls. He walked near the bed. The pair were engulfed, as was the king-size bed, in a sea of blood.

Trevino narrated. "The husband's head's been severed from his body. His legs were hacked off, too. Presumably as a safety measure. The wife being half off the bed means she woke up to the slaughter. And neither could defend themselves."

With a deep sigh, Tony walked out of the room and stood by the wall with his head down. He did not know whether he wanted to cry or vomit. He heard Trevino's voice as if he was in a wind tunnel.

"Are you okay?"

"Yeah. How am I going to work the angle on this one?"

"Very carefully."

"When were they found?"

"About an hour ago by the housekeeper."

"Milagros? You talk to her yet?"

"No. She was on the verge of hysteria. I couldn't make out a thing she said."

"Where is she?"

"She's in the kitchen. I have Officer Montalvo with her."

"Why are you here?"

"Closer than James and Dante's out with his wife."

"Oh, yeah. Good call. Where's your partner?"

"I told her to stay home. This is the anniversary of her husband's death. She sure didn't need to see this."

"Right. I need to speak to the housekeeper." Tony stopped. "Where are the kids? Did you get a chance to question them?"

"Yes. Judge Young came for them. The kids didn't hear, see, or know anything was amiss."

"Do they know about their parents?"

"Unfortunately, they do now. Psychologists are with them at the judge's home. I called Michael Minnelli and his wife, Diana Minnelli. We use them in court cases involving children."

"Oh, great. I'll call Michael later. Let me speak to Milagros."

"Tony, you know this is the fourth woman to be murdered this year?"

"Well, this time he struck both targets, so it might not be the same killer as the others."

"You're not thinking of a copycat, are you?"

"I don't know what I'm thinking right now, Luis. Stay close."

Trevino nodded and watched Tony run down the long hall to take the back stairs to the kitchen below. He walked back into the bloody bedroom.

The housekeeper, Milagros de la Pena, was near hysteria in the kitchen, sobbing and speaking incoherently to the police officer. Milagros was stout and short, with medium brown skin, black heavy hair streaked with gray and worn in a bun at the nape of her neck. Her gold hoop earrings flashed in her ears as she turned at the sound of footsteps. She was seated at the counter but jumped off the stool when she saw Tony. Speaking in rapid fire Spanish, while simultaneously crying, she flung herself in Tony's arms.

"My God! My God! Lieutenant! What is happening?"

"*Calm down, Milagros. Where were the children?*"

"*Lieutenant, they were sleeping soundly. The poor children heard nothing. My God! My God!*"

"*Where are the children now?*"

"*The Judge came for them.*"

"*Weren't they going on a camping trip?*"

"*Yes, Lieutenant.*"

"*The Young's were also going away?*"

"*Yes.*"

"*When were they expected to return?*"

"*In about two or three weeks. Mr. Young was leaving today for a convention in Arizona with Mrs. Young.*" With tears streaming down her face, the housekeeper looked up at Tony in full anguish. "*And they were going on a second honeymoon kind of trip, Lieutenant. They were so happy, so happy. My God! My God!*"

She began to cry again, making the sign of the cross on her chest. Tony signaled for the police officer to come close. He spoke in Spanish to the officer to soothe the housekeeper and keep her aware of what was happening.

"*Officer Montalvo, please keep Mrs. Milagros with you at all times. She is in police custody for her own safety. I will check in with you both later. Thank you.*"

The women walked past Trevino who stood at the kitchen door.

Tony turned to Trevino. "Good call with Montalvo."

"Ana was on duty. If not, the new guy Cousins also speaks Spanish."

"Good to know. Send a text to Robin and get her over here. She's got to be visually prepared."

"You're right. This looks worse than a slaughterhouse."

"Get Trudy and her Canine Unit down here. Have Hank do an aerial surveillance around this property." Tony took off his hazmat suit. A technician appeared and took the goggles, gloves, and boots. Tony turned back to Trevino. "I saw Doctor Symonds downstairs. I want first dibs on all information she gathers. I'm going home before Marissa finds out. You need me, call."

They parted ways with Tony leaving out through the side door which he had entered the home. Trevino walked into a room off the kitchen, and realized it was the family room. It was spacious with a nice array of seating and side tables. His attention was caught by the French patio doors. They led to a private area enclosed in flowering shrubbery. The scenery made him momentarily reminisce about his native Puerto Rico.

As he retraced his steps to the kitchen, he spied the credenza packed with photographs. He turned on the lamp. The detective stared for a moment at the one of Stacie in her wedding dress surrounded by her bridal party. He noticed who were seated closest to the victim in most of the settings.

A few minutes later Trevino was back in the bedroom watching the technicians collect evidence when Santorelli walked in the room. She swooned a little. The detective caught her around the waist and guided her to a chair.

"Are you okay Doctor? You looked like you were going to faint."

"That's my friend. Oh, my!"

The doctor put her face in her hands and cried. She tried to gain her composure.

"Doctor, let one of your assistants handle this one. It's gruesome over there."

"I'll be alright," she said as tears fell from her eyes.

The detective was adamant. "No, Doctor. You're not alright. Either you send one of your people in to do this preliminary examination, or we pull you off homicide. It's your decision."

Santorelli wiped her eyes quickly and nodded her head. She reached in her pocket for her phone. Trevino stood at the top of the stairs and waited for the assistant. He was as tall as the detective but much bigger. Trevino wondered if he played collegiate sports as he could tell the young man was powerfully built in the white hazmat uniform. The pathologist initially paused when he saw all the blood.

Trevino greeted him. "I'm Detective Trevino, and you?"

"Hi, I'm Doctor Mike LeClerc. Everything happened in here?"

"Yes. The children were untouched."

"That's a relief."

LeClerc pulled on his gloves, slid on a face shield, and walked toward the bed. Trevino sat in the same chair Santorelli had sat in. He surveyed the room from his seated position. He slowly scanned the base of the room when something caught his eye at the door frame. He followed the thin almost translucent wire behind the dresser to the fireplace where it disappeared.

He got down on his hands and knees and carefully traced the wire's path. He found the slim black case among the lattice work on the elaborate grill gates. He smiled. Great camouflage. He put the box in his coat pocket, and quickly returned to his seat. People in dark suits walked in followed by Holtz, Murray, and Hall. Trevino eased out of the room.

Tony entered the kitchen. He could hear Marissa typing. He drank some water, unstrapped his holster, and laid it on the kitchen counter. He walked into the family room, sat on the couch, and pulled off his sneakers. He laid back, closed his eyes, and put his feet up on the ottoman. He heard the typing stop and opened his eyes. Marissa stood before him. She was wearing one of his old white dress shirts. He pulled her down on his lap.

"Writer's block over?"

"I'm writing an article for the Winding Falls Gazette. Where have you been?"

"What's the article about?"

"Proper grammar as a second language. Where have you been?"

"What's for breakfast besides you?"

"Breakfast? It's almost lunchtime. How about a stuffed omelet with wheat muffins? That should keep you satisfied until dinner."

He kissed her neck snuggling his head on her shoulder.

She looked at him. "What's the matter?"

"What makes you think anything's the matter?"

"You have that look. What's wrong?"

"What look is that baby? Tell me, I'm curious about that look."

"I hate you sometimes."

"Sure you do."

He grinned and wrapped his arms tighter around her. He kissed her neck letting his lips linger. She moved off his lap and walked to the patio door. He looked at her legs as she leaned seductively against the door.

"What are you wearing under that shirt?"

"Nothing. Why? A woman can't be half naked in her own home?"

173

They grinned at each other. Tony eased off the couch. Grinning she ran across the room, behind the kitchen counter, and up the back stairs with him following.

Marissa opened her eyes, stretched and looked over to where Tony should have been. She glanced at the nightstand. It was past nine in the evening. She had slept for most of the day. There was no note which meant Tony was downstairs. She took a shower, threw on a robe, and walked downstairs. She found him in the kitchen.

Tony was in a towel and the news was on. He turned off the set when he saw her. She looked past him to the counter. There was no food anywhere. He took her by the hand and sat on the couch. He gazed at her in a thoughtful pleasant way, and she began to feel as if she could not breathe. She pulled her hand away from him. Her throat felt as if it had closed.

"Tony, you want me to fix you something to eat. There's tomato salad in the fridge. I have chicken thawed out... and..."

She swallowed trying to dislodge the lump in her throat. Tony was quiet. She needed sound.

"It's not too late for dinner. People in Europe eat late and call it dinner. The meal we eat earlier here in America called dinner is called supper over there."

Silence. Tony stared at her. She swallowed and held her breath.

"What's the matter, Tony? You know I don't do suspense well."

"I have something bad to tell you."

"Yeah? What?"

"James Alan and Stacie were found murdered in their home."

Tony was unprepared for Marissa's reaction.

Chapter 27

Tony pulled into the parking lot of Winding Falls Police Station. He surveyed the parking spots as he walked to the elevator. He said a quick prayer before the doors opened. His team was ready and waiting at their desks. He heard a few wolf whistles as he strode across the squad room.

Sloan said, "Wow! I haven't seen you in your police uniform in a while. You clean up nicely, Lieutenant."

"He's a handsome cop, for sure," echoed Benson.

Johnston said, "I don't know how your wife allowed you out the house this morning."

"A uniform always does something for a man," said Trevino as he sipped his coffee.

Di Giovanni handed him a coffee. He and Sloan were in their police uniforms as well.

Tony smiled. "Good morning, everyone. The captain and I will be in the State Capitol today. Based on the phone call I received from the mayor in route here, this might be an all-day session. It's going to be a rough day for sure. Luis and Priscilla are the leads on the Young's homicide. James could you and your partner prepare a fact sheet analysis for me on these four women? Get as much information compiled as you can on these recent homicides. If I don't see you all this evening, have a good night."

Tony saw Murray hang up his phone as he approached. Di Giovanni and Sloan pulled off ahead of him with Gerard and Johnston's vehicle following. Murray gave Tony a hawk-eyed look before climbing into the passenger seat of the cruiser.

"You, okay?" Tony asked as he put the truck in gear. He stopped and looked at Fred. "Why are they going in the opposite direction?"

"The State Building was bombed a few hours ago."

"What?"

"No casualties reported so far." Murray looked out his side window. "The governor wants us to meet at the Bell Building. It's heavily guarded and you can bet everyone's on high alert."

Tony turned the cruiser to the right to hit the highway. He drove in silence as the captain stared out the window. After a while he looked at Tony.

"What's your take on what happened last night with James Alan and Stacie?"

"I don't have one yet. I'm still in shock, I guess."

"You know James Alan was being primed for a bigger role... I mean, he would've been the perfect candidate. Poor, beautiful Stacie... who would do something so horrific."

"I don't know, Fred."

"How's Marissa?"

"She fainted when I told her. I called her parents. It's all I know how to do."

"You did good. Rose will take care of her daughter. Trust me on that. But this can't be good for Marissa's mental or emotional health."

Tony squirmed. "Her father's a psychiatrist. He helps others. I'm sure he'll take good care of his daughter."

Something in Tony's tone made Murray glance at him sideways. He decided to change the subject.

"With the suits at this meeting, my best advice is to answer as clearly and honestly as possible any questions asked. It may not appear to be an inquisition, but believe me, it is."

Tony smiled. "Life is short, Fred. Why worry about what we can't change?"

Murray leaned his head against the seat's headrest and watched the river as they crossed the bridge into the city district.

Trevino showed his badge to the parking attendant in the private lot next to City Hall. He placed the police placard on the dashboard and pinned his badge to the outside of his jacket. He stored his police weapon in the concealed part of the vehicle. He waited five minutes at the checkpoint line to enter the building. Once his credentials were approved, he took the elevator to the ninth floor staffed by an undercover cop. The deadly quiet that comes with lockdown situations was clear throughout the building.

The deputy mayor's office was the typical professional space with dark furnishings against grayish matte walls. The desk was flanked by the American, state and township flags. The detective walked across the room and sat behind the desk. The drawers were unlocked and stocked full of writing implements. The top of the desk was neat with law books closed and stacked to one side. The computer was password-protected. Its screen blinked the Winding Falls township logo. His eyes roamed the room. A short knock and an Asian man entered.

"Are you Detective Trevino?" the man asked.

"Yes. Who are you?"

"My name is David Chen. I am... I was Mr. Young's personal assistant."

"Come in and closed the door."

Trevino pointed to one of the chairs in front of the desk. David Chen was slight of build and upon closer inspection had hair with light streaks of gray situated between the dark strands. The plain black suit, white shirt, and black thin tie gave him a low-key executive look. Chen carried himself stiff and once he sat down, he looked at Trevino through slightly almond shaped eyes.

"How long have you worked for the deputy mayor?"

"This would've been eight years."

"What did you do before working for Mr. Young?"

"I was his paralegal at the law firm."

"So, in total, how long have you worked for Mr. Young?"

"This would be twelve years."

"Did you make all his travel arrangements?"

"Yes."

"Do you have his itinerary for the conference he was to attend?"

"Yes. The conference was for a weekend. But he'd planned an anniversary surprise for his wife."

"What was that?"

"Two weeks in Paris. That was where they spent their honeymoon. They were also spending a week in Belize before returning home. Because it was a last-minute surprise, I had to cancel his original flight and rebook it to include his wife."

"Which meant instead of him leaving the day of his murder, he would have left the following day with his wife."

"Precisely."

"When did you last speak to Mr. Young?"

"The evening before his... before his... death."

"Were you on the phone or in person?"

"I went to his home to drop off the plane tickets and their passports for the Paris trip."

"How was his mood?"

"He was very happy. He told me a joke about a fish and a shoe. I don't remember it now, but it was very funny. He always told jokes when he was happy."

"Did you see Mrs. Young?"

"No. He answered the door, took the tickets, walked me to my car and that was that."

"Did anyone else know of his recent change of travel plans?"

"No one that I can think of."

"Here's my card, Mr. Chen. If you remember anything else, no matter how tiny you call that number and leave a message. I will return your call."

"Thank you, Detective. Please catch whoever did this. Mr. Young was a good and decent man. I will miss him."

Chen left as quickly and quietly as he arrived. Trevino turned off the tape recorder in his pocket. He scanned the room. His eyes leveled with many small photographs on a side table. They were all the deputy mayor and his family.

As Trevino was about to turn away, he saw a picture of James Alan in a tuxedo surrounded by his groomsmen. To the side of that picture was the entire wedding party. The photograph highlighted the elegance of the bridal party. The detective studied the picture for some time.

Not far away, in the law firm of Hugo, Larsen, and Young where Stacie was a partner, a woman greeted Perez at the elevator.

"Good morning, Detective. I'm Lisa Douglas, I work for Ms. Young. Please follow me."

Perez felt like a giant ogre following the slim and trim figure of the woman. The navy pinstripe pantsuit fit her like a glove. Perez watched the long wavy brown ponytail as it swung from side to side. She looked down at the high-heeled stiletto pumps and smirked. She almost walked into her when she stopped in front of the double doors.

"How long have you worked for Ms. Young?"

"Six years."

"Where did you work before here?"

"I was in grad school. I interned for Judge Mendoza."

"Are you in school now?"

"I graduate with my law degree in the fall."

"Any future plans?"

"I was offered a position here in the tax fraud division."

"When was the last time you had contact with Ms. Young?"

"The day before she... before she.....Thursday evening."

"Tell me about the contact."

"She cleared her calendar of any calls. We coordinated her meetings for when she returned. She was happy as she was going on a little vacation with her husband."

"So, she was in the office?"

"Yes."

"Did you speak to her at all the next day?"

"No. She had given me Friday off so I would have a nice weekend. My boyfriend and I were recently engaged."

"Congratulations. Your last contact with Ms. Young was last Thursday. How was her mood?"

"She was happy. She loved going on any kind of trips with her husband and children, although this time the children were to remain at home."

"Thank you, Ms. Douglas. If you think of anything else, please don't hesitate to call."

"Thank you, Detective."

Perez stood in the doorway for a minute examining the interior. On a wall she looked at the number of commendations Stacie received from various children and youth organizations. On her desk she read a lunch appointment circled in red on the calendar. She took a picture of the sheet.

On the credenza were grouped photographs of family and close friends. One of them caught her attention. It was a recent vacation picture. A group of friends gathered on a boat. The women were standing in the middle of the boat with their arms around each other's waists, and the men were behind them grinning at the camera. The deputy mayor and his wife were on holiday with Tony and Marissa Marigny.

Chapter 28

Winding Falls Evening News studios were found at the far end of Center City on a huge multiplex lot. Trevino and Perez walked up to the receptionist desk, showed their police badges, and received name tags and directions. Walking down a long hall, the detectives met a woman wearing all black with headphones on. She waved at them to follow her.

"Are you the detectives here to see Sallie Anne?" she asked, listening to whoever was screaming in her ear. "My name's Anya. I'm her personal assistant. Follow me."

She led them down a hall with names on doors and stopped in front of one with Sallie Anne Lewis in gold script across the center. The woman knocked and opened the door.

"Stay here, please. Make yourself comfortable. There are beverages on that cart and rolled sandwiches and pastries. Fresh fruit to the right of that. Through that door is the bathroom. Sallie Anne will be with you shortly. She's completing a mike check."

She left the room. Trevino and Perez looked around. The walls were painted in a light-yellow sateen color. The overhead ceiling lights as well as a makeup table with a mirror framed in lights brightened the room and illuminated a coat rack that held a bright red shawl and oversize beige tote. Johnston walked over to a soft yellow sofa framed in lighting and sat down. The coffee table held a blue vase of white and yellow silk roses.

Perez looked at the wall opposite the sofa where several photos of different sizes earmarked Sallie Anne's years at the station. Around the photos were awards and plaques. On a small table to the side of the sofa were a collage of framed pictures of social events not shown on media networks.

After fifteen minutes Perez stood to stretch and noticed the double doors painted the same color as the walls. Behind the doors an array of dresses and jackets made up two racks of clothes. On the floor was a two-drawer chest. Lined inside were several pairs of heels in the same style but different colors. Opening a side door, she discovered a bathroom complete with shower.

It was thirty minutes later when Sallie Anne appeared. She rushed into the room all smiles and perfume followed by the personal assistant. Perez studied the news anchor. She was undoubtedly tall and still willowy of frame. Her dark red hair styled in a shaggy layered cut to her shoulders was set off perfectly by the deep yellow dress. Light hazel eyes vied for attention with her bright smile.

"Hello, I'm Sallie Anne Lewis. I'm sorry for the delay. Won't you please sit down?" The voice was golden smooth and pitched to perfection.

"Trevino and Perez. Ms. Lewis, we'd like to ask you a few questions about your relationship with the late Stacie Young?"

"Of course, Detectives. Whatever I can do to be of help." The anchor sat at her makeup table and studied herself. She looked at her nails and played with the top of her hair.

"How were you acquainted with Ms. Young?"

"Childhood friends." She turned to look at them. The smile was golden.

"Did you attend college together?"

"Yes, we did."

"What college was this?"

"Winding Falls University."

"You stayed in touch after graduation?"

"Of course."

The anchor walked over to a plush chair directly opposite them and sat down. She laid back on the sofa cushions. The woman in black without ceremony removed her shoes and propped her feet into fuzzy slippers, laying them gently on a small ottoman.

Noting the quietness of her partner, Perez peeked at him sideways. He sat transfixed gazing at the anchor.

"How would you describe your relationship with the victim?"

"We were great friends."

"Was Ms. Young having an affair?"

"No. I don't think so. She and James were devoted to each other."

"When did the victim meet her husband?"

"In college."

"Do you know where and how they met?"

"I believe they were introduced by friends at a party. They were at once attracted to each other. Perfect match."

"You knew the husband personally then?"

"Only through my brother. They were in the same fraternity. Were you in a fraternity, Detective Trevino?"

The anchor favored him with a glowing smile. Trevino smiled in return. Perez cleared her throat.

"Ms. Lewis, this is a criminal investigation. The deputy mayor and his wife were brutally assaulted in their home. We have reason to believe you had a close relationship with Stacie Young. We would appreciate your cooperation."

The light hazel eyes stared at Perez as if seeing her for the first time. She slowly looked at the detective from head to toe before smiling. She resorted to her professional anchor voice.

"What do you want to know, Detective?"

"You left a message for Ms. Young the day before her death. Would you mind telling us what that was about?"

"The only message I remember leaving for Stacie was about a piece on grandparenting. She had told me she and James were going out of town. I just needed to coordinate my calendar for when she and I could meet when they returned."

The anchor stopped talking to listen to what her personal assistant whispered in her ear. She sat up and put on deep yellow pumps.

"Detectives, I'm sorry, but I must prepare for my appearance. My co-anchor is here. Are you football fans?"

Trevino's eyes lit up. "Bill Braxton is here?"

She turned on her dazzling smile. "He's right next door. Anya, please ask Bill to come here."

"Oh no, we couldn't impose," Perez said, as the door opened admitting a huge mammoth of a man.

The man seemed to dwarf Sallie Anne. He gazed at them with a pleasant look on his handsome face.

"Hi Bill, I wanted you to meet two of Winding Falls finest police officers. These detectives are looking into the deaths of my college friends."

"Bill Braxton," said the news anchor as he grasped their hands. "Detectives, it's so good to meet you."

"It's such an honor to meet you," said Trevino.

"Oh no," said the news anchor in his deep bass voice. "It is an honor for me to meet you both. Keeping our community safe by putting your life on the line is more than I could ever do."

"True, Bill," Sallie Anne said. "We have American heroes right here in our news station."

They looked at Trevino and Perez with broad grins. The detectives instinctively felt like prey. The anchor turned to her colleague. "Bill, do you have something to say to these fine detectives?"

Without missing a beat, in his deep bass voice, the anchor said, "I would say that you have the support of the entire news station as you seek to solve these heinous crimes against our community."

The detectives managed to get out of the room. They hastily walked down the hall. They were only too aware of various other people who had appeared in the hall.

Trevino merged into noonday traffic. Perez looked at her partner.

"What are you thinking, Luis?"

"The lovely anchor was skirting around something. Pardon the pun. She was trying to appear calm, but I had a feeling she was waiting for us to say something."

"Say something? Like what?"

"I don't know. I just have a strange feeling about all this. Something's wrong here. Five people dead, no witnesses, no surveillance footage."

"Five people? I thought we were investigating the Young case."

"The deputy mayor and his wife knew Spencer Carr and his wife."

"Three lawyers."

"Exactly, but there's more. The murdered women, including the book publicist, all knew each other. How it all ties in is the big question."

"How do you know they all knew each other?"

"Photos in the deputy mayor's office."

"Oh, boy!"

Chapter 29

In the soundproof private office of Mayor Bill Holtz of Winding Falls, the session of inquiries were tight, strained, and repetitive. By the end of the day the team was placed in a smaller room.

Murray was pleased. "We did a grand job in there, but it's not over yet. The Mayor is catching heat from the Governor, and if we don't solve these murders, they will take this case out of our hands."

"I gathered the Governor was getting heat when I saw who all entered the room," said Tony.

"We should have had the entire team here," said di Giovanni.

"On the contrary, Kevin's assessment of the need for updated surveillance cameras and alarms was spot on. The diagrams he showed were remarkable in their clarity. Having an engineer as a detective is an extreme asset for this team," said Murray.

He looked at Gerard, Sloan, and Trevino who sat across the room from them; each on their phones.

Murray said to di Giovanni. "The media releases your partner sends out have served to steady the positive image between the police and the Winding Falls community."

"In other words," Tony smiled. "We did alright with the team we had. Never underestimate what you bring to the table, Detectives."

"I'm still doing what I love many years later," crooned Johnston while tap dancing.

The captain laughed. "I'm glad you're all in high spirits and kept your cool in there. Everyone's shaky after the bomb attack."

Di Giovanni passed his phone to Murray. "Robin and I took a little detour. It's leveled to the ground over there." He pointed to a spot. "We were stopped before we could head over there."

"Yeah, we had to take a detour as well," said Johnston. "Do you know what's in that building?"

Murray's blue eyes darkened to a deeper blue. He stared at them. "That's the governor's remodeled private office. He was supposed to be in closed door sessions yesterday evening but his assistant became ill. In taking her to the hospital his office was bombed."

"Whoa," said Johnston. "I would be spooked, too."

The news quieted the team. Tony found a quiet spot and sat back. He closed his eyes.

A half hour later, a knock on the door and a tall, slender man entered the room. Senator James Whitman was joined by Mayor Holtz.

"Fred, excellent job, as always," said Holtz as he shook Murray's hand vigorously.

"It's easy to serve when you have a great team, Bill," said Murray.

"The team is only as good as the leadership," said Whitman, who also shook the detectives' hands. He and Tony hugged.

The mayor turned to Tony. "Tony, I'm always in awe of your ability to remain cool and calm under pressure." He turned to the other detectives and shook each of their hands. "Let me just say you each inspire and motivate me as your mayor. You received exemplary high marks, and praise from that group in there."

"The team will stay together as is," said Whitman with finality. "Good job, everyone. Tony, call me tomorrow morning." He looked at Sloan. "Detective Sloan, may I speak with you a moment, please?"

Holtz turned to Murray. "I'll send you the list of concessions agreed on and copies of the new vendor contracts. Have a good evening, everyone."

Sloan and Whitman had a short conversation. Whitman walked to the elevator, his phone in his ear, and his bodyguard nearby. Sloan sat down and opened her tablet. The mayor returned to his office.

In their squad car with the captain driving this time, Tony took off his hat and gazed out the window.

"Don't second guess yourself, Tony. I heard what you said to your team. It's great to boost their morale, but I specifically fought for you to head this team because of your work in California and Chicago. You're a law enforcement officer, Tony. It's in your blood. You remind me so much of your father, and that's high praise. Your team believes in you, and they have faith in your judgment. You make me proud, son."

"Thanks, Fred."

"You're far away. What's bothering you?"

"Ever since James and Stacie's deaths, Marissa's been on high stress alert. I know the signs. The last time she was like this I was preparing to go undercover for several months, and she knew it."

"It's the nature of the job, and it's why some of us lose our spouses."

"I don't want to lose her, Fred, but I love what I do."

"I understand that. It's why I'm still here after three divorces. You'd think I'd have learned my lesson."

Tony half-smiled. "In regard to this case, I have the feeling there's something I'm missing. Some hidden clue. It's right in front of my face, but I'm not seeing it."

"Some cases are like that, Tony. Don't worry about today's meeting. They occasionally will pull you in for a rough show and tell, but it's all smoke and mirrors."

"Oh, I figured someone would want answers sooner or later with the Young's double murders. Not to mention the murder of Spencer Carr's wife in broad daylight with no witnesses. It was just a matter of time."

Murray's blue eyes stared at Tony's profile for a second. "You're an unusual young man, Tony."

The closing statement from Tony on the subject was "hmm."

The captain smiled. "I pretty much read all the files you sent me."

"Just wanting to get some kind of clue as to how this guy is operating."

"Yeah. The news coverage about Janelle Carr's murder is being replayed for some reason. It's a pity we couldn't get surveillance at their home."

Tony thumped the top of his cap in frustration. "That's just it, Fred. With technology readily available at our fingertips a minor glitch and we're literally in the dark."

Murray frowned. "What?"

"James and Vee found out there was some minor blackout that destroyed the outside video of the overhead cameras. Remember when they told us about the zap delay?"

"Yeah... Leave it to mother nature to screw you up."

"It wasn't mother nature, Fred. Someone programmed the glitch into the system. It was like a blink of an eye, so no one would've noticed their appliances were off by a millisecond."

"Jeez! Yeah, I forgot about that. I must be getting old."

"Kevin also has a tracking device found on the Asian victim's car."

"Asian victim? You mean the schoolteacher?"

"Yes. Anna Yang. Either she's a new type of spy or someone planted that device knowing we would find it and target her."

"Calm down. It's what we used to call batting zero to zilch. With some cases, you have long frustrating days. You know that."

"Yeah, I do." Tony slumped down in his seat.

The captain dropped Tony off in the police parking lot and decided to call it a day. Murray parked the cruiser and climbed into his personal car. He honked once as he drove by Tony. Physically tired, but mentally wired, Tony climbed into his vehicle and called Marissa.

"Hi baby, how are you feeling?"

"Hi Tony, I'm okay. How was it at city hall?"

"The normal inquisition, but they didn't fire us."

"That's good news."

"Yeah. In fact, we received praise for the work we've been doing. The captain is pleased. He took the rest of the day off."

Tony laughed with good humor. There was a pause which Tony caught too late.

"Why didn't you take the rest of the day off? It's late."

"I have a job to do, Marissa."

"Doesn't the captain have a job to do as well?"

"I can't answer for him. I'm my own man. Besides, this is my unit. I'm responsible."

"Okay. Stop it. I don't need another one of your he-man lectures."

The silence stretched on. Tony said, "Baby, I love you. I know you're hurting right now, especially with losing Janelle. Tell me what you need."

"I need you to come home to me."

"Okay. Let me talk to my team. I'll be on the way home then. Okay?"

"Okay. I love you, Tony."

"I love you, too, baby."

Tony sat in the parking lot a minute more. He took the back elevator upstairs. He usually took the stairs for a little cardio workout, but the quiet impact of his phone conversation with Marissa made him feel uncomfortable. No one was in the squad room. On his desk were several folders which Tony put in his briefcase, turned off the lights, and headed home.

The double funeral for James Alan Young, and his wife, Stacie Young, was broadcast on every news channel in Winding Falls Township. The American flag draped caskets were laid side by side to rest in the family's ancestral plot. The couple's four children were kept away from public scrutiny. Tony arrived late to the ceremony. He saw the mayor and other government officials. He saw his team in black spread out among the mourners. He found a discarded funeral program and stashed it in his briefcase. He looked for Marissa and saw her seated up front. Tony stood beside Marissa as she read an opening passage in her second book dedicated to *Stacie Royal Young,* whom she described as, *"my lifelong friend who was blonde, beautiful, and brilliant."*

Chapter 30

Must turn up the volume now. Everyone's too relaxed. The holidays are around the corner. I want to celebrate them in peace. I didn't want to kill James. Why the hell was he home? These men and their women. He shouldn't have lied to me. He would still be alive. Waiting on this one. She hasn't jogged or whatever she calls it in a few days.

Wait a minute! What's the princess doing jogging this time of night? Love the red set on her but, it's too late to be running. The mountain cats come out at night. I'd hate to have to save her only to kill her later. Ha, ha, ha. Now that's funny. Well, this is a good opportunity for me. Now to jog up the path and round the back. Easy to walk into these homes since this group acts as if the world loves them.

Hmm... Beautiful home. She has an eye for color. Okay, let's check the den. Wow! The leather and wood decor spells man cave in here. All the drawers unlocked on the desk means the bulk of his files are in his work office. Hmm... what's down this hall? I like this kitchen. Wow! Refrigerator packed with food. She likes to cook. Good for her. Something's in the oven. The aromas are delicious. Cozy family room. I wonder why they have no children. They need some. This is an ideal home to raise a family. What room is this? Ah, blue and yellow. I can guess who this room was designed for. There's the multitude of photos of the fabulous twenty. Just look at them. A bunch of lying, hypocritical, two-faced, backstabbing, double-dealing, murdering... whew! Let me calm down. They're getting their due rewards now. You can bet on it!

Might as well check out upstairs. The nursery is set up here. Tony never mentioned losing a baby. Furnished bedroom. Must be the in-law suite. Master bedroom. Love monotone colors. Soothing room. Every drawer scented. They make a good-looking couple. Too bad for them. Two more empty bedrooms. How many bedrooms do a childless couple need? I guess that's none of my business. On second thought, maybe they planned on having lots of children. Well, that won't happen now. Tony can make them with his next wife.

Okay, back downstairs. Let me leave her a gift. What's this? Is she writing another book? Well, my dear, here's my calling card. All right, I'm out, but I'll be back!

When O'Malley burst through the lieutenant's office door the team had their guns trained on the cop as did the man who sat behind the desk. Tony moved so quickly O'Malley knew he was dead. He kept his hands in the air and his eyes closed on the gun aimed at his forehead.

His body trembled with fear. In a shaky voice he managed to speak. "Lieutenant, please! Your phone is off ... There's been an alert at your house...*home invasion...*"

Before he could finish, Tony and his team were taking the stairs. O'Malley sank to his knees. An arm was gently placed around his shoulders. He looked into the dark eyes of Benson with her gun lowered at her side. He closed his eyes and bowed his head in prayer. O'Neill, with one eye on him, was on the phone.

Downstairs in the parking lot Tony was roughly shoved by Trevino in the back of a squad car with di Giovanni at the helm. Sloan jumped in the passenger seat, and they took off. They were followed by Trevino, Perez, Johnston and Gerard.

Di Giovanni used silent flashers to move swiftly through highway traffic until he came to a side ramp. Making a series of deft moves he turned off the flashers and sped silently through hilly, rocky terrain until he entered a
clearing. He sped up the winding trail leading to Mockingbird Road in Oxford Circle. Tony sat resolutely in the passenger seat with his eyes closed. As soon as the vehicle stopped, he jumped out, followed closely by his detectives.

Marissa was in the living room. She ran to Tony who hugged her.

His voice hoarse with emotion he gave her a once-over noting the jogging outfit. "You alright? What happened?"

"I think someone was in the house. I took a quick run to clear my head. When I returned, I could tell somebody had been in here."

"What?"

"I looked at my laptop, and its wiped clean of what I had written before I left."

Tony stared at her. He turned and nodded to a tall, blonde woman with a tapered short haircut.

"Trudy, get your team to check the premises The guy may still be in the area."

"Okay, Lieutenant."

The police officer glanced at Marissa in passing as she alerted her Canine Unit. Tony left the room without another word to Marissa who returned to the living room couch.

A half-hour later, fewer police strolled around the premises. Benson, with O'Neill in the passenger seat, drove up the driveway to the white column Georgian style mansion. It loomed larger than life against the late evening dusk. They walked through the double front doors and Benson's mouth almost fell open. She gazed around in amazement. She had never been to Marissa's home in the twenty years of her membership in the book club.

She stood in the doorway and viewed the winding staircase centered as the home's entryway. She looked around. O'Neill had disappeared. To her right was the largest living room she had ever been in. It was finished in shades of white, cream and black. She turned to the left. She saw di Giovanni near wall-to-ceiling bookcases deeply engrossed in a book. Behind him glass partitions looked out on a garden of blooming foliage. Seated to his left on a plush white sectional Sloan was on her laptop.

Benson walked further and to her right, flanked by columns, was a room that resembled an art gallery. She looked at Perez mesmerized by a large, sculpted vase atop an elaborate-designed pedestal. The walls were covered with artwork and below them rested colorful benches. She noticed other pieces of artwork lined the bottom walls. Benson walked past the staircase into the spacious dining room in a beige and cocoa-color themed motif. She saw in an alcove a window seat which held an open laptop. Across was a built-in butler's pantry. The dining table held seating for a dozen or more people and was placed in front of an ornate fireplace. Atop the fireplace was a black and white portrait of Tony and Marissa on their wedding day.

She heard voices and walked down the short hall of closed doors. She entered the expansive all-white kitchen where she found her colleagues. Johnston and Trevino's attentions were directed on a small object they hovered over on top of a nine-foot marble counter. Benson looked beyond them to a bevy of picture windows and saw Gerard with a plate of food sitting in the breakfast nook. The evening light flooded into the kitchen by way of wall-to-wall sliding glass doors.

"Where's the Lieutenant?" asked Benson in a slight whisper. She was beyond astounded.

"In his den talking to the suits," said Gerard, his eyes on his phone screen. "Walk back to the staircase and hang right. The bath is on your left, and the Lieutenant's den is opposite. Or you could take the short hall behind you. Leads you directly to his den and some other room."

"Where's the Lieutenant's wife?" asked Benson. She could not get over how large this area was.

Gerard pointed ahead. "In one of these rooms with the Captain and James."

Benson walked past Trevino and Johnston to the family room. It was an open space design with beige plush seating facing a wall mounted television screen that appeared as large as the sectional beneath it. There was a game table on one side of the room and a card table on the other. The entire left of the room was sliding glass doors. There was another area shrouded in shadows.

Benson turned on the light switch and studied the room. This was Marissa's sitting room. She remembered Jacky speaking on it. In here were pale off-white matte walls and soft, plush carpeting to match. The sectional was burgundy jacquard. Plush pillows were tossed elegantly at each end. Two sets of off-white plush chairs were set at opposite ends of the sectional. The built-in bookshelves flanked a television over a decorative fireplace. She walked over to the wall. It was lined with various size pictures. Benson examined the photographs of Marissa's parents and grandparents. She looked at similar ones of Tony's family.

She almost missed the long credenza placed behind the sectional. She turned on the lamp. The pictures were mostly of Marissa and Janelle. Then she spied the formal portrait of the members. Benson smirked at the dozens of others of Marissa and her clique.

Tony walked into the kitchen with O'Neill. He looked slightly embarrassed, but his smile was intact.

"Hi everyone. It was a false alarm mistakenly reported as a home invasion when it wasn't."

"I've found women's intuition to be highly accurate," said O'Neill.

"True," said Benson with amusement as she watched Tony's face.

Gerard finished his plate, walked past Tony, and set it on a rack in the dishwasher. Tony frowned slightly.

"Well, we're out. Glad your wife's alright." said Benson. She looked at her partner who had appeared from behind Tony. "Are you going home?"

"I'm okay. Take the cruiser."

She hesitated. "Not a problem." She turned and walked out.

O'Neill said, "Hank and his team scanned the area but didn't see anything suspicious. You want them called off?"

"Yes. I sent Trudy and her team home as well. Thanks for covering the air."

O'Neill leaned closer and whispered to Tony who nodded. O'Neill waved to the team and walked out using a side door.

"Do you use your front door much?" asked Johnston.

"No, we use the side door entrance or the garage nearly all the time. Why?"

Trevino handed him the black box. "We found this under that armchair. It automatically collapses whatever security system you have and unlocks the doors and windows. This is the same gadget I found in the deputy mayor's home."

Tony examined it closely. "Who knows about this, Luis?"

"For now? Just the people in this room. Kevin..."

Trevino glanced over at Gerard who sat in the family room with his phone and a large hunk of pie.

Tony nearly smiled. "What about Kevin?" he asked.

"He's an engineer, and he's as intrigued as we are," said Trevino. "When he stops eating, that is."

"Leave him alone. Let him eat. Remember, he and Robin are still twenty-somethings. They're still growing," said Johnston.

"Humph."

"Can we reprogram it?" asked Tony trying hard not to smile.

Johnston said, "We can let Kevin do that."

"You want me to do a sweep?" asked Trevino.

"Why do I have a feeling you've done one?"

Trevino smiled. "You know me, brother. Why wait?"

Perez entered the kitchen from the hall. She gazed across the expansive kitchen into the family room where Gerard now exited. He put his dessert dish in the dishwasher with his plate as his colleagues' stifled smirks.

"Night, Tony," Johnston said.

"Priscilla, you coming?"

Tony followed his team to the front of the house. He saw di Giovanni with a book in his hand. He waved it at Tony.

"May I borrow this?"

"Sure. Where's Robin?"

"She's on her way home. James picked her up." He was holding another book. "Why didn't you tell me you had written a text on forensic science?"

"It was a long time ago. Who's James?"

"Fourth printing, I see. Not bad. James is Senator Whitman. They met when we were called to city hall. They showed up at the Art Gallery Exhibition together, so I imagine they're dating. I haven't officially asked her yet."

"You attended the event?"

"Yes, Gina and I attended. You showed up in time for the photo-op."

"Oh, now I remember. I couldn't find my suit..."

Di Giovanni laughed. "Stop it, Tony. We both know you tried to figure out a way not to attend."

"That's not actually true, Dante. Anyway, what printing is your latest book currently in?"

Di Giovanni grinned. "Third, last time I checked. Look don't be too hard on Marissa."

"Good night, Dante. Say hello to Gina for me."

"I would be jumpy too if I suspected someone had been in my home with what happened with James Alan and Stacie."

Tony walked him to the door. "Good night, Dante."

"Good night, Tony."

Tony joined his wife and Murray in the kitchen. Murray, clearly shaken, spent most of the time talking to Marissa. He told her funny cop stories to make her laugh. They invited him to a late-night breakfast. After the meal, he left them.

Chapter 31

Tony stood in the kitchen doorway with his hands in his pocket. He took Marissa's hand and led her to the family room couch. He sat on the ottoman. He studied his fingernails. He gave her a pleasant look. The usual glass green eyes were now a bright green and seem to assume his entire face now flushed with a reddish cast. She stood up.

"Sit down."

"What's the matter with you, Tony?"

"You tell me."

"I haven't a clue."

"Do you respect what I do for a living?"

"Tony..." she stood up again.

"Sit down, please."

"What did I do wrong?"

"What did you do wrong?" he repeated. He almost smiled. His voice was quiet and sent chills up her spine. She could tell he was angry, but she could not figure out why.

"You are aware we have people dying right and left in Winding Falls, aren't you? And you're calling the police on a whim?"

"I did not call the police on a whim! I told you. I believe someone was in here. They erased the beginning pages of the manuscript I was working on."

"You never lock the damn doors, and you believe someone was in here?"

"This is a safe area. Not like where you work."

"And yet you believed someone had broken in? You had near the entire police force here tonight."

"Tony..."

"I'm the head of my own homicide unit, Marissa! A team I created and yet that flies right over your head."

"Tony..."

"We deal with murder and mayhem every day. You think what I do is a joke?"

"No, I don't. It's... I mean I..."

"You've lost friends to this maniac, and yet you're not taking your personal safety serious?"

"That's not fair..." she stood up.

Tony was at his breaking point. He needed to calm down, but something inside spurned him on.

"Sit down, and I'm not saying it again! Why were you out running in the middle of the night?"

Marissa had enough. Her temper exploded. "For the same reason you weren't here! It's my job!"

"Don't you dare get cute with me, Marissa! Do you know how embarrassing this was tonight? Every one of my detectives in my home on a whim?"

"In your home? This is my home too, or have you forgotten that? You're away so much I guess you forget I'm here, too."

"No one expects a police officer to be living in a mansion! Are you crazy?"

"It's a house. It's our home. We have money. What about it?"

"And on top of it the deputy mayor and his wife lived next door! It's only a matter of time before they find out half your friends are millionaires!"

"Stop shouting at me," she glared. "What about your friends that *my* friends are married to? What are you ashamed of, anyway? You come from money. So what? You've made a name for yourself as a police officer and..."

"Let me explain something to you which you should know after ten years of marriage. I don't like people invading my privacy."

"Invading your   how narcissistic are you? Why all the secrecy about your personal life to the people whose job it is to have each other's backs?"

"Why can't my personal space be as private as yours is?"

198

"Tony, you've written books that are still selling. Your education and experience allows you to be a consultant on criminal issues. Why shouldn't your detectives be aware of all this about the man who leads them?"

"Does anyone outside your inner circle know where you live, and what you do besides write one book a year? Do your friends know you also write under a pen name? Do they know what that pen name is?"

Marissa lost this argument, but she was not about to throw in the towel yet.

"Alright, look I'm sorry," she said, smiling meekly. "When I returned from my run, I could feel the presence of someone having been in the house."

"Oh, that's great! The police force was out here because you felt like someone was in the house! A house you never lock the doors on."

"Dante and James live in the neighborhood too or did you forget that? The captain also lives in the area..."

"And no one knows it!" yelled Tony.

"No one locks their doors around here. Stop acting so high and mighty!"

"Stop acting like a moron!"

He stopped. Her eyes widened in disbelief and hurt. She swallowed and a sad look came over her face. Before he could say another word, she ran out of the room and up the stairs. He ran behind her, but he heard the lock on the bedroom door click midway to the top. He sat on the step. He heard her crying and put his head in his hands.

After a few minutes Tony went to his den and laid down on the leather couch. He sighed. He remembered how terrified he was when he imagined finding her in a similar fate of her friends. He could not let her see his fear, and that was the problem.

From the outset, her father had voiced concerns to him about his only child marrying a career lawman. Yet here they were a decade later. Tony loved Marissa with all his heart and soul. He could never have given her up, no matter who objected. Without intending to, he fell asleep on the couch.

Tony woke up with a headache, a stiff neck and a backache. He did a series of stretches to loosen his joints. He stumbled into the kitchen. He craved a hot cup of coffee and breakfast. He looked around. Marissa had not been downstairs. He climbed the back stairs to the bedrooms. The door was unlocked on their bedroom. The bed had not been slept in. He walked down the hall. The two middle rooms were empty. He crossed to the one past the bathroom. The lock was on. It was the guest bedroom.

He took a shower with thoughts of her on his mind. For the first time in his career, Tony dragged his feet. He sat in the driveway and thought of their other fights. She would cry, he would apologize, and they would make up. This time the look in her eyes unnerved him. He had never called her out of her name before. He realized with deep sadness he had lost the edge he prided himself on.

Her friends had arrived by the time Marissa entered Tessa's spacious sitting room. The women embraced each other with warm hugs. Marissa sat on a comfy chaise and pulled out her attendance roster. She drew pink hearts around Janelle's name before doing the same with Anna and Stacie's names. She took out her novel. The room became quiet as the women looked at each other. Carla was the first to speak.

"I'm sorry, ladies, but with all that's been going on, I haven't been able to read this book."

"You're not alone, Carla," said Lynda. She sighed. "What are we doing? We've lost Janelle, Stacie and Anna. We've had to cancel our events. It's been a horrible year."

"Poor, poor Stacie," said LisaMarie with tears in her eyes. Her best friend, Emily put a comforting arm around her shoulder.

Elsa pushed hair out of her face. "Are you sure you're okay, Marissa? My heart was in my stomach when I heard about the break-in."

The women's attention at once focused on Marissa who squirmed slightly on the chaise. She wordlessly nodded.

"Mine, too," echoed Diana. The sapphire eyes squinted at her. They elevated the high cheekbones chiseled in the perfect face. "If you ever need to talk you know I'm always here for you."

"I'm okay, ladies. The only pain I'm feeling is a sense of betrayal. Tony behaved as if I made up the whole thing to get attention. It's humiliating."

Patricia's eyes narrowed. "Hush, Marissa! After what happened to Stacie, are you so unaware of the danger that's happening around us? Some nut is killing women in our town."

"We live only a house or two away. Suppose this psycho is targeting our community?" said Beth. Our deep blue eyes scanned the room.

"Exactly! Tony was right to be worried." Emily's sweet voice was elevated in soft indignation.

"You mustn't be upset with him," said Sierra. The purple bow in her carrot-red hair matched the purple ball of yarn she held. "He loves you, girl."

"Yes," Catori said as she helped Sierra rewind the ball of yarn. "You know Tony is crazy about you. I'm sure he was upset when he imagined you were hurt or possibly…"

"And he has every right to be upset." Angela injected with her usual straight forwardness.

"I just returned to work full time from maternity leave," said Lynda with a loud sigh. "My return was anything but peaceful. I'm closing the office earlier and earlier because the staff is afraid to leave later in the evenings."

"What? You mean at five o'clock?" asked Angela with a look of incredulity on her face. "It's still early!"

"Staff parking is behind the building, Angela, facing the back wall of that utility shop. No one is ever out. Plus, there's little to no adequate lighting, and my staff is majority women," said Lynda.

"She's right," said Janelle. "I had to park in the back when we met up last week. The lighting is bad back there after four in the afternoon."

Angela raised both hands. "I'm sorry. I surrender with a full apology."

Janelle smiled. Lynda turned to Catori. "Thank you, Catori, for those sleeping aids. I'm no good for my family or colleagues without rest."

Angela said, "I think of poor Anna every time I drop my kids off at school these days."

"What do you do in the afternoons when they get out of school?" asked Tessa.

"Jesus' parents or mine pick them up. They've worked out a chart between them. The girls love it."

Carla smiled. "It's a great system, Angela. My parents live next door to us. They've always picked up the kids. I've been blessed in that manner."

Sallie Anne said, "I think we've all managed to find ways to keep our children safe. Beth, Patricia and I have our housekeepers rotate picking up the kids which works out well as everyone knows the other."

"Well, let me be the first to give you and Beth flowers for that special you did on ways to keep our children safe," said Sierra. She put down her yarn and clapped.

The women followed suit. Sallie Anne and Beth looked happily flustered. Angela leaned forward and with customary stance stared across at Benson.

"What are the police doing about all this, Vanessa?"

The other women in the room turned to stare at Benson. She returned her friends stares.

"We're doing the best we can, ladies. We don't have anything to go on. Who would hurt Janelle? For that matter, why little Anna? The police are looking at James Alan as being the real target and Stacie being hurt by default."

"You mean, because she was home, too?" asked Sallie Anne with a frown.

"I'm afraid so."

"Ladies...," began Priscilla.

"Wait a minute, suppose it's the same thing with Janelle?" said Sierra. Her eyes widen. "Spencer is a lawyer as was Stacie and James Alan."

"If Stacie and her husband were the real targets, how is the district attorney's office going to oversee the safety of all lawyers in Winding Falls?" Catori asked.

"Let's not exaggerate," said Priscilla and rolled her eyes. "We will prosecute whoever the police find to the fullest extent of the law. Don't worry about that! Now can we please move on? Everyone in this room knows Vanessa and I cannot speak on active investigations."

"Please, let's not do this, ladies." The calming voice of Kristen intruded. "Let's not fight among ourselves."

"She's right," said Diana. "We can't allow stress to take us out of ourselves. If any of you need to talk, you know I'm always available," she repeated.

"We can always go shopping or better yet, come into the shop and get your hair styled, nails manicured, or a full body massage," said Tessa. The women smiled.

"Hey, in obedience to the suggestion to change the subject, I heard James is dating a cop. Is that true, Marissa?" asked LisaMarie, glancing sideways at Patricia.

Marissa smiled. "I had nothing to do with it. I must admit I failed in my matchmaking duties this time. He met Robin at that city hall meeting a couple of weeks ago."

"James, who?" asked Emily.

"James Whitman, the state senator."

Emily's mouth formed an O. Beth giggled.

"Yes, I was there. It seems they were both smitten. They couldn't keep their eyes off each other," said Patricia with a smirk.

"Where was there?" Diana asked.

"He brought her to the Art Gallery Exhibition," said Kristen with a smug look. "The one you missed because you and Mike insisted on attending your son's school play."

Diana laughed.

"It was a good production." Elsa said in defense of her best friend. "Michael was the lead and as handsome as his father. The girls in the audience were swooning in their seats."

"I thought a few of the mothers were as well," said Lynda with a grin.

"Oh! "I'm so sorry I missed the play and the exhibition," said LisaMarie, with a pout. "Dan had a business-related dinner that night I had to attend."

"Well, the loss goes to all of you," said Kristen with a saucy grin.

"Behave, Kristen." Tessa said with a smile. "They looked as if they were enjoying each other's company."

"Ah! So that's who that stunning blonde was," Beth said with a murmur. "Are you sure she's a cop? She's gorgeous."

Marissa said, "She's a detective with Tony's unit."

"A senator and a police detective. That should make media headlines," said Sallie Anne. "Where's she from?"

"I don't have all the digits..." Marissa said. "At least, not yet. We all know James has been a bachelor for a while."

"I'm going to throw a dinner party and invite James. I'm sure he'll bring her," said Sallie Anne.

"You and your dinner parties, girl. They're the stuff of dreams!" Diana gushed. "Make sure to invite Michael and me."

"You're not writing another psych book, are you?" asked Emily with a hopeful grin on her face.

Diana beamed. "No, girl, I'm not. I just want to be in the same room with the senator and his future wife!"

Amid the general laughter following Diana's remark, Elsa said, "I'm glad we got together again. I missed us more than I thought."

"Me, too. I know it's not been long but ..." said Angela with a shoulder shrug.

"Well, I know this is going to sound awful, but I can't help but think if we had only gotten Jacky out of our hair a long time ago. Seems the curse of knowing her..."

"Stop that, Carla! We can't put what's happened to our friends on Jacky. We chose to help her," responded Sierra.

"Besides," added Catori, "that's in the past."

"Chose to help her do what?" asked Benson. She looked around the room.

Marissa, across the room, raised her hand for attention. "Whatever the reason we've lost our friends, we still have each other. I'm confident Tony and his team will find out what happened to them."

Tessa, seated quietly beside Marissa, stood up. "Okay, I move we temporarily halt the book club for this year. Let's properly grieve for our friends."

"That's a great idea, Tess."

"Marissa, I've been meaning to ask you something..." began Diana. "It's about your new publicist."

"Is it personal, Diana?"

"No. It's a general question to be heard by all," said Diana. She took a deep breath. "I was wondering if we're going to vote in your new publicist to our book club. She will be replacing Jacky."

Sallie Anne said, "Normally I'm generous with my friendships, however, this time we need to still be as is. As Tessa suggested and we agreed, we need to properly mourn our friends passing."

"I agree," said Catori. "Let's not rush into it. Also, we might want to vote in more members and for that we need to go public, I think."

"Is that something we have to discuss right now?" asked Kristen.

"No," said Marissa. "In fact, I'll make a notation to discuss it next year this time. Let's give ourselves breathing room. I'm still missing Janelle like crazy."

"I know I miss Stacie so darn much!" said Patricia in a hoarse voice. "I still can't believe she's gone. This time of year, we were planning trips with our daughters."

The room quieted down. Patricia's grieved voice haunted the room. Two of the women sniffled, and Catori and Lynda blew their noses. Sierra's eyes watered slightly. The women sat with bowed heads. Suddenly sobriety fell. Marissa softly nudged Tessa who leaned forward and spoke in a gentle voice.

"Good points about the membership. I don't believe we'll ever find anyone to replace our friends. They were a special part of our lives within this group and beyond."

"Let's find something pleasant to talk about. For instance, when is the christening for little baby Christopher?" Carla asked.

A big smile spread across Lynda's face. "I was sending out save-the-date cards this week. Of course, you all are invited. This time the lucky picks for godparents go to Michael and Diana Minnelli."

Amid claps and cheers of congratulations, Diana and Lynda hugged. "It's a good thing we have reasonably flexible schedules. Michael is thrilled to be a godfather."

"Wait a minute! He has four brothers. He's never been asked to be a godfather to one of their children?" asked Tessa with a shocked look on her face.

"Michael is the youngest. His oldest brother's kids were born before he could walk, and Vincent lives in Italy and Nico is a confirmed bachelor."

"Well, glad I got to you before you guys were too old to see the baby."

"Lynda!"

"I hate to change such glorious subjects as babies, christenings, and old age," said Beth laughing merrily along with the others, "but are we eating lunch anytime today? I'm starving."

"A hungry voice calls out from the wilderness," sang LisaMarie.

"Girl, you never could sing."

"Hey!" LisaMarie with mocked outrage sat up straight.

At that moment, Ida Mae opened the doors. The ladies cheered and walked in unison to the dining room stopping to chat with or hug Ida Mae. Benson walked slowly behind the group and watched. She pulled Carla to the side.

"What's the matter, Vanessa?"

"What happened a long time ago?"

"What?"

"You guys said you helped Jacky a long time ago."

Carla frowned and shrugged. "Girl, I have no idea what you're talking about. Come on, let's go eat. I'm starving."

Carla walked ahead of her into the dining room linking arms with Angela. Benson hesitated and then followed her friends. She was unaware Marissa, Tessa, and Patricia watched her from across the room.

Chapter 32

After a long and weary day, Tony could not wait to get home. He parked in the garage alongside Marissa's car. He gathered the big bouquet of wildflowers from the passenger seat. The kitchen smelled delicious. A prepared plate of food sat in the oven. He was about to go upstairs when he spied Marissa on the enclosed patio. She was typing on her tablet.

"Hello, Mrs. Marigny." Tony smiled, offering Marissa the bouquet.

She looked up and smiled tentatively. "Thank you."

Tony sat in the chair next to hers. He looked at the up swept curls. She was wearing a short blue dress ruffled at the hem. The long legs ended in bare feet. Around one of her ankles was a gold anklet with a heart attachment. He remembered when he gave it to her. He studied the toenails painted white. He could smell her perfume. He put his arm across the back of her chair and leaned closer. He wanted to take her in his arms. She closed the lid on the tablet and stood up.

"Listen, Marissa, I was thinking..." he began, speaking softly. He stood up. "Why don't we spend the weekend at our favorite spot at Sandstone Resort?"

"That's nice, but I'm really not in the mood."

"I'll make all the arrangements."

"No. I really need to finish this chapter."

"Are you still angry with me?"

"No."

"Where are you going? Have dinner with me."

"Maria left you a plate in the oven."

She turned back to look at him at the door. Her face bore a pensive look. They stared at each other. With a sad smile she said, "I'm not angry or upset anymore, Tony. Please don't think about that. I've had a long day. One of my closest friends christened her fourth child today. A little boy. He's gorgeous."

"I'm sorry I didn't make the christening. I had..."

She cut him off. "Please be quiet. I didn't expect you would show up. You never have in the past. To get you to attend a family event or special occasion I must beg and plead right up to the time of the affair. Even then, I'm on pins and needles if you'll show up."

"Marissa..."

"Not to mention any social gathering, charity or fundraiser." She stopped and sighed. "Meanwhile, another one of my closest friends has been... Well, anyway, it's late. I don't want to argue anymore. You are who you are."

"Marissa..."

"I used to be embarrassed to have Maria see me eat alone night after night. But about two years ago, I stopped caring. I'm going to bed. Have a good night."

Tony watched her take the backstairs to the rooms above. He sat down heavily. He noticed she left the bouquet of wildflowers on the table. He closed his eyes. He sat on the patio until the violet blue of late evening gave way to the midnight black of nightfall.

Chapter 33

The summer was long and hot. The team took vacations in rotation as they always did. Marissa did not plan anything for the summer, and while Tony was home, stayed in the guest bedroom or went out alone during the day. He ignored her silence. He called up Trevino and two other men to take part in a golf tournament. He visited the shooting range, upgraded the home gym equipment, and with his dad built a tool shed behind a large tree in the backyard.

The sensational deaths of the deputy mayor and his wife were the headline for the nightly news during the remaining weeks of summer. Tony watched it in his den so as not to upset Marissa. The broadcast highlighted the lives of four of the five victims. The publicist death was not mentioned.

The first week into the fall season, Tony gathered his team in the police squad room.

"The captain will be on vacation starting mid-week. He's asked that we supply him with a condensed report of our open cases. We currently have four open cases. I asked Stefanie Symonds from the Crime Lab to send us their final analysis on the open cases. Luis and Priscilla, are you ready?"

Lead criminologist Trevino addressed his colleagues. "The first victim, Janelle Carr, was manually strangled in her home in Washington Heights. The Crime Lab lifted handprints, but the identity of the assailant is not in the database. We have nothing else to go on. Spencer Carr moved his family to Oxford Circle and hired a live-in nanny. He's also offered a substantial reward for information leading to the capture and arrest of his wife's killer. The case will remain open until its closed."

"Since he was a former prosecutor, have we looked at any of the people he put away?" asked Gerard.

"Yes, Kevin. It was one of the first moves we made," O'Neill said. "It was standard reasoning given he managed high-profiled cases. We also went a step further and investigated the mayor."

"The mayor?" echoed Sloan.

"Good housekeeping," said di Giovanni. "What about the publicist? Has her mode of death been officially confirmed yet?"

Perez said, "The publicist, Jacky Crenshaw, found hanging from the chandelier in her living room had rope burns around her neck. Our investigation uncovered the rope was a commonplace style sold everywhere. No DNA was found at the scene. We were told she was a party girl by nearly everyone we questioned, but we have not been able to substantiate or verify who she partied with."

"Did you guys receive any further details on the letter you found in Crenshaw's purse?"

"The handwriting expert confirmed it was written about nineteen years ago. Given that Crenshaw was thirty-six-years old at the time of her death, it makes sense she was writing to her high school boyfriend," said Trevino.

"Were you able to narrow down a boyfriend?"

"Yes, but he hadn't had contact with her in years."

"What about the bundle of letters and the ring you found in her work office?"

"Just her prints." He nodded towards O'Neill. "We gave the stash to James."

"These letters were dated about a year after the single letter to the high school beau. Based on the fact the letters were found with the ring, we've concluded this was a first-year college romance."

"So, what happened next?" asked Gerard.

"I examined each letter line-by-line," said O'Neill. "There was no mention of a name. I thought young girls were infamous for writing their lovers names repeatedly wherever they could find space."

"James, you're not too far off. I've wondered why there's no mention of a man's name in all the love letters," said Perez. "We noticed she called him by pet names like sweetie and lover boy but not his actual name. Not even a first name on the envelope."

"Maybe he had a girlfriend already or was one of her teachers. She would not want his identity known," said Sloan.

"Good points, Robin," said O'Neill. "Someone among her friends knew who this guy was. I doubt seriously young girls are that secretive with each other."

"Yeah," mused Benson with a faraway look. "She told someone."

"What about the women you've questioned already? What were their stories?" asked Gerard.

Trevino quietly said, "None knew anything about Crenshaw's love life, or seem to want to acknowledge they knew her. The engagement ring was appraised at today's market value. It's worth six million dollars. It's an heirloom is all we know."

Sloan, Benson, and Johnston reacted simultaneously. "What?" The women stared at Trevino with open mouths.

Trevino grinned. "The third victim is Anna Yang. She was a fourth-grade schoolteacher found hanging in her classroom. It was later determined by the coroner she was manually strangled before the hanging took place. We confiscated her home tablet. It was full of school-related curriculum, and food recipes. No DNA was found on the victim or at the crime scene. Kevin, tell them about your find."

"The victim's car was taken to the crime lab where we found a tracking device shaped like a gold coin."

Di Giovanni reached for the photo of the coin. "The writing looks like old Greek or Sicilian. It's not Latin."

"Kevin and I, along with the techs in the lab are trying to decipher the writing. Stefanie is researching the coin material."

"Seems like someone was following the teacher. Why?"

"That's what we're trying to determine," said Johnston. "The victim had no criminal record or law enforcement training. Her late father was a pharmacist and mother a homemaker. She and her husband, also a teacher, lived normal, middle-class lives with their two children."

"A case of mistaken identity?"

"That's what we're leaning toward but the mode of her death is identical to the first two women."

"The case remains open."

"The fourth and final victims are James and Stacie Young."

They were found butchered to death in their bedroom while their four children laid sleeping in their rooms. None of the kids heard anything. The housekeeper found the couple the next morning. No DNA was found despite the brutality of the scene. The children are undergoing therapy with child psychologists, Michael and Diana Minnelli, close family friends. Judge Young is having them homeschooled."

"Sounds like the Young's deaths was different from the three previous ones."

Tony sat on a stool with his chin in his hand. He straightened up. "Okay, I asked James and Vee to investigate the backgrounds of these women. What were your results?"

Benson said, "The commonality in these cases is that these victims all lived in Washington Heights and were the same age. All were married with children except for the publicist. All were employed full-time except for the librarian who worked part-time."

"We also have different sites for where each was killed," said O'Neill.

"Meaning we've got five deaths and an unknown killer," said di Giovanni. "We can't forget the deputy mayor was murdered alongside his wife."

Trevino exhaled. "We've got a smart murderer who knows how to cover his tracks. No DNA was found at any of the crime scenes. Either he's a cop, a scientist, or someone who's studied how to murder someone and get away with it."

"Could be someone with a medical background."

"Good suggestion, Kevin. But we need a motive."

"I believe it's someone these women knew," said Perez, frowning.

"Suppose it's not a man?" said Sloan. "Our killer could be a woman."

Benson looked across her desk at her coworker. A look of incredulity spread across her face. "Did you check their heights, Robin? Carr and Young were five feet ten inches each, Crenshaw was five feet eleven inches."

"What does their heights have to do with anything? I'm almost five eleven in bare feet. "I could lift you without a problem."

"Oh, really, blondie? Come over here and try it."

"Detectives, you're both forgetting about the lack of DNA found at these crime scenes," said Johnston. "Neither of you would be able to lift the other without depositing DNA on each other plus all the heavy lifting. Someone lifted Crenshaw to her death, and someone laid the Carr woman gently on the kitchen floor. That's why there's a strong hypothesis this is a male killer."

"What about Marissa Marigny who reported the home invasion?" asked Sloan. She tossed a candy bar to Benson who smiled. "Suppose she was next?"

"That's right. We can't forget about her," said Gerard. "The house alarm alerted the police station."

"Were the phones disconnected in your residence, Tony?"

Tony nodded his head. "No."

Gerard said, "The alarm to the station house was sent from an outside phone. When Stan tried to call home, our lines were blocked. Someone was working our phone lines by remote."

"Could you trace the lines?"

"It was set up as a temporary ruse and self-destructed as soon as we opened the cable box."

"What?"

"Her not being in the home probably saved her life," muttered Benson.

"Um... never thought about it that way. How tall is your wife, Tony?"

"She's five feet ten inches."

"How many women do you know who fit these height descriptions?"

"Athletes and models," said Sloan with her eyes on her computer screen.

"You've made good points," agreed Trevino, "but we still don't have a motive why these women and the deputy mayor were killed."

"Other than the fact they knew each other," said Tony, "and they went to college together."

"They attended the same university?"

"Yes. Winding Falls."

"How tall was the deputy mayor?"

"Six feet three inches and a cool two hundred twelve pounds," answered Trevino. "We can correctly assume it's why he was dealt with first. The hacking of his legs says as much."

"If we include Marissa, who's five feet ten inches, I'm wondering if any of them were college athletes."

Sloan and Perez looked at Tony. He said, "Marissa was on the women's basketball team. But I think we need to investigate the other victim's bios before we make assumptions based on their heights."

"I agree with Tony because I remember when Janelle Carr and Marissa Marigny were elected campus beauty queens," said Benson.

"Nice." Perez said, "I thought you were a beauty queen too, Vee."

"I was in beauty pageants, Priscilla. That's how I got to college. Can we get back to this case?"

"He's committed all his murders in broad daylight." Sloan studied her notes. "That's a pretty spunky thing to do, if you ask me."

"Except for Young... she was killed in the evening with her husband beside her."

"Hold on, all the victims were killed in their homes except for the third victim who was on her worksite." Gerard drew a diagram on his tablet. "We also don't know definitively when the publicist was killed."

"Could be the Carr woman being alone during morning hours was a murder of opportunity. The Crenshaw woman might have brought the killer home with her," Trevino said. "Remember the half-eaten food containers, Priscilla?"

"The classroom was empty," said Gerard. "I checked with the principal and at least two other teachers were in their classrooms. No one saw or heard anything."

Di Giovanni twirled his pen as he spoke. "Obviously he followed the others to get their addresses. The teacher was interesting because anyone could have seen him enter and exit the building."

"That's a recurring problem," said Trevino. "There's no surveillance at any of the crime scenes."

"Unfortunate," said Sloan.

Di Giovanni smiled. "Theory of opportunity anyone?"

"Where are we with motive? These women aren't connected career wise. hat I want is to be able to connect them to the killer. So far, I don't see a link"

"I don't either," said O'Neill.

"How is your wife, Tony?" asked Johnston.

"As good as can be expected. She was best friends with Janelle Carr. Well, we were both friends with the Carr's and the Young's."

"Spencer Carr sold the family home a month after her... murder."

"It stands to reason, Priscilla," said Tony. "He lost the love of his life. Would you want to stay amid memories of a bygone past, especially if that past was a happy one?"

Perez nodded. A month after losing her husband she sold their quaint cottage and bought her current home.

Tony stood and stretched. "These cases are open until we can close them or send them to the cold case crew. Anything else?"

Benson stood up. "My classes start tomorrow evening. I'll try and stay in the loop though."

"Are you returning back to school?" asked Perez.

"Yes."

"What are you studying, Vee?" Sloan asked.

"I've decided to train in the martial arts."

"What's your hours?"

"Right now, it's only twice a week."

"You'll do fine."

"It's about time," said O'Neill, smiling at her.

"You need any time-off you can always ask for it," said Tony. "We're proud of you, Vee."

"Good for you," said Gerard, grinning broadly. "You need a study partner, let me know."

"Same here," said Trevino giving her the thumbs-up.

"Thanks, Kevin, Luis. See you all later."

Benson smiled as her colleagues clapped and banged on their desks. She pulled a leather tote from under her desk. On the way to the elevators, her eyes were bright with happy tears.

"Hey, wait for me, Vee. I have something to tell you." Sloan grabbed her tote, waved to her colleagues and ran to catch up with Benson.

Chapter 34

Tony pulled into the driveway. He craved a hot bath, warm food, and his wife. She had been frosty the last few weeks. On the weekends she barely spoke. As summer faded into fall and the weeks rolled by, he was tired of the silent treatment. More bleak was the semi-darkness of the house when he arrived home in the evenings.

Maria was coming down the driveway as he pulled up to the gate. She stopped her vehicle and rolled down her window.

"Hey, Maria. Am I that late, or are you?"

"I'm late. I had to run extra chores for Ms. Marissa."

"Extra chores?"

"The holidays are coming fast, Mr. Tony. We always begin preparing for them around this time of year."

Tony felt a chill he could not explain. He looked down at Maria and smiled.

"Have a good night, Maria."

"You too."

Tony watched as she sped off up the road. He drove the rest of the way deep in thought. With the holidays near, he was hoping to end this war of silence between them. He wanted to make the upcoming weekend a romantic one. He gathered the bouquet of yellow roses.

The trunk on her car was open with two blue and yellow print suitcases in it. She walked past him to deposit a makeup case on top of the luggage. As she leaned into the trunk, his eyes roamed her figure hungrily. The blue knit pullover tucked into blue slacks hugged her curves. She had gained weight. He liked it.

"Hey baby. What are you doing?"

"What does it look like I'm doing?"

"It's the middle of the night."

"I waited long as I could."

"Marissa, let's go inside and talk."

"You've talked enough for me."

"I'm sorry, baby. I'm sorry for yelling at you. Please, let's go inside."

She walked ahead of him into the house. He looked at the luggage as he closed the trunk. She stopped in the living room and sat in an armchair. He pulled an ottoman over to her.

"Look, I truly apologize for losing my temper. I'm worried about you. All these women getting killed and finding all these bodies. The reason I'm late tonight is..."

She raised her hand. "You investigate crime."

"The call for a home invasion in my house with my wife... Marissa, I didn't know what to think, baby! I was terrified. It's not an excuse. I just need you to know I love you, Marissa. This is our neighborhood, but how safe is it when the deputy mayor and his wife are murdered right next door? James and Stacie were killed a half a mile from us."

She looked at him. "I'm petrified Tony, but you don't see me shouting at you. And these are my friends that have gotten murdered. How do you think that makes me feel? You're not the only one in this marriage worried. I'm fearful every time there's a murder or bank robbery. I know you love what you do but yelling at me because the house alarm went off doesn't make sense to me."

"Where are you going?"

"My parents. I think we need a little time apart. This case has gotten to you in the worse way. You've never been like this. I can't live on the edge anymore."

"Baby, please. I'm sorry."

"I know, and I'm sorry too, but I think this is best. That way you won't have to worry about me. You can catch your bad guys."

"It's not that. It's just..."

"Tony, drop it. It's obvious all the years you've been with your team they don't know anything about you. You were more approachable when you were a patrol officer."

"Now you're exaggerating. Look, I don't want to argue. I was thinking why don't we..."

"You think I'm stupid?" Marissa stood up and moved away from him.

Tony was quiet. "I know you're not stupid."

"I'll bet none of your detectives know Perez is my cousin, do they?"

"They don't need to. I don't give her preferential treatment, and she doesn't expect it."

"You don't get it, do you? That's the side of you that needs to change. Putting people in tight boxes." Marissa shook her head. She grabbed her long wool coat and a short jacket out of the hall closet. "I need some time alone."

"Okay. I'll drive you."

"No, you won't! I want my car in case I want to go somewhere."

"Go somewhere? Like where?"

"Shopping, eating out, a drive. What do you mean like where? You're gone all day long, and well into the night most times. Do you know what I do all day? Do you think I stay indoors and write and in-between writing I cook and do laundry? Is that how you want me to spend my life? I want my car. I'm an adult. I want my car!"

"Okay, okay. Calm down. Don't scream. Look, I'm sorry. Tell you what. How about I drive behind you?"

"It's a free road. Now I'd better go. I called my dad."

"Marissa?"

"What?"

"Are you leaving me?"

She looked at him, and tears came in her eyes. "No, Tony. I love you."

"I love you too, baby. More than anything in the world."

"That's why I've got to leave. I need some space between us."

She hunched her shoulders. Tony reached out and pulled her to him. He held her tightly in his arms. She dropped the coats and wrapped her arms around him. They stood that way for a long time.

Chapter 35

What a long morning thought Sierra Smith as she hurried through the halls of Winding Falls Hospital and Medical Center to the front desk. She had left the bathroom key in the desk for Julie yesterday. Hopefully, Julie remembered to return it. Ah, yes! Here it was. Sierra was due for her break and could she use it! She made her way to the locker room, opened her locker and took out the bag of almonds, and the crossword puzzle book. She pushed her lunch kit back onto the shelf.

Sierra walked up a flight of stairs to the third floor and to the end of the hall. She walked through the automatic sliding doors stepping out onto the veranda, a glass enclosed structure that was drafty at times. The sun was out, and the unseasonably warm weather was exhilarating as fall had arrived windy and chilly. She looked at the pumpkin displays and loved the addition of the bats lining the ceiling and walls. Halloween was one of her favorite holidays.

Sierra pulled on her purple cable cardigan and sat in her favorite spot all the way in the back of the room. She took her carrot red hair out of its bun and loosened it about her shoulders. She opened the bag of almonds and bent over a crossword puzzle.

At the nurses' station, Julie Mulkowski looked at her watch. Where was Sierra? Jennifer Stanley walked in the door. Jennifer was always early for shift changes. She looked at Julie quizzically.

"Are you okay, Julie? Where's Sierra?"

"She took her break a good fifteen minutes ago."

"Did you text her?"

"Yes, but her phone is going to voicemail."

Jennifer brought her jacket and belongings to the locker room while Julie tried sending Sierra another text message. By now, two other nurses had come on duty. When Jennifer returned, Julie asked one of the nurses to stay at the desk. Julie and Jennifer went in search of Sierra. They were about to board the elevator when Jennifer saw the nurse on the outdoor veranda.

"Look, Julie," she said, pointing outside. "Sierra must have fallen asleep."

"In the middle of the day?" said Julie and started to smile. "Someone could be expecting soon."

Both ladies hurried to their co-worker who was slumped forward in her chair. Her long red hair was draped over her shoulders onto her lap.

"Well Sierra, you certainly had me going," said Julie and shook Sierra's shoulder playfully.

The ladies watched in horror as Sierra fell to the side, and they saw the huge knife embedded in her chest. Their screams were heard throughout the hospital.

Gerard and Johnston entered the emergency section of Winding Falls Hospital and found it in a state of near chaos. They reached the third floor, and an intern directed them to the veranda. Hospital staff were restrained outside the veranda by police, concern etched on their faces. The sound system came on, and hospital personnel cleared the area.

Johnson and Gerard saw the prone figure of the woman outfitted in a blue two-piece nursing uniform and bulky purple cardigan. She sat slack in the chair, her head downward on her chest. The sunlight flooded the glass enclosed veranda and illuminated the thick mass of red hair hung in deep waves across the nurse's face and neck.

Johnston said, "I know this young nurse. I remember she was a scout leader. I always bought cookies from her girls."

"Is that right?"

"She was a nice young woman."

Johnston checked her hands and fingers for signs of forensic evidence. She noted the long delicate fingers with tips scrubbed clean of nail polish. The gold wedding band was slim and delicate like its owner. The butcher knife was embedded deep in the woman's chest allowing but a trickle of blood to ooze out onto her blue scrubs.

Johnston said, "This is her bag of half-empty almonds on the table."

Gerard pointed to a blood drenched item on the floor by the woman's feet. Johnston picked up the crossword booklet. She returned it to the floor. Santorelli rushed off the elevator and all but barreled down the police restraining the crowd. The detectives watched as she fell to her knees, and gently pushed the woman's hair back from across her face.

"How long has she been dead, Doctor. Santorelli?"

"I would say less than three hours."

"Cause of death?"

"From here it looks like a punctured heart. I will confirm after the autopsy."

"Thanks."

A commotion across the room caught their attention. Johnston walked over to a tall, blonde man restrained by two officers.

"Mr. Smith, please give us a second. You will be with your wife in a moment."

The man focused his attention on her. His brown eyes held a faraway gaze as he held back tears. A look of anguish crossed his features, as his mouth opened, but no words formed.

Johnston and Gerard took the elevator to the next floor where they were to speak to the nurse supervisor. Gerard spotted the woman in lavender scrubs at the end of the hall. She was tall and broad-shouldered with black wavy hair she held at the nape of her neck with a beaded hair clip.

"Are you the nurse manager?" asked Johnston, showing her badge.

The nurse extended her hand. "I'm Catori Moon Perry, nurse supervisor for this unit. How may I help you?"

Gerard said, "Is there somewhere we could speak privately?"

"Of course. Please follow me."

They followed her midway down the hall. She seated them and waited. Her turquoise drop earrings emphasized the smooth light brown skin and dark almond-shaped eyes. Gerard noted her hands were free of rings except for a slim wedding band; fingernails clipped short and void of nail polish.

"Nurse Perry, have you heard of this morning's incident?"

"I was informed about twenty minutes ago, Detective. I was in surgery when all this occurred."

"Then you know the victim has been identified as Sierra Smith, a nurse here at the hospital?"

"Yes. Sierra was one of my seasoned nurses."

"How long had Ms. Smith been employed at the hospital?"

"Sierra joined us fifteen years ago right after she graduated nursing school."

"How long has she worked on the maternity ward?"

"The last ten years. Before that, she was on the emergency ward."

"Any marital problems you're aware of?"

"None or she didn't bring them to work. Very pleasant woman."

"How did she get on with her co-workers?"

"Sierra had a light, bubbly personality. She was a good friend and a good co-worker."

"Did you and the deceased have a relationship outside of work?"

"Yes, we were good friends. She often babysat my children as she and her husband didn't have any."

"Did you know each other prior to her working here at the hospital?"

"Yes. We met in college our first year in nursing school."

"What college was this?"

"Winding Falls University School of Nursing."

"Have there been any issues with patients? Anyone disgruntled?"

"No, but babies are always disgruntled leaving the warmth and security of the womb. Sierra had a wonderful disposition with them."

"How did she get on with hospital staff?"

"As I've mentioned, Sierra's personality was one of joy. She was in love with her husband, and he was with her. She loved being a nurse, and her little patients loved her."

"If there's anything else you'd wish to share, please don't hesitate to call. Thank you for your time."

"Thank you, and you're welcome, Detective."

Johnston said, "Before we leave, I'd like to see the area where the nurses stash their belongings."

"And would it be possible to interview the nurses who found the victim?" asked Gerard.

"I'll have someone direct you to the locker room." Nurse Perry paged a nurse. She looked at Gerard. "I'm afraid our young nurses were traumatized at discovering the body of their colleague. We sent them both home. If you need to speak with them, I can give you, their information."

Johnston said, "That's not necessary. If we need further information from them, we'll reach out. Thank you for your cooperation."

"No problem, Detective." She looked at the African man in scrubs who stood in the doorway. "David, please show these detectives to the staff locker rooms."

They were led to their destination on the second floor. The nurse was paged. With a smile he left them walking swiftly down the hall. Gerard sat in the hall and began typing his notes.

In the locker room, Johnston pulled on plastic gloves. She was dismayed to find a Winding Falls University student badge, registration papers, and three textbooks. A small duffle bag held a change of clothing, and toiletries. As she closed the locker, she spied the photographs neatly taped to the inside of the door. Most were of the nurse and her husband. The four spread across the top of the locker were of Sierra with a group of women. The photographs were old and blurred with age. Johnston smiled and closed the locker.

The detectives found the security office three floors up. As they stepped off the elevator they were greeted by a tall, broad-shouldered man in a dark police uniform. His black hair was streaked with gray with the lower part of his face completely gray. The beard was trimmed neatly, and the black uniform cleaned and pressed.

"Detectives? I'm Sergeant Alex Macchio. The receptionist told me you were looking for me?"

"Johnston and Gerard. We'd like to speak with you in private, if you don't mind."

"Of course. Right this way."

The sergeant led them down the hall. The office was plain and accommodated a desk, office chair and two stationery chairs. A phone and laptop completed the office decor. The sergeant sat behind his desk.

"What can we do for you, Detectives?"

Gerard stared at him. Johnston sat down. She opened her phone to record the session. The sergeant had a slight smile on his face.

Gerard said, "A homicide just occurred in this hospital..."

"Of course. We've been busy putting up barricades, and..."

"One of the nurses here was fatally injured," continued Gerard. "She's on the fourth floor. Does this hospital have surveillance on that floor?"

"Where was she found, exactly?"

He opened his laptop. Johnston tried not to look at him. He brought back memories of her late husband.

"The veranda," said Gerard.

"No, we have no video coverage in that area. We only have coverage in the halls. The veranda is considered private space."

"Could we have the film for that hallway?"

"I'll make you a copy."

"Another question. Since you're aware there's no video surveillance in that area, what do you do about security?"

The sergeant gave Gerard a serious look. There was no response. He handed the tape to Johnston. Their eyes met and held. Johnston took the tape, gave him a tight-lipped smile, and walked ahead of Gerard out of the office.

Chapter 36

The mood in the office was somber as the detectives viewed the photograph of the recent homicide victim. She looked at the camera with unabashed joy. It was a look that projected happiness.

Johnston, seated in front of Murray's desk, said, "This is Sierra Smith, thirty-six years old. She was a registered nurse at Winding Falls Hospital and Medical Center."

"Married?"

"Yes. Husband's name is Thomas Smith, same age."

"Any children?"

"No."

"What does the husband do for a living?"

"He's a math professor at Exeter College."

"Have you checked his whereabouts at the time of his wife's death?"

"It's an hour's drive one way from here to Exeter. There's a toll station between here and Exeter. They have him clocked in one hour before his wife's death."

Murray looked up. "That's not what I asked. Was he in class?"

"Yes. He was in his office with the dean while his wife was headed to work. He was teaching a class as she was being assaulted. He appeared at the hospital ninety minutes after her death."

"Where is he now?"

"He's at their home in Delsea Park. He's taken a leave of absence from the university."

"Any problems in the marriage?"

"None reported."

"Victim's cause of death?" asked Tony.

Gerard read his notes. "Cause of death was a butcher knife thrust in the center of her heart. Died on impact."

"Front or back entry?" asked Murray.

"Front chest. It was so deep all you saw was the handle."

"In order for anyone to be stabbed in the chest at close range, you have to have some familiarity with the attacker," Murray said dryly.

"There's surveillance on every floor but no one has stood out yet."

"Correction," said Gerard. "There are entire sections in the hospital that's not under surveillance. For instance, this section where the nurse was attacked. It's an unsecured area down one end of a closed hall." Johnston side-eyed her partner but said nothing.

"There you have it," said Murray throwing up his hands. "No one saw anything, and no one knows anything."

"We've been anxious all summer and nothing happens. Then school opens again, and we're on standby alerts but again, nothing happens."

"Except now it's two weeks before Halloween and everyone is gearing up getting ready for trick or treat," said Johnston.

With a subdued tone as he studied the recently added photograph on his tablet, Di Giovanni said, "I'm sensing a deep emotional element to these killings as if he wants to erase their very existence."

"She's the sixth victim of this mad man," said Johnston.

"What are we saying to the community?" asked Gerard. "The holidays are around the corner."

"Standard police lingo," said Murray. "We don't have anything, Kevin. No DNA evidence at the scene, no witnesses, nothing. What are we telling the public? We can't have mass panic."

"They're all graduates of Winding Falls University."

"So is half the town who attended college. What else?"

"Nothing, I guess."

"How tall was this victim?"

"Oh, here we go with the height thing again."

"She was five feet ten inches."

"And that does what for you, Luis?"

"Don't know yet."

"I did find this in her locker," said Johnston.

She laid out the pictures she had found in the locker on the whiteboard. The team studied the photos. They spotted the redhead in a soccer uniform among other women.

"Those are old photos," murmured Murray as he squinted his eyes. "I can't make out anyone's features. Can you?"

"Not I," said Sloan and sighed. "I can barely see the coach."

Gerard pointed to the last photo. "That one looks more modern because she's older there."

"College, maybe?"

"That university does have a women's soccer team."

"What are we doing? I doubt if a member of her former high school or college soccer team did her in."

"Good point, Luis. I think we're grasping at straws. She did know her attacker and I'm thinking it could be someone in the hospital."

"That's a more likely motive."

Gerard said, "We talked to the guy in security. He doesn't seem like the ambitious type to me. He knows there's no surveillance in certain areas."

"In all fairness, Kevin, hospitals are owned by private entities. The owners think the security they have is enough. He's doing the best he can with what he has."

"Aren't we all?"

"Normally it is."

"Are we thinking this is the same individual who's murdered six other people?"

"Other than this on-site murder in the hospital the teacher was killed early in the morning in her classroom. This murder was committed mid-morning with the hospital full of staff and visitors."

"Yet, no one saw anything suspicious."

"Who could move around a hospital with complete anonymity?"

"Medical staff."

"Bingo!"

"Well, that doesn't help us because medical staff is supposed to be in the hospital."

"Wait a minute, have we checked for anyone in areas they're not supposed to be in?"

"Like where, Vee? The surveillance cameras are mainly at entrances and exits."

"Hospitals have to be alert to any HIPPA violation as it concerns patient privacy and safety regulations, Vee," said Johnston. "And, as Tony just said, this is a privately-run hospital. They aren't trying to be sued out of business."

"This seems like a crime of passion. Another nurse, maybe?"

"Then we're back to looking at the husband."

"Let's check out the good professor a bit more closely. I don't think he personally got rid of his wife but if he were playing around, his mistress wouldn't have the same reservations."

"Mistress? Could be a man. Let's not be archaic here."

"Heck, the entire university is now under the radar?"

"Don't we have other cases?"

"Game over."

Tony grunted a smile. "Alright, all right. We're all tired. Let's call it a night."

Murray said, "Have a good weekend, folks. Tony, could you see me in about thirty minutes?"

Murray waved good night as he rushed to catch the elevator. Tony looked in the squad room. The lights were dimmed. He was alone. He looked at the report in his hands. A rustle caused him to look up. Santorelli was standing at his door. She walked in and closed it behind her. She was dressed more conservatively in a black silk blouse and belted skirt. Somehow, she looked sexier.

Tony frowned. "What do you want this time, Elsa?"

"I don't want anything. I was in the building, so I stopped by."

"Thanks for the medical records on the Smith case."

"She was such a lovely person."

"Did you know her? Oh, of course you did. You both work at the same hospital."

She smiled. When she moved, he saw she had her purse at her side. Tony busied himself clearing off his desk. He looked across at her. She was smiling with her eyes half-closed. He put on his answering service, stood, and pulled on his leather jacket.

"Are you attending the Halloween party this year?"

"No."

"That's a shame. It's for spouses only this year. I'm sure Marissa would love it. She always loved dressing up for Halloween."

Something in her tone irritated Tony. He grabbed his briefcase and walked past her to the door. He waited while she walked by him. He could smell her perfume. She walked with him to the elevator.

On the elevator he looked at Santorelli. She was talking, but he did not understand one word. His mind was caught up in images of Marissa.

"Tony, if you change your mind, Chris can't attend this year. You can have his costume."

"Good night, Elsa."

He was unaware of what she said or in which direction she went. He drove and watched the lights on the highway traffic. In his mind he replayed the argument that brought about his separation from his one true love.

On a blustery chilly morning the day before Halloween, a visibly grieving husband buried his wife in the Smith family plot. Marissa and her friends each carried a bouquet of yellow mixed wildflowers. Later that same day at the family home, Marissa read a passage from her thirteenth best-selling novel. It was written after the sadness of her second miscarriage. The passage was to the nurse who had taken care of her during her hospital stay. The dedication page read, "*Sierra Whittier Smith, angel of medicine, who brought peace after the storm.*"

Chapter 37

Emily Wilkinson was afraid, and she did not try to hide it. She jumped if the wind blew a leaf her way. She had begun closing the bookstore after the last customer walked out the door. When poor Sierra died in the hospital surrounded by medical professionals, Emily feared being alone in the bookstore in the afternoons.

This would be the last week for the store to be opened. She had talked it over with her husband, Clay, and had decided to sell it after the holidays. It had been her dream since she was a little girl to grow up and be able to own the place where she had nurtured and developed her dreams. That dream came true. Now it was time to grow up. She had a family and three children of her own to raise. With this decision she looked forward to spending more time with her family. They had put up the Christmas tree last weekend. This weekend they were driving to Exeter to see them light the Christmas tree in their town square. They took the kids every year and spent the weekend at the Wilkinson family home there.

She turned her attention to the last customer who was ready to leave. She walked her to the door and locked it behind her. Whew! It was three fifty-five, but that was okay. She texted Clay she was on the way home and sent another one to her oldest child to take the roast out of the fridge and place it in the oven.

She hurried back to retrieve her belongings and car keys. She pulled on her wool coat, and looked in her purse for her lipstick, and heard a rustle behind her. She turned around trying to see everything at once. Fear gripped her senses, and she decided to leave the store. Wait a minute, she heard that rustling sound again. Who was there?

Emily Wilkinson's quaint little bookstore was in the middle of a bakery and a daycare center in Olde City. This strip of shops and quaint bistro was never in the news except to promote the bed and breakfast inns, and family-style restaurants. With the winter holidays firmly in place, the shops were adorned with Christmas lights and colorful posters. The decor cast a festive glow on the street creating a picturesque wintry landscape complete with tinsel-decked lampposts.

O'Neill and Benson walked into the little shop and were directed to the back. A dark-haired police officer was nearby writing in a notepad.

"What happened here, Officer?" asked Benson.

"The alarm system was triggered. By the time we got here the front door was open and…"

"Hey, Susan," said O'Neill. He bent down to get a closer look. He noticed the victim on her side curled in a fetal position. A thick wiry cord was embedded deep in her neck. "How long you been here?"

"Hi, James. Ollie and I arrived about twenty minutes before you folks. Looks like she's been strangled."

"Hmm," said O'Neill. The soft blonde curls emphasized the beauty of the angelic face. The large gray eyes were open with a single teardrop on her cheek. He laid a hand gently over the victim's eyelids, closing them.

"Has her husband been called?"

"That was him in the ambulance that passed you. He found her. Poor guy went berserk."

Tony walked into the little shop with Santorelli who gasped and staggered backwards when she saw the body on the floor. Tony laid his hand flat on her back to steady her.

"Are you alright? Do you know this lady?"

"Yes," her voice came to him faintly. "We were in school together."

The female cop began reading from her notes. "She's wearing a buttoned-up overcoat. Her purse strap is still on her shoulder. She's wearing one glove."

"Thank you. That's enough." Santorelli dismissed her with a wave of her hand. "Detective."

The officer looked at Tony who nodded. She snapped her tablet closed and rolled her eyes at the back of the medical examiner's head as she walked out the door.

O'Neill caught Tony's eye and beckoned him to walk outside.

"The doctor just told me she attended school with the deceased."

"I know it's hard to see someone you know like that. Is Vee okay otherwise?"

"Yeah, but you must wonder how she's feeling. This is another woman she's attended school with."

"I wonder how these events are shaping up for the women in this town, as well as the ones we work with," mused O'Neill.

"Well, you have a counselor in your midst. I think if he felt one of you were in trouble he would say something."

O'Neill smirked. "You know I always forget Dante's a psych guy."

"I think that's the point. Have you had a chance to speak to her husband??"

"No. Officer Drayton and her partner were here ahead of us. The husband had to be sedated. He found her."

"Here comes the doctor."

"Detectives." Santorelli removed her face mask. "This was pretty gruesome though it doesn't look like it."

"What was the cause of death?"

"Strangulation using a metal wire embedded in rope. It wasn't a slow death."

"What do you mean?"

"He tortured her before allowing her to die. The pain of the wire coupled with consciousness and terror would have been excruciating."

"How long would she have suffered?"

"A good thirty minutes," Santorelli turned and walked away.

Tony watched her dropped shoulders as she exited the shop. "This can't be good for Santorelli either James. She knew the victim as well."

"Isn't she going on some kind of vacation?"

"She's been going on vacation for the last few months. See if it's at all possible to find customers who were in this shop today. If we're lucky we might stumble on the last person to see this lady alive."

Tony silently surveyed the activity swarming around the outside of the shop. The signs of the coming holidays were displayed in each shop and storefront window. Up and down the cobbled street, he saw on the faces of shopkeepers and visitors alike, the look of silent fear mingled with curiosity. The images merged and contrasted with the joyful signs. Tony sighed inwardly. Who was this monster?

O'Neill retraced his steps going to the backroom that was Emily's office. He stood in the doorway and surveyed the room. The area was well-lit with an overhead fan. Books lined the built-in wall shelf behind the small wood desk. He looked at a few receipts found in her checkbook. He looked around. To the right of her desk was a locked window. The third wall held photographs. One picture was of a group of twenty women smiling at the camera. The pictures were old and grainy. He looked at the chalk outline on the floor. Something played in the dim recesses of his mind. What was he missing here?

O'Neill walked back into the main part of the bookstore. He caught glimpse of a police officer with his back to him.

"Hey, Officer Brown," he called out.

The officer turned around. A smile spread across his face. He and O'Neill shook hands.

"Hi, James. I saw your partner earlier. She told me she knew the lady."

"Susan told me you got here a little ahead of us. Did you see anyone around? The last customer, for instance?"

"Yeah. Do you see those two ladies over there? I was speaking to them. One of them was in this shop shortly before it closed. She's upset, too."

"Which one?"

"The smaller one. She was returning a book. Her name's Gladys Walker. If you don't need me, I'm out."

"Thanks, Ollie."

"No problem, James."

O'Neill studied the women as he crossed the street. They were medium height, and both were slim. They were in casual shirts and pants. One had shoulder-length deep brown hair, and the other had long wavy blonde hair. They were extremely attractive. He took out his police badge.

"Good evening, ladies. My name's Sergeant O'Neill. Would you mind answering some questions for me?"

"What's happened over there?" asked the dark-haired woman. "The police have been there for hours but won't tell us anything."

"What do you do?" asked the blonde.

"Investigate homicides."

They looked at each other in awe before the dark-haired one mutely nodded. Her friend followed her lead.

"What are your names?"

"I'm Emma Brown," said the dark-haired one. She pointed to her blonde friend. "She's Gladys Walker."

"Have either of you visited this bookstore today?"

"Yes, I have," said the blonde. "I was in there this morning."

"How long did you stay?"

"I was in there approximately two hours."

"How do you know the approximate time?"

"I came in at ten o'clock and left at twelve noon to attend my son's parent-teacher conference."

"What were you doing for two hours in the bookstore?"

"I was going through party planning books. Our church is hosting a fundraiser, and I was looking up a few things."

"Was that the only time you were in the shop today or this week?"

"Yes."

"What brought you back here this evening?"

"I wanted to speak to Emily... I wanted to speak to Emily about..."

She stopped talking and lowered her head. Her breath came in ragged gasps. She put her hand on her friend's shoulder.

"Who is Emily?" asked O'Neill. He kept his face blank.

"The bookshop owner, Emily Wilkinson!" replied Brown with indignation. "Where is she anyway? We haven't seen her yet."

Ignoring her friend, O'Neill asked Walker, "Did you get an opportunity to speak with the owner?"

"No. When I arrived there were police everywhere. I walked over here and called Emma."

"Why did you call your friend?"

"I was scared. I don't know why but I was scared. I don't know..."

"Where do you both live?"

"Washington Heights," said Brown.

"Did either of you notice anyone lurking about? Anyone you've never seen before?"

Walker shook her head. "This area is full of shops but there are also homes on the other side. People are always about."

"But we didn't notice anyone out of place if that's what you mean," replied Brown.

O'Neill handed them his card. "If you think of anything, please don't hesitate to call me."

"Thank you, Sergeant O'Neill," said Brown with a smile.

The detective put on his dark shades and walked away. He sat in the squad car and watched as the quaint cobblestone street neighborhood quieted down for the evening.

The squad room was deserted. Seated in O'Neill's office were Tony and Trevino.

"Emily Wilkinson was a married mother of three and a bookstore owner. Killed in her back office after close of business day." O'Neill spoke in monotone.

"Method?"

"She was strangled using a thick cord wrapped around a plastic-coated metal wire that was later found to be a coat hanger. The wire cut into her throat severing her spinal column."

"How tall was this woman?"

"She was five feet ten and one-half inches, Luis."

"Where's Vee?"

"I sent her home. Vee didn't complain so you know she wasn't in a good place mentally."

"Damn," said Trevino under his breath. "Right before Christmas..."

O'Neill showed them the photos from the bookstore. The detectives studied them, each lost in their own thoughts.

"Can't make out their faces. Where is this from?"

"The victim's office in the back of the bookstore. The pics are old and fuzzy, and you can't make out any of the men in between the women."

"You couldn't clear this up, James?"

"No. I sent them to the Crime Lab and Stefanie couldn't either."

Trevino said, "I think we need to haul the good doctor in here for questioning."

"There's no reason to question her. Of course, she knows the victims. She went to school with them," O'Neill said. "Let's go home. I'm tired."

Trevino gave O'Neill a squinty eye look. He looked at Tony who remained silent.

Chapter 38

The business owners in the Olde City community came out in the pouring rain to pay respects to the Wilkinson family. Clay Wilkinson, sedated to get through the church service, managed to speak of their great love for each other. Tony attended the funeral and sat high in the church balcony. He paid close attention to the women seated around Marissa. Tony could not take his eyes off his wife. She looked breathtaking to him. She appeared to have gained more weight. He saw it in the roundness of her face. Rose would make certain her daughter ate three meals a day.

Tony saw Benson approach Marissa and the women briefly hugged before Marissa turned to embrace another woman. Marissa in a black wool unstructured coat read an excerpt from her tenth best-selling novel. It was dedicated to *Emilia McCoy Wilkinson, "the most loving and kindest person I've ever known."*

The mood was as melancholy as the weather. In the graveyard, Tony scanned the visitors. Few had bothered to attend the final going away part of the funeral. The chilly weather and constant rain meant a sea of black umbrellas made it difficult for Tony to keep Marissa in view. He saw Benson who stood among the women gathered around her. He realized with a start that there were more women in the graveyard than had been in the church. After the brief service Tony caught up with Benson as she crossed the pathway to her car.

"Hi, Vee. I didn't know you would be here."

"Hi, Tony. Wonderful day for a funeral."

"This must have been difficult to attend."

"No more difficult than attending any other friend's funeral. I don't think they're pleasant. Do you?"

"No, I don't. James told me you knew this lady personally."

"I didn't know Emily personally. We met in college on the soccer team."

"Did you keep in contact after college?"

"Somewhat. She owned a bookstore, remember?"

"Good point. I was surprised to see you at the funeral."

"Why be surprised? This is a small town. She was a local girl who done well for herself."

"Can you tell me anything else about Emily?"

"Is that why you're here? Why not ask Marissa?"

She stopped talking when she saw how deeply green Tony's eyes had become. She learned long ago it was always a sure sign he was angry. Benson looked around and sighed.

"Emily was a sweetheart. For those of us who were in any classes or activities with her, she was the kind of person who didn't make enemies. That's why they're so many women here. I remember her as a great leader on the soccer field, besides being your friendly neighborhood bookworm."

"So, you can't think of anyone who would've wanted to harm her in any way?"

"No. Sorry. That's why I attended this funeral. I needed to see her for myself."

"Thanks, Vee." Tony smiled. "That's all I wanted to know. We need to catch whoever did this."

"Yeah. She didn't deserve this." Benson stood with a lowered head. "I've got to run. Talk to you later."

He nodded. Tony looked around. Marissa was gone. He sat in his truck and played back the conversation he had taped with Benson. Thoughts ran concurrently in his mind's eye. He remembered when Marissa felt someone had been in their home. A chill ran down his spine, and not for the first time.

Tony was staring at the same words in the paragraph for a good twenty minutes before he gave up. He grabbed a folder to look at a crime scene, but after a minute pushed everything aside. He simply could not concentrate. He missed Marissa with every fiber of his being. A knock and Trevino entered. The all-black ensemble he wore made him look larger. Tony noticed his hair was slicked back and he was holding a black wool hat with a red feather on the brim.

"Are you sure you don't want to attend this holiday party? I still have the invitation." Trevino slid the black and gold envelope across his desk.

"Thanks, but no thanks, Luis. I'm heading home."

"Okay. Happy holidays to you and Marissa."

"Same to you, Luis."

Tony sat at his desk trying to think of something to do. Marissa flashed across his mind's eye. He thought of the last year when she greeted him in a skimpy holiday outfit. He smiled at the memory. He decided to call her. He was about to pick up the desk phone when Santorelli entered his office.

With a smile she closed the door and sat in the chair in front of his desk. The white silk blouse was cut invitingly low. Tony smiled and she returned his smile. He was glad she sat down. The desk covered her shapely legs, and she did not know how much he enjoyed the shape of women's legs, especially Marissa's. But smiling encouraged Santorelli which he thought about too late. She leaned forward and the golden thick head of hair fell over one eye.

"I know you've been working extremely late recently. Is everything okay at home?"

Tony stared at her. He weighed how much she might know since she and Marissa were friends.

"What do you want, Elsa?"

"Since you don't drink, let's have dinner together. There's nothing wrong with..."

Tony raised his hand. "Go home to your husband. I'm not interested."

"You're not interested in eating? Come on now, Tony. We're not children. Sharing a meal is a social event. Besides, I want to exchange one or two ideas with you about this killer."

Tony stared at her. He thought of his conversation with Benson. "How long did you know our last victim, Emily Wilkinson?"

"She was a college friend. I occasionally went into her bookstore for a novel, or..." She looked down at her hands in her lap.

"Did you two ever hang out together?"

"No. We did the usual small talk like women do. Mostly about our children. Nothing more. I always received advance notice when Marissa was launching a new book. Emily was so good with that."

Santorelli's voice drifted off. They sat in silence. Santorelli straightened up and smiled at Tony. The light blue eyes radiated joy. She tossed her hair forward.

"Okay, Lieutenant, time's up. Let's find something yummy to eat. The Riviera Restaurant is an excellent choice because …"

"Elsa, I'm not in the mood right now for social bantering."

"Oh, come on! It's the holidays. Everyone needs time off."

"I'm in the middle of something. Find your way out of my office, please. If I feel like eating, I know how to order food."

They stared at each other. Tony's green eyes were piercing in their intensity. She realized he was serious. She got up and walked out. Tony placed an order for pickup at the Deli, locked his office, and used the backstairs to the lobby.

The holidays were in full swing, but Tony scarcely noticed. He missed Marissa more than he thought possible. He spent every weekend alone. He tried calling her, but she had turned off her phone. He drove by her parents' home and the house was lit with bright lights and the Christmas tree decorated in the living room window. He drove by her home one week after Christmas to see it shrouded in darkness. He received an early holiday card postmarked from a ski resort and realized her family had gone skiing. He thought of calling lodges to find them, and remembered they owned a cabin. He could not recall where it was because he was always working, and Marissa would go without him. That memory was painful. How had he neglected her for so long, and she had not left before now?

Chapter 39

It had been a long day and a longer evening. Tony was ready to head home. He had managed to get through the annual holiday office party listening to all the jokes, smiling at the new baby pictures, and laughing at the shenanigans. He was standing by himself when the Captain appeared and threw an arm around his shoulders. He signaled to someone to turn the music down.

"Make the announcement now, Tony. I'm ready to get this party started right!"

"Our Captain has put in a promotion request which has been approved. Let's congratulate Sergeant Luis Trevino."

A happy melee occurred which took Tony out of the doldrums. Murray gave Trevino a large bottle of imported whiskey which brought cheers and jeers from the assembled cops in the room. O'Neill and Tony congratulated the detective with a box of Cuban cigars. Di Giovanni and Gerard gave him a classic black tie which made Trevino howl with laughter. The women gave him hugs and kisses which made him blush. The team took the new sergeant out for a celebratory dinner at the Policeman's Pub. The captain, energized, told jokes as he sat in the passenger seat of Tony's car with Benson and Perez in the backseats.

Unlike most bars, the Policeman's Pub was well-known for its robust and hearty meals served in the private room reserved for special occasions. It drew clientele as hungry as they were thirsty. Everyone ordered steaks and tried to outdo each other with cop humor.

Tony was grinning at a slightly racy joke told by O'Neill when a dark-haired brunette caught his attention. Instantly, he thought of Marissa, and how much he missed her.

Tony exited the men's room and almost fell into Santorelli standing outside the door.

"This is the men's room." he said as he tried to step around her.

"I know."

"What's the matter? Women's room crowded?"

She giggled as she leaned into him. The dress was black, low cut and snugly hugged her curves. He could smell the exotic scent of the perfume wafting off her skin.

"You're so silly. I was waiting for you."

Tony moved back. Images of Marissa flooded his vision, and a desperate longing filled his body. He breathed out.

"I'm heading out, Elsa."

"So, Marissa's home? Good for her. I heard the happy news."

Tony was half listening as he scanned the slightly darkened room. "Thank you. Now if you'll excuse me..."

"Let's drink to your new...your good fortune."

"I don't drink, Elsa."

"What were you doing with your team tonight? I watched you. You were drinking with them."

"I was drinking ginger ale which was the drink of choice around the table. You should have asked the servers instead of assuming."

"You have the most beautiful eyes I've ever seen. Your body is nice too. I love it when I look up..."

"Move out of my way, Elsa."

"Don't be mean, Tony. I'm a little lightheaded. You see, I *was* drinking. Scotch and water all night long."

She laughed a little and staggered forward. Tony held her by the shoulders to keep her from lying on him. He was aware there was nothing but a dark alcove behind him. He could feel her weight lean into him.

"You're not drunk, Elsa. Cut it out! Let me call Chris to come get you."

"You can bring me home, Tony."

"I'm going home to my wife, Elsa."

"YOU STILL HERE?"

Trevino's shout at the back of her head caused Santorelli to shudder and blink rapidly several times. Tony worked hard to keep from laughing. He took the opportunity to push Santarelli hard onto Trevino who grabbed her shoulders from the back. Trevino winked at him as Santorelli strained to twist from his grip. Tony moved quickly around them. He snaked his way through the crowd, grabbed his coat off the rack, and practically ran to his vehicle parked at the corner.

In the driveway of his house, Tony sent a message to Marissa's phone. It bounced back. Her phone was still turned off. He was devastated. He sat in his den watching the new year arrive on television.

February came in and found him unaware of the lover's holiday that brightened the month. One evening he found himself driving past Marissa's parents' home. The holiday ornaments had been removed, but now the house and surrounding landscape was cloaked in decorative lighting. All loomed larger than life against the dark sky. He parked across the street and struggled with his emotions. He looked across at the house. He wanted to see her. He needed to see her. He loved the look of her. No matter how hard or long he worked, she was always at the forefront of his heart. He loved her so much, and these last weeks had been unbearable. He sat there and slowly tears rolled down his face. He wiped them away hurriedly. When he saw dawn break, he turned on his ignition, and silently eased down the street with his headlights off.

Chapter 40

The squad room was empty. The housekeeping crew had finished on the floor. The lights were dimmed. Tony was in his office trying to concentrate on reading a file. He closed the folder. He picked up the paperback di Giovanni had loaned him.

A short time later, Murray stuck his head in the door as Tony watched a video on serial killers.

"What the hell are you doing here this time of night?" he bellowed.

"Just catching up on videos. Did you know one strong attribute about serial killers is they stalk their victims to learn their habits? It's not always random acts. Where are you going?"

"Home for a quick.... Wait a minute! It's almost four in the morning, why aren't you home?"

"I was just about to call it a night when I noticed..."

"Never mind that. Go home." Murray almost closed the door before re-opening it. "Aren't you on vacation?"

"I was hoping you'd forgotten."

Murray looked over at him with his stern look. The blue eyes squint daggers across the room.

"Say hello to Marissa for me. And enjoy your time off. You need a break."

"I'm good. We've got too much to do here."

"Go on vacation or I fire you, *and* for a lot longer than your vacation would be!"

Murray slammed the door so hard a plaque fell from the wall.

Tony took the long way home. He missed Marissa. He tried talking to her on the phone, but she was either out or asleep. Since their marriage they had never lived apart, and these months without her left him empty and drained inside. He understood he hurt her deeply, but when would she forgive him? He was tired of living in an empty house. He drove up the driveway and parked. He turned off the ignition, closed his eyes, and leaned back against the headrest. He could not tell anyone she had left him. He was so lonely and lost without her. What would he do with a vacation by himself?

He walked into the house through the side patio door bypassing the garage. He hated the empty space where her car used to sit. The first thing that hit him was the bright lighting in the kitchen. The aroma of home cooked food assailed his senses. He saw the pots on the stove and the oven light on. The downstairs was immaculate which meant Maria had been called for the housekeeping. He ran upstairs and stood in the doorway watching her. She had not heard him and was busy folding clothes. She was wearing one of his white shirts. It made her look plump. Her face was rounder, and her hair was thick and wild about her shoulders cascading down her back. It was longer and thicker than he remembered. He looked at her legs. They were fuller. He stepped closer. He could not stop gazing at her. He walked into the room and shrugged out of his coat.

She looked up and gave him a half smile. "Tony, we need to talk."

He unfastened his holster. "I've missed you more than I thought possible. I'm more than sorry. You are my life, my dream, my heart, and my soul. If I need to spend the rest of my life making it up to you, I will. Just please, come back to me. Life has no meaning without you."

"Tony, I have something to tell you that you might not like."

She did not look at him, and still folded clothes. He felt weak. He slumped down on the edge of the bed.

"What? You've filed for divorce already? Is that why you're folding clothes? You're leaving me?"

He could hardly breathe, let alone speak. Marissa looked at him. In the next instant, she threw her head back and let loose with a robust laugh.

"You wish! No silly. I am as of this morning exactly four months pregnant."

"Marissa! Why didn't you tell me?"

She sat down on the edge of the bed beside him. "I didn't know until a week ago when I kept vomiting all over the place. I was so sad about everything that's been happening I didn't pay any attention to what was happening in my body."

Tony slid off the bed and kneeled before her wrapping his arms around her. He could now feel the slight roundness of her stomach.

"Baby..."

"The doctor says we're going to be okay this time. This baby is a lot stronger than the others. Are you okay?"

"I love you so much."

"I love you too. The captain told me you're on vacation starting today."

"What?" He looked up at her, "How did ...?"

Marissa giggled. "He's called me at least twice a week to check up on me. He was concerned I was leaving you, too. He took me to lunch last week and the nail shop." She showed him her nails. "He's loads of fun."

"I'll bet he is. When did you come home?"

"The captain called me after Emily's funeral and told me how pitiful you were. But I had to wait for the doctor's okay to travel. After Emily's death, he and dad recommended that I come home. Fred has been an amazing friend. He came around the day before yesterday to take me to my doctor's appointment. This morning, he came by with my dad and helped me get settled in. Then he took me to the supermarket and helped me cook and clean up. I called Maria, and she came over and deep cleaned."

She stopped talking and looked down at him. They laced their fingers together.

"Tony, you're going to be a father soon. That's why I'm here. But things will have to change between us for me to stay."

Tony listened to her studying her face. In the back of his mind, he thought about the captain's empty office the last few days. He smiled looking up at his wife.

"Anything for you. I never want you to leave me again."

"And I don't want to leave you. We've had fights in our marriage Tony, but you've never called me names."

"That was inexcusable on my part, and I'm sorry. But please, don't leave. Let's talk our way through misunderstandings. We love each other and neither one of us is perfect. We must learn to forgive each other, not run away."

She put her arms around his neck. "That's what my dad said too. I'm sorry for leaving you. But now, I'm back and home to stay."

"What do you want to do on our vacation, pretty lady?"

"First things first?"

"Of course!"

"Let's eat. I'm starving!"

"So am I."

He sat on the bed beside her and wrapped his arms around her.

Tony and Marissa decided to spend their reunion somewhere special. They spent the first week at their favorite beach resort on a little tropical island. On the first morning of their vacation, Tony sat up in bed squinting against the bright sunlight. He looked for the bedside clock.

"Good morning my love," said Marissa brightly. She was drinking coffee and wearing a long pink and orange floral robe.

"Good morning. Um...is coffee good for the baby?"

"Yes! She will grow up strong and feisty like her mother."

Tony laughed. "What's for breakfast? Or have you eaten already?"

"No, we've managed to wait for you. Tony? Are you sure you're happy about the baby?"

"Are you kidding? I didn't think we'd ever pull it off."

"I love you, Tony."

"Same here baby. How about a funnel cake?"

"Oh, boy!"

Their vacation time was peaceful with the days spent on the beach or in the water, and the nights laying out on the sand. When they returned home, they set about planning the design of the nursery. The time passed quickly but not once did Tony think about the police station, or murder.

O'Neill hung up the phone and gathered the detectives in the squad room for a quick meeting.

"I know it's late and the beginning of the weekend, so I'll be brief. Tony and Marissa are expecting."

A collective cheer erupted from the group. O'Neill raised his hands, smiling despite himself.

"Yeah, it's great news. But as we all know they've had a history of ...of...they've had a tough time. Tony doesn't want Marissa upset. He'll be in the office next week. She'll be out of the danger zone then."

Johnston said, "I'm guessing Marissa knew the last victim."

"We knew them all," said Benson to the room. "I went to college with those ladies too."

"Jeez, Vee," said Sloan. "Did you know any of them personally?"

"No. I just attended school with them." Benson stood up and pulled her jacket on. "Time to hit happy hour at the Policeman's Pub."

"Wait for me, Vee," said Sloan. "I have some juicy cop gossip I know you haven't heard!"

Benson laughed. "The first round is on me, then."

"Wait a minute," said Perez, retrieving her jacket. "I need to hear this, too. Are you coming with us, Kevin?"

"Not tonight," said Gerard, pulling on his jacket. "Going to a game. Hold the elevator, please."

Trevino hung up his phone. "Night."

"Right behind you," said di Giovanni, pulling on his coat.

"Hold up!" O'Neill held the elevator door open for the captain.

Tony's return to the precinct was greeted with good cheer. He stepped off the elevator to shouts of "He's back," "It's about time," and "The place fell apart without you!" To the last admission Tony laughed gaily. Perez greeted him with a colorful gift bag.

"Congratulations, soon-to-be Dad!" she said.

"You'd better be ready to get back to work after taking half the year off," said Murray to great laughter.

He gave Tony a brown gift bag, patted him on the back, and headed to his office. Johnston gave him a white shopping bag with a card attached from all the detectives.

"Here's to many little Marigny's!"

Stan handed him a large gift bag. "My wife is thrilled and wants dibs on being a godmother."

"Thank you! Thank you!" said Tony. "You'll receive Marissa's thank-you cards in the mail."

Much later in the day, the team was alerted to a brief staff meeting with Captain Murray. While Tony was on vacation, Murray had been called to Washington, D.C. to attend a special joint law enforcement conference. His appearance at the staff meeting was met with curiosity. The detectives sat at their desks with coffee cups and tablets. The mikes were set up around the captain to catch every word.

"Good evening," said Murray. His blue eyes scanned the room, smiling as he did so. "I won't be before you long. I want to give you an update on how Washington thinks we ought to manage these murders. Pay close attention, take notes if you want, and then do as the lieutenant instructs. We catch criminals on the ground not from behind desks!"

There was general laughter around the room. The captain smiled again before he continued. "Let me go over these guidelines, answer any questions you may have, and get out of your way."

Murray finished his presentation and responded to questions. After twenty minutes the session was over.

Tony walked across the squad room to the open door. Murray looked up as he entered.

"I'm going home. If you need anything, Rob's here."

"Fred, I wanted to thank you for taking care of Marissa."

Murray held up his hand. "Stop. Please. I wish someone had helped me with any one of my marriages. But hey, you live and learn." he shook his head slightly as if to get rid of unwanted memories. "Your wife is expecting your child. The child you two have always wanted. Family is everything. Don't neglect them riding the wave of popularity and media attention. Believe me, it's not worth it in the end. Learn to take time off between these cases. Murder and mayhem will always be here."

Murray grabbed his jacket and briefcase and smiled at Tony. "Lock up for me, please. I've got a hot date. I need to get to the barber NOW!"

Tony smiled and shook his head. Where Murray found the energy was beyond him.

Chapter 41

Kristen O'Leary was busy matching the numbers on one page with the numbers on another page. Her assistant entered her office and stood in front of her desk. Kristen could not stand hovering. She looked under eye at her.

"What do you want, Pat?"

"I wanted to say good night. Don't stay in here too late. You have your first meeting at seven-thirty in the morning. You need to get some sleep."

She smiled. "I know Pat, I know. I'll leave in twenty minutes."

"I'm calling back here."

"Good night, Pat."

"Good night, Kristen and go home!"

Kristen smiled. She loved her career at Stonehedge Martine Accountants. She was a mathematician at her heart. She glanced at the clock. She did have to get home though. Thank goodness for live-in nannies. She would be a wreck without Hilda. One more page to go.

Sometime later Kristen rose from her hunched position over the ledgers and looked across her desk at the clock on the wall. It was three thirty in the morning. Wow! Time to get out of here. She put on some lipstick, threw her overcoat over her arm, and picked up her purse. She locked the door to her office and stepped on the elevator. It took her to the parking garage on the roof.

The lot was flooded with light from illumination supplied by neighboring buildings. She reached her car, tossed her items in, and caught a moving figure out of her peripheral vision. She turned and gave blow for blow until she realized she was at a disadvantage. She was wearing heels and a snug-fitting dress. A vision of her three children flooded her mind, and she lowered her head, and continued the fight.

He was taller and stronger. He also owned a vast array of fighting techniques. She was trying not to panic. He was pushing her backwards with each assault. The heel on one of her pumps broke, and she staggered enough for him to deliver a swift blow to her temple that nearly knocked her out. She fell backwards, but sprang to her feet groggy, and decided to subdue this stranger.

She barely felt the blows to her shoulders as she countered a jab to her rib cage. She received another hit to her temple that staggered her. This time he moved in swiftly, grabbed the front of her dress, and tossed her effortlessly over the roof railing.

The police officer on security detail made his rounds at three forty-five in the morning. He noticed the lone car in the garage lot with the open door. He took out his weapon and carefully scouted the premises. He looked over the railing and saw the crumbled body lying below. He sent for back-up.

Johnston and Gerard were escorted to the spot where the twisted form of the woman laid. They silently examined the scene.

Finally, Johnston said, "She has red bruises on both sides of both hands. Her neck is bruised, and the left side of her face."

"Looks like she was in a helluva fight," Gerard said as he typed. "Any broken nails?"

"All of them."

Johnston collected forensic evidence from the woman's broken nails. She put the little bags in her jacket pocket.

"Come on," she said to Gerard. "Her car is parked on the roof."

They took the elevator to the parking garage. The expensive black sports car sat alone with the car door on the driver's side still open.

Gerard whistled as he looked inside. "This car is clean. The victim's purse and briefcase are on the passenger seat. I don't see the keys though."

He tossed the purse to Johnston. She looked inside. "Her driver's license says she's Kristen O'Leary, thirty-six years of age. She lives in Oxford Circle. I remember this name..."

They walked around the car looking for her car keys. Gerard found a black button on the ground and bagged it for Johnston. They continued searching until a police officer brought them a plastic bag with car keys inside. They returned to the crime scene. LeClerc had arrived and was examining the body.

"Hey guys. Looks like the impact of the fall broke her neck and collar bone. She was obviously in a physical altercation, but I won't know the full extent until I get her on the table," he said.

"How long has she been deceased?"

"I'd say about one to two hours."

"Thanks, Mike."

The detectives nodded as the morgue workers arrived to take away the victim. Gerard put in a call.

"Get a forensics team to Stonehedge Martine Accountants. There's been a homicide on the roof of the parking garage. Yes. Right. Thanks."

Johnston looked at Gerard. "Where are you going? We need to speak to the security detail."

"No need. He was pretty shaken up. They're sending relief for him. He also wrote out a statement the best he could. He didn't see anything." Gerard pressed the button for the elevator. "We need to check out the victim's office."

"How do you know what floor she's on?"

"It's on the badge pinned to her collarbone."

Johnston said nothing. Gerard was more observant than she realized sometimes. She wondered how much he knew of her personal life.

Johnson and Gerard walked into Kristen's office. It was a large, sterile environment. One wall was lined with ledgers stacked in floor-to-ceiling bookcases. The other wall held four large abstract paintings. The last wall was floor length glass-windowpanes that looked out onto the world far below. The square l-shaped desk was in front of the window. To the right of the desk was a white tree decorated with fairy lighting. The lights from the tree illuminated the room.

On top of the desk was a closed tablet and a world globe. The drawers were locked. As they were turning to leave, they spied a small table and chair off to the side with a tall lamp beside it. On the table was a photograph of twenty women in white. Alongside it was a framed photo of Kristen and her family, and next to it a smaller picture of the victim sitting on a bench looking directly at the camera. The honey tan skin, striking sea blue eyes offset by a thick head of black wavy hair was breathtaking. Gerard took photos of the pictures.

A police officer appeared in the door. "The assistant is here."

"Thanks," said Johnston. To Gerard she said, "you do the interview. I'll speak when necessary."

"I thought he was going to say her husband is waiting," said Gerard.

They rode the elevator to the lobby area in silence.

The assistant was as put-together as her late boss. A dark eyed, dark-haired brunette, she was dressed in a black knit suit with a muted print scarf draped about her shoulders. She looked visibly upset as she gazed with sad eyes at the body bag as it passed by. She watched as the morgue workers move it into their truck. The man standing with her was her height with heavy gray hair. The woman looked up as they approached.

"We're Detectives Gerard and Johnston. May I have your name?" asked Gerard.

"Patricia Brownstein. This is my husband," said the woman, sniffling through sad tears. Up close, the detectives noted the assistant's dark hair was streaked heavily with gray strands. "Kristen called me Pat, except when she was irritated with me for making her go home sometimes. She was such a workaholic."

"You're her secretary?"

"I'm her personal assistant."

"How long were you working for her?"

"She's been my boss for the last fifteen years. Honestly? I have a business degree, and I could have gone anywhere to work."

"Why did you stay here as her personal assistant?"

"Because of her, Detective! She taught me the financial side of business in corporate America. She was excellent at what she did. She fought for me with pay raises, titles, promotions and much more. She was truly my hero." Tears welled up in her eyes and her husband wrapped her in his arms speaking low in her ear. She managed to gain control of her emotions. "I'm sorry, Detective. This is such a shock."

253

Gerard nodded. "I understand. You've been together a long time."

"Yes, we were college interns here together. I was going to move on after graduation, but she made me an offer I couldn't refuse."

The assistant's laughter turned into tears. Her husband held her again.

Gerard said, "What was the victim's position at this firm?"

"This is an accounting firm. She's the vice president in the finance department."

"Ms. Brownstein, was the victim involved in any kind of interoffice conflict?"

"Kristen? No. She's a ... she was a certified public accountant."

"What about her marriage?"

"No scandals. They're a happy couple, Detectives. He's an accountant too. He's a vice president for Solomon, Stewart, and Stein."

"Did she mention in the past few days or weeks anyone problematic entering her life?"

"Like whom?"

"Someone from college? High school?"

"No."

"When was the last time you saw your boss?"

"Earlier tonight. I was here until a little after midnight."

"Was it normal for her to work that late?"

"Not just her," came the reply. "Last year when we were conducting a major audit, I don't think anyone went home for several days."

"Staying well past midnight was a normal occurrence?"

"For Kristen? Yes."

"What's security like here?"

"I don't know. You'd have to check with Peg in human resources."

"Peg?"

"I'm sorry. Margaret Atwell. She's our human resources director."

Answering their questions appeared to bring a quiet composure to her. She smiled sadly at them with a wearied expression. Johnston beckoned to Gerard and stepped in front of him.

"Ms. Brownstein, please accept our deepest condolences. We're sorry to have had to call you down here for such grisly news."

"Do you know where her husband is?" asked Gerard.

The woman turned around with surprised eyes. "Oh my God! David, her husband, David! He took the kids on a week's vacation to visit his parents in Oklahoma because they were taking them to Canada for spring break. She spoke to him this morning... I mean, yesterday morning. Kristen has an early meeting scheduled for seven thirty this morning. After the meeting, she was catching the first flight out to Oklahoma. If you're finished with your questions, I've got a slew of calls to get through."

Gerard said, "Ms. Brownstein, we need a number where we can reach Mr. O'Leary. Would you have that?"

"Oh, yes, of course." She handed them a business card. "That's David's information. The information for his family in Oklahoma is on the back of the card."

Johnston nodded. "Thank you, Ms. Brownstein, for your cooperation. If you remember anything, please call us. Here's my card. Again, condolences on the loss of your friend and boss."

The assistant looked at Johnston with a face of sorrow, and fighting back tears walked away with her husband, arm in arm. Johnston and Gerard stood there a moment staring after them.

The detectives were still on the sidewalk when a petite blonde in four-inch black heels walked up to a police officer and showed him identification. He turned and pointed at them. He moved the police barricade for her to pass through.

"You take this one," whispered Gerard and moved slightly to the side.

The woman was medium in height and so thin she looked gaunt. The shoulder-length blonde hair was professionally styled and rested full and thick on her shoulders. The deep pea green outfit was expensively tailored and reached mid-calf. The tan calf-leather boots bore a low heel. She carried a tan handbag and matching briefcase.

"You're the detectives?" She walked up to them and gave each a no-nonsense full-body scan. In a voice use to giving commands she asked, "What's happened here?"

"Who are you?" asked Johnston.

"Margaret Atwell. I'm the human resource director. Who are you two?"

"Detectives Johnston and Gerard from Winding Falls Major Crimes. What do you know of why you're down here?"

"Someone called and said Kristen had been hurt."

Gerard cut in. "Excuse me, let's try to respond appropriately. Who called you? What did they say, and who is Kristen?"

The woman blushed to the roots of her hairline. "I received a phone call from Pat Brownstein who is Kristen O'Leary's assistant. She told me something had happened to Kristen, but she didn't say what."

Johnston said, "Ms. O'Leary was fatally attacked earlier tonight. That's why we're here."

"She was attacked. By whom? The security is tight here." She looked from one to the other. "You said your major crimes? What does that mean?"

"We're homicide detectives. When a homicide is committed, they call us. Ms. O'Leary's body was found by the security officer on-duty."

"Her body was found?" her voice came to them faintly. "Who was the officer?"

"Ed Flynn. Do you know him?"

"Yes. Ed is an actual police officer. Stonehedge Martine Accountants hired him straight out of the Police Academy. He's been here almost twenty years."

"How is it you know this officer's resume by heart?"

"I hired him. He graduated from the same class as my brother except my brother died in a traffic accident soon after. Careless driver speeding..."

Johnston smiled. "What else Ms. Atwell?"

Atwell smiled and turned her head. "He's my husband's protege. Sam Greenlee is my husband and the director of security here. He called me to tell me about Ed. He's downstairs now."

"What can you tell us about the victim?"

"Beautiful lady in looks and personality. Everyone liked her."

"Not everyone," said Gerard, "or she wouldn't be dead."

Atwell blinked rapidly and swallowed.

On the second floor the detectives stepped off the elevator onto a glass-enclosed foyer. The room was large with computer terminals on one side of a long wall. A man in full uniform walked towards them. He stopped by a wall and pressed a button. The glass partition parted, and they entered. He greeted them with a smile and an extended hand.

"Good evening or good morning. I'm not sure what time it is. I'm Lieutenant Greenlee."

"Detectives Gerard and Johnston. Tell me, how many people are in this department?" asked Gerard.

"We have a full staff of seven who work on rotation during the weekdays. The weekends its usually Sergeant Ed Flynn."

"Are you aware of who works late consistently in this building?"

"Of course. Ms. O'Leary is a vice president, and she's always worked late for as long as I've known her."

"Anyone else?"

"Not on this floor. Ms. O'Leary was our sole workaholic."

"Did she work holidays as well?"

He smiled. "No, and she took vacation breaks. She usually took two weeks in the summer and a week in the winter."

"Have you ever had a complaint or concern about her safety or another woman's safety in this building?" asked Gerard.

"No. We've never had a break-in, bomb threat, triggered alarm, threatening phone calls, or worker unrest."

"Are any of those terminals operating?"

"No."

"Why not?"

"We've never had reason to have them on."

"There was a murder tonight that took place in this building," Gerard said. "The victim fought for her life. Perhaps if these monitors had been on, someone might've been able to help her, or at least, save her life."

For the first time in their interactions the lieutenant stopped smiling. He subconsciously rolled his shoulders and stared at them. The silence that followed his remark seemed to envelop the room.

Chapter 42

Johnston and Gerard split their tasks and by noon, Johnston was in the Crime Lab bent over a microscope. She was slightly startled by a light shoulder tap. It was the morgue supervisor, Abdul Al-Hasan. He stood with an armful of files. He smiled as he shuffled the bundle.

"Detective? Doctor LeClerc would like to see you, please."

"Thanks, Brother Abdul."

"Do you need any other files, Detective?"

"Oh, no. This is just what I was looking for. Thanks."

"Then, please, follow me."

Twenty minutes later, Johnston found LeClerc in Santorelli's office seated behind her desk. He looked up with a smile when she entered.

"Hi, Mike," said Johnston.

"Hi, Jeanette. Come in and take a seat, please. Thanks, Brother Abdul."

LeClerc waited until the door closed to speak. He looked at the opened file on his desk.

"I sent the completed file by courier to Lieutenant Marigny. He asked me to inform you personally of my findings. Detective Gerard will be here in about twenty minutes. He's being briefed by the Lieutenant, so let's get down to business."

Johnston watched LeClerc with a slight frown. He spoke calmly, but she read the dark panic in his eyes and watched his heart pump hard through his shirt and white jacket. He cleared his throat.

"The victim is Kristen O'Leary, a thirty-seven-year-old female. Her height is five feet ten and one-half inches and body weight is one hundred-ninety pounds of muscle. First, let me make it clear this victim was in excellent physical condition. Ms. O'Leary suffered bodily trauma indicative of a serious physical altercation. Meaning she was bruised and battered like she'd been in a street fight. The fall from the roof was not accidental slipping. The angle at which she fell suggests she was thrown. Her neck and shoulders were broken prior to the fall. From the angle of the bruises, we deduced the killer is at least six feet three inches in height, and two hundred plus pounds."

"Hmm... a martial arts expert?" asked Johnston.

LeClerc looked directly at her. "A skilled killer. He hit pressure points on her body designed to weaken her. His intention wasn't to maim, but to kill. I've seen this pattern in nearly all the victims of this madman."

Johnston left the forensics lab with Gerard, visibly shaken. She could not breathe.

In the elevator she asked her partner, "Where are we headed?"

"Tony wants us to interview the husband. His plane landed a few hours ago. He was in to identify his wife this morning. He's expecting us."

They were quiet on the way to the residence.

The O'Leary home was in the middle of a cul-de-sac in Oxford Circle. The stucco facade on the two-story home boasted gabled roof lines with a classic look. The front door was opened by a well-dressed, attractive young woman with two small children clinging to each of her legs.

"Good morning, may I help you?"

They showed her their badges. Johnston said, "We're here to speak with David O'Leary. Who are you?"

"Hilda Osborn. I'm the nanny. I'm sorry but Mr. O'Leary isn't here."

"Where is he?"

"Tending to his wife's.... tending to personal matters. I must take the children to their grandparents. Our car has just arrived. Shall I leave a message for Mr. O'Leary?"

Gerard frowned. Johnston smiled. "That won't be necessary. Which set of grandparents are you visiting?"

"We're taking a return flight to Oklahoma. Now, if you'll excuse us."

"Excuse me," said Gerard as he stepped in front of the woman and children. "Why aren't you taking them to their grandparents here in Winding Falls?"

"I'm following the instructions given me by Mr. O'Leary."

She walked around Gerard with the children. They watched the private car until it drove out of sight.

Tony looked up at the light tap on his office door. Gerard and Johnston entered with their tablets in hand. Gerard sat down and opened his tablet. After a slight hesitation, Johnston followed suit. Tony closed an open file on his computer and turned to his detectives.

"I have a question," said Tony. "Where's the witness statement from the cop on duty?"

"The witness statement from the cop on duty would've been empty paperwork as he saw and heard nothing," said Gerard. "The building doesn't have a surveillance system, but they do have hired security detail. In fact, the cop on duty is Officer Ed Flynn, thirty-nine years old, and a graduate of the Police Academy. He has been with this corporation for the last twenty years and works solely for them."

"Does he have scheduled rounds?"

"Yes. He provided me with this sheet." Gerard passed a sheet across Tony's desk. "He also supervises seven other officers. Their names, addresses, and security clearances are in this folder."

"Security clearances?"

"This is the richest accounting firm in this region. Most of the executives and staff are bonded."

Tony stared at Gerard. "Was the victim?"

"Yes."

"Tell me about this guard. Did he know the victim?"

"Officer Flynn knew of the victim; meaning he knew who she was. He described her as a non-problematic workaholic."

"So he was used to seeing her late in her office?"

"Yes."

"So when Flynn discovered the victim, she was already deceased?"

"Yes. The medical examiner said the time as between one and two hours."

"Who knew she would be working late?"

Johnston found her voice. "According to her personal assistant, Pat Brownstein, the deceased was always one of the last people in the building. She also described her as a workaholic. This night was like any other. We also spoke to Sam Greenlee who's the director of security operations. He also described her as a workaholic."

"I took a page out of Luis' book and examined the woman's personal life away from the office," said Gerard. Johnston side-eyed him and watched Tony. "O'Leary was orphaned at age twelve when her parents private jet malfunctioned. She's a millionaire twice over and together with her husband own a sizable fortune. We're waiting on a copy of the Will."

"You've been busy," said Johnston.

Gerard seemed not to hear her. "Here's the part I want to emphasize. O'Leary was a trained martial artist, and before the birth of her two children, was a four-time state and two-time national martial arts champion. She held Black belts in karate and judo before quitting to take on motherhood. She knew how to fight, and the killer spared no punches."

In a lowered tone Johnston said, "what Kevin means is the victim fought for her life because she knew how. But she suffered significant traumatic injuries to her body. Her neck and both shoulders were broken prior to the fall from the rooftop."

"I went to the morgue," Gerard continued with a voice full of emotion. "What we had not seen due to how her body was positioned on the ground was her right cheekbone had been smashed and her nose broken in three places. The rest of her body from the neck down was swollen with most of the lumps turning purple or black. She had a collapsed lung, yet she fought to the bitter end because she had something to live for... her two kids who are now motherless. That lady fought for her life."

Gerard stood up and walked out of the room. Johnston lowered her head. In a subdued voice, Trevino spoke from the door where he stood.

"This killer means to inflict pain and suffering on his victims... to the death."

"Or his desire to kill is stronger than we've initially processed," di Giovanni said as he entered and leaned on the file cabinet.

"Are you coming from the angle of blood lust?" Tony asked him.

"Yes and no," replied di Giovanni. "We know based on science that the sight and smell of blood can have a sexually stimulating effect on some individuals. However, I don't believe our killer is driven by blood lust. Seems he's on a revenge type path. Which presupposes these women caused his desire for vengeance."

"Mike's report echoes your statement," replied Tony. "This is a skilled killer. He's either targeted these women for some past grievance, or they're crimes of opportunity."

Johnston looked up at Tony. "Don't be hard on Kevin. He lost both his parents in similar fashion."

"Not really," Trevino said, "This lady was an accountant. Kevin's parents were trained undercover operatives in Haiti trying to weed out the corruption. Good luck with that."

Di Giovanni caught Trevino's attention as Gerard entered the room with his tablet and sat down. Tony glanced at him.

"I understand the great strain these homicides are placing on all of you, but we've got to control our emotions to find this killer. Right now, we're holding straws because we don't know his identity."

Gerard said, "We know something about him. We know he's targeting professional women, and we know all these women knew each other."

"Of course they knew each other. They all graduated from the same university."

"Well, that is one common factor among these women and might be important as we move forward in this investigation," said Tony.

"May I continue?" asked Gerard. "All the women affected by this madman have been tall and in excellent physical shape. So much so, I looked into their college backgrounds and discovered they were college athletes."

"I don't believe them being college athletes has anything to do with ...," Tony stopped speaking and shook his head. "I don't know, Kevin. That seems like a long stretch. Twenty years later someone is picking off college athletes. What's the motive?"

"Money?" She was an orphan who inherited lots of money. Married money and they're making even more money," said Gerard.

"No." Johnston shook her head. "The only people benefiting from these folks money are their families and maybe some foundation. I think we could look into another disgruntled player?"

Trevino smiled. "I think we're all tired now. Have a good night, all."

Di Giovanni smiled and followed Trevino. Tony looked at Gerard and Johnston. Gerard walked out first. Johnston closed his door on her way out.

Tony had been up for a few hours watching the weather reports on television in his den. He walked into the living room. Marissa was seated on the sofa with a forlorn look on her face. Tony had not wanted Marissa to attend this funeral as she was still in the early weeks of the pregnancy. But she insisted. Tony sat beside her.

"I know I'm going to hate seeing her... that way."

"Then stay home. You don't have to attend this funeral. It's damp, rainy and cold. It's going to be a graveside service, so you'll need to bundle up and wear your boots."

"Stop talking to me as if I'm a child, Tony." She walked to the fireplace and looked at the mantel adorned with a blend of pinecones, branches, and candles. She looked back at him. "There is no question I'm attending this funeral. Kristen didn't deserve this any more than my other friends. We've been together since college. I won't abandon her now."

Tony held his temper in check. The doorbell rang and his parents followed by his in-laws entered the living room. The resultant greetings and hugs eased the tensions between them. Mark went with his son to City Hall for a meeting with officials while Maurice went with the women to the funeral service.

Marissa wrote her seventh novel in honor of the birth of Bridget, the oldest daughter of Kristen and David O'Leary. Sallie Anne and Beth each held an umbrella over her while she stood at the grave. Marissa cried reading the passage dedicated to *Kristen Walsh O'Leary, "a steady influence despite the pain."*

The repast at the O'Leary residence followed shortly after the service. Tony arrived a half-hour later. He sat on an ornate bench by the front hall where he could see into the great room where everyone was gathered. He watched as Benson stopped to chat with Marissa. It was brief because Patricia grabbed Marissa by the hand and took her to a table where other women were seated. He noted Benson's expressionless face as she weaved through the gathering and disappeared.

Tony slowly walked to a window overlooking the driveway. He watched Benson exit the house and head toward the parked cars. He returned to the hall and walked over to Marissa seated between Sallie Anne and another woman. The women around them jumped up and each one playfully pushed the other to get in line to hug him.

"Congratulations, Poppa Bear," said Patricia. "Eric and I are planning a welcome to the world baby party soon and, you two will be our guests of honor!"

"Move Patricia, let me at him!" said Sallie Anne, swooping in for a hug.

Sallie Anne's husband leaned around his wife to shake Tony's hand vigorously.

"Congratulations, old man! It's about time."

Beth kissed his cheek, and her husband hugged him with all smiles. The women were now hugging him two at a time, and Tony could not help but laugh as they swarmed him. The men manage to ease Tony away from the women to ask him about the police investigation into the murders. Tony had to ease their fears diplomatically but truthfully.

Tony brought his wife home and changed his clothes. Marissa happily talked about the upcoming parties they were to be the guests of honor at. He walked into the bedroom from the closet.

"How are you feeling?" he asked her.

She had changed into a powder blue silk caftan. She pulled her hair into a low ponytail and turned to face him.

"I feel great. I'm not hungry, but if you are, we can..."

"No. I'm fine. It's still misty outside. You're not going for a run later, are you?"

Marissa laughed. "No, silly. Whatever exercise I do can be done here. I was going to watch a movie. Are you going out?"

"No. Why?"

"Could you go to the store for me?"

"What's the craving this time?"

She smiled. "I wanted some vanilla ice cream to go with the chocolate chip coconut cookies I'm about to bake."

"What a wild woman you are!" Tony laughed. "Okay, I'll pick up the ice cream, you make the cookies, and we'll watch your movie together."

"Oh, boy!"

Chapter 43

Angela Rojas was glad it was Friday! What a long week it had been. Two months had passed since Kristen's death, but it still seemed surreal to her. And poor Emily, who in their right mind would ever want to harm her. Angela had become so despondent; her family became worried. Her husband made reservations at a beach resort for the upcoming four-day holiday weekend. They had planned it months ago, but in all the sadness, Angela had forgotten about it.

Everyone had been grumpy of late as the previous weekends were eclipsed by thunderstorms and heavy torrential rains. She looked up at the bright sky. She could not be more thankful for the weather as the effects of a frosty winter slowly gave way to sunshine and warm spring temperatures.

She parked in the driveway and collected the mail. She returned to the van and gathered her purse and bag of groceries resting on the passenger seat. Angela knew her family and had stopped at the drug store to replenish the household supply of sunblock and buy a pair of non-prescription sunglasses for eight-year-old Amy and thirteen-year-old Damaris. She also stopped by the supermarket and picked up snack items for the long drive.

For once the girls had not been fighting this morning or last night. They loved going to the beach. She wondered if she should still wear her red bikini or the new one-piece purple one, she had recently bought on a shopping trip with Lynda.

Waving at her neighbors across the street, Angela walked around the side of the house to the door which led into the home through the laundry room. She was the only one in the family who used this entrance. Jesus and the girls preferred the garage which led directly into the kitchen and din-

ing rooms. The moment she stepped into the laundry room she could see one or both of her children had been in the house. Their dirty laundry was spread over the floor instead of being placed in the hamper.

She put her bag of groceries on the kitchen counter, along with the mail and her purse, and walked into the dining room. She sensed rather than heard the presence of someone behind her. The tap on her shoulder sent icicles of fear coursing through her body. She turned to look. She opened her mouth and let out a soundless scream.

The first thought that went through Benson's head when they turned down the street in Delsea Park North was how storybook picturesque the homes looked. She parked the cruiser behind a fire truck as they made their way under the yellow police tape and up the walkway lined with colorful wild-flowers. The porch echoed the walkway with wildflowers placed in wooden baskets flanking the two rocking chairs and low-slung porch swing.

Inside the house were floral-patterned sofas, and over-stuffed chairs, white tables and lamps, and colorful abstract paintings on the walls. She saw a dollhouse in the corner of the living room and smiled. O'Neill pointed out photographs on the fireplace mantel. He noted the same type of fuzzy pictures he had seen in other offices and snapped four to compare.

Officer Brown walked in. "You want the details, James."

"If you don't mind, Ollie."

The officer smirked. "Her name is Angela Rojas, thirty-six years old, married to Jesus Rojas, a computer programmer. They have two children."

"Who found her?"

"The husband. They were planning a weekend and he and the daughters had picked up the grandparents who were going on the trip too."

"Where was she coming from?"

"Work. She's a social worker."

"Is the red van hers?"

"Yes. Here's the registration and insurance."

"Thanks, Ollie. Until next time."

O'Neill joined Benson in the dining room. The dining room blinds were closed. O'Neill opened the double French doors. They led to a patio which led to an in-ground swimming pool. The pool was still covered. He quickly spotted the shed. Everything was neat and orderly. He closed the doors. On the far side of the room, they saw the blood smeared and splattered on the wall. Benson stopped in her tracks. O'Neill knelt close enough to get a good look and then straightened up. He sighed as he walked past Benson out of the house. Benson could not stop staring at the woman on the floor.

Angela Rojas huge curly brown Afro was covered in blood as if poured over her head. Her hazel eyes stared out at the world vacant and cold. Her mouth in a perpetual soundless scream. Benson's eyes traveled further down and saw the huge butcher knife planted at the base of Angela's throat and dropped her head. She closed her eyes to stop herself from tearing up.

"Are you alright, Detective Benson?" She felt a hand on her shoulder.

She looked up into the dark eyes of the new assistant to Santorelli. At five foot eleven inches tall, Benson did not often find men her height let alone taller than she was who were single, and she was certain LeClerc was single.

"Yes, thank you." She gathered herself. "I know this woman. Her name's Angela Rojas."

"Me, too. Angela and I grew up together. Her husband Jesus is outside with your partner. Let me look at her. I'll join you in a minute."

"Thanks."

She left the room and walked into the kitchen. She saw the car keys and Angela's purse on the counter.

O'Neill was standing on the curb watching Jesus Rojas who was seated in a police car with his head in his hands as Benson walked up. She saw their two daughters, Amy, and Damaris, seated with their grandparents. Damaris was the splitting image of her mother.

O'Neill nodded to her, and said, "Mr. Rojas, my name is Sergeant O'Neill, and this is my partner, Detective Benson."

The man looked up at Benson. He got out of the car and hugged her to him. O'Neill taken aback; watched silently.

"Why would someone do something like this? Angie would never hurt anybody. Why, Vee? Why?"

"We're sorry for your loss, Jesus," said Benson.

"Thanks, Vanessa," he stammered. He looked at the house with tears in his eyes. The police and technicians entered and exited the home through the front door and the garage area.

"Mr. Rojas, could you please tell us what you found when you came home this evening?" asked O'Neill.

"I saw Angie's van in the driveway, so I knew she was home. I waved to our neighbors across the street and went inside."

They looked across the street. "The people sitting on the porch?"

"Yes. Stan and Debbie. Thank God the girls were out here with my parents. I wouldn't have wanted them to see their mother like that." He rocked back and forth, closing his eyes to the images in his mind.

"What was your wife's occupation?"

"She was a clinical social worker for a child welfare agency in the city."

"Did she ever mention having any issues with her clients?"

"No. Angie was easygoing."

"What about her coworkers?"

"Again, no. She's been with her staff a long time."

"What's your occupation? Where do you work?"

"I work at Exeter Business Systems. I'm a computer programmer."

"What's your neighbors full names?"

"Stan and Debbie Forrester." He hung his head. "Is that it? I need to go be with my children."

They nodded. He said something to Benson who responded in Spanish which O'Neill did not hear. The widower walked over to his daughters. They ran to their father holding tightly onto him as he joined his parents standing a little way off.

The medical examiner walked towards them.

"Detectives, I wanted to catch you before you left." He peeled off his gloves and put them in an open bag a technician was holding. "The victim was assaulted with the large butcher knife, as you saw. Death was certain but she felt the pain."

"What do you mean?" asked O'Neill.

"The angle of the knife plus its size meant he wanted her to feel the pain, and to know she was dying."

"How long did it take, or would it take?" asked O'Neill.

"Twenty minutes or more. Slow and agonizing," said LeClerc. "We'll talk later."

Benson said to O'Neill. "The neighbors were out."

"What did you say to the husband."

"Condolences from us."

"Thanks. Let's go speak to the neighbors."

The detectives crossed the street to the neighbors seated in lawn chairs on their front porch. They sat up expectantly when the detectives approached. They were barefoot and dressed in shorts and tank tops. The husband had shoulder-length, wavy hair and the wife's hair was piled on top of her head in a messy style bun with curls around her face.

"I'm Detective Benson and this is my partner, Sergeant O'Neill. We'd like to ask you a few questions."

Stan, blonde and blue-eyed, smiled. "We're Stan and Debbie Forrester. How can we help you detectives?"

"How long have you lived on this block?"

Stan looked at Debbie. "Oh, ah... I would say ten or twelve years."

"No dear," interjected brown-haired Debbie, shaking her loose curls off her suntanned freckled shoulders. "We moved here exactly fifteen years ago today."

"When did you come outside today?"

"We've been out here all day. We've been planting our tulips and geraniums."

"Were either of you outside when your neighbor across the street, Jesus Rojas, came home this evening?"

"Yes," said Stan. "In fact, we were outside when Angela came home too."

"Was she alone?"

"Yes, she was alone in her van. She'd been shopping. She waved at us."

"Have either of you noticed anyone different on the block today?"

"No. It's been quiet."

Debbie frowned; her brown eyes squinting close. "You know they weren't your typical Hispanic family."

"Why do you say that?"

"They're always inside. We hardly ever see them."

"Last year they had a sleepover for Damaris, and we didn't know anything about it!"

"Your daughters weren't invited?" asked O'Neill.

"We don't have children," Stan said quickly with a subtle frown at his wife.

"Do you recall seeing a strange car or a stranger on the block?"

"No strange automobiles or persons," said Debbie. "We know everyone on the block and the Rojas have been on the block as long as we have. They moved in a year before or after we did."

"Very quiet family," said Stan, musing over his statement. "They'll like regular people. And they're always in their backyard. I don't think they have a swimming pool like the rest of us along here."

"Indeed. Which is odd given their Hispanic. Those people love the water coming from those islands," agreed Debbie. She continued in a friendly way. "You know they're the only Hispanic family on the block? We're very progressive in this community."

Stan frowned and shook his blonde bangs out of his eyes. "No, hon. They're not the only Hispanic family. We have at least two other families, and there's an African family two doors down."

"Yes, we're becoming very diverse along here." She batted an imaginary fly from the side of her head while her husband shook his long hair from shoulder to shoulder. Benson tried to keep a straight face. O'Neill wrote on his pad to avoid looking at them.

"Did you hear anything out of the ordinary?" asked O'Neill in a deadpan voice.

"Like what?"

"Like a scream of someone being tortured or killed?" asked Benson.

Stan stared vacantly in Benson's face, trying to recall whether he heard screams. After a minute, he tossed his full blonde head of hair from side to side again. It swayed about his shoulders.

"Nope, didn't hear a peep."

Debbie bent toward the detectives, speaking in a near whisper. "That's another thing. They were quiet folks even when other people were over there."

"What other people?" asked O'Neill sharply.

"Their family members," said Stan. His face reddened slightly.

Debbie was undaunted. She looked across the street with pursed lips. "If you don't mind us asking, what happened over there?"

"According to you, nothing!" snapped Benson and walked away.

Debbie blushed redder than the top she wore. The husband looked wide-eyed up the street. O'Neill followed his partner and tried to suppress a smile.

Tony was in his office when O'Neill and Benson entered and closed the door.

"This homicide victim's death is like the Young's and the nurse. Both were killed with butcher knives," said Tony.

"We asked Stefanie if the knives were by the same maker. The answer is no. The one that was used on the Young's is older than dirt and according to Stefanie looks like it was picked from a trash bin."

"Ouch!"

"That's what we said. The knife used on the nurse was stolen from a museum collection."

He studied the photographs spread across his desk. He looked at Benson with a frown. "What?"

"You heard her. The knife was stolen from a collection piece in the Art Museum about seven months ago."

"Was the theft reported?"

"It was given a byline on the news but nothing major."

Tony stared at O'Neill and Benson not seeing them. He turned to his computer. He pulled up a medical report.

"Seems he used one of the Rojas kitchen knives this time," he said.

"There was no DNA found on the knife."

Tony said, "I'm beginning to wonder if we're dealing with a serial killer or a killer for hire."

"She's a social worker and her husband's a computer programmer. The suspect could be one of her clients," said Benson.

"I know you two know this but check out the wife and the husband's work sites. We need to clear them if nothing else."

"What do you mean if nothing else, Tony?" asked Benson, puzzled.

"I don't believe these are random murders or a serial killer. My gut tells me these women knew their killer."

"Personally, I believe it's a rejected lover," said O'Neill. He stood up. "Someone they all knew. Anyway, it's been a long day. I'm headed out. The boys have baseball practice this evening. Are you leaving now Vee?"

"Yes. Let me see if Priscilla's ready."

Tony watched his team as they shut down the systems and turned on answering services. He locked his door and sent Marissa a text saying he was on the way home.

Chapter 44

Early the next morning O'Neill and Benson drove to Center City. The Child Welfare Agency was on the second floor of the Human Services building. A woman of medium height with smooth brown skin, mahogany brown curly hair streaked with gray, and a slim physique walked toward them.

She extended her hand. "Good morning. I'm Margaret Sanders, the personnel manager. Please come into my office."

Once seated, she gazed at them with a pleasant expression in her deep brown eyes.

"How may I help you this morning, Detectives?"

"Angela Rojas death has been confirmed as a homicide."

Sanders swallowed and blinked her eyes rapidly a few times before struggling to keep the easy smile she wanted to convey.

"What was the victim's position here?"

"Angela was a clinical social worker."

"How long did she work here?"

"Angela was hired right out of school."

"Who hired her? You?"

"No. Doctor Frances Welcher hired her."

"We'd like to speak with Doctor Welcher."

"Doctor Welcher retired a few years ago." Sanders smiled at Benson.

O'Neill's voice cut through the air. "Lady, we're investigating a murder. If you think this is a joke, you can answer our questions at the station."

"Lynda Molina assumed Welcher's position."

"And what position is that?"

"Director of social services here."

"What else can you tell us about the victim with respect to her work here?"

"Angela earned a graduate degree in clinical social work."

"Friendships outside the workplace?"

"I didn't know Ms. Rojas personally."

"We'd like to speak with the director."

"Doctor Molina's office is directly above mine."

O'Neill and Benson stood up. "Thank you for your time. As per our phone conversation, we'd like to see Ms. Rojas office before we leave."

Sanders smiled and nodded her head in agreement. "It's the second door on your right as you walk down the hall. Meanwhile, I'll put in a call to Doctor Molina's office. Have a good day, Detectives."

The late social worker's workspace was medium-sized. A Puerto Rican flag was draped across the top of the room's single window. Various watercolor prints were tacked on the corkboard near her desk.

"Bright office," said O'Neill. He sat at the desk. "No paperwork out. Desk drawers full of office supplies. I suppose the major work is on her laptop. Do you see one?"

"No." Benson said. "I like the Latin flavor she incorporated in here."

"Come here and look at these photos," said O'Neill still seated behind the desk. "It's the same one of the women we've seen in the all-white photo. This one is more colorful though." O'Neill looked at Benson. "I can see you're in this one."

Benson blushed. "Angela insisted I be a bridesmaid and wouldn't take no for an answer. If you'll notice, there's ten of us."

"What's special about the number ten?"

"We were all members of the soccer team. She wanted us as her bridesmaids. This is her bridal shower." Benson placed a finger on the picture. "Right, there is the lady we're about to see, Lynda Molina. She was Angela's best friend and had just gotten engaged herself."

"You know more about her than the colleague down the hall. I should have questioned you."

Benson grunted and her partner smiled. O'Neill studied the photos. He could barely make out the victim's face. He found her sitting directly in front of a younger Benson. He saw gift bags, colorful balloons, and tables adorned with white cut flowers in the background. The second photo was of bride Angela in a white wedding gown standing among a group of women in bright pink bridesmaids' gowns.

The woman who greeted them at the elevators was small boned with a curly pixie cut. The plain black dress was offset by a striped cardigan. She led the way down the hall. She stopped and opened the door. With a smile she ushered them inside the room.

The interior was smaller than Benson expected. The decor colors were gray, taupe, and pink. Two taupe-clothed chairs were in front of the desk. The chair was in a dusky pink fabric with a vase of pink silk tulips on the edge of the desk. There were various pink artifacts on the built-in shelves behind the chair which sat in front of a window with rose strewn valance.

Across the room stood Lynda Molina, tall and trim. The curly brown hair fell to her waist. The powder blue pantsuit was styled with shoulder epaulets and French-cuffs on the button front jacket and paired with straight leg creased slacks. The beige leather moccasins held a blue decal across the instep. She greeted them with an easy smile and a firm handshake and nodded to the chairs.

"Hi, Vanessa, it's good to see you. Though it's unfortunate under these circumstances. Sergeant O'Neill, it's a pleasure. Do say hello to Judge Byrne for me. Please have a seat. How can our department help you?"

"We're trying to find a motive for Angela's murder. The only thing we have is that she was a clinical social worker here."

Lynda looked at Benson the entire time she spoke with a smile on her face. She looked at O'Neill with the same smile.

"Angela was incredibly good at what she did. She had a great deal of empathy and respect for her clients. They saw it and felt it. She will be missed. She had just been promoted to a senior level position."

"As a social worker, did she have any difficult clients or perhaps, their family members?"

"No. It would have been written up at once. The safety of our clients and staff we take as top priority."

"Who were her clients?"

"Due to HIPPA violations, I can't give you specific client information."

"Can you tell us who she serviced?"

"Her client base were the elderly and the handicapped."

"We'd like to know if Ms. Rojas' spoke to you of any complaints she might have had with clients, or their families?"

"You're asking the same question. The answer will always be Angela never had any issues with her clients... or with their families."

"What was her relationship like with her coworkers?"

"As far as I know, she had a good working relationship with everyone here. Her assistant is out today. She was terribly upset, as you can imagine."

"What is the assistant's name?"

"Carmen Villanueva."

"How long has the assistant been working with Ms. Rojas?"

"Carmen's been with Angela going on nine years now. In fact, she was mentored by Angela while finishing her degree. We hired Carmen as Angela's assistant the day she graduated."

"What about Angela's marriage?"

"Again, as far as I know, Angela and Jesus had a good marriage. Jesus is a close friend of one of my cousins, and it was he that introduced them."

O'Neill asked, "Outside of the workplace, you and the victim were good friends?"

"We were best friends, Detective. We lived next door to each other. If you've been to their home, mine is the adobe brick style with the wrought iron gates."

"Can you tell us the last time you saw or spoke with Ms. Rojas outside of the work environment?"

"A week ago, tomorrow. We had a fire drill, so she and I decided to go shopping. That was such a fun day."

Lynda put her head down. Benson stood up as did O'Neill.

"Thank you for your time, and condolences on your loss," said O'Neill.

There was no response. Benson looked back. Lynda had turned her chair around facing the window.

The drive to Exeter Township was forty-five minutes one way. O'Neill drove and there was no talking. Benson glanced at him occasionally but enjoyed the view of the countryside.

276

Exeter Business Systems was found on the outskirts of the town on a two-acre lot. The building was two-stories connected to another building by a walk-through bridge. A tall thin man directed them to Jesus Rojas office. The programmer sat in front of three screens with a headset on. He waved at his colleague before ushering them in.

"Hi. Sorry I didn't meet you in the lobby. I needed to complete that phone call. I asked Mike to bring you up. You folks want any coffee? It should be freshly brewed right about now."

"No, thanks," said Benson, and smiled.

O'Neill looked at Rojas. He had aged in the week following his wife's death. His disheveled appearance and eyes circled in gray showed his deep grief.

"We apologize for any inconvenience," said Benson.

"It's all right Vanessa. I don't mind your questions. I want to know who did this to my wife, to me, and our beautiful family. I don't know how to move forward. I don't know what to do. How will I raise my daughters without their mother?"

"You'll be okay, Jesus. You have your parents and hers."

"That's true. Her parents are flying in from ..."

"Excuse me," O'Neill interrupted. "This is a murder investigation and we're homicide cops. Right now, I need to ask you questions to help solve your wife's murder. Do you understand me?"

"Yes. Yes, I understand."

"The first question is where were you when your wife was murdered?"

"I don't know when she was ..."

"What time did you get off work?"

"I left an hour early because we had planned a little family vacation. You can check with my supervisor."

"Why did you leave work early?"

"I picked up my girls from school..."

"And then what?"

"I picked up my parents. They were coming with us .... and... and... The highway was packed. We crawled for an hour... then the road opened... I got home and saw Angie's van..." Rojas went silent. He looked down at his hands and slowly folded them together. "I saw Angie's van and knew she was home. I ... told everyone to wait in the car because I was bringing out all the suitcases... and..."

"Okay. That's enough. I need to ask you if you saw anything out of order when you entered your home. Think carefully. Go over it in your mind's eye. Before you saw your wife, was there anything that made you pause for a minute," asked O'Neill.

Rojas looked at him with eyes heavily outlined in gray shadows. His hollowed-out cheeks gave him a macabre look. He closed his eyes and slightly swayed from side to side.

"Yeah... Angie had text she was stopping at the market to get snacks for the girls. I remember wondering why she hadn't done that...then...I saw her..." He gasped and put his face in his hands.

"What were you looking for, Mr. Rojas?"

He dropped his hands. "Bags. I was looking for shopping bags, but I didn't see anything...and then I saw... Angie."

O'Neill stood up. "Thank you for seeing us Mr. Rojas and answering our questions. If you remember anything else, please don't hesitate to call us. This is a number for a child psychologist. I suggest you make an appointment for your daughters."

Rojas nodded, took the card but kept his head down as he turned to his desk. Gasps turned into sobs. The detectives did not look back.

The squad room was still as the somber voice of O'Neill addressed the room.

"Angela Rojas was attacked in her home just an hour before the arrival of her family. The weapon was a large butcher knife. Mike says she was dead for a little under one hour. There aren't any suspects currently. The only possible eyewitnesses were neighbors who told us they didn't see anyone entering or exiting the home during the hours they were outside."

"There's a discrepancy between the neighbor's accounts of seeing the victim and what the husband saw."

"What's the discrepancy?" asked Perez.

"The neighbors said she'd been shopping. Her husband sent us text messages from his wife detailing what she was buying for their trip. But when he walked in the home, he didn't see a shopping bag."

"Neither did we," said O'Neill. "The victim's purse and car keys were on the counter but no sign of a market bag."

"We checked with the local markets. We have her on surveillance footage paying for items identical to what she texted her husband she was getting. We have that same footage showing her stashing the items in her vehicle. The question now is where are the bags?"

"No question needed," said Trevino. "The killer took the bags."

"Our serial killer is back, Gerard said. "We haven't had anything for months and now this homicide."

"Was anything like this missing at the other crime scenes?"

"If it was no one has mentioned it."

Trevino's voice boomed throughout the room. "Wait a minute. A file addressed to Tony was reported missing from the Minnelli's home."

"The Minnelli case," murmured Benson. She scrolled through her online files. "The psychologist was doing a file on who?"

Tony said, "That's what we don't know. I assume it was on the murderer of these women. She and I never discussed these cases."

"Weren't they called in for Spencer Carr's children?"

"Yes. This same social worker was also there. She's the children's godparent." Benson stopped speaking. She frowned with concern. "Something's wrong here."

"What's this victim's height?"

"She was exactly five feet eleven inches."

"The killer is definitely much taller than the victims."

"If it's the same guy you mean."

Sloan rushed into the squad room from the elevators. Her light blue eyes wide with concern. She gasped for air.

"Sorry to interrupt, but this is important,"

"What's the matter, Robin?"

"The local news stations are running bylines on the murder of Angela Rojas." She turned her tablet for them to see the screen. "Someone's leaking information. I never sent anything in yet on this new case."

"Who's feeding the news stations?"

"Not to mention our phone lines are now busy with incoming calls from terrified women," said Johnston, as she hung up her phone.

"Oh, crap!" breathed O'Neill.

"Precisely." Tony breathed out through his mouth.

Murray opened his office door with a bang, and yelled for Tony, Trevino, and O'Neill.

More than an hour passed without the trio leaving the office. When the squad room cleared for the night the captain's office was brightly lit and the blinds drawn tight.

The funeral for Angela was private and attended by her family, coworkers, and the women who had shared her life since college. Jesus asked Marissa to read a passage from her twelfth book she dedicated to his wife on the birth of their second child. Marissa, surrounded by her friends, read the inscription to *Angelina Deleon Rojas* whom she described as *"a beautiful woman with the conscience of a saint."*

Chapter 45

Lord, what a long day! LisaMarie Butler was glad the day was over. All she could think about was getting home to Dan and their two spunky sons. They were taking the boys to the cabin for the weekend. The weather was now stable with sunshine and blue skies every day. Dan wanted to get the canoe on the water, and she looked forward to getting the cabin cleaned for the summer ahead.

Her protégé stepped on the elevator with her. "Enjoy your summer off, LisaMarie. I can't wait for next week to get here."

"Are you almost finished with the reception details?"

"Yes, we've planned the menu already. Tonight is cake tasting time."

"Oh, Belinda that's the best part. Be careful though. You don't want to gain weight. You have that beautiful gown to get into."

The young woman laughed merrily. "Brian will be doing all the taste testing, that's for sure."

The elevator stopped on the woman's floor, and she stepped off.

"Have a good weekend, Belinda. Say hello to Brian for me."

"Same to you, and I will."

LisaMarie was happy. Three blissful weeks with her family. Although she knew Dan would be back in the office by the third week, she still looked forward to spending quality time together. The elevator doors opened, and she stepped out into the still, clammy garage. She glanced furtively about.

She loved her job as postal inspector, but she wished they had adequate lighting in this garage. She did not mind walking through here in the company of her colleagues. But on evenings like now when she was the last person in her department to leave the building and the garage was nearly empty of cars, she hated it.

She walked straight and fast toward her vehicle. Her gold highlighted russet curls swayed slightly from the light breeze wafting through the garage. Good, she was almost there. She looked down to put her key in the lock. Someone was behind her.

Next time tell me the truth. Be gracious enough to answer without a judgmental look or haughty attitude while lying for your friends.

The broad expanse of land known as the Industrial Park Business District sat on six thousand acres of land. It was home to eighty businesses with warehouses and factories at the far end. On a one-acre lot next to an air freight business sat the Winding Falls Postal Service. Trevino and Perez followed police through the underground clearance to the crime site. The area swarmed with various vehicles of all shapes and sizes.

Tony drove up in a cruiser. The three detectives were directed to the tarp covered body on the ground near a large, tan vehicle. A bloody mass of shattered bone and tissue replaced what was once the victim's head. Perez turned away. She could taste the vomit in the back of her throat. Trevino and Tony stooped down and studied the scene closer. The dark brown uniform was drenched in blood as was the beige trench coat.

The victim had long curly reddish-blonde hair which absorbed the blood as it seeped down from her head at a steady clip. On the hand rested across her chest was a diamond engagement ring and wedding band set in white platinum. Tony, with a gloved hand, reached under the victim. He handed the purse and belongings to a nearby technician. Trevino pointed to the pooled blood.

"Maybe we should get something out before the public rips us to shreds."

Tony nodded. "I'll get Robin to draft something."

"She never made it inside her vehicle," Trevino sighed. "She was attacked while the key was still in the latch."

"Why destroy her face like that?" said Perez, in a ragged voice. She tried to control the urge to vomit. "Someone hated this lady."

"Take a breath, Priscilla." Trevino put a hand on her shoulder to steady her. "She looks pretty messed up to say there are no defensive wounds. That could only mean it was someone she knew."

"Had to be a woman though," offered Tony. "This is a different murder pattern than we've seen in the other women victims."

Trevino frowned. "Good point. We need to see how she died. I didn't see any kind of weapon around. Did you?"

"No."

"Santorelli's arrived," murmured Perez.

The detectives watched as Santorelli, outfitted in a hazmat suit, waved to them as she walked toward the body. She was joined by another figure in the same uniform. They bent over the figure on the ground.

"Who called this in?" asked Tony.

"We got this call about fifteen minutes ago. A coworker leaving for the night," said Trevino. "Name is Belinda Carson. That's her sports car over there. It's parked directly across from the van."

"Did you check out the car?" asked Tony.

"You know me, brother. It belongs to the young woman who called in. She's twenty-six, and lives with her parents in Delsea Park North. Clean record. Winding Falls graduate."

Perez found her voice. "The girl dropped her purse and car keys by the door of her car." She showed Tony the items.

"Poor kid," said Tony.

"We'll talk to her in a minute. I wanted to give her a chance to pull herself together. She was near hysteria on the call."

"Where is she now?"

"Back in her office. I have an officer with her

"Good. Santorelli's ready for us."

The medical examiner walked over to them. The look on her face was somber.

"I heard you had to delay your vacation again. I'm sorry, Elsa"

"Thanks, Tony, but this is what we do," she said wearily. "The victim's name is LisaMarie Butler. She's thirty-seven-years old and lives in Oxford Circle."

"How did she die?"

"The victim died from a massive hemorrhage caused when her skull was split in two. She's been dead about an hour and a half now. Believe it or not, this was a quick and painless death. Brutal as it looks."

"And all the blood on her head and face?"

"From the impact of being hit in the face with a blunt force object after she was down with repeated blows," said Santorelli. She held up a long blood-drenched object in a plastic bag. "This tire iron caused all that damage. We've taken pics of it for your files, but this is going to the crime lab for analysis."

"Thanks, Elsa." Tony sighed deeply. "Priscilla, contact her husband. His name is Dan Butler over at Stone Harris York Investment."

"Law   firm?"

"Investment banking."

Perez moved away. Trevino opened the trunk of the van and looked inside. He gave a low growl before slamming down the trunk lid.

Tony asked, "Did you find her tire iron?"

"No."

Perez returned. "The husband's headed to the hospital now."

"He's bringing a photo, I'm sure," Trevino said, dryly. "There'll be no identification being done from this end."

"Have a talk with building security," said Tony. He pointed to a wall shrouded in darkness. "I noticed there's a camera over there on the other side of her van. What kind of security system are they using? No one's arrived yet."

"Where are you headed?" Trevino asked him.

"The hospital to check on her husband. Call the captain and get the flags lowered to half-staff."

Trevino nodded as he pulled out his phone. Perez watched Tony run to his car and speed away. She turned to her partner.

"That's the first time in all our years working crime scenes I've seen Tony wear dark glasses."

"He knows them, Priscilla," said Trevino. "They're close friends with this couple." In the silence that followed, he said, "There's the elevator... to your right."

Trevino and Perez rode the elevator to the second floor. The police officer stood guard in the hall and was on the alert when the doors opened. He nodded toward the young woman who rose to meet them.

She was slight of build with a light beige complexion. Her black curly hair sat about her shoulders enveloping her face in its fullness. She was pretty with a softness to her face that matched her voice. Her eyes were moist from crying, and the tip of her nose pink. As she clasped her hands together in despair, Perez noticed the pear-shaped diamond ring on her left hand.

"Hello, are you the detectives? Lieutenant Marigny told me you would want to speak to me. I'm Belinda Carson."

"Hello, Ms. Carson. Our names are Trevino and Perez. We need to ask you some questions."

"Okay," said Belinda, sniffling. "Please follow me to my office."

She led the way to her office. It was a mid-size room that was comfortably lit. The built-in bookshelves and the desk were dark mahogany wood. One wall held the young woman's education degrees and abstract prints. The desk was clear but for a computer, a blank pad and two framed photo- graphs. She seated them in two golden chairs placed in front of her desk.

"What is your position here?"

"Postal inspector."

"How long have you worked with Ms. Butler?"

"Five years. She was my trainer for a year."

"What was your working relationship like?"

"I honestly loved her. She was the most pleasant person to be around. Always full of laughter. Just a good person."

"Do you know of any problems she may have had with a coworker or businessperson?"

"Oh, no. She was well-liked, and she knew her craft."

"Did you two socialize after hours?"

"No, not after hours. We went to lunch occasionally."

"We understand you found Ms. Butler?"

"Yes. I was walking to my car and looked over ..." She stopped and swallowed a few times.

"Was there anyone else in the parking garage?" asked Perez.

"I didn't see anyone else around."

"Is it always empty when you get off work?"

"I usually leave around five o'clock with everyone else. There's a bunch of us who leave at the same time on this floor."

"What floor is Ms. Butler on?"

"She's on the sixth floor."

"What time did you leave today and why?"

"I was leaving at seven o'clock for two reasons. First, I was working on an assignment with LisaMarie involving a retail firm. Second, my fiancé and I are going to a wedding planning event that starts later tonight. That's why I was still here." She tried to stop the flow of tears. "She's so sweet. She's been helping me with stuff like wedding invitations."

"Thank you for your time, Ms. Carson. If you think of anything else, please don't hesitate to call us."

The young woman began crying softly. "Thank you."

As they were leaving the floor, a well-dressed young man rushed off the elevator and sped by them. They watched as the man embraced the woman in a lover's knot.

"Must be the fiancé," Perez murmured as the doors closed. "Beautiful engagement ring."

On the sixth floor, the custodian on duty was oblivious to the chaos in the building parking lot. She was busy with her tasks. All the office doors were standing open. She gave them directions to the victim's office.

The room they entered was roomy with bookcases covering one entire wall from floor to ceiling. A large picture window offered scenic views of the mountains. Trevino inspected the bookcase behind the spacious desk. On a wall were commendations and awards from various children and youth organizations. Perez was in the private bathroom looking in the medicine cabinet. She joined Trevino in the main office. He was seated behind the desk with his hands folded. She sat in one of the plush golden leather chairs.

She looked at her partner. His dark blue eyes were slits atop the high cheekbones. The jet-black hair falling in deep waves to his shirt collar. Perez stared at him. The older he became, the more handsome, but she would never tell him that.

"This office reminds me of the publicist's office," said Perez, sinking deeper in the leather chair.

"There's a difference here though," said Trevino.

"What's the difference?"

"This office is more in step with a family setting. Look at this wall of photographs behind me. Many are social events, but the majority are family oriented. The social events seem to include the same women and

286

men. Look at this one." He pointed to an assortment of pictures at the lower end of the built-in. "It's a collage of what appears to be the same group of people year after year. In these pics Tony and his wife are front and center."

"What does that have to do with anything, Luis?"

"Ms. Marigny was close friends with the Carr and Crenshaw women. When questioned about her relationship with them, she appeared to know a lot about the Carr woman but not the other one."

"Marigny and Carr were best friends as I recall."

"Yet, all three knew each other from their college days, and that includes that news producer you interviewed. Now this woman was part of that circle."

"This is a small college town, Luis. They all attended the same college. So what? I don't hang with most of the women I hung out with in college...and I bet, neither do you."

"There's nothing small about Winding Falls. Second, were you in a sorority, Priscilla?"

"No, Luis. I attended college as a scholarship kid being from a poor Indigenous community."

"Well, I was in one. The Omega Pi Fraternity. The Alpha Nu Sorority is our sister sorority. This is their crest and paddle. These are their colors."

Trevino pointed to photographs on the wall. Perez studied the wall and looked closely at all the items. She looked at her partner who stared at the ceiling.

"Are you building a case against Tony's wife?"

Trevino focused his gaze on Perez. He sighed and looked at his hands.

"I don't know where I'm going. Just throwing out bait, Priscilla." He looked back at the photographs of LisaMarie with her family. "This lady was family oriented. Reminds me of the first victim."

"Janelle Carr with the four boys."

"Exactly. There's something about all this that's bothering me."

"I can see that. Do you know what it is?"

"No, not yet. It's like a puzzle piece that's missing. You know it's somewhere among the other pieces. You just must find it."

"Maybe it's nothing, but again, maybe it's something. Time will tell," said Perez.

"Time is something we don't have Priscilla." He rose from the desk. "Come on, let's get out of here."

He palmed a small frame as the forensic team appeared in the room.

Trevino and Perez stepped off the elevator as a large black Range Rover entered the parking lot and stopped. Every police officer watched the vehicle until the driver opened the door and stepped into view. He was a short man with a bald head. Packed with muscle he strolled with a stance of authority across the parking lot. He walked up to the detectives, dismissed Perez with a look, and glared with scorn at Trevino.

"I received a call one of my men was hurt tonight," he growled by way of introduction.

"Who are you?" asked Trevino as he looked calmly down at him.

"Louis Matteo, Chief Postal Inspector," he barked. "Who are you?"

"Detectives Trevino and Perez. Homicide."

Matteo stared at Trevino. "Homicide?"

"Your *man*, LisaMarie Butler, was murdered earlier tonight."

Matteo's face turned beet red. He looked from one detective to another. Finally, he said, "LisaMarie's gone?"

"Is it customary for female employees to use this underground garage after the rush hour?" Trevino asked as he stared down at Matteo.

"We all use this garage." Matteo said loudly. He tried to regain his former arrogance.

"Let me ask you another way," said Trevino. "Where are the security guards for this area?"

"Due to recent budget cuts none of our facilities are currently using security guards. We do have a strong police presence in this area though."

"Yeah, we noticed their absence on the way in here," said Trevino.

"Our boss noticed the one camera in darkness over there," said Perez. "We'd like to take a look at it."

Matteo frowned and shook his head fiercely. Elevating his voice, he said, "I can't allow that. Its federal property on a federal installation."

"Pardon me if I ignore your protocols, but one of your federal employees was brutally murdered on this site." Trevino raised his voice. "Now, either we look at the system now or return with a warrant. Then we'll look at everything."

288

Police turned to look at them. There was an awkward silence. Matteo rubbed a hand over his face.

"Come inside."

They followed him into the building and rode a tight elevator that smelled of wet cement and pine cleaner to the ninth floor. A tiny door opened into a larger room lined with computer terminals, and empty of personnel. Matteo walked to a computer and punched the keys. The screen opened and the trio surveyed the parking garage from the angle of the cameras. There was no sound and less visual.

"Her family van blocked views of this attack and the attacker," said Matteo. He almost sighed with relief.

"But these cameras, what there are of them, are placed in the most inconvenient and unsafe locations." Perez said. "She could have been on a bike, and you wouldn't see anything."

"The one that could have nabbed this guy is in darkness," added Trevino, "and tilted to the ceiling. And these two cameras are inoperable."

Matteo let out a long sigh of grief.

Chapter 46

The eight figures moved silently through the parking garage. One used his palm print to electronically run the elevator. When they arrived on their floor, they found Tony in his office with the door open and his head bent over a book. The aroma of fresh brewed coffee guided them into the squad room. The corner table held a buffet of dinner foods.

Thirty minutes later, Tony joined them in the squad room. Holding onto a large mug of steaming coffee, he seated himself beside Johnston's desk.

"I have some thoughts I wanted to share before we hit the weekend. I think we're all aware we have a major problem. It's been almost a year since the murder of Janelle Carr. The captain is catching heat. James Alan Young was being groomed for the mayor's office. His wife's partnership with Hugo, Larsen and Young was extremely successful. Their grisly deaths has caused a political domino effect."

"No disrespect to the deputy mayor and his wife," said Gerard, cutting Tony off, "but what about the poor women who have been murdered in cold blood since?"

O'Neill's deep voice added, "Our last victim's agonizing demise fits with the modus operandi of earlier murders. We have several connecting pieces with these homicides. All these women knew each other in college. One or two may have known each other after college. All except two were married with children. All met violent deaths."

"LisaMarie Butler is our last victim," boomed Trevino. "She's the postal worker who got her skull bashed in with her own tire iron. There weren't any prints found but hers, which includes the murder weapon. Her husband and the Postal Service are offering a substantial reward for information and capture of her killer." He turned to the room. "We need to be careful here.

These women and their husbands were homegrown and affluent. We can't just shrug off their deaths as random nut jobs."

"They were all graduates of Winding Falls University which educates some of the wealthiest in the quad-county region," Benson added. She scrolled down her tablet. "The university is privately funded and has an endowment of six billion."

"We need to remember Crenshaw was an out-of-towner. She made Winding Falls Township her home," said O'Neill. "Both her parents are now retired. Her father was a dentist and mother a school principal. She has one older brother who's been enquiring into her murder."

"Oh, oh," said Johnston. "Why do I get the feeling it's more than the Young's we have to worry about?"

"That's right. Crenshaw's brother is State Senator Edwin Crenshaw, and he wants to know what happened to his sister. Can you blame him?"

"There's another piece to this puzzle as well," said O'Neill. "The Rojas murder shows the lady texting her husband in the market."

"And the surveillance tapes at the market clearly show her at the register and later, loading bags in her car," said Benson.

"We have witness statements from the neighbors who saw the victim when she arrived home with her purchases."

"But there were no bags in the home."

"The killer was hungry?"

"Or mocking us."

"Can we return to a point I wanted to make about the postal inspector's death? Although these facilities have cameras now, we didn't get any kind of decent footage at the postal site."

"That's another sore point. The parking garage where the woman was killed placed the camera too low, and in an inappropriate place."

"What?"

"She drove a family van and was parked right near the camera monitor, but we didn't see anything because the camera was placed too low on the wall, and it was in a dark corner. You couldn't even make out shadows. There was nothing!"

"Oh, Christ!"

"Exactly. Even if the assault had been recorded, the footage would've been at knee level. While we're speaking on security, the Young's didn't have their security system set or turned on! So, we got nothing there either."

"Alright, everyone," interrupted Tony in a loud voice. "Let's focus. Dante, I asked you to give me a psych profile. How about informing the team?"

"Quite seriously, we have someone on a revenge warpath. Either one or all of these women hurt this individual, and he or she is returning the favor with deadly consequences."

"That's too simple, Dante," said O'Neill.

"Right," added Gerard. "I think we need to look at the crimes outside the realm of psychology. The killer is no stranger to his victims. We need to find the missing connection between these women and the killer."

"Excuse me," said di Giovanni. "Not only am I a psychologist but I've been trained as a profiler. What seems simple is often what is overlooked. Revenge is a powerful motivator for destruction just ask a country or a person who's been the object of scorn."

O'Neill raised both his hands. "Okay, Dante. I got the message. I apologize for my comment."

"Can we get back to the case? I get what Dante is saying," said Perez. "These women were targeted for a reason. We must find out the reason."

"Well, how are we going to do that when they're dead?" asked Gerard.

"Well, for one they were all classmates in college. Maybe he's connected with their past in some way," said Sloan.

"Why can't this killer be a woman?" said Perez. "The victims weren't assaulted, and they all died violent deaths as if they were being made to suffer physical pain."

"That's good, Priscilla," said Benson. "Beauty hurts."

"I don't think this killer is a woman..." began Sloan.

Tony raised his hand and the room became quiet. "I believe James has some interesting figures for us. James?"

"I was able to look up the school's sports teams fifteen years ago."

"Fifteen years ago? Where'd you come up with that?"

"From Crenshaw's love letters. The second victim found strangled in her home."

"I had forgotten about her. I thought she was the suicide victim. Is she now homicide?"

"Yes, Kevin. In lieu of these other murders and her proximity to some of these women, we're ruling her death a homicide as well."

"Let's hear James out."

"The university had a winning women's basketball team. For the four years they attended Winding Falls, these five ladies were basketball legends. They were Janelle Carr, Jacky Crenshaw, Kristen O'Leary, Marissa Marigny, and Stacie Young. Four of these five have been murdered."

There was silence. O'Neill cleared his throat. "There's more. I have the positions they played."

Sloan whistled. She read from her screen. "Wow! They were called the Fantastic Five! They played together the entire time they were in college."

"I have a film clip of one of their last games. I downloaded the highlights to your sites," said O'Neill.

Tony watched the film over Johnston's shoulder. He noticed how well-coordinated they were as a team.

It was Gerard who whistled. "This is fascinating how good they were. Who's the girl with the long black plait? She seems to be playing nearly every position. She's number fourteen."

"That's Marissa Marigny the power forward. Her buddy Carr is number three and she's the shooting guard. Young is the point guard. She's number ten. Crenshaw is number thirty-three."

"The center..." murmured di Giovanni.

The game ended with Winding Falls University scoring eighty-one points to their opponents sixty-three points.

"Your wife still play? Even recreationally?" asked Gerard.

"No."

"They could have joined a professional team."

"I'm sure they received offers. They were that good."

Benson waited a minute and cleared her throat. "Besides their athletic ability you might want to consider Carr, O'Leary and Crenshaw studied the martial arts. Carr earned a Black belt in judo, Crenshaw earned a Black belt in jiu jitsu and judo, and O'Leary earned a Black belt in karate and judo."

"Three women knew the martial arts?"

"Carr and Crenshaw were the first two victims," said Trevino. "This means they knew their killer."

"It also means," interjected di Giovanni, "the element of trust is why the victims weren't threatened by their killer. The question then becomes who would they have felt safe with not to resort to immediate defensive/offensive fight tactics?"

"We could very well be looking for a woman," Tony mused. "With the exception of one victim, the rest of these ladies are above average in height. Two thoughts I'm having. Someone who got cut from a team and someone from any of the opposing schools they played against."

Trevino tossed a paper clip in the trash. "Well, that idea is shot."

"Why is that, Luis?" asked Sloan. "We can easily input the data information and pull out..."

O'Neill looked at Sloan. "Robin, we can't just go into student records. We also have no real idea of who we're looking for."

Trevino raised his voice to a small roar. "The reason the idea is shot is because the women killed took part in competitive sports throughout high school and college. Different schools and different coaches. Also, their killer is a skilled one. He *or she* is also well-trained in martial arts. She must be to wield a knife the way she does, *and* there was no DNA found on any of the knives."

Into the quiet that followed di Giovanni said, "We do know we're looking for a female because she's only targeting women."

"The deputy mayor was a man, Dante."

"Who was attacked first to incapacitate him, my dear. I can assure you men are not the target of this person."

"her rage is against these former athletes. But why wait so long?"

"Who says they've been waiting? Suppose they've struck other counties; we just haven't heard about it yet?"

"Aw, come off it. Unless there have been isolated killings, we would have heard about it before now."

"We've thrown out a lot of hypotheses but nothing to work with."

Tony suddenly stood up. "All these women had children. It could be a jealous parent."

"Sierra Smith didn't have kids," said Gerard.

"No, she just worked around them all day, every day," said Sloan.

Benson added, "Jacky Crenshaw wasn't married and didn't have kids."

"We keep forgetting about the second victim who I'm beginning to think was actually the first victim," said Trevino. "She was the beginning of all this. The method of her death was echoed in the following victims."

"Why do you say the second victim? Are you saying Jacky Crenshaw was the first?" asked Benson.

"Yes, because she was dead weeks before we found her."

"I get the feeling there's a method to all this," murmured di Giovanni.

"A soccer mom who practices judo and karate offs these women for what purpose?" Johnston asked, "and I'm not being sarcastic either."

Trevino stood up. "I'm officially off the clock or we'll be here all weekend. But we'll all rest easy knowing we have a serial killer on the loose in Winding Falls targeting athletic women."

Tony held up his hand. "Wait a minute, Luis. A few months ago, we spoke about the graduating class these women were in. Do we have that information yet?"

Benson raised her hand. A few snickers went around the room. Tony's eyes flashed green streaks of light, and the laughter died down.

"I found a group photo of the graduating class these women were in. I checked with the school and fifteen years ago, approximately four thousand eight hundred students graduated that year. The total number of undergraduates was two thousand two hundred and sixty-five. The number of male undergraduates was one thousand two hundred and thirty-two against the one thousand thirty-three females."

Tony sighed. "Thank you. Rounding up, that's close to twenty-three hundred graduates. This is a needle in a haystack. We need to examine each of these victims more closely. What common factor is threading each together besides being members of this graduating class? What activities or clubs did they belong to besides sports? Who did they date?"

"As to the athletics programs in our schools and colleges, we're no different than any other town."

"The martial arts is a lifelong commitment for many," said Gerard.

"Good point, Kevin."

"Is this homework for the weekend?" Sloan asked.

"Let me repeat myself." Trevino stood up again. "Good night, all."

"It's only a matter of time before the media does exactly what we're doing," said Sloan. "They're almost there now. The weekly panic reports are creating havoc in the town."

"We need to alert the public," said Perez watching her colleague get on the elevator.

"Alert them to what, Priscilla?" asked Benson. She pulled on her jacket. "So far, the ones needing to be on the alert are working women."

"Working women? I don't know if we want to put it out there like that," Gerard said. "We have a million threads, and those threads have arms. Have a good weekend, guys." He put his tablet in its cover and headed for the elevator.

Johnston looked at Tony's pleasant face as the rest of the team prepared to leave for the night.

"Robin, I need to see you and Dante in my office. Thanks, Priscilla, for the suggestion. We do need to alert the public but there's a way of doing so that we don't create further panic and confusion. Good night to the rest of you."

He waved as he walked toward his office followed by Sloan, di Giovanni, and O'Neill.

Chapter 47

Murray looked across his desk at Tony with a look of wearied disgust. They were in Murray's office going over the condensed report Tony had sent earlier.

"What's the matter with this case? We're looking at a group of professional women who've been targeted by some mad man, and your team is studying their college sports teams. How does that make any sense, Tony?"

"When you put it like that it makes plenty of sense. If we count Marissa's claim about the break-in then we have five women on that basketball team who were targeted with four now dead. For all we know, Marissa could have been..." He stopped talking.

Murray softened his tone. "What about the other women? Were they involved in sports or only these five?"

"All of them engaged in competitive sports."

Murray studied a point on the wall above Tony's head. "I think you and Dante may be on to something. If this is a woman, it could be another player. Maybe a coach..."

Tony felt his adrenaline begin to flow. "You think we should look into possible female rivals of these ladies?"

"Why not? We both know how jealousy and envy can be over the top and with these young athletes i t ' s worth a try. What do we have to lose at this point?" He blew through his mouth. "While you're at it, see if any of those girls from those rival teams was studying martial arts in college."

"I'll get them on it first thing Monday morning. Thanks, Fred, for listening. Sometimes I just need a clear perspective."

"Don't we all?" Murray popped a stick of chewing gum in his mouth. He looked thoughtfully at Tony. "How's Marissa doing?"

"She's doing well. Her friends have been checking on her, giving her new mother advice. She's calmer than I've seen her in a while."

"Was this postal woman a friend of hers?"

"There's something I wanted to talk to you about regarding some of these victims."

"Sure. Shoot."

"Marissa and I knew the Carr's, Young's, and the Butler's..."

"Sure. I knew the Carr's and the Young's as well. What's your point?"

"We knew them on a personal level. You knew Spencer because you collaborated with his father. Same as with James Alan..."

"Oh, I see... I'm sorry, I didn't understand what you meant..."

"Don't apologize, Fred. These murders have been hard on us all."

"But especially difficult when they're your longtime friends. I get your point well. Look, whenever you need to take the time, do it. Our mental health is very important in this occupation, and your wife is the most important asset you have."

Tony could not explain it, but the silent look Murray gave him sent chills up his spine.

Tony was writing his summary on a case file when he saw his door open out of his peripheral. He smelled the perfume, and did not look up. He finished typing the paragraph and turned around.

Santorelli was standing by the door. The striped silk blouse was open to bare cleavage and the black knit skirt emphasized her hour-glass figure. She walked to the chair in front of the desk and sat down with a little smile playing around her lips.

"What's the matter, Elsa?"

"Nothing's the matter. I stopped by to say hello. I also wanted to apologize for my despicable behavior a few weeks ago. I've been swamped in the lab, or I would've come by sooner."

"That's okay, Elsa. No need to apologize for having a good time."

"We didn't have a good time, Tony. I got a bit intoxicated, and your detective brought me home with his partner as his chaperone. I guess I'm deemed as a dangerous woman by your staff."

Tony smiled. "Not dangerous but a femme fatale nonetheless."

To his surprise Santorelli laughed. "I like that." She got up to leave. "Well, thanks for understanding. Got to get back to work."

Tony was relieved she did not stay but puzzled by the change in her attitude. Perhaps his becoming a father sobered her up a bit. He took the opportunity to lock his office and leave for the evening.

In a packed graveyard with the sweltering heat of summer reflected in the bright sunlight, Tony and Marissa stood alongside widower Dan Butler and his sons. Marissa read from her eighth book dedicated to her *long-time friend, LisaMarie Valentine Butler,* whom she described as *"beautiful and bubbly, no matter the outcome."*

Dan swayed slightly as his wife's casket was lowered into the grave and his youngest son wiped away tears from his eyes. Beside them, Tony remembered the days he and Marissa babysat for the couple. A strange feeling engulfed him standing at the grave site. He closed his eyes. What was he missing?

After the funeral service Tony and Marissa returned home to change their somber attire and pack their bags. At his parents' home, they were delighted by the surprise baby shower hosted by both sets of soon-to-be grandparents. The day was lighthearted and full of heartfelt surprises for the soon

Chapter 48

Monday morning Tony was in his office as his team entered the floor. He Tony met with them in the squad room where he had set up a whiteboard with composite photos of the murdered women. The detectives greeted the display with visible smirks.

"Haven't seen one of those since I was a beat cop."

"Stone Age detective investigations, anyone?"

"I hear they only use them on television cop shows," said di Giovanni. He hummed an upbeat music hall show tune, and the room exploded with laughter. Tony took out his handwritten notes and cleared his throat.

"We have approached summer. We have to hope our elusive killer stays put for the duration of the season."

"Well, we can't depend on his laxity. Last year this time he killed the Young's."

"Ten women and one man have met with fatalities with one woman a possible near-miss. Based on your reports, these women have things in common: they're local to Winding Falls, graduates of the university, and former scholar-athletes. All but two were married with children, and all were professionals."

"There's another commonality."

"What?"

"They're all extremely good-looking; tall, fit and healthy."

"They weren't all tall. The Yang lady came in at four feet eleven."

"Yeah, but she was a student-athlete in gymnastics plus she fit all the other criteria."

"The publicist is the only woman who was from out-of-town. When she graduated, she opted to still be in the township making it her home," said Trevino.

"You mentioned these women were student-athletes. What sports?"

Trevino walked to the board and rearranged the pictures. "Well, as we've discussed before there as the popular basketball team starring Carr, Crenshaw, O'Leary, Marigny, and Young. But on the soccer team was Sierra Smith, Emily Wilkinson, LisaMarie Butler, and Angela Rojas. For the entire time of their college life, these ladies were solid members of their school teams."

He rearranged four photos at the bottom of the board. "Here we have Yang the gymnast."

"And, before I forget," added Trevino, "their athleticism didn't begin in college. These women were lifelong athletes. The Yang woman was a child gymnast with great potential, but her parents opted for education over sports. This lady here," Trevino pointed to Kristen, "was an award-winning martial arts expert as a child and an adult. Her agility and speed were second to none."

"Which explains her ability to sustain a fighting stance the medical report confirms was a good intense hour," said Gerard.

Sloan looked at her colleague. "Kevin, aren't you a martial artist yourself?"

Gerard smiled but remained silent. Benson said, "He's very good at it too. He's helped me with my techniques."

"Can we get back to work?" asked di Giovanni with tongue in cheek.

"Have we checked out the athletics department of the college?"

Benson, with a smirk, said, "The director of the college athletics department is a retired male living in Florida with his wife and dogs. The assistant basketball coach predeceased these women by twelve years. The second assistant was a man who now lives in Arizona in a nursing home. The soccer coach lives in Pearl Valley with her husband. She's also half-blind with a degenerative condition."

"A dead end it seems."

"Only if we assumed the killer was related to these women through their sports accomplishments."

"Well, we can't investigate the other teams they played against. That would be suicide for us."

"What about the other team members? The relief members, equipment person, medic team... I don't know. There's a lot of people around athletes."

"That's just it," said Tony. "We can't build a case off suppositions. We don't know if this person goes as far back as their college years, earlier than their college years, or sometime afterward."

"That's a good one, Tony. Suppose as single new professionals one of them dated someone who the rest didn't like..."

"Please stop."

"We have another issue," said O'Neill.

"Yeah? What's that?"

"The killer is taunting us. Remember what happened with the market bags at Rojas' home? They didn't disappear. The killer took the shopping bags on purpose."

"But why?"

"I think to let us know he's on to us."

"Or she."

"But we need to come together with a plan. I get where you're headed, but we're all over the place now. Are we dealing with a man, or a woman is first on the ballot..."

"Lieutenant!" yelled Sloan as she slammed down her phone receiver. "Your wife just went into labor. Her father's taking her to the hospital."

Trevino and O'Neill drove a frantic Tony to Winding Falls Hospital.

Chapter 49

Two weeks later Tony was in his den watching football highlights when Marissa appeared in the doorway. She stood there quietly. He turned to say something to her and noticed the grimace on her face. She was trying to breathe out, and he realized she was in labor. Tony bundled Marissa into the passenger side of the car and drove to the hospital trying not to speed.

"Are you okay?"

"Shut up, Tony, and drive!" Marissa panted through clenched teeth.

He spun into the emergency parking lot and walked her into the lobby. A nurse hurried over with a wheelchair. Another nurse handed him a clipboard of paperwork. Tony sat in the waiting room and made phone calls.

Marissa's parents entered the waiting room moments later. Maurice took the half-completed clipboard from Tony, found a chair and began to write information on the forms.

"Don't you worry, she'll be fine." Rose said. She put an arm through his and sat comfortably with him in the waiting room.

The emergency room doors opened again and a tall man with a light tan complexion and bright green eyes entered the hospital. He wore a black tuxedo. Close beside him was a trim woman with clear, ivory skin and golden-brown hair fashioned into a sedate chignon. She wore a cream-colored sequined gown.

Mark and Lisa Marigny approached their son. Mark's face seldom bored the look of stress regardless of the situation or circumstance. His wife, Lisa on the other hand, was the opposite of her husband and son. She rushed to hug her son and then Rose. The two women clasped on to each other tightly.

"Dad, Mom, I thought you were out of town," said a surprised Tony.

"Don't be silly," said Lisa, her clear light blue eyes glowing. "Did you really think we would miss the birth of our first grandchildren."

"Especially after that close call a few days ago," said Mark.

"We called them on the way here," said Rose, gleefully.

Rose and Lisa, with arms tight around each other's waists, found seats in a corner of the waiting room; their heads bent in quiet conversation. Mark and Maurice hugged. Mark took the clipboard from Maurice and completed the rest of the forms. Tony sat down and tried to steady his breathing. Maurice sat beside him and pulled out his phone. Tony looked at nothing. What was taking so long? Tony looked at his wedding band.

He thought about when he first saw Marissa stepping out of her parents' car. He remembered she wore a blue plaid shirt and blue denim shorts and carried a brown teddy bear. He could not take his eyes off her. She glanced up at him, and he lost his train of thought. All he remembered was the long black plait that swung as she walked. He sat on the wall waiting to see her again, wanting to see her again. In the back of his mind, he knew he had found his forever love.

He looked up. He saw his team of detectives shaking hands and exchanging hugs with his parents. They were all in casual wear. He looked at them but could not make out what was being said. He vaguely wondered why they were in the hospital.

A nurse appeared through the double doors. Tony jumped up in alarm. The nurse wore full scrubs. She smiled at Tony.

"Lieutenant Marigny, I'm Nurse Stanley. Would you come with me, please? The babies are about to make their appearance."

Rose and Lisa hugged Tony. Their husbands pulled their arms from around his body.

Tony walked down the hall outfitted in surgical scrubs. The doctor in a face mask and gloves nodded at Tony's entrance.

"Marissa is doing fine. She's coming through with flying colors. We should be welcoming the babies any second now."

Tony walked over to Marissa whose eyes were closed. Her hair was spread out over the top of her head and spilled over the edge of the bed. The nurse across from him brushed the damp tendrils around her face. Marissa pushed her hand away. Tony glanced at the doctor. It took a minute for the news to sink in.

"Babies?" echoed Tony.

The doctor grinned. "I see Marissa opted not to tell you."

Several hours later, Marissa and Tony welcomed identical twin boys. The new parents named their sons Philip and Paul Marigny.

The maternity ward nurses brought the Marigny babies into the viewing area. They were pleasantly surprised by the large mass of people gathered at the window. Both sets of grandparents' video recorded the nurses holding the babies.

Down the hall in the maternity wing, Marissa was sitting up in bed watching the door. Her hair was pushed into a messy curly bun on top her head. Her cheeks were flushed, but when Tony appeared, a smile lit up her face.

"Have you seen them yet?" she asked.

"Yes. I saw them when you delivered them," he said. He smiled and kissed her. "You look great. I thought you'd be worn out and sleepy."

She gave a little laugh. "No, I'm happy it's over."

She looked at him. He was holding her hand and looking at the palm. He looked at the name tag on her wrist. "Tony? Tell me what you're thinking. I know it's not about our sons."

"I'm wondering when you started lying to me."

"The babies are yours," she said with a huge grin.

He stared pleasantly at her but did not smile. The grin on her face faded. The silence stretched on. Two nurses appeared with the babies. Tony looked at his sons as the nurses placed them in separate baby baskets. Marissa watched Tony with a sad expression on her face.

The viewing room was empty and quiet. Tony stood at the window looking at his sons. They were white as ghosts with scrunched up faces. Wrapped in hospital blankets with tiny blue caps on their heads, Tony thought they looked like little gnomes. He felt a presence and turned sharply before smiling.

"Hi, Fred. They just brought them back from their feeding. Marissa's finally asleep I think."

Murray smiled. "I was able to say good night before Lisa and Rose threw me out."

Tony laughed. "Don't tangle with first-time grandmothers."

Murray laughed gaily. "Marissa looks beautiful. Congratulations, Tony. Not one, but two sons. I'm happy for you."

"Marissa did all the work." Tony looked down at his sons. In a choked voice he said, "Fred, I'm so happy I can't believe we finally have our family."

Murray smiled. "Look, I was thinking. Spend time with your family. Marissa and your sons are going to need you for the first few days, if not, weeks. Enjoy this first year as a father. You deserve it."

"Thanks, Fred. I'll take a week off. You know me."

"I do know you. A week is good, but two weeks are better. Can you tell them apart yet?"

"Are you kidding me? Maybe by next month. All these babies look alike to me."

Murray looked around at the other babies. "Hey, you know, I never realized how alike all newborns look."

"When you were married you ever think about starting a family?"

"No. Never wanted children. I was lucky the women I married didn't want them either."

"I never asked, but... why did they leave?"

Murray was looking thoughtfully at the babies. "The first one died in a car accident. The second one left me for a traveling salesperson. The last one got tired of being alone. She just left."

"I almost lost Marissa. I think her getting pregnant is why she returned."

"Things always have a way of working out, Tony. That's your motto, remember? Let me get out of here. I'm helping your team gather data on those athletes. Dante thinks we should look at the coaches of the other teams those girls played against."

"Sounds like too much of a long shot."

"Long shots all we got for now, Tony. We got to work with what we've got."

"That's true. Thanks for coming by."

"Are you kidding? When Jeanette texted me about the babies, I came right over."

"Where were you?"

"Bowling alley up the street with Stan and the guys. Our championship game is in two weeks."

Tony looked sideways at Murray. "When do you sleep? Didn't you just come off a camping trip?"

"It's the summer!" Murray looked at him with surprised eyes. "I work hard for the money."

It was Tony's turn to laugh. Murray patted him on the back with a big grin on his face. "Happy Fatherhood, Tony." At the door he turned back. "Enjoy your summer with your family. Take more than a week. I mean it. Enjoy life for a change."

"Thanks, Fred. I hope your team wins the championship."

"Oh, we will. We're undefeated after twenty-two seasons." He snapped his fingers. "That reminds me, I need a new pair of bowling shoes."

Tony smiled and shook his head. He could only hope to be as active as his father and Murray were when he reached their ages. He happily stared down at his sons.

Tony arrived early to pick up Marissa and the boys. He sat in a chair and held one of his sons in his arms while Marissa nursed the other. She could tell them apart, but he could not. Tony looked down at the tiny bundle in his arms. He was not nervous as he held his child. He felt a great deal of pride and love for the wonderful gifts he and Marissa shared.

The nurse Jennifer appeared with another nurse to help the new parents escort their babies home. Tony pushed the wheelchair Marissa was in to the front of the hospital where his truck was parked. Marissa positioned herself in the car with Tony's help. He pulled the seatbelt across her lap. The nurses buckled the twins in their car seats.

It was precisely at that moment Tony felt a shiver of fear run down his spine. He was incapable of raising a child, let alone two of them at once. He sat in the car beside Marissa and looked at her. She was leant back in the seat with her eyes closed. She looked at him.

"What's the matter?"

"Nothing. You look tired. Are you okay?"

"I'm fine. I want to get home is all."

"Okay. You know they're all ours now."

Marissa laughed. "It's going to be alright."

The nurse closed the back door and walked up to Marissa's window. She smiled.

"You're all set, Mrs. Marigny. Congratulations, and enjoy your family."

"Thank you, Nurse. I really appreciated your help today."

"The pleasure's all mine. Bye, folks. Bye, guys."

As Tony inched from the curb, he thought of his marriage. He remembered the failed pregnancies. He kept his eyes on the road and on the traffic. He wanted nothing to happen to his family. This year had taken on a different meaning.

Both sets of grandparents were at their home when they arrived. Mark and Maurice rushed to unstrap the babies and get them in the house following directives from Rose and Lisa. Marissa laughed with her happy face.

"Oh! You don't have to be here. I've got everything in order."

"I'm sure you do with your endless lists," said Rose. "However, you've never given birth before."

"And certainly not to two babies at once!" said Lisa.

"Oh, my! I couldn't even imagine," said Rose.

"Mark and I are staying in the guest room for a few days until you get on your feet."

"Thank you, Lisa," said Rose. "Once the babies are on schedule with feeding, she'll be fine."

"True," said Lisa. "Did you want to stay with her this first week?"

"Oh, no! That's fine, Lisa. It will give me a chance to get my recipe card file together. Enjoy your week with the babies."

"Okay, thank you sweetie."

Then both mothers looked at Marissa. They guided Marissa upstairs and put her to bed. Mark and Maurice carried the babies and followed the women. Tony brought up Marissa's hospital tote bag. The men stood in the doorway until Maria approached from the end of the hall. She directed them to the room next door. In the nursery, colorful carousels were set up over each baby's crib. Rose and Lisa appeared. The women shooed the men out of the room.

Chapter 50

Hours later Tony was in bed beside his wife filled with unspeakable joy. It took time for them to get here, but they had joined the tribe called parents, and he was grateful. He spoke to his team via social media and managed to sneak a short video of the twins. The women were visibly moved. The men exchanged jokes. He closed his eyes and drifted drowsily off to sleep.

A constant, low hum sounded in his subconscious. It was a minute before he realized it was his personal phone. He eased out of bed, retrieved it and walked into the bathroom.

"Hello?"

"Tony, it's Antonio Santini. I heard the good news. Congratulations!"

"Thank you, sir."

"How come you leave town without forwarding your address?"

"I apologize. I got an offer I couldn't refuse."

Santini laughed merrily. "You're a card. Family is the greatest blessing for a man. You have sons. They are double blessings. Next, you and your gorgeous wife will create a beautiful daughter. I tell you she will break your heart."

"I think my heart is already broken with my sons."

Santini laughed. "No, it is called pride when you have sons. Now listen, I must be serious with you. This is very important."

Tony knew for Santini to call him there was a problem.

"What is it, Mr. Santini? What do you need help with?"

"It is not me this time, Tony. But listen I have advice for you, no?"

"Yes?"

"Someone close to you is killing those women. All the bodies, all the pretty ladies dying. It's not us."

"Do you know who it is?"

"All I can think of is you are being set up. None of the houses have beef with each other."

"How do you know it is someone close to me?"

"When I hang up, go watch your news. Nick Moreno was my man. I had him keeping your wife under surveillance. Someone was tracking her."

"What?"

"Listen! My man was killed a day before your wife went into the hospital, or maybe it was the night she was in there."

Tony tried to control his breathing. "How long has she been..."

"Listen and stop talking! My man only said he may be one of your team because of his skills. Then nothing. Go watch the news. I'm an old man, Tony. We aren't doing this to these women. I swear it. You call me if you need me."

"Thank you, Mr. Santini."

Tony hung up. He threw on a robe and took the backstairs to his den. He turned on the taped evening news broadcast. The two anchors stood side by side with microphones in hand.

Bill Braxton in a dark gray, double-breasted suit with black lapels looked into the camera with a somber expression on his face. The black wavy hair was trimmed close but tapered down to long sideburns.

"Sallie Anne, it appears Winding Falls is yet again under assault as another victim has been found in Winding Falls Park. Police have been baffled by the lack of evidence in these murders."

The camera panned to the beautiful anchor, Sallie Anne Lewis, wearing a deep blue silk dress. The fiery dark red hair was shaped into a long version of a pixie cut and rested becomingly on her shoulders. She gave her colleague a grim look before facing the camera.

"That's right, Bill. Last year this time, Stacie Young along with her husband, deputy mayor James Alan Young, was fatally assaulted in their Oxford Circle home. Their murders are still unsolved, and the police tell us it's an ongoing investigation. Well, tonight we bring you another such case. Thirty-nine-year-old Nicolas Moreno was brutally beaten and left for dead in Winding Falls Park just under midnight four days ago. Police confirmed with us that Nicolas, the son of Rick Moreno who owns the popular Jazzie's Club in Crestwood, is believed to have been targeted for

theft. Police confirmed an undisclosed amount of cash is missing along with a gold watch and his wedding band."

An image appeared on the screen of a tall, heavily built man in black formal wear. His facial features were blurred, but Tony knew who he was. Nicolas Moreno trained as a boxer and had won local small-town fights before retiring. He'd married the following year and kept a low profile. The camera returned to the anchor's face.

"The police are asking the public for their help. If you know anything about the murder of Nicolas Moreno, please call the numbers listed at the bottom of this screen. All information will be held in the strictest confidence. As always, we will keep you abreast of this continuing story."

Bill returned to sign off. *"That's tonight's coverage. Be safe everybody. Sallie Anne and I wish you all a good night!"*

Sallie Anne smiled engagingly at the camera. *"Good night, everyone."*

Tony turned off the set and sat back. He closed his eyes and remembered years past. Driving home from football practice he took a detour to pass the home of a girl he had a crush on. He spotted a vehicle crashed into a tree, and a man behind the wheel. He dragged the man who was delirious and speaking incoherently to safety. Multilingual Tony understood much of what the man said. He took him home and put him in the family's vacant pool house.

With his best friend, O'Neill, they nursed the mobster back to health. Along the way a friendship developed between the teenagers and Antonio Santini. One week later, Tony returned from school to find the pool house empty. One thing he noticed at once was that the place had been immaculately cleaned.

Throughout the years the law enforcement officer and the mobster would form a unique friendship built on mutual trust. Tony discovered Santini lived by Old World customs. If Santini said he was not involved in a matter, whether criminal or not, it turned out to be the truth.

Tony opened his eyes. Moreno was killed tracking a man following Marissa. Peaks of anxiety brought a chill through Tony's body. He needed to formulate a game plan and ensure his family's safety. He walked around his den in deep thought. He stopped in front of his college class photo. He studied the familiar face among the young men in his core group of friends. He sent a text. *I need your help. T*

www.ingramcontent.com/pod-product-compliance
Lightning Source LLC
Chambersburg PA
CBHW070737180626
46818CB00007B/2883